The Dunwich Cycle

Where the Old Gods Wait

Chaosium Cycle Books

THE HASTUR CYCLE
ROBERT BLOCH'S MYSTERIES OF THE WORM
CTHULHU'S HEIRS
THE SHUB-NIGGURATH CYCLE
THE ENCYCLOPEDIA CTHULHIANA
THE AZATHOTH CYCLE
THE BOOK OF IOD
MADE IN GOATSWOOD
THE DISCIPLES OF CTHULHU Second Edition

Tales That Define the Cthulhu Mythos

CALL OF CTHULHU® FICTION

The Dunwich Cycle

WHERE THE OLD GODS WAIT

by

August W. Derleth
C. J. Henderson
Ben Indick
Richard A. Lupoff
Arthur Machen
H. P. Lovecraft
W. H. Pugmire
Robert M. Price

Selected and edited by Robert M. Price
Chapter decorations by Earl Geier

A Chaosium Book

1995

Cover art by H. E. Fassl. Frontispiece by Allen Koszowski. Interior art by Earl Geier. Cover layout by Eric Vogt. Editing and layout by Janice Sellers. Proofreading by James Naureckas. Editor in chief Lynn Willis.

Please address questions and comments concerning this book, as well as requests for free notices of Chaosium publications, by mail to: Chaosium, Inc., 950-A 56th Street, Oakland, CA 94608-3129, U.S.A.

FIRST EDITION
1 2 3 4 5 6 7 8 9 10

Chaosium Publication 6010. Published in November 1995.
ISBN 0-56882-047-X.
Printed in the United States of America.

CONTENTS

Dedicated to

DIRK W. MOSIG,

father of modern Lovecraftian criticism

What Roodmas Horror

I will confess that among the tales of H. P. Lovecraft, "The Dunwich Horror" remains my favorite. Thus I have always been excited to see any pastiche-sequel or related tale. In this volume, *The Dunwich Cycle*, I have gathered most of these fellow travelers of Wilbur Whateley. Of course, none of them can count as a true sequel, what "actually" happened next. This would be equally true even had Lovecraft himself later penned a sequel, unless he had planned a "part two" at the same time, in which case it would not really be a sequel at all, but rather a continuation. Any later add-on, even by HPL himself, must count as an afterthought, not what did happen next. For nothing happened next: The narrative world of the original tale is self-contained, an island universe unto itself. But rather what *might* have happened. It's just fun to speculate. That is what sequels do.

I have for some time wanted to assemble a book of sequels to "The Dunwich Horror" once I began to realize how many stories would qualify. Then, one cannot leave out prequels. These are the stories of which Lovecraft's "The Dunwich Horror" is itself a pastiche. I refer to the tales of Arthur Machen, particularly "The Great God Pan", "The White People", "The Novel of the Black Seal", and *The Terror*. We simply do not have the space to include all of them, but "The Novel of the Black Seal" does appear in an earlier volume in this series, *The Hastur Cycle*. A word about them before we embark on the rutted and weed-grown road to Dunwich Village.

I believe the debt owed by Lovecraft to Machen in "The Dunwich Horror", though acknowledged, is underestimated. Indeed, I would go so far as to say that "The Dunwich Horror" is in every sense an homage to Machen and even a pastiche. There is little in Lovecraft's wonderful story that does not come directly out of Machen's fiction. If we are used to saying that "The Outsider" could stand as a stray Poe manuscript, I am near to saying that "The Dunwich Horror" might be read as an adjunct to the Machen canon. We might even compare what Lovecraft has done here with August Derleth's attempts to ape Lovecraft himself, one of which you will read in this book. (I will have more to say on Lovecraft's use of elements from "The Great God Pan" and "The White People" in my introductory notes to those tales.)

As S. T. Joshi notes in his masterful sketch *H. P. Lovecraft* (Starmont House Reader's Guide series), "The Whisperer in Darkness" owes much to Machen's "The Novel of the Black Seal." I explored this debt in my introduction to *The Hastur Cycle*. As I mentioned there and must repeat here, "The Dunwich Horror" bears some ancestral resemblance to "The Novel of the Black Seal" as well. Specifically, the monstrous appearance of Wilbur Whateley is surely derived from Machen's description of cretinous rustic Jervase Cradock. As it happens, Mr. Cradock is a Whateley twin in more than one respect. He, too, is the result of horrific miscegenation, his mother having been raped by one of the elusive Little People of the hills. Jervase has a fantastic death scene, too: "I saw his body swell and become distended as a bladder, while the face blackened before my eyes .... The sight I had to witness was horrible, almost beyond the power of human conception and the most fearful fantasy. Something pushed out from the body there on the floor, and stretched forth a slimy, wavering tentacle, across the room ...." I submit that what of Wilbur's passing we cannot match from the swan song of Helen Vaughan in "The Great God Pan" (see my introduction to that story below) we find made up here.

The stricken Mrs. Cradock was found and helped home by "a farmer, who had lost a couple of sheep, supposed to have wandered from the flock, [and] was walking over the Grey Hills, with a lantern and his dog." Here we have to think back to Dunwich farmer Silas Bishop, who happened to see Wilbur and Lavinia trick or treating in the hills: "Silas was rounding up a stray heifer, but he nearly forgot his mission when he fleetingly spied the two figures in the dim light of his lantern."

The very notion of the Old Ones, mankind's predecessors, now having retreated, but still lurking invisibly between the spaces that we know, seems to me a direct combining of equal portions of the invisible satyrs of Pan's realm in "The Great God Pan" and the furtive Little People of "The Novel of the Black Seal." Just as Lovecraft's invisible "airy rushing presences" are detected by their reptilian musk, Machen's Little People leave a "queer sort of smell .... [Once] we went into the snake-house to see the snakes, and it was just the same sort of smell."

In sum, then, I cannot help thinking of "The Dunwich Horror" as an attempt by Lovecraft to write a Machen story, exactly in the manner of August Derleth, who tried to assume the mantle of Lovecraft. If there is in Lovecraft's story something of a Derlethian species of flattery by imitation, can we also find in it any intimation of Derleth's own Mythos? Does "The Dunwich Horror" perhaps count as the first tale in the Derlethian Cthulhu Mythos? Some of the very same scholars who are most eager to dissociate Lovecraft from Derleth's interpretation of him are also, ironically, willing to admit that in "The Dunwich

Horror" HPL seems to stray from the purity of his cosmic vision as evidenced in other stories. In short, in "The Dunwich Horror", Lovecraft sounds too much like Derleth! There is all that talk by Armitage about good versus evil, something Lovecraft really shouldn't have his characters talking about if he were as nihilistic and anti-humanistic as Dirk Mosig painted him. And the flotsam-and-jetsam humans manage to win one! They aren't supposed to, according to Lovecraft's cosmic futilitarianism. Of course, it may be one battle in an unwinnable war, as some critics suggest, but the story seems to me to assume that what the Whateleys did was a rarity unlikely to be repeated.

But there are other Derlethianisms (as we may call them, reversing the historical perspective) in "The Dunwich Horror." Poor Derleth is excoriated by Lovecraft purists for introducing the idea that Cthulhu and his Old Ones were banished to the briny deeps as a punishment by enemies of greater power. True, in "The Call of Cthulhu" R'lyeh simply sank in a geological upheaval, and Cthulhu drowsed according to some cosmic hibernation schedule to awake again when the stars are right. But in "The Dunwich Horror", do we not read from the *Necronomicon* itself that Cthulhu is imprisoned in a sealed tower beneath the sea, exiled by the Old Ones, his more powerful cousins? Here is the passage I am thinking of: "And the sunken isles of Ocean hold stones whereon Their seal is engraven, but who hath seen ... the sealed tower long garlanded with seaweed and barnacles? Great Cthulhu is Their cousin, yet can he spy Them only dimly."

Even the figure of Henry Armitage is in some ways more like Derleth's Dr. Laban Shrewsbury than Lovecraft's Albert Wilmarth, whom we tend to take as the model Lovecraft protagonist. The difference is that Wilmarth starts out blissfully ignorant and only too late learns the terrible truth, and that only after a long battle with his initial rationalistic skepticism. Shrewsbury, on the other hand, already knows the lore of the Old Ones and is under no illusion as to the danger posed by Cthulhu cult-types. Now which of these gentlemen sounds more like Dr. Henry Armitage? Surprisingly—the latter! As soon as he sees Wilbur he pretty much knows what's up. "The bent, goatish giant before him seemed like the spawn of another planet or dimension; like something only partly of mankind, and linked to black gulfs of essence and entity that stretch like titan phantasms beyond all spheres of force and matter, space and time." That about sums it up! Why won't Armitage let Wilbur take the book with him? Because he already knows he will play hell with it. "There was too much responsibility in giving such a being the key to such blasphemous outer spheres."

Armitage is far from writing off Wilbur as some kind of religious nut. He shares the same nutty convictions!

At any rate, "The Dunwich Horror" has spawned an unnatural brood fully as eldritch as Wilbur himself. There have been numerous media adaptations, including spoken word recordings; a radio drama on the old *Suspense* program; a 1970 movie starring Dean Stockwell as Wilbur, Sam Jaffe as Old Whateley, and Ed Bagley as Dr. Armitage; and Brecchia's beautiful comic book adaptation. We can reproduce none of these here. But awaiting you are a writhing nest of foundlings from the hidden spheres of blasphemy, stories by Machen, Derleth, Richard Lupoff, Ben Indick, C. J. Henderson, and yours truly. You have already read "The Dunwich Horror" on its own many times, I'm sure. This time, why don't you have a little fun and read the story in a new way, intertextually with the other tales collected here, because they all pretty much fit together. Why don't you pretend they are chapters of one Dunwich novel? If we have done our work well, maybe you'll be sitting up all night, like Henry Armitage perusing Wilbur's diary, in a cold sweat and a state of "acute spiritual fear."

— Robert M. Price

ALLEN K.
86

Arthur Machen (1863-1947) was perhaps, as has been said about Lovecraft, "his own most fantastic creation", embodying many of the traits one might expect in a weird fiction protagonist. He was a mystic and initiate into the Order of the Golden Dawn and an adherent of the theory of the Grail Legend as the charter of an independent, pre-Catholic Celtic Christianity. It almost seems as if Poe and M. R. James got together to create Machen on paper, and then, like the Golem, he sprang to life. His fiction is incandescent with the witchfire glow of the numinous and partakes of the substance of genuine revelation. It is always a cause of rejoicing when his fiction comes back into print, though altogether too little of it has.

Lovecraft was by no means loath to acknowledge the dependence of "The Dunwich Horror" on a Machen prototype. As the disappointed Wilbur Whateley departs the university library, Henry Armitage watches him go and marvels that anyone can look at the goatish giant and not guess the truth: "'Inbreeding?' Armitage muttered half aloud to himself. 'Great God, what simpletons! Shew them Arthur Machen's Great God Pan and they'll think it a common Dunwich scandal!'" And indeed we cannot fail to recognize in Wilbur, son of Yog-Sothoth and Lavinia, a male counterpart to Machen's Helen Vaughan, daughter of Pan and Dr. Raymond's young ward Mary. Mary was impregnated by the Great God during a visionary moment following a brain operation allowing her to pierce the mundane veil of perception and to behold Pan. Wizard Whateley employed more traditional methods of magical invocation to make Yog-Sothoth come a-courting.

Wilbur's spectacular ending parallels Helen's just as strikingly as does his beginning. Both are observed in terrible death throes in which their physiognomies and anatomies are revealed as "teratologically fabulous" (to use Lovecraft's adjectivally fabulous expression), manifesting the anatomy of various evolutionary stages, Helen's in turn, Wilbur's simultaneously, and finally resolving themselves into disintegrating ooze.

Between beginning and end there is at least another direct borrowing. In Machen's tale, a seven-year-old named Trevor is at play in the woods when he begins screaming, having, as he later informs his father, spied Helen "playing on the grass with a 'strange naked man', whom he seemed unable to describe more fully." Lovecraft has divided this scene into two moments in "The Dunwich Horror", the first being the report of Silas Bishop who swore he had glimpsed, one Halloween night, "two figures" who "darted almost noiselessly through the underbrush, and the astonished watcher seemed to think they were entirely unclothed. Afterward he could not be sure about the boy, who may have had some kind of a fringed belt and a pair of dark trunks or trousers on." The description of young Wilbur is already enough to suggest a satyr, which is just what Helen's companion is later revealed to be as well. The Trevor character has been transformed into two youngsters, Luther Brown and Chauncey Sawyer, both of whom breathlessly report astounding sights.

These sightings of the aftermath of what seems an invisible cloud of destruction may have been suggested by a minor passage in Machen's The Terror, from which the very name of Lovecraft's eponymous town is no doubt drawn as well: "Some say they've seen the gas. I heard a man living in Dunwich saw it one night like a black cloud with sparks of fire in it floating over the tops of the trees by Dunwich Common." Here we think also of the chance phrase, just quoted above, "a common Dunwich scandal." (Dunwich is the name of a real coastal English village, the old capital of East Anglia, victim of shore erosion, and now completely sunken off the coast.) Machen's character was describing what he might have called, in view of the book's title, "The Dunwich Terror." Too close for comfort, I'd say. How about you, Lavinny?

The Great God Pan

by Arthur Machen

I

The Experiment

I am glad you came, Clarke; very glad indeed. I was not sure you could spare the time."

"I was able to make arrangements for a few days; things are not very lively just now. But have you no misgivings, Raymond? Is it absolutely safe?"

The two men were slowly pacing the terrace in front of Dr. Raymond's house. The sun still hung above the western mountain line, but it shone with a dull red glow that cast no shadows, and all the air was quiet; a sweet breath came from the great wood on the hillside above, and with it, at intervals, the soft murmuring call of the wild doves. Below, in the long lovely valley, the river wound in and out between the lonely hills, and, as the sun hovered and vanished into the west, a faint mist, pure white, began to rise from the banks. Dr. Raymond turned sharply to his friend.

"Safe? Of course it is. In itself the operation is a perfectly simple one; any surgeon could do it.

"And there is no danger whatever, I give you my word. You are always timid, Clarke, always; but you know my history. I have devoted myself to transcendental medicine for the last twenty years. I have heard myself called quack and charlatan and imposter, but all the while I knew I was on the right path. Five years ago I reached the goal, and since then every day has been a preparation for what we shall do to-night."

"I should like to believe it is all true." Clarke knit his brows, and looked doubtfully at Dr. Raymond. "Are you perfectly sure, Raymond, that your theory is not a phantasmagoria—a splendid vision, certainly, but a mere vision after all?"

Dr Raymond stopped in his walk and turned sharply. He was a middle-aged man, gaunt and thin, of a pale yellow complexion, but as he answered Clarke and faced him, there was a flush on his cheek.

"Look about you, Clarke. You see the mountain, and hill following after hill, as wave on wave, you see the woods and orchards, the fields of ripe corn, and the meadows reaching to the reed beds by the river. You see me standing here beside you, and hear my voice; but I tell you that all these things—yes, from that star that has just shone out in the sky to the solid ground beneath our feet—I say that all these are but dreams and shadows that hide the real world from our eyes. There is a real world, but it is beyond this glamour and this vision, beyond these 'chases in Arras, dreams in a career', beyond them all as beyond a veil. I do not know whether any human being has ever lifted that veil; but I do know, Clarke, that you and I shall see it lifted this very night from before another's eyes. You may think all this strange nonsense; it may be strange, but it is true, and the ancients knew what lifting the veil means. They called it seeing the God Pan."

Clarke shivered; the white mist gathering over the river was chilly.

"It is wonderful indeed," he said. "We are standing on the brink of a strange world, Raymond, if what you say is true. I suppose the knife is absolutely necessary?"

"Yes; a slight lesion in the grey matter, that is all; a trifling rearrangement of certain cells, a microscopical alteration that would escape the attention of ninety-nine brain specialists out of a hundred. I don't want to bother you with 'shop', Clarke; I might give you a mass of technical detail which would sound very imposing, and would leave you as enlightened as you are now. But I suppose you have read, casually, in out-of-the-way corners of your paper, that immense strides have been made recently in the physiology of the brain. I saw a paragraph the other day about Digby's theory, and Browne Faber's discoveries. Theories and discoveries! Where they are standing now, I stood fifteen years ago, and I need not tell you that I have not been standing still for the last fifteen years. It is enough if I say that five years ago I made the discovery to which I alluded when I said that then I reached the goal. After years of labour, after years of toiling and groping in the dark, after days and nights of disappointment and sometimes despair, in which I used now and then to tremble and grow cold with the thought that perhaps there were others seeking for what I sought, at last, after so long, a pang of sudden joy thrilled my soul, and I knew the long journey was at an end. By what seemed then and still seems a chance, the suggestion of a moment's idle thought followed up upon familiar lines and paths that I had tracked a hundred times already, the great truth burst upon me, and I saw, mapped out in lines of light, a whole world, a sphere unknown; continents and islands, and great oceans in which no ship had sailed—to my belief—since Man first lifted up his eyes and beheld the sun, and the stars of heaven, and the quiet earth beneath. You will think all this high-flown language, Clarke, but it is hard to be literal. And yet; I do not know whether what I am hinting at cannot be set forth in plain and homely terms. For instance, this world of ours is pretty well girded now with the telegraph wires and cables; thought, with something less than the speed of thoughts, flashes from sunrise to sunset, from north to south, across the floods and the desert places. Suppose that an electrician of today were suddenly to perceive that he and his friends have merely been playing with pebbles and mistaking them for the foundations of the world; suppose that such a man saw uttermost space lie open before the current, and words of men flash forth to the sun and beyond the sun into the systems beyond, and the voices of articulate-speaking men echo in the waste void that bounds our thought. As analogies go, that is a pretty good analogy of what I have done; you can understand now a little of what I felt as I stood here one evening; it was a summer evening, and the valley looked much as it does now; I stood here, and saw before me the unutterable, the unthinkable gulf that yawns profound between two worlds, the world of matter and the world of spirit; I saw the great empty deep stretch dim before me, and in that instant a bridge of light leapt from the earth to the unknown shore, and the abyss was spanned. You may look in Browne Faber's book, if you like, and you will find that to the present day men of science are unable to account for the presence, or to specify the functions, of a certain group of nerve cells in the brain. That group is, as it were, land to let, a mere wasteland for fanciful theories. I am not in the position of Browne Faber and the specialists, I am perfectly instructed as to the possible functions of those nerve centres in the scheme of things. With a touch I can bring them into play, with a touch, I say, I can set free the current, with a touch I can complete the communication between this world of sense and—we shall be able to finish this sentence later on. Yes, the knife is necessary; but think what the knife will effect. It will level utterly the solid wall of sense, and probably, for the first time since man was made, a spirit will gaze on a spirit world. Clarke, Mary will see the God Pan!"

"But you remember what you wrote to me? I thought it would be requisite that she—"

He whispered into the doctor's ear.

"Not at all, not at all. That is nonsense, I assure you. Indeed, it is better as it is; I am quite certain of that."

"Consider the matter well, Raymond. It's a great responsibility. Something might go wrong; you would be a miserable man for the rest of your days."

"No, I think not, even if the worst happened. As you know, I rescued Mary from the gutter, and from almost certain starvation, when she was a child; I think her life is mine, to use as I see fit. Come, it is getting late; we had better go in."

Dr. Raymond led the way into the house, through the hall, and down a long dark passage. He took a key from his pocket and opened a heavy door, and motioned Clarke into his laboratory. It had once been a billiard room, and was lighted by a glass dome in the centre of the ceiling, whence there still shone a sad grey light on the figure of the doctor as he lit a lamp with a heavy shade and placed it on a table in the middle of the room.

Clarke looked about him. Scarcely a foot of wall remained bare; there were shelves all around laden with bottles and phials of all shapes and colours, and at one end stood a little Chippendale bookcase. Raymond pointed to this.

"You see that parchment by Oswald Crollius? He was one of the first to show me the way, though I don't think he ever found it himself. That is a strange saying of his: 'In every grain of wheat there lies hidden the soul of a star.'"

There was not much of furniture in the laboratory. The table in the centre, a stone slab with a drain in one corner, the two armchairs on which Raymond and Clarke were sitting; that was all, except an odd-looking chair at the furthest end of the room. Clarke looked at it and raised his eyebrows.

"Yes, that is the chair," said Raymond. "We may as well place it in position." He got up and wheeled the chair to the light, and began raising and lowering it, letting down the seat, setting the back at various angles, and adjusting the footrest. It looked comfortable enough, and Clarke passed his hand over the soft green velvet, as the doctor manipulated the levers.

"Now, Clarke, make yourself quite comfortable. I have a couple of hours' work before me; I was obliged to leave certain matters to the last."

Raymond went to the stone slab, and Clarke watched him drearily as he bent over a row of phials and lit the flame under the crucible. The doctor had a small hand-lamp, shaded as the larger one, on the ledge above his apparatus, and Clarke, who sat in the shadows, looked down the great dreary room, wondering at the bizarre effects of brilliant light and undefined darkness contrasting with one another. Soon he became conscious of an odd odour, at first the merest suggestion of odour, in the room; and as it grew more decided he felt surprised that he was not reminded of the chemist's shop or the surgery. Clarke found himself idly endeavouring to analyse the sensation, and, half conscious, he began to think of a day, fifteen years ago, that he had spent in roaming through the woods and meadows near his old home. It was a burning day at the beginning of August, the heat had dimmed the outlines of all things and all distances with a faint mist, and people who observed the thermometer spoke of an abnormal register, of a temperature that was almost tropical. Strangely that wonderful hot day of the 'fifties rose up on Clarke's imagination; the sense of dazzling all-pervading sunlight seemed to blot out the shadows and lights of the laboratory, and he felt again the heated air beating in gusts about his face, saw the shimmer rising from the turf, and heard the myriad murmur of the summer.

"I hope that smell doesn't annoy you, Clarke; there's nothing unwholesome about it. It may make you a bit sleepy, that's all."

Clarke heard the words quite distinctly, and knew that Raymond was speaking to him, but for the life of him he could not rouse himself from his lethargy. He could only think of the lonely walk he had taken fifteen years ago; it was his last look at the fields and woods he had known since he was a child, and now it all stood out in brilliant light, as a picture, before him. Above all there came to his nostrils the scent of summer, the smell of flowers mingled, and the odour of the woods, of cool shaded places, deep in the green depths, drawn forth by the sun's heat; and the scent of the good earth, as it were with arms stretched forth, and smiling lips, overpowered all. His fancies made him wander, as he had wandered long ago, from the fields into the wood, tracking a little path between the shining undergrowth of beech trees; and the trickle of water dropping from the limestone rock sounded as a clear melody in the dream. Thoughts began to go astray and to mingle with other recollections; the beech alley was transformed to a path beneath ilex trees, and here and there a vine climbed from bough to bough, and sent up waving tendrils and drooped with purple grapes, and the sparse grey-green leaves of a wild olive tree stood out against the dark shadows of the ilex. Clarke, in the deep folds of dream, was conscious that the path from his father's house had led him into an undiscovered country, and he was wondering at the strangeness of it all, when suddenly, in place of the hum and murmur of the summer, an infinite silence seemed to fall on things, and the wood was hushed, and for a moment of time he stood face to face there with a presence, that was neither man nor beast, neither the living nor the dead, but all things mingled, the form of all things but devoid of all form. And in that moment, the sacrament of body and soul was dissolved, and a voice seemed to cry "Let us go hence," and then the darkness of darkness beyond the stars, the darkness of everlasting.

When Clarke woke up with a start he saw Raymond pouring a few drops of some oily fluid into a green phial, which he stoppered tightly.

"You have been dozing," he said; "the journey must have tired you out. It is done now. I am going to fetch Mary; I shall be back in ten minutes."

Clarke lay back in his chair and wondered. It seemed as if he had but passed from one dream into another, he half expected to see the walls of the laboratory melt and disappear, and to awake in London, shuddering at his own sleeping fancies. But at last the door opened, and the doctor returned, and behind him came a girl of about seventeen, dressed all in white. She was so beautiful that Clarke did not wonder at what the doctor had written to him. She was blushing now over face and neck and arms, but Raymond seemed unmoved.

"Mary," he said, "the time has come. You are quite free. Are you willing to trust yourself to me entirely?"

"Yes, dear."

"You hear that, Clarke? You are my witness. Here is the chair, Mary. It is quite easy. Just sit in and lean back. Are you ready?"

"Yes, dear, quite ready. Give me a kiss before you begin."

The doctor stopped and kissed her mouth, kindly enough. "Now shut your eyes," he said. The girl closed her eyelids, as if she were tired, and longed for sleep, and Raymond held the green phial to her nostrils. Her face grew white, whiter than her dress; she struggled faintly, and then with the feeling of submission strong within her, crossed her arms across her breast as a little child about to say her prayers. The bright light of the lamp beat full upon her, and Clarke watched changes fleeting over that face as the changes of the hills when the summer clouds float across the sun. And then she lay all white and still, and the doctor turned up one of her eyelids. She was quite unconscious. Raymond pressed hard on one of the levers and the chair instantly sank back. Clark saw him cutting away a circle, like a tonsure, from her hair, and the lamp was moved nearer. Raymond took a small glittering instrument from a little case, and Clarke turned away shuddering. When he looked again the doctor was binding up the wound he had made.

"She will wake in five minutes." Raymond was still perfectly cool. "There is nothing more to be done; we can only wait."

The minutes passed slowly; they could hear a slow, heavy ticking. There was an old clock in the passage. Clarke felt sick and faint; his knees shook beneath him, he could hardly stand.

Suddenly, as they watched, they heard a long drawn sigh, and suddenly did the colour that had vanished return to the girl's cheeks, and suddenly her eyes opened. Clarke quailed before them. They shone with an awful light, looking far away, and a great wonder fell upon her face, and her hands stretched out as if to touch what was invisible; but in an instant the wonder faded, and gave place to the most awful terror. The muscles of her face were hideously convulsed, she shook from head to foot; the soul seemed struggling and shuddering within the house of flesh. It was a horrible sight, and Clarke rushed forward, as she fell shrieking to the floor.

Three days later Raymond took Clarke to Mary's bedside. She was wide awake, rolling her head from side to side, and grinning vacantly.

"Yes," said the doctor, still quite cool, "it is a great pity; she is a hopeless idiot. However, it could not be helped; and, after all, she has seen the Great God Pan."

II

Clarke's Memoirs

Mr. Clarke, the gentleman chosen by Dr. Raymond to witness the strange experiment of the God Pan, was a person in whose character caution and curiosity were oddly mingled; in his sober moments he thought of the unusual and the eccentric with undisguised aversion, and yet, deep in his heart, there was a wide-eyed inquisitiveness with respect to all the more recondite and esoteric elements in the nature of men. The latter tendency had prevailed when he accepted Raymond's invitation, for though his considered judgement had always repudiated the doctor's theories as the wildest nonsense, yet he secretly hugged a belief in fantasy, and would have rejoiced to see that belief confirmed. The horrors that he witnessed in the dreary laboratory were to a certain extent salutary; he was conscious of being involved in an affair not altogether reputable, and for many years afterwards he clung bravely to the commonplace, and rejected all occasions of occult investigation. Indeed, on some homeopathic principle, he for some time attended the seances of distinguished mediums, hoping that the clumsy tricks of these gentlemen would make him altogether disgusted with mysticism of every kind, but the remedy, though caustic, was not efficacious. Clarke knew that he still pined for the unseen, and little by little, the old passion began to reassert itself, as the face of Mary, shuddering and convulsed with an unknowable terror, faded slowly from his memory. Occupied all day in pursuits both serious and lucrative, the temptation to relax in the evening was too great, especially in the winter

months, when the fire cast a warm glow over his snug bachelor
apartment, and a bottle of some choice claret stood ready by his elbow.
His dinner digested, he would make a brief pretence of reading the
evening paper, but the mere catalogue of news soon palled upon him,
and Clarke would find himself casting glances of warm desire in the
direction of an old Japanese bureau, which stood at a pleasant distance
from the hearth. Like a boy before a jam closet, for a few minutes he
would hover indecisive, but lust always prevailed, and Clarke ended
by drawing up his chair, lighting a candle, and sitting down before the
bureau. Its pigeonholes and drawers teemed with documents on the
most morbid subjects, and in the well reposed a large manuscript
volume, in which he had painfully entered the gems of his collection.
Clarke had a fine contempt for published literature; the most ghostly
story ceased to interest him if it happened to be printed; his sole
pleasure was in the reading, compiling, and rearranging of what he
called his "Memoirs to Prove the Existence of the Devil", and engaged
in this pursuit the evening seemed to fly and the night appeared too
short.

On one particular evening, an ugly December night, black with fog,
and raw with frost, Clarke hurried over his dinner, and scarcely deigned
to observe his customary ritual of taking up the paper and laying it
down again. He paced two or three times up and down the room, and
opened the bureau, stood still a moment, and sat down. He leant back,
absorbed in one of those dreams to which he was subject, and at length
drew out his book, and opened it at the last entry. There were three or
four pages densely covered with Clarke's round, set penmanship, and
at the beginning he had written in a somewhat larger hand:

*Singular Narrative told me by my Friend, Dr. Phillips. He assures me that
all the facts related therein are strictly and wholly True, but refuses to give
either the Surnames of the Persons concerned, or the Place where these Extraordinary Events occurred.*

Mr. Clarke began to read over the account for the tenth time, glancing
now and then at the pencil notes he had made when it was told him by
his friend. It was one of his humours to pride himself on a certain literary
ability; he thought well of his style, and took pains in arranging the
circumstances in dramatic order. He read the following story:

*The persons concerned in this statement are Helen V., who, if she is still
alive, must now be a woman of twenty-three; Rachel M., since deceased, who*

was a year younger than the above; and Trevor W., an imbecile, aged eighteen. These persons were at a period of the story inhabitants of a village on the borders of Wales, a place of some importance in the time of the Roman occupation, but now a scattered hamlet, of not more than five hundred souls. It is situated on rising ground, about six miles from the sea, and is sheltered by a large and picturesque forest.

Some eleven years ago, Helen V. came to the village under rather peculiar circumstances. It is understood that she, being an orphan, was adopted in her infancy by a distant relative, who brought her up in his own house till she was twelve years old. Thinking, however, that it would be better for the child to have playmates of her own age, he advertised in several local papers for a good home in a comfortable farmhouse for a girl of twelve, and this advertisement was answered by Mr. R., a well-to-do farmer in the above mentioned village. His references proving satisfactory, the gentleman sent his adopted daughter to Mr. R., with a letter, in which he stipulated that the girl should have a room to herself, and stated that her guardians need be at no trouble in the matter of education, as she was already sufficiently educated for the position in life she would occupy. In fact, Mr. R. was given to understand that the girl was to be allowed to find her own occupations, and to spend her time almost as she liked. Mr. R. duly met her at the nearest station, a town some seven miles away from his house, and seems to have remarked nothing extraordinary about the child, except that she was reticent as to her former life and her adopted father. She was, however, of a very different type from the inhabitants of the village; her skin was pale, clear olive, and her features were strongly marked, and of a somewhat foreign character. She appears to have settled down easily enough into farmhouse life, and became a favourite with the children, who sometimes went with her on her rambles in the forest, for this was her amusement. Mr. R. states that he has known her to go out by herself directly after their early breakfast, and not return till after dusk, and that, feeling uneasy at a young girl being out alone for so many hours, he communicated with her adopted father, who replied in a brief note that Helen must do as she chose. In the winter, when the forest paths are impassable, she spent most of her time in her bedroom, where she slept alone, according to the instructions of her relative. It was on one of these expeditions to the forest that the first of the singular incidents with which this girl is connected occurred, the date being about a year after her arrival at the village. The preceding winter had been remarkably severe, the snow drifting to a great depth, and the frost continuing for an unexampled period, and the summer following was as noteworthy for its extreme heat. On one of the very hottest days in this summer, Helen V. left the farmhouse for one of her long rambles in the forest, taking with her, as usual, some bread and meat for lunch. She was seen by some men in the fields making for the old Roman Road, a green causeway which traverses the highest part of the wood, and they were astonished to observe that the girl had taken off her hat, though the heat of the sun was already almost tropical. As it happened, a labourer, Joseph W. by name, was working in the forest near the Roman Road, and at twelve o'clock his little son, Trevor, brought the man his dinner of bread and cheese. After the meal, the boy, who was about seven years old at the time, left his father at work, and, as he said, went to look for flowers in the wood, and the man, who could hear him shouting with delight over his discoveries, felt no uneasiness. Suddenly, however, he was horrified at hearing the most dreadful screams, evidently the result of great terror, proceeding from the direction in which his son had gone, and he hastily threw down his tools and ran to see what had happened. Tracing his path by the sound, he met the little boy, who was running headlong, and was evidently terribly frightened, and on questioning him the man at last elicited that after picking a posy of flowers he felt tired, and lay down on the grass and fell asleep. He was suddenly awakened, as he stated, by a peculiar noise, a sort of singing he called it, and on peeping through the branches he saw Helen V. playing on the grass with a "strange naked man", whom he seemed unable to describe more fully. He said he felt dreadfully frightened, and ran away crying for his father. Joseph W. proceeded in the direction indicated by his son, and found Helen V. sitting on the grass in the middle of a glade or open space left by charcoal burners. He angrily charged her with frightening his little boy, but she entirely denied the accusation and laughed at the child's story of a "strange man", to which he himself did not attach much credence. Joseph W. came to the conclusion that the boy had woken up with a sudden fright, as children sometimes do, but Trevor persisted in his story, and continued in such evident distress that at last his father took him home, hoping that his mother would be able to soothe him. For many weeks, however, the boy gave his parents much anxiety; he became nervous and strange in his manner, refusing to leave the cottage by himself, and constantly alarming the household by waking in the night with cries of "The man in the wood! Father! Father!"

In course of time, however, the impression seemed to have worn off, and about three months later he accompanied his father to the house of a gentleman in the neighbourhood, for whom Joseph W. occasionally did work. The man was shown into the study, and the little boy was left sitting in the hall, and a few minutes later, while the gentleman was giving W. his instructions, they were both horrified by a piercing shriek and the sound of a fall, and rushing out they found the child senseless on the floor, his face contorted with terror. The doctor was immediately summoned, and after some examination he pronounced the child to be suffering from a kind of fit, apparently produced by a sudden shock. The boy was taken to one of the bedrooms, and after some time recovered consciousness, but only to pass into a condition described by the medical man as

*one of violent hysteria. The doctor exhibited a strong sedative, and in the course
of two hours pronounced him fit to walk home, but in passing through the hall
the paroxysms of fright returned and with additional violence. The father
perceived that the child was pointing at some object and heard the old cry, "The
man in the wood," and looking in the direction indicated saw a stone head of
grotesque appearance, which had been built into the wall above one of the doors.
It seems that the owner of the house had recently made alterations in his premises,
and on digging the foundation for some offices, the men had found a curious
head, evidently of Roman period, which had been placed in the hall in the
manner described. The head is pronounced by the most experienced archaeologists
of the district to be that of a faun or satyr. (Dr. Phillips tells me that he has
seen the head in question, and assures me that he has never received such a vivid
presentment of intense evil.)*

*From whatever cause arising, this second shock seemed too severe for the boy Trevor,
and at the present date he suffers from a weakness of intellect, which gives but little
promise of amending. The matter caused a good deal of sensation at the time, and
the girl Helen was closely questioned by Mr. R., but to no purpose, she steadfastly
denying that she had frightened or in any way molested Trevor.*

*The second event with which this girl's name is connected took place about
six years ago, and is of a still more extraordinary character.*

*At the beginning of the summer of 1882 Helen contracted a friendship of a
peculiarly intimate character with Rachel M., the daughter of a prosperous
farmer in the neighbourhood. This girl, who was a year younger than Helen,
was considered by most people to be the prettier of the two, though Helen's features
had to a great extent softened as she became older. The two girls, who were
together on every available opportunity, presented a singular contrast, the one
with her clear, olive skin and almost Italian appearance, and the other of the
proverbial red and white of our rural districts. It must be stated that the
payments made to Mr. R. for the maintenance of Helen were known in the village
for their excessive liberality, and the impression was general that she would one
day inherit a large sum of money from her relative. The parents of Rachel were
therefore not averse from their daughter's friendship with the girl, and even
encouraged the intimacy, though they now bitterly regret having done so. Helen
still retained her extraordinary fondness for the forest, and on several occasions
Rachel accompanied her, the two friends setting out early in the morning, and
remaining in the wood till dusk. Once or twice after these excursions Mrs. M.
thought her daughter's manner rather peculiar; she seemed languid and dreamy,
and as it has been expressed, "different from herself", but these peculiarities seem
to have been thought too trifling for remark. One evening, however, after Rachel
had come home, her mother heard a noise which sounded like suppressed weeping
in the girl's room, and on going in found her , half undressed, upon the bed,*

*evidently in the greatest distress. As soon as she saw her mother, she exclaimed,
"Ah, Mother, Mother, why did you let me go to the forest with Helen?" Mrs.
M. was astonished at so strange a question, and proceeded to make inquiries.
Rachel told her a wild story. She said—*

Clarke closed the book with a snap, and turned his chair towards the
fire. When his friend sat one evening in that very chair, and told his
story, Clarke had interrupted him at a point a little subsequent to this,
had cut short his words in a paroxysm of horror. "My God!" he had
exclaimed, "think, think what you are saying. It is too incredible, too
monstrous; such things can never be in this quiet world, where men
and women live and die, and struggle, and conquer, or maybe fail, and
fall down under sorrow, and grieve and suffer strange fortunes for many
a year; but not this, Phillips, not such things as this. There must be
some explanation, some way out of the terror. Why, man, if such a case
were possible, our earth would be a nightmare."

But Phillips had told his story to the end, concluding:

"Her flight remains a mystery to this day; she vanished in broad
sunlight; they saw her walking in a meadow, and a few moments later
she was not there."

Clarke tried to conceive the thing again, as he sat by the fire, and
again his mind shuddered and shrank back, appalled before the sight
of such awful, unspeakable elements enthroned as it were, and trium-
phant in human flesh. Before him stretched the long dim vista of the
green causeway in the forest, as his friend had described it; he saw the
swaying leaves and the quivering shadows on the grass, he saw the
sunlight and the flowers, and far away, far in the long distance, the two
figures moved toward him. One was Rachel, but the other?

Clarke had tried his best to disbelieve it all, but at the end of the
account, as he had written it in his book, he had placed the inscription:

ET DIABOLUS INCARNATUS EST. ET HOMO FACTUS EST.

III

City of Resurrections

"Herbert! Good God! Is it possible?"

"Yes, my name's Herbert. I think I know your face too, but I don't
remember your name. My memory is very queer."

"Don't you recollect Villiers of Wadham?"

"So it is, so it is. I beg your pardon, Villiers, I didn't think I was begging of an old college friend. Goodnight."

"My dear fellow, this haste is unnecessary. My rooms are close by, but we won't go there just yet. Suppose we walk up Shaftesbury Avenue a little way? But how in heaven's name have you come to this pass, Herbert?"

"It's a long story, Villiers, and a strange one too, but you can hear it if you like."

"Come on, then. Take my arm, you don't seem very strong."

The ill-assorted pair moved slowly up Rupert Street; the one in dirty, evil-looking rags, the other attired in the regulation uniform of a man about town, trim, glossy, and eminently well-to-do. Villiers had emerged from his restaurant after an excellent dinner of many courses, assisted by an ingratiating little flask of Chianti, and, in that frame of mind which was with him almost chronic, had delayed a moment by the door, peering round in the dimly lighted street in search of those mysterious incidents and persons with which the streets of London teem in every quarter and at every hour. Villiers prided himself as a practised explorer of such obscure mazes and byways of London life, and in this unprofitable pursuit he displayed an assiduity which was worthy of more serious employment. Thus he stood beside the lamp-post surveying the passers-by with undisguised curiosity, and with that gravity only known to the systematic diner, had just enunciated in his mind the formula: "London has been called the city of encounters; it is more than that, it is the city of resurrections," when these reflections were suddenly interrupted by a piteous whine at his elbow, and a deplorable appeal for alms. He looked around in some irritation, and with a sudden shock found himself confronted with the embodied proof of his somewhat stilted fancies. There, close beside him, his face altered and disfigured by poverty and disgrace, his body barely covered by greasy ill-fitting rags, stood his old friend Charles Herbert, who had matriculated on the same day as himself, with whom he had been merry and wise for twelve revolving terms. Different occupations and varying interests had interrupted the friendship, and it was six years since Villiers had seen Herbert; and now he looked upon this wreck of a man with grief and dismay, mingled with a certain inquisitiveness as to what dreary chain of circumstance had dragged him down to such a doleful pass. Villiers felt together with compassion all the relish of the amateur in mysteries, and congratulated himself on his leisurely speculations outside the restaurant.

They walked on in silence for some time, and more than one passer-by stared in astonishment at the unaccustomed spectacle of a well dressed man with an unmistakable beggar hanging on to his arm, and, observing this, Villiers led the way to an obscure street in Soho. Here he repeated his question.

"How on earth has it happened, Herbert? I always understood you would succeed to an excellent position in Dorsetshire. Did your father disinherit you? Surely not?"

"No, Villiers; I came into all the property at my poor father's death; he died a year after I left Oxford. He was a very good father to me, and I mourned his death sincerely enough. But you know what young men are; a few months later I came up to town and went a good deal into society. Of course I had excellent introductions, and I managed to enjoy myself very much in a harmless sort of way. I played a little, certainly, but never for heavy stakes, and the few bets I made on races brought me in money—only a few pounds, you know, but enough to pay for cigars and such petty pleasures. It was in my second season that the tide turned. Of course you have heard of my marriage?"

"No, I never heard anything about it."

"Yes, I married, Villiers. I met a girl, a girl of the most wonderful and most strange beauty, at the house of some people whom I knew. I cannot tell you her age; I never knew it, but, so far as I can guess, I should think she must have been about nineteen when I made her acquaintance. My friends had come to know her at Florence; she told them she was an orphan, the child of an English father and an Italian mother, and she charmed them as she charmed me. The first time I saw her was at an evening party. I was standing above the hum and babble of conversation when I heard a voice which seemed to thrill to my heart. She was singing an Italian song. I was introduced to her that evening, and in three months I married Helen. Villiers, that woman, if I can call her a 'woman', corrupted my soul. The night of the wedding I found myself sitting in her bedroom in the hotel, listening to her talk. She was sitting up in bed, and I listened to her as she spoke in her beautiful voice, spoke of things which even now I would not dare whisper in blackest night, though I stood in the midst of wilderness. You, Villiers, you may think you know life, and London, and what goes on day and night in this dreadful city; for all I can say you may have heard the talk of the vilest, but I can tell you can have no conception of what I know, not in your most fantastic, hideous dreams can you have imaged forth the faintest shadow of what I have heard—and seen. Yes, seen. I have seen the incredible, such horrors that even I myself sometimes stop in the middle of the street, and ask whether it is possible for a man to hold such things and live. In a year, Villiers, I was a ruined man, in body and soul—in body and soul."

"But your property, Herbert? You had land in Dorset."

"I sold it all; the fields and woods, the dear old house—everything."

"And the money?"

"She took it all from me."

"And then left you?"

"Yes; she disappeared one night. I don't know where she went but I am sure if I saw her again it would kill me. The rest of my story is of no interest; sordid misery, that is all. You may think, Villiers, that I have exaggerated and talked for effect; but I have not told you half. I could tell you certain things which would convince you, but you would never know a happy day again. You would pass the rest of your life, as I pass mine, a haunted man, a man who has seen Hell."

Villiers took the unfortunate man to his rooms, and gave him a meal. Herbert could eat little, and scarcely touched the glass of wine set before him. He sat moody and silent by the fire, and seemed relieved when Villiers sent him away with a small present of money.

"By the way, Herbert," said Villiers, as they parted at the door, "what was your wife's name? You said Helen, I think? Helen what?"

"The name she passed under when I met her was Helen Vaughan, but what her real name was I can't say. I don't think she had a name. No, no, not in that sense. Only human beings have names, Villiers; I can't say any more. Goodbye; yes, I will not fail to call if I see any way in which you can help me. Goodnight."

The man went out into the bitter night, and Villiers returned to his fireside. There was something about Herbert which shocked him inexpressibly; not his poor rags nor the marks which poverty had set upon his face, but rather an indefinite terror which hung about him like a mist. He had acknowledged that he himself was not devoid of blame; the woman, he had avowed, had corrupted him body and soul, and Villiers felt that this man, once his friend, had been an actor in scenes evil beyond the power of words. His story needed no confirmation: he himself was the embodied proof of it. Villiers mused curiously over the story he had heard, and wondered whether he had heard both the first and last of it. *No*, he thought, *certainly not the last, probably only the beginning. A case like this is like a nest of Chinese boxes; you open one after another and find a quainter workmanship in every box. Most likely poor Herbert is merely one of the outside boxes; there are stranger ones to follow.*

Villiers could not take his mind away from Herbert and his story, which seemed to grow wilder as the night wore on. The fire began to burn low, and the chilly air of the morning crept into the room; Villiers got up with a glance over his shoulder, and shivering slightly, went to bed.

A few days later he saw at his club a gentleman of his acquaintance, named Austin, who was famous for his intimate knowledge of London life, both in its tenebrous and luminous phases. Villiers, still full of his encounter in Soho and its consequences, thought Austin might possibly be able to shed some light on Herbert's history, and so after some casual talk he suddenly put the question:

"Do you happen to know anything of a man named Herbert—Charles Herbert?"

Austin turned round sharply and stared at Villiers with some astonishment.

"Charles Herbert? Weren't you in town three years ago? No; then you have not heard of the Paul Street case? It caused a good deal of sensation at the time."

"What was the case?"

"Well, a gentleman, a man of very good position, was found dead, stark dead, in the area of a certain house on Paul Street, off Tottenham Court Road. Of course the police did not make the discovery; if you happen to be sitting up all night and have a light in your window, the constable will ring the bell, but if you happen to be dead in somebody's area, you will be left alone. In this instance as in many others the alarm was raised by some kind of vagabond; I don't mean a common tramp, or a public-house loafer, but a gentleman, whose business or pleasure, or both, made him a spectator of the London streets at five o'clock in the morning. This individual was, as he said, 'going home', it did not appear whence or whither, and had occasion to pass through Paul Street between four and five a.m. Something or other caught his eye at Number 20; he said, absurdly enough, that the house had the most unpleasant physiognomy he had ever observed, but, at any rate, he glanced down the area, and was a good deal astonished to see a man on the stones, his limbs all huddled together, and his face turned up. Our gentleman thought his face looked peculiarly ghastly, and so set off at a run in search of the nearest policeman. The constable was at first inclined to treat the matter lightly, suspecting common drunkenness; however, he came, and after looking at the man's face, changed his tone, quickly enough. The early bird, who had picked up this fine worm, was sent off for a doctor, and the policeman rang and knocked at the door till a slatternly servant girl came down looking more than half asleep. The constable pointed out the contents of the area to the maid, who screamed loudly enough to wake up the street, but she knew nothing of the man; had never seen him at the house, and so forth. Meanwhile the original discoverer had come back with a medical man, and the next thing was to get into the area. The gate was open, so the whole quartet stumped down the steps. The doctor hardly needed a moment's examination; he said the poor fellow had been dead for several hours, and it was then the case began to get interesting. The dead man had not been robbed, and in one of his pockets were papers identifying him as—well, as a man of good family means, a favourite in society, and nobody's enemy, so far as could be known. I don't give his name, Villiers, because it has nothing to do with the story, and because it's no good raking up these affairs about the dead when there are no relations living. The next curious point was that the medical men couldn't agree as to how he met his death. There were some slight bruises on his shoulders, but they were so slight that it looked as if he had been pushed roughly out of the kitchen door, and not thrown over the railings from the street or even dragged down the steps. But there were positively no other marks of violence about him, certainly none that would account for his death; and when they came to the autopsy there wasn't a trace of poison of any kind. Of course the police wanted to know all about the people at Number 20, and here again, so I have heard from private sources, one or two other very curious points came out. It appears that the occupants of the house were Mr. and Mrs. Charles Herbert; he was said to be a landed proprietor, though it struck most people that Paul Street was not exactly the place to look for country gentry. As for Mrs. Herbert, nobody seemed to know who or what she was, and, between ourselves, I fancy the divers after her history found themselves in rather strange waters. Of course they both denied knowing anything about the deceased, and in default of any evidence against them they were discharged. But some very odd things came out about them. Though it was between five and six in the morning when the dead man was removed, a large crowd had collected, and several of the neighbours ran to see what was going on. They were pretty free with their comments, by all accounts, and from these it appeared that Number 20 was in very bad odour in Paul Street. The detectives tried to trace down these rumours to some solid foundation of fact, but could not get hold of anything. People shook their heads and raised their eyebrows and thought the Herberts rather 'queer', 'would rather not be seen going into their house', and so on, but there was nothing tangible. The authorities were morally certain that the man met his death in some way or another in the house and was thrown out by the kitchen door, but they couldn't prove it, and the absence of any indications of violence or poisoning left them helpless. An odd case, wasn't it? But curiously enough, there's something more that I haven't told you. I happened to know one of the doctors who was consulted as to the cause of death, and some time after the inquest I met him, and asked him about it. 'Do you really mean to tell me,' I said, 'that you were baffled by the case, that you actually don't know what the man died of?' 'Pardon me,' he replied, 'I know perfectly well what caused the death. B—— died of fright, of sheer, awful terror; I never saw features so hideously contorted in the entire course of my practise, and I have seen the faces of a whole host of dead.' The doctor was usually a cool customer enough, and a certain vehemence in his manner struck me, but I couldn't get anything more out of him. I suppose the Treasury didn't see their way to prosecuting the Herberts for frightening a man to death; at any rate, nothing was done, and the case dropped out of the men's minds. Do you happen to know anything of Herbert?"

"Well," replied Villiers, "he was an old college friend of mine."

"You don't say so? Have you ever seen his wife?"

"No, I haven't. I have lost sight of Herbert for many years."

"It's queer, isn't it, parting with a man at the college gate or at Paddington, seeing nothing of him for years, and then finding him pop his head in such an odd place. But I should like to have seen Mrs. Herbert; people said extraordinary things about her."

"What sort of things?"

"Well, I hardly know how to tell you. Every one who saw her at the police court said she was at once the most beautiful woman and the most repulsive they had ever set eyes on. I have spoken to a man who saw her, and I assure you he positively shuddered as he tried to describe the woman, but he couldn't tell why. She seems to have been a sort of enigma; and I expect if that one dead man could have told tales, he would have told some uncommonly queer ones. And there you are again in another puzzle; what could a respectable country gentleman like Mr. Blank—we'll call him that if you don't mind—want in such a very queer house as Number 20? It's altogether a very odd case, isn't it?"

"It is indeed, Austin; an extraordinary case. I didn't think, when I asked you about my old friend, I should strike on such strange metal. Well, I must be off; good -day."

Villiers went away, thinking of his own conceit of the Chinese boxes; here was quaint workmanship indeed.

IV

The Discovery in Paul Street

A few months after Villiers' meeting with Herbert, Mr. Clarke was sitting, as usual, by his after-dinner hearth, resolutely guarding his fancies from wandering in the direction of the bureau. For more than a week he had succeeded in keeping away from the "Memoirs", and he cherished hopes of a complete self-reformation; but, in spite of his endeavours, he could not hush the wonder and the strange curiosity that that last case he had written down had excited within him. He had put the case, or rather the outline of it, conjecturally to a scientific friend, who shook his head, and thought Clarke getting queer, and on this particular evening Clarke was making an effort to rationalize the story, when a sudden knock at his door roused him from his meditations.

"Mr. Villiers to see you, sir."

"Dear me, Villiers, it is very kind of you to look me up; I have not seen you for many months; I should think nearly a year. Come in, come in. And how are you, Villiers? Want any advice about investments?"

"No, thanks, I fancy everything I have in that way is pretty safe. No, Clarke, I have really come to consult you about a rather curious matter that has been brought under my notice of late. I am afraid you will think it all rather absurd when I tell my tale. I sometimes think so myself, and that's just why I made up my mind to come to you, as I know you're a practical man."

Mr. Villiers was ignorant of the "Memoirs to Prove the Existence of the Devil."

"Well, Villiers, I shall be happy to give you my advice, to the best of my ability. What is the nature of the case?"

"It's an extraordinary thing altogether. You know my ways; I always keep my eyes open in the streets, and in my time I have chanced upon some queer customers, and queer cases too, but this, I think, beats all. I was coming out of a restaurant one nasty winter night about three months ago; I had a capital dinner and a good bottle of Chianti, and I stood for a moment on the pavement, thinking what a mystery there is about London streets and the companies that pass along them. A bottle of red wine encourages these fancies, Clarke, and I dare say I should have thought a page of small type, but I was cut short by a beggar who had come behind me, and was making the usual appeals. Of course I looked round, and this beggar turned out to be what was left of an old friend of mine, a man named Herbert. I asked him how he had come to such a wretched pass, and he told me. We walked up and down one of those long dark Soho streets, and there I listened to his story. He said he had married a beautiful girl, some years younger than himself, and, as he put it, she had corrupted him body and soul. He wouldn't go into details; he said he dare not, that what he had seen and heard haunted him by night and day, and when I looked in his face I knew he was speaking the truth. There was something about the man that made me shiver. I don't know why, but it was there. I gave him a little money and sent him away, and I assure you that when he was gone I gasped for breath. His presence seemed to chill one's blood."

"Isn't all this just a little fanciful, Villiers? I suppose the poor fellow had made an imprudent marriage, and, in plain English, gone to the bad."

"Well, listen to this." Villiers told Clarke the story he had heard from Austin.

"You see," he concluded, "there can be but little doubt that this Mr. Blank, whoever he was, died of sheer terror; he saw something so awful, so terrible, that it cut short his life. And what he saw, he most certainly saw in that house, which, somehow or other, had got a bad name in the neighbourhood. I had the curiosity to go and look at the place for myself. It's a saddening kind of street; the houses are old enough to be mean and dreary, but not old enough to be quaint. As far as I could see most of them are let in lodgings, furnished and unfurnished, and almost every door has three bells to it. Here and there the ground floors have been made into shops of the commonest kind; it's a dismal street in every way. I found Number 20 was to let, and I went to the agent's and got the key. Of course I should have heard nothing of the Herberts in that quarter, but I asked the man, fair and square, how long they had left the house, and whether there had been other tenants in the meanwhile. He looked at me queerly for a minute, and told me the Herberts had left immediately after the unpleasantness, as he called it, and since then the house had been empty."

Mr. Villiers paused for a moment.

"I have always been rather fond of going over empty houses; there's a sort of fascination about the desolate empty rooms, with the nails sticking in the walls, and the dust thick upon the window sill. But I didn't enjoy going over Number 20, Paul Street. I had hardly put my foot inside the passage before I noticed a queer, heavy feeling about the air of the house. Of course all empty houses are stuffy, and so forth, but this was something quite different; I can't describe it to you, but it seemed to stop the breath. I went into the front room and the back room, and the kitchens downstairs; they were all dirty and dusty enough, as you would expect, but there was something strange about them all. I couldn't define it to you, I only know I felt queer. It was one of the rooms on the first floor, though, that was the worst. It was a largish room, and once on a time the paper must have been cheerful enough, but when I saw it, paint, paper, and everything were almost doleful. But the room was full of horror; I felt my teeth grinding as I put my hand on the door, and when I went in, I thought I should have fallen fainting to the floor. However, I pulled myself together, and stood against the end wall, wondering what on earth there could be about the room to make my limbs tremble, and my heart beat as if I were at the hour of death. In one corner there was a pile of newspapers littered about on the floor, and I began looking at them; they were papers of three or four years ago, some of them half torn, and some crumpled as if they had been used for packing. I turned the whole pile over, and amongst them I found a curious drawing; I will show it you presently. But I was thankful to come out, safe and sound, into the open air. People stared at me as I walked along the street, and one man said I was drunk. I was staggering about from one side of the pavement to the other, and it was as much as I could do to take the key back to the agent and get home. I was in bed for a week, suffering from what my doctor called nervous shock and exhaustion. One of those days I was reading the evening paper, and happened to notice a paragraph headed: *'Starved to Death.'* It was the usual style of thing; a model lodging-house in Marylebone, a door locked for several days, and a dead man in his chair when they broke in. *'The deceased,'* said the paragraph, *'was known as Charles Herbert, and is believed to have been once a prosperous country gentleman. His name was familiar to the public three years ago in connexion with the mysterious death in Paul Street, Tottenham Court Road, the deceased being the tenant of the house Number 20, in the area of which a gentleman of good position was found dead under circumstances not devoid of suspicion.'* A tragic ending, wasn't it? But after all, if what he told me were true, which I am sure it was, the man's life was all tragedy, and a tragedy of a stranger sort than they put on the boards."

"And that is the story, is it?" said Clarke musingly.

"Yes, that is the story."

"Well, really, Villiers, I scarcely know what to say about it. There are, no doubt, circumstances in the case which seem peculiar, the finding of the dead man in the area of Herbert's house, for instance, and the extraordinary opinion of the physician as to the cause of death; but, after all, it is conceivable that the facts may be explained in a straightforward manner. As to your own sensations, when you went to see the house, I would suggest that they were due to a vivid imagination; you must have been brooding, in a semi-conscious way, over what you had heard. I don't exactly see what more can be said or done in the matter; you evidently think there is a mystery of some kind, but Herbert is dead; where do you propose to look?"

"I propose to look for the woman; the woman whom he married. She is the mystery."

The two men sat silent by the fireside; Clarke secretly congratulating himself on having successfully kept up the character of advocate of the commonplace, and Villiers wrapt in his gloomy fancies.

"I think I will have a cigarette," he said at last, and put his hand in his pocket to feel for the cigarette case.

"Ah!" he said, starting slightly, "I forgot I had something to show you. You remember my saying that I found a rather curious sketch amongst a pile of old newspapers at the house in Paul Street? Here it is."

Villiers drew out a small thin parcel from his pocket. It was covered with brown paper, and secured with string, and the knots were troublesome. In spite of himself Clarke felt inquisitive; he bent forward on his chair as Villiers painfully undid the string, and unfolded the outer covering. Inside was a second wrapping of tissue, and Villiers took it off and handed the small piece of paper to Clarke without a word.

There was dead silence in the room for five minutes or more; the two men sat so still that they could hear the ticking of the tall old-fashioned clock that stood outside in the hall, and in the mind of one of them the slow monotony of sound woke up a far, far memory. He was looking intently at the small pen-and-ink sketch of the woman's head; it had evidently been drawn with great care, and by a true artist, for the woman's soul looked out of the eyes, and the lips were parted with a strange smile. Clarke gazed still at the face; it brought to his memory one summer evening long ago; he saw again the long lovely valley, the river winding between the hills, the meadows and the cornfields, the dull red sun, and the cold white mist rising from the water. He heard a voice speaking to him across the waves of many years, and saying: *"Clarke, Mary will see the God Pan!"* and then he was standing in the grim room beside the doctor, listening to the heavy ticking of the clock, waiting and watching, watching the figure on the green chair beneath the lamplight. Mary rose up, and he looked into her eyes, and his heart grew cold within him.

"Who is this woman?" he said at last. His voice was dry and hoarse.

"That's the woman whom Herbert married."

Clarke looked again at the sketch; it was not Mary after all. There
certainly was Mary's face, but there was something else, something he
had not seen on Mary's features when the white-clad girl entered the
laboratory with the doctor, nor at her terrible awakening, nor when
she lay grinning on the bed. Whatever it was, the glance that came
from those eyes, the smile on the full lips, or the expression of the whole
face, Clarke shuddered before it in his inmost soul, and thought,
unconsciously, of Dr. Phillips's words, *the most vivid presentment of evil
I have ever seen.*" He turned the paper over mechanically in his hand and
glanced at the back.

"Good God! Clarke, what is the matter? You are as white as death."

Villiers had started wildly from his chair, as Clarke fell back with a
groan, and let the paper drop from his hands.

"I don't feel very well, Villiers, I am subject to these attacks. Pour me
out a little wine; thanks, that will do. I shall feel better in a few minutes."

Villiers picked up the fallen sketch and turned it over as Clarke
had done.

"You saw that?" he said. "That's how I identified it as being a portrait
of Herbert's wife, or should I say his widow. How do you feel now?"

"Better, thanks, it was only a passing faintness. I don't think I quite catch
your meaning. What did you say enabled you to identify the picture?"

"This word—'Helen'—written on the back. Didn't I tell you her
name was Helen? Yes; Helen Vaughan."

Clarke groaned; there could be no shadow of a doubt.

"Now, don't you agree with me," said Villiers, "that in the story I
have told you tonight, and in the part this woman plays in it, there are
some very strange points?"

"Yes, Villiers," Clarke muttered, "it is a strange story indeed; a strange
story indeed. You must give me time to think it over; I may be able to
help you or I may not. Must you be going now? Well, goodnight,
Villiers, goodnight. Come and see me in the course of a week."

V

The Letter Of Advice

"Do you know, Austin," said Villiers, as the two friends were pacing
sedately along Piccadilly one pleasant morning in May, "do you know
I am convinced that what you told me about Paul Street and the

Herberts is a mere episode in an extraordinary history? I may as well
confess to you that when I asked you about Herbert a few months ago
I had just seen him."

"You had seen him? Where?"

"He begged of me in the street one night. He was in the most
pitiable plight, but I recognized the man, and I got him to tell me his
history, or at least the outline of it. In brief, it amounted to this—he
had been ruined by his wife."

"In what manner?"

"He would not tell me; he would only say that she had destroyed
him, body and soul. The man is dead now."

"And what has become of his wife?"

"Ah, that's what I should like to know, and I mean to find her sooner
or later. I know a man named Clarke, a dry fellow, in fact a man of
business, but shrewd enough. You understand my meaning; not
shrewd in the mere business sense of the word, but a man who really
knows something about men and life. Well, I laid the case before him,
and he was evidently impressed. He said it needed consideration, and
asked me to come again in the course of a week. A few days later, I
received this extraordinary letter."

Austin took the envelope, drew out the letter, and read it curiously.
It ran as follows:

*My dear Villiers,—I have thought over the matter on which you consulted
me the other night, and my advice to you is this. Throw the portrait into the
fire, blot out the story from your mind. Never give it another thought, Villiers,
or you will be sorry. You will think, no doubt, that I am in possession of some
secret information, and to a certain extent that is the case. But I only know a
little; I am like a traveller who has peered over an abyss, and has drawn back
in terror. What I know is strange enough and horrible enough, but beyond my
knowledge there are depths and horrors more frightful still, more incredible than
any tale told of winter nights about the fire. I have resolved, and nothing shall
shake that resolve, to explore no whit further, and if you value your happiness
you will make the same determination. Come and see me by all means; but we
will talk on more cheerful topics than this.*

Austin folded the letter methodically, and returned it to Villiers.

"It is certainly an extraordinary letter," he said; "what does he mean
by 'the portrait?'"

"Ah! I forgot to tell you, I have been to Paul Street and have made
a discovery."

Villiers told his story as he had told it to Clarke, and Austin listened in silence. He seemed puzzled.

"How very curious that you should experience such an unpleasant sensation in that room!" he said at length. "I hardly gather that it was a mere matter of the imagination; a feeling of repulsion, in short."

"No, it was more physical than mental. It was as if I were inhaling at every breath some deadly fume, which seemed to penetrate to every nerve and bone and sinew of my body. I felt racked from head to foot, my eyes began to grow dim; it was like the entrance of death."

"Yes, yes, very strange, certainly. You see, your friend confesses that there is some very black story connected with this woman. Did you notice any particular emotion in him when you were telling your tale?"

"Yes, I did. He became very faint, but he assured me that it was a mere passing attack to which he was subject."

"Did you believe him?"

"I did at the time, but I don't now. He heard what I had to say with a good deal of indifference, till I showed him the portrait. It was then he was seized with the attack of which I spoke. He looked ghastly, I assure you."

"Then he must have seen the woman before. But there might be another explanation; it might have been the name, and not the face, which was familiar to him. What do you think?"

"I couldn't say. To the best of my belief it was after turning the portrait in his hands that he nearly dropped from his chair. The name, you know, was written on the back."

"Quite so. After all, it is impossible to come to any resolution in a case like this. I hate melodrama, and nothing strikes me as more commonplace and tedious than the ordinary ghost story of commerce; but really, Villiers, it looks as if there were something very queer at the bottom of this."

The two men had, without noticing it, turned up Ashley Street, leading northward from Piccadilly. It was a long street, and rather a gloomy one, but here and there a brighter taste had illuminated the dark houses with flowers, and gay curtains, and a cheerful paint on the doors. Villiers glanced up as Austin stopped speaking, and looked at one of these houses; geraniums, red and white, dropped from every sill, and daffodil-coloured curtains were draped back from each window.

"It looks cheerful, doesn't it?" he said.

"Yes, and the inside is still more cheery. One of the pleasantest houses of the season, so I have heard. I haven't been there myself, but I've met several men who have, and they tell me it's uncommonly jovial."

"Whose house is it?"

"A Mrs. Beaumont's."

"And who is she?"

"I couldn't tell you. I have heard she comes from South America, but, after all, who she is is of little consequence. She is a very wealthy woman, there's no doubt of that, and some of the best people have taken her up. I heard she has some wonderful claret, really marvellous wine, which must have cost a fabulous sum. Lord Argentine was telling me about it; he was there last Sunday evening. He assures me he has never tasted such a wine, and Argentine, as you know, is an expert. By the way, that reminds me, she must be an oddish sort of woman, this Mrs. Beaumont. Argentine asked her how old the wine was, and what do you think she said? 'About a thousand years, I believe.' Lord Argentine thought she was chaffing him, you know, but when he laughed she said she was speaking quite seriously, and offered to show him the jar. Of course, he couldn't say anything more after that; but it seems rather antiquated for a beverage, doesn't it? Why, here we are at my rooms. Come in, won't you?"

"Thanks, I think I will. I haven't seen the curiosity shop for some time."

It was a room furnished richly, yet oddly, where every chair and bookcase and table, and every rug and jar and ornament seemed to be a thing apart, preserving each its own individuality.

"Anything fresh lately?" said Villiers after a while.

"No; I think not; you saw those queer jugs, didn't you? I thought so. I don't think I have come across anything for the last few weeks."

Austin glanced round the room from cupboard to cupboard, from shelf to shelf, in search of some new oddity. His eyes fell last on an old chest, pleasantly and quaintly carved, which stood in a dark corner of the room.

"Ah," he said, "I was forgetting, I have something to show you." Austin unlocked the chest, drew out a thick quarto volume, laid it on the table, and resumed the cigar he had put down.

"Did you know Arthur Meyrick the painter, Villiers?"

"A little; I met him two or three times at the house of a friend of mine. What has become of him? I haven't heard his name mentioned for some time."

"He's dead."

"You don't say so! Quite young, wasn't he?"

"Yes; only thirty when he died."

"What did he die of?"

"I don't know. He was an intimate friend of mine, and a thoroughly good fellow. He used to come here and talk to me for hours, and he was one of the best talkers I have met. He could even talk about painting, and that's more than can be said of most painters. About eighteen months ago he was feeling rather overworked, and partly at my suggestion he went off on a sort of roving expedition, with no very definite end or aim about it. I believe New York was to be his first port, but I never heard from him. Three months ago I got this book, with a very civil letter from an English doctor practising at Buenos Aires, stating that he had attended the late Mr. Meyrick during his illness, and that the deceased had expressed an earnest wish that the enclosed packet should be sent to me after his death. That was all."

"And haven't you written for further particulars?"

"I have been thinking of doing so. You would advise me to write to the doctor?"

"Certainly. And what about the book?"

"It was sealed up when I got it. I don't think the doctor had seen it."

"Is it something very rare? Meyrick was a collector, perhaps?"

"No, I think not, hardly a collector. Now, what do you think of those Ainu jugs?"

"They are peculiar, but I like them. But aren't you going to show me poor Meyrick's legacy?"

"Yes, yes, to be sure. The fact is, it's rather a peculiar sort of thing, and I haven't shown it to anyone. I wouldn't say anything about it if I were you. There it is."

Villiers took the book, and opened it at haphazard.

"It isn't a printed volume, then?" he said.

"No. It is a collection of drawings in black and white by my poor friend Meyrick."

Villiers turned to the first page, it was blank; the second bore a brief inscription, which he read:

Silet per diem universus, nec sine horrore secretus est; lucet nocturnis ignibus, chorus Ægipanum undique personatur: audiuntur et cantus tibiarum, et tinnitus cymbalorum per oram maritimam.

On the third page was a design which made Villiers start and look up at Austin; he was gazing abstractedly out of the window. Villiers turned page after page, absorbed, in spite of himself, in the frightful Walpurgis-night of evil, strange monstrous evil, that the dead artist had set forth in hard black and white. The figures of fauns and satyrs and Ægipans danced before his eyes, the darkness of the thicket, the dance on the mountain-top, the scenes by lonely shores, in green vineyards, by rocks and desert places, passed before him: a world before which the human soul seemed to shrink back and shudder. Villiers whirled over the remaining pages; he had seen enough, but the picture on the last leaf caught his eye, as he almost closed the book.

"Austin!"

"Well, what is it?"

"Do you know who that is?"

It was a woman's face, alone on the white page.

"Know who it is? No, of course not."

"I do."

"Who is it?"

"It is Mrs. Herbert."

"Are you sure?"

"I am perfectly certain of it. Poor Meyrick! He is one more chapter in her history."

"But what do you think of the designs?"

"They are frightful. Lock the book up again, Austin. If I were you I would burn it; it must be a terrible companion even though it be in a chest."

"Yes, they are singular drawings. But I wonder what connection there could be between Meyrick and Mrs. Herbert, or what link between her and those designs?"

"Ah, who can say? It is possible that the matter may end here, and we shall never know, but in my own opinion this Helen Vaughan, or Mrs. Herbert, is only the beginning. She will come back to London, Austin; depend upon it, she will come back, and we shall hear more about her then. I don't think it will be very pleasant news."

VI

The Suicides

Lord Argentine was a great favourite in London Society. At twenty he had been a poor man, decked with the surname of an illustrious family, but forced to earn a livelihood as best he could, and the most speculative of money-lenders would not have entrusted him with fifty pounds on the chance of his ever changing his name for a title, and his poverty for a great fortune. His father had been near enough to the fountain of good things to secure one of the family livings, but the son, even if he had taken orders, would scarcely have obtained so much as this, and

moreover felt no vocation for the ecclesiastical estate. Thus he fronted
the world with no better armour than the bachelor's gown and the wits
of a younger son's grandson, with which equipment he contrived in
some way to make a very tolerable fight of it. At twenty-five Mr.
Charles Aubernoun saw himself still a man of struggles and of warfare
with the world, but out of the seven who stood between him and the
high places of his family three only remained. These three, however,
were "good lives", but yet not proof against the Zulu assegais and
typhoid fever, and so one morning Aubernoun woke up and found
himself Lord Argentine, a man of thirty who had faced the difficulties
of existence, and had conquered. The situation amused him immensely,
and he resolved that riches should be as pleasant to him as poverty had
always been. Argentine, after some little consideration, came to the
conclusion that dining, regarded as a fine art, was perhaps the most
amusing pursuit open to fallen humanity, and thus his dinners became
famous in London, and an invitation to his table a thing covetously
desired. After ten years of Lordship and dinners Argentine still declined
to be jaded, still persisted in enjoying life, and by a kind of infection
had become recognized as the cause of joy in others, in short, as the
best company. His sudden and tragical death therefore caused a wide
and deep sensation. People could scarce believe it, even though the
newspaper was before their eyes, and the cry of "Mysterious Death of
a Nobleman" came ringing up from the street. But there stood the
brief paragraph: *"Lord Argentine was found dead this morning by his valet
under distressing circumstances. It is stated that there can be no doubt that his
lordship committed suicide, though no motive can be assigned for the act. The
deceased nobleman was widely known in society, and much liked for his genial
manner and sumptuous hospitality. He is succeeded by,"* etc., etc.

By slow degrees the details came to light, but the case still remained
a mystery. The chief witness at the inquest was the dead nobleman's
valet, who said that the night before his death Lord Argentine had
dined with a lady of good position, whose name was suppressed in
newspaper reports. At about eleven o'clock Lord Argentine had returned, and informed his man that he should not require his services
till the next morning. A little later the valet had occasion to cross the
hall and was somewhat astonished to see his master quietly letting
himself out at the front door. He had taken off his evening clothes, and
was dressed in a Norfolk coat and knickerbockers, and wore a low
brown hat. The valet had no reason to suppose that Lord Argentine
had seen him, and though his master rarely kept late hours, thought
little of the occurrence till the next morning, when he knocked at the

bedroom door at a quarter to nine as usual. He received no answer, and, after knocking two or three times, entered the room, and saw Lord Argentine's body leaning forward at an angle from the bottom of the bed. He found that his master had tied a rope securely to one of the short bedposts, and, after making a running noose and slipping it round his neck, the unfortunate man must have resolutely fallen forward, to die by slow strangulation. He was dressed in the light suit in which the valet had seen him go out, and the doctor who was summoned pronounced that life had been extinct for more than four hours. All papers, letters, and so forth seemed in perfect order, and nothing was discovered which pointed in the most remote way to any scandal either great or small. Here the evidence ended; nothing more could be discovered. Several persons had been present at the dinner party at which Lord Argentine had assisted, and to all these he seemed in his usual genial spirits. The valet, indeed, said he thought his master appeared a little excited when he came home, but he confessed that the alteration in his manner was very slight, hardly noticeable, indeed. It seemed hopeless to seek for any clue, and the suggestion that Lord Argentine had been suddenly attacked by acute suicidal mania was generally accepted.

It was otherwise, however, when within three weeks, three more gentlemen, one of them a nobleman, and the two others men of good position and ample means, perished miserably in almost precisely the same manner. Lord Swanleigh was found one morning in his dressing-room, hanging from a peg affixed to the wall, and Mr. Collier-Stuart and Mr. Herries had chosen to die as Lord Argentine. There was no explanation in either case; a few bald facts; a living man in the evening, and a dead body with a black swollen face in the morning. The police had been forced to confess themselves powerless to arrest or explain the sordid murders of Whitechapel; but before the horrible suicides of Piccadilly and Mayfair they were dumbfounded, for not even the mere ferocity which did duty as an explanation of the crimes of the East End, could be of service in the West. Each of these men who had resolved to die a tortured shameful death was rich, prosperous, and to all appearances in love with the world, and not the acutest research could ferret out any shadow of a lurking motive in either case. There was a horror in the air, and men looked at one another's faces when they met, each wondering whether the other was to be the victim of the fifth nameless tragedy. Journalists sought in vain in their scrapbooks for materials whereof to concoct reminiscent articles; and the morning paper was unfolded in many a house with a feeling of awe; no man knew when or where the blow would next light.

A short while after the last of these terrible events, Austin came to see
Mr. Villiers. He was curious to know whether Villiers had succeeded in
discovering any fresh traces of Mrs. Herbert, either through Clarke or by
any other sources, and he asked the question soon after he had sat down.

"No," said Villiers, "I wrote to Clarke, but he remains obdurate, and
I have tried other channels, but without any result. I can't find out
what became of Helen Vaughan after she left Paul Street, but I think
she must have gone abroad. But to tell the truth, Austin, I haven't paid
very much attention to the matter for the last few weeks; I knew poor
Herries intimately, and his terrible death has been a great shock to me,
a great shock."

"I can well believe it," answered Austin gravely; "you know Argentine was a friend of mine. If I remember rightly, we were speaking of
him that day you came to my rooms."

"Yes; it was in connection with that house on Ashley Street, Mrs.
Beaumont's house. You said something about Argentine's dining there."

"Quite so. Of course you know it was there Argentine dined the
night before—before his death."

"No, I haven't heard that."

"Oh yes; the name was kept out of the papers to spare Mrs.
Beaumont. Argentine was a great favourite of hers, and it is said she
was in a terrible state for some time after."

A curious look came over Villiers' face; he seemed undecided
whether to speak out or not. Austin began again.

"I never experienced such a feeling of horror as when I read the
account of Argentine's death. I didn't understand it at the time, and I
don't now. I knew him well, and it completely passes my understanding for what possible cause he—or any of the others for the matter
of that—could have resolved in cold blood to die in such an awful
manner. You know how men babble away each other's characters in
London, you may be sure any buried scandal or hidden skeleton would
have been brought to light in such a case as this; but nothing of the
sort has taken place. As for the theory of mania, that is very well, of
course, for the coroner's jury, but everybody knows that it's all nonsense. Suicidal mania is not smallpox."

Austin relapsed into gloomy silence. Villiers sat silent also, watching
his friend. The expression of indecision still fleeted across his face; he
seemed as if weighing his thoughts in the balance, and the considera-
tions he was revolving left him still silent. Austin tried to shake off the
remembrance of tragedies as hopeless and perplexed as the labyrinth

of Daedalus, and began to talk in an indifferent voice of the more pleasant incidents and adventures of the season.

"That Mrs. Beaumont," he said, "of whom we were speaking, is a great success; she has taken London almost by storm. I met her the other night at Fulham's; she is really a remarkable woman."

"You have met Mrs. Beaumont?"

"Yes; she had quite a court around her. She would be called very handsome, I suppose, and yet there is something about her face which I didn't like. The features are exquisite, but the expression is strange. And all the time I was looking at her, and afterwards, when I was going home, I had a curious feeling that very expression was in some way or other familiar to me."

"You must have seen her in the Row."

"No, I am sure I never set eyes on the woman before; it is that which makes it puzzling. And to the best of my belief I have never seen anybody like her; what I felt was a kind of dim far-off memory, vague but persistent. The only sensation I can compare it to, is that odd feeling one sometimes has in a dream, when fantastic cities and wondrous lands and phantom personages appear familiar and accustomed."

Villiers nodded and glanced aimlessly round the room, possibly in search of something on which to turn the conversation. His eyes fell on an old chest somewhat like that in which the artist's strange legacy lay hidden beneath a Gothic scutcheon.

"Have you written to the doctor about poor Meyrick?" he asked.

"Yes; I wrote asking for full particulars as to his illness and death. I don't expect to have an answer for another three weeks or a month. I thought I might as well enquire whether Meyrick knew an English-woman named Herbert, and if so, whether the doctor could give me any information about her at New York, or Mexico, or San Francisco. I have no idea as to the extent or direction of his travels."

"Yes, and it's very possible that the woman may have more than one name."

"Exactly. I wish I had thought of asking you to lend me the portrait of her which you possess. I might have enclosed it in my letter to Dr. Matthews."

"So you might; that never occurred to me. We might send it now. Hark! What are those boys calling?"

While the two men had been talking together a confused noise of shouting had been gradually growing louder. The noise rose from the eastward and swelled down Piccadilly, drawing nearer and nearer, a very torrent of sound; surging up streets usually quiet, and making

every window a frame for a face, curious or excited. The cries and voices
came echoing up the silent street where Villiers lived, growing more
distinct as they advanced, and, as Villiers spoke, an answer rang up
from the pavement:

"THE WEST END HORRORS; ANOTHER AWFUL SUICIDE;
FULL DETAILS!"

Austin rushed down the stairs and bought a paper and read out the
paragraph to Villiers as the uproar in the street rose and fell. The
window was open and the air seemed full of noise and terror.

*"Another gentleman has fallen a victim to the terrible epidemic of suicide
which for the last month has prevailed in the West End. Mr. Sidney Crawshaw
of Stoke House, Fulham, and King's Pomeroy, Devon, was found, after a
prolonged search, hanging from the branch of a tree in his garden at one
o'clock today. The deceased gentleman dined last night at the Carlton Club
and seemed in his usual health and spirits. He left the Club at about ten o'clock,
and was seen walking leisurely up St. James's Street a little later. Subsequent
to this his movements cannot be traced. On the discovery of the body medical aid
was at once summoned, but life had evidently been long extinct. So far as is
known, Mr. Crawshaw had not trouble or anxiety of any kind. This painful
suicide, it will be remembered, is the fifth of the kind in the last month. The
authorities of Scotland Yard are unable to suggest any explanation of these
terrible occurrences."*

Austin put down the paper in mute horror.

"I shall leave London tomorrow," he said, "it is a city of nightmares.
How awful this is, Villiers!"

Mr. Villiers was sitting by the window quietly looking out into the
street. He had listened to the newspaper report attentively, and the
hint of indecision was no longer on his face.

"Wait a moment, Austin," he replied, "I have made up my mind to
mention a little matter that occurred last night. It is stated, I think,
that Crawshaw was last seen alive in St. James's Street shortly after ten?"

"Yes, I think so. I will look again. Yes, you are quite right."

"Quite so. Well, I am in a position to contradict that statement at
all events. Crawshaw was seen after that; considerably later indeed."

"How do you know?"

"Because I happened to see Crawshaw myself at about two o'clock
this morning."

"You saw Crawshaw? You, Villiers?"

"Yes, I saw him quite distinctly; indeed, there were but a few feet
between us."

"Where, in Heaven's name, did you see him?"

"Not far from here. I saw him in Ashley Street. He was just leaving a house."

"Did you notice which house it was?"

"Yes. It was Mrs. Beaumont's."

"Villiers! Think what you are saying; there must be some mistake. How could Crawshaw be in Mrs. Beaumont's house at two o'clock in the morning? Surely, surely, you must have been dreaming, Villiers, you were always rather fanciful."

"No; I was wide awake enough. Even if I had been dreaming as you say, what I saw would have roused me effectually."

"What you saw? What did you see? Was there anything strange about Crawshaw? But I can't believe it; it is impossible."

"Well, if you like I will tell you what I saw, or if you please, what I think I saw, and you can judge for yourself."

"Very good, Villiers."

The noise and clamour of the street had died away, though now and then the sound of shouting still came from the distance, and the dull, leaden silence seemed like the quiet after an earthquake or a storm. Villiers turned from the window and began speaking.

"I was at a house near Regent's Park last night, and when I came away the fancy took me to walk home instead of taking a hansom. It was a clear pleasant night enough, and after a few minutes I had the streets pretty much to myself. It's a curious thing, Austin, to be alone in London at night, the gas lamps stretching away in perspective, and the dead silence, and then perhaps the rush and clatter of a hansom on the stones, and the fire starting up under the horse's hoofs. I walked along pretty briskly, for I was feeling a little tired of being out in the night, and as the clocks were striking two I turned down Ashley Street, which, you know, is on my way. It was quieter than ever there, and the lamps were fewer; altogether, it looked as dark and gloomy as a forest in winter. I had done about half the length of the street when I heard a door closed very softly, and naturally I looked up to see who was abroad like myself at such an hour. As it happens, there is a street lamp close to the house in question, and I saw a man standing on the step. He had just shut the door and his face was towards me, and I recognized Crawshaw directly. I never knew him to speak to, but I had often seen him, and I am positive that I was not mistaken in my man. I looked into his face for a moment, and then—I will confess the truth—I set off at a good run, and kept it up till I was within my own door."

"Why?"

"Why? Because it made my blood run cold to see that man's face. I could never have supposed that such an infernal medley of passions could have glared out of any human eyes; I almost fainted as I looked. I knew I had looked into the eyes of a lost soul, Austin, the man's outward form remained, but all hell was within it. Furious lust, and hate that was like fire, and the loss of all hope and horror that seemed to shriek aloud to the night, though his teeth were shut; and the utter blackness of despair. I am sure he did not see me; he saw nothing that you or I can see, but he saw what I hope we never shall. I do not know when he died; I suppose in an hour, or perhaps two, but when I passed down Ashley Street and heard the closing door, that man no longer belonged to this world; it was a devil's face I looked upon."

There was an interval of silence in the room when Villiers ceased speaking. The light was failing, and all the tumult of an hour ago was quite hushed. Austin had bent his head at the close of the story, and his hand covered his eyes.

"What can it mean?" he said at length.

"Who knows, Austin, who knows? It's a black business, but I think we had better keep it to ourselves, for the present at any rate. I will see if I cannot learn anything about that house through private channels of information, and if I do light upon anything I will let you know."

VII

The Encounter in Soho

Three weeks later Austin received a note from Villiers, asking him to call either that afternoon or the next. He chose the nearer date, and found Villiers sitting as usual by the window, apparently lost in meditation on the drowsy traffic of the street. There was a bamboo table by his side, a fantastic thing, enriched with gilding and queer painted scenes, and on it lay a little pile of papers arranged and docketed as neatly as anything in Mr. Clarke's office.

"Well, Villiers, have you made any discoveries in the last three weeks?"

"I think so; I have here one or two memoranda which struck me as singular, and there is a statement to which I shall call your attention."

"And these documents relate to Mrs. Beaumont? It was really Crawshaw whom you saw that night standing on the doorstep of the house in Ashley Street?"

"As to that matter my belief remains unchanged, but neither my inquiries nor their results have any special relation to Crawshaw. But my investigations have had a strange issue. I have found out who Mrs. Beaumont is!"

"Who she is? What do you mean?"

"I mean that you and I know her better under another name."

"What name is that?"

"Herbert."

"Herbert!" Austin repeated the word, dazed with astonishment.

"Yes, Mrs. Herbert of Paul Street, Helen Vaughan of earlier adventures unknown to me. You had reason to recognize the expression on her face; when you go home look at the face in Meyrick's book of horrors, and you will know the sources of your recollection."

"And you have proof of this?"

"Yes, the best of proof; I have seen Mrs. Beaumont, or shall we say Mrs. Herbert?"

"Where did you see her?"

"Hardly in a place where you would expect to see a lady who lives in Ashley Street, Piccadilly. I saw her entering a house in one of the meanest and most disreputable streets in Soho. In fact, I had made an appointment, though not with her, and she was precise both to time and place."

"All this seems very wonderful, but I cannot call it incredible. You must remember, Villiers, that I have seen this woman, in the ordinary adventure of London society, talking and laughing, and sipping her coffee in a commonplace drawing room with commonplace people. But you know what you are saying."

"I do; I have not allowed myself to be led by surmises or fancies. It was with no thought of finding Helen Vaughan that I searched for Mrs. Beaumont in the dark waters of the life of London, but such has been the issue."

"You must have been in strange places, Villiers."

"Yes, I have been in very strange places. It would have been useless, you know, to go to Ashley Street, and ask Mrs. Beaumont to give me a short sketch of her previous history. No; assuming, as I do assume, that her record was not of the cleanest, it would be pretty certain that at some previous time she must have moved in circles not quite so refined as her present ones. If you see mud on the top of a stream, you may be sure that it was once at the bottom. I went to the bottom. I have always been fond of diving into Queer Street for my amusement, and I found my knowledge of that locality and its inhabitants very useful. It is, perhaps, needless to say that my friends had never heard the name of Beaumont, and as I had never seen the lady, and was quite unable to describe her, I had to set to work in an indirect way. The people there know me; I have been able to do some of them service now and again, so they made no difficulty about giving their information; they were aware I had no communication direct or indirect with Scotland Yard. I had to cast out a good many lines, though, before I got what I wanted, and when I landed the fish I did not for a moment suppose it was my fish. But I listened to what I was told out of a constitutional liking for useless information, and I found myself in possession of a very curious story, though, as I imagined, not the story I was looking for. It was to this effect. Some five or six years ago, a woman named Raymond suddenly made her appearance in the neighbourhood to which I am referring. She was described to me as being quite young, probably not more than seventeen or eighteen, very handsome, and looking as if she came from the country. I should be wrong in saying that she found her level in going to this particular quarter, or associating with these people, for from what I was told, I should think the worst den in London far too good for her. The person from whom I got my information—as you may suppose, no great Puritan—shuddered and grew sick in telling me of the nameless infamies which were laid to her charge. After living there for a year, or perhaps a little more, she disappeared as suddenly as she came, and they saw nothing of her till about the time of the Paul Street case. At first she came to her old haunts only occasionally, then more frequently, and finally took up her abode there as before, and remained for six or eight months. It's of no use my going into details as to the life that woman led; if you want particulars, you can look at Meyrick's legacy. Those designs were not drawn from his imagination. She again disappeared, and the people of the place saw nothing of her till a few months ago. My informant told me that she had taken some rooms in a house which he pointed out, and these rooms she was in the habit of visiting two or three times a week and always at ten in the morning. I was led to expect that one of these visits would be paid on a certain day about a week ago, and I accordingly managed to be on the look-out in company with my cicerone at quarter to ten, and the hour and the lady came with equal punctuality. My friend and I were standing under an archway, a little way back from the street, but she saw us, and gave us a glance that I shall be long in forgetting. That look was quite enough for me; I knew Miss Raymond to be Mrs. Herbert; as for Mrs. Beaumont, she had quite gone out of my head. She went into the house, and I watched it till four o'clock, when she came out, and then I followed her. It was a long chase, and I had to be very careful to keep a long way in the background, and yet not lose sight

of the woman. She took me down to the Strand, and then to Westmin-
ster, and then up St. James's Street, and along Piccadilly. I felt queerish
when I saw her turn up Ashley Street; the thought that Mrs. Herbert
was Mrs. Beaumont came into my mind, but it seemed too improbable
to be true. I waited at the corner, keeping my eye on her all the time,
and I took particular care to note the house at which she stopped. It
was the house with the gay curtains, the house of flowers, the house
out of which Crawshaw came the night he hanged himself in his garden.
I was just going away with my discovery, when I saw an empty carriage
come round and draw up in front of the house, and I came to the conclusion
that Mrs. Herbert was going out for a drive, and I was right. I took a
hansom and followed the carriage into the Park. There, as it happened, I
met a man I know, and we stood talking together a little distance from
the carriage-way, to which I had my back. We had not been there for ten
minutes when my friend took off his hat, and I glanced round and saw
the lady I had been following all day. 'Who is that?' I said, and his answer
was, 'Mrs. Beaumont; lives in Ashley Street.' Of course there could be no
doubt after that. I don't know whether she saw me, but I don't think she
did. I went home at once, and, on consideration, I thought that I had a
sufficiently good case with which to go to Clarke."

"Why to Clarke?"

"Because I am sure that Clarke is in possession of facts about this
woman, facts of which I know nothing."

"Well, what then?"

Mr. Villiers leaned back in his chair and looked reflectively at Austin
for a moment before he answered:

"My idea was that Clarke and I should call on Mrs. Beaumont."

"You would never go into such a house as that? No, no, Villiers, you
cannot do it. Besides, consider; what result—"

"I will tell you soon. But I was going to say that my information
does not end here; it has been completed in an extraordinary manner.

"Look at this neat little packet of manuscript; it is paginated you
see, and I have indulged in the civil coquetry of a ribbon of red tape.
It has almost a legal air, hasn't it? Run your eye over it, Austin. It is
an account of the entertainment Mrs. Beaumont provided for her
choicer guests. The man who wrote this escaped with his life, but I do
not think he will live many years. The doctors tell him he must have
sustained some severe shock to his nerves."

Austin took the manuscript, but never read it. Opening the neat
pages at haphazard his eye was caught by a word and a phrase that

followed it; and, sick at heart, with white lips and a cold sweat pouring like water from his temples, he flung the paper down.

"Take it away, Villiers, never speak of this again. Are you made of stone, man? Why, the dread and horror of death itself, the thought of the man who stands in the keen morning air on the black platform, bound, the bell tolling in his ears, and waits for the harsh rattle of the bolt, are as nothing compared to this. I will not read it; I should never sleep again."

"Very good. I can fancy what you saw. Yes; it is horrible enough; but after all, it is an old story, an old mystery played in our day, and in dim London streets instead of amidst the vineyards and the olive gardens. We know what happened to those who chanced to meet the Great God Pan, and those who are wise know that all symbols are symbols of something, not of nothing. It was, indeed, an exquisite symbol beneath which men long ago veiled their knowledge of the most awful, most secret forces which lie at the heart of all things; forces before which the souls of men must wither and die and blacken, as their bodies blacken under the electric current. Such forces cannot be named, cannot be spoken, cannot be imagined except under a veil and a symbol, a symbol to the most of us appearing a quaint, poetic fancy, to some a foolish tale. But you and I, at all events, have known something of the terror that may dwell in the secret place of life, manifested under human flesh; that which is without form taking to itself a form. Oh, Austin, how can it be? How is it that the very sunlight does not turn to blackness before this thing, the hard earth melt and boil beneath such a burden?"

Villiers was pacing up and down the room, and the beads of sweat stood out on his forehead. Austin sat silent for a while, but Villiers saw him make a sign upon his breast.

"I say again, Villiers, you will surely never enter such a house as that? You would never pass out alive."

"Yes, Austin, I shall go out alive—I, and Clarke with me."

"What do you mean? You cannot, you would not dare—"

"Wait a moment. The air was very pleasant and fresh this morning; there was a breeze blowing, even through this dull street, and I thought I would take a walk. Piccadilly stretched before me a clear, bright vista, and the sun flashed on the carriages and on the quivering leaves in the park. It was a joyous morning, and men and women looked at the sky and smiled as they went about their work or their pleasure, and the wind blew as blithely as upon the meadows and the scented gorse. But somehow or other I got out of the bustle and the gaiety, and found myself walking slowly along a quiet, dull street, where there seemed to be no sunshine and no air, and where the few foot-passengers loitered as they walked, and hung indecisively about corners and archways. I walked along, hardly knowing where I was going or what I did there, but feeling impelled, as one sometimes is, to explore still further, with a vague idea of reaching some unknown goal. Thus I forged up the street, noting the small traffic of the milk shop, and wondering at the incongruous medley of penny pipes, black tobacco, sweets, newspapers, and comic songs which here and there jostled one another in the short compass of a single window. I think it was a cold shudder that suddenly passed through me that first told me that I had found what I wanted. I looked up from the pavement and stopped before a dusty shop, above which the lettering had faded, where the windows had gathered to themselves the fog and the dirt of winters innumerable. I saw what I required; but I think it was five minutes before I had steadied myself and could walk in and ask for it in a cool voice and with a calm face. I think there must even then have been a tremor in my words, for the old man who came out from his back parlour, and fumbled slowly amongst his goods, looked oddly at me as he tied the parcel. I paid what he asked, and stood leaning by the counter, with a strange reluctance to take up my goods and go. I asked about the business, and learnt that trade was bad and the profits cut down sadly; but then the street was not what it was before traffic had been diverted, but that was done forty years ago, 'just before my father died,' he said. I got away at last, and walked along sharply; it was a dismal street indeed, and I was glad to return to the bustle and the noise. Would you like to see my purchase?"

Austin said nothing, but nodded his head slightly; he still looked white and sick. Villiers pulled out a drawer in the bamboo table, and showed Austin a long coil of cord, hard and new; and at one end was a running noose.

"It is the best hempen cord," said Villiers, "just as it used to be made for the old trade, the man told me. Not an inch of jute from end to end."

Austin set his teeth hard, and stared at Villiers, growing whiter as he looked.

"You would not do it," he murmured at last. "You would not have blood on your hands. My God!" he exclaimed, with sudden vehemence, "you cannot mean this, Villiers, that you will make yourself a hangman?"

"No. I shall offer that choice, and leave Helen Vaughan alone with this cord in a locked room for fifteen minutes. If when we go in it is not done, I shall call the nearest policeman. That is all."

"I must go now. I cannot stay here any longer; I cannot hear this. Goodnight."

"Goodnight, Austin."

The door shut, but in a moment it was opened again, and Austin stood, white and ghastly in the entrance.

"I was forgetting," he said, "that I too have something to tell. I have received a letter from Dr. Harding of Buenos Aires. He says that he attended Meyrick for three weeks before his death."

"And does he say what carried him off in the prime of his life? It was not fever?"

"No, it was not fever. According to the doctor, it was an utter collapse of the whole system, probably caused by some severe shock. But he states that the patient would tell him nothing, and that he was consequently at some disadvantage in treating the case."

"Is there anything more?"

"Yes. Dr. Harding ends his letter by saying: 'I think this is all the information I can give you about your poor friend. He had not been long in Buenos Aires, and knew scarcely any one, with the exception of a person who did not bear the best of characters, and has since left—a Mrs. Vaughan.'"

VIII

The Fragments

Amongst the papers of the well-known physician, Dr. Robert Matheson, of Ashley Street, Piccadilly, who died suddenly, of apoplectic seizure, at the beginning of 1892, a leaf of manuscript paper was found, covered with pencil jottings. These notes were in Latin, much abbreviated, and had evidently been made in great haste. The MS. was only deciphered with great difficulty, and some words have up to the present time evaded all the efforts of the expert employed. The date, "XXV Jul. 1888," is written on the right-hand corner of the MS. The following is a translation of Dr. Matheson's manuscript:

Whether science would benefit by these brief notes if they could be published, I do not know, but rather doubt. But certainly I shall never take the responsibility of publishing or divulging one word of what is here written, not only on account of my oath freely given to those two persons who were present, but also because the details are too abominable. It is probably that, upon mature consideration, and after weighing the good and evil, I shall one day destroy this paper, or at least leave it under seal to my friend D., trusting his discretion, to use it or to burn it, as he may think fit.

As was befitting, I did all that my knowledge suggested to make sure that I was suffering under no delusion. At first astounded, I could hardly think, but in a minute's time I was sure that my pulse was steady and regular, and that I was in my real and true senses. I then fixed my eyes quietly on what was before me.

Though horror and revolting nausea rose up within me, and an odour of corruption choked my breath, I remained firm. I was then privileged or accursed, I dare not say which, to see that which was on the bed, there black like ink, transformed before my eyes. The skin, and the flesh, and the muscles, and the bones, and the firm structure of the human body that I had thought to be unchangeable, and permanent as adamant, began to melt and dissolve.

I knew that the body may be separated into its elements by external agencies, but I should have refused to believe what I saw. For here there was some internal force, of which I knew nothing, that caused dissolution and change.

Here too was all the work by which man had been made repeated before my eyes. I saw the form waver from sex to sex, dividing itself from itself, and then again reunited. Then I saw the body descend to the beasts whence it ascended, and that which was on the heights go down to the depths, even to the abyss of all being. The principle of life, which makes organism, always remained, while the outward form changed.

The light within the room had turned to blackness, not the darkness of night, in which objects are seen dimly, for I could see clearly and without difficulty. But it was the negation of light; objects were presented to my eyes, if I may say so, without any medium, in such a manner that if there had been a prism in the room I should have seen no colours represented in it.

I watched, and at last I saw nothing but a substance as jelly. Then the ladder was ascended again ... [here the MS. is illegible] ... for one instant I saw a Form, shaped in dimness before me, which I will not farther describe. But the symbol of this form may be seen in ancient sculptures, and in paintings which survived beneath the lava, too foul to be spoken of ... as a horrible and unspeakable shape, neither man nor beast, was changed into human form, there came finally death.

I who saw all this, not without great horror and loathing of soul, here write my name, declaring all that I have set on this paper to be true.

— *Robert Matheson, Med Dr.*

... Such, Raymond, is the story of what I know and what I have seen. The burden of it was too heavy for me to bear alone, and yet I could tell it to none but you. Villiers, who was with me at the last, knows nothing of that awful secret of the wood, of how what we both saw die,

lay upon the smooth, sweet turf amidst the summer flowers, half in
sun and half in shadow, and holding the girl Rachel's hand, called and
summoned those companions, and shaped in solid form, upon the earth
we tread on, the horror which we can but hint at, which we can only
name under a figure. I would not tell Villiers of this, nor of that
resemblance, which struck me as with a blow upon my heart, when I
saw the portrait, which filled the cup of terror at the end. What this
can mean I dare not guess. I know that what I saw perish was not Mary,
and yet in the last agony Mary's eyes looked into mine. Whether there
be any one who can show the last link in this chain of awful mystery,
I do not know, but if there be anyone who can do this, you, Raymond,
are the man. And if you know the secret, it rests with you to tell it or
not, as you please.

I am writing this letter to you immediately on my getting back to
town. I have been in the country for the last few days; perhaps you may
be able to guess in what part. While the horror and wonder of London
was at its height—for "Mrs. Beaumont," as I have told you, was well
known in society—I wrote to my friend Dr. Phillips, giving some brief
outline, or rather hint, of what had happened, and asking him to tell
me the name of the village where the events he had related to me
occurred. He gave me the name, as he said with the less hesitation,
because Rachel's parents, he said, had undoubtedly died of grief and
horror caused by the terrible death of their daughter, and by what had
gone before that death. On the evening of the day on which I received
Phillips' letter I was at Caermaen, and standing beneath the mouldering Roman walls, white with the winters of seventeen hundred years,
I looked over the meadow where once had stood the older temple of
the "God of the Deeps", and saw a house gleaming in the sunlight. It
was the house where Helen had lived. I stayed at Caermaen for several
days. The people of the place, I found, knew little and had guessed less.
Those whom I spoke to on the matter seemed surprised that an
antiquarian (as I professed myself to be) should trouble about a village
tragedy, of which they gave a very commonplace version, and, as you
may imagine, I told nothing of what I knew. Most of my time was
spent in the great wood that rises just above the village and climbs the
hillside, and goes down to the river in the valley; such another long
valley, Raymond, as that on which we looked one summer night,
walking to and fro before your house. For many an hour I strayed
through the maze of the forest, turning now to right and now to left,
pacing slowly down long alleys of undergrowth, shadowy and chill,
even under the midday sun, and halting beneath great oaks; on the

short turf of a clearing where the faint sweet scent of wild roses came
to me on the wind and mixed with the heavy perfume of the elder,
whose mingled odour is like the odour of the room of the dead, a vapour
of incense and corruption. I stood at the edges of the wood, gazing at
all the pomp and procession of the foxgloves towering amidst the
bracken and shining red in the broad sunshine, and beyond them into
deep thickets of close undergrowth where springs boil up from the rock
and nourish the water-weeds, dank and evil. But in all my wanderings
I avoided one part of the wood; it was not till yesterday that I climbed
to the summit of the hill, and stood upon the ancient Roman road that
threads the highest ridge of the wood. Here they had walked, Helen
and Rachel, along this quiet causeway, upon the pavement of green
turf, shut in on either side by high banks of red earth, and tall hedges
of shining beech, and here I followed in their steps, looking out, now
and again, through partings in the boughs, and seeing on one side the
sweep of the wood stretching far to right and left, and sinking into the
broad level, and beyond, the yellow sea, and the land over the sea. On
the other side was the valley and the river and hill following hill as
wave on wave, and wood and meadow, and cornfield, and white houses
gleaming, and a great wall of mountain, and far blue peaks in the north.
And so at last I came to the place. The track went up a gentle slope,
and widened out into an open space with a wall of thick undergrowth
around it, and then, narrowing again, passed on into the distance and
the faint blue mist of summer heat. And into this pleasant summer
glade Rachel passed a girl, and left it, who shall say what? I did not
stay there long.

In a small town near Caermaen there is a museum, containing for
the most part Roman remains which have been found in the neighbourhood at various times. On the day after my arrival at Caermaen I
walked over to the town in question, and took the opportunity of
inspecting this museum. After I had seen most of the sculptured stones,
the coffins, rings, coins, and fragments of tessellated pavement which
the place contains, I was shown a small square pillar of white stone,
which had been recently discovered in the wood of which I have been
speaking, and, as I found on inquiry, in that open space where the
Roman road broadens out. On one side of the pillar was an inscription,
of which I took a note. Some of the letters have been defaced, but I do
not think there can be any doubt as to those which I supply. The
inscription is as follows:

DEVOMNODENT*i*
FLA*v*IVSSENILISPOSSV*it*
PROPTERNVP*tias*
*quas*VIDITSVBVMB*ra*

*"To the great god Nodens (the god of the great Deep or Abyss) Flavius
Senilis has erected this pillar on account of the marriage which he saw beneath
the shade."*

The custodian of the museum informed me that local antiquaries
were much puzzled, not by the inscription, or by any difficulty in
translating it, but as to the circumstance or rite to which allusion
is made.

... And now, my dear Clarke, as to what you tell me about Helen
Vaughan, whom you say you saw die under circumstances of the utmost
and incredible horror. I was interested in your account, but a good deal,
nay all, of what you told me I knew already. I can understand the
strange likeness you remarked both in the portrait and in the actual
face; you have seen Helen's mother. You remember Mary. She was the
mother of Helen Vaughan, who was born nine months after that night.

Mary never recovered her reason. She lay, as you saw her, all the while
upon her bed, and a few days after the child was born she died. I fancy
that just at the last she knew me; I was standing by the bed, and the
old look came into her eyes for a second, and then she shuddered and
groaned and died. It was an ill work I did that night when you were
present; I broke open the door of the house of life, without knowing
or caring what might pass forth or enter in. I recollect your telling me
at the time, sharply enough, and rightly enough too, in one sense, that
I had ruined the reason of a human being by a foolish experiment, based
on an absurd theory. You did well to blame me, but my theory was not
all absurdity. What I said Mary would see, she saw, but I forgot that
no human eyes could look on such a vision with impunity. And I forgot,
as I have just said, that when the house of life is thus thrown open,
there may enter in that for which we have no name, and human flesh
may become the veil of a horror one dare not express. I played with
energies which I did not understand, and you have seen the ending of
it. Helen Vaughan did well to bind the cord about her neck and die,
though the death was horrible. The blackened face, the hideous form
upon the bed, changing and melting before your eyes from woman to
man, from man to beast, and from beast to worse than beast, all the
strange horror that you witnessed, surprises me but little. What you
say the doctor whom you sent for saw and shuddered at I noticed long

ago; I knew what I had done the moment the child was born, and when it was scarcely five years old I surprised it, not once or twice but several times with a playmate, you may guess of what kind. It was for me a constant, an incarnate horror, and after a few years I felt I could bear it no longer, and I sent Helen Vaughan away. You know now what frightened the boy in the wood. The rest of the strange story, and all else that you tell me, as discovered by your friend, I have contrived to learn from time to time, almost to the last chapter. And now Helen is with her companions ....

NOTE: Helen Vaughan was born on August 5th, 1865, at the Red House, Breconshire, and died on July 25th, 1888, in her house in a street off Piccadilly, called Ashley Street in the story.

A surprisingly large amount of the following story is taken up with the text of a diary, and it is not exactly easy reading. It is the diary of a child who is rather more eloquent than we might expect in real life, but who nonetheless writes in a childish run-on sort of way. The result is a distancing device unmatched in eerie effect. There is no evident artifice in it, no attempt at all to convince, and this makes it all the more convincing. Out of the mouths of babes. Machen uses a brilliant variation on the "unreliable narrator" device, a gimmick designed to create an ironic distance between author and fictive narrator on the one hand and between narrator and reader on the other. The unreliable narrator understands the action less than the reader does (as in "The Haunter of the Dark"). But Machen's diarist knows both much less and much more than the reader.

And in this diary we have no trouble seeing the prototype of Wilbur Whateley's cryptic diary with its references to "the Voorish sign" and "the Aklo Sabaoth." Machen reproduces a considerably longer diary excerpt than Lovecraft, but in Machen's we read of "the kingdom of Voor" and of a "wicked voorish dome in Deep Dendo", as well as "the Aklo letters." And finally, in the post-game preachment of Dr. Armitage, when he admonishes the cowed Dunwich populace, "We have no business calling in such things from outside, and only very wicked people and very wicked cults ever try to," we cannot fail to think of Ambrose's disquisition on "real sin" and "great sinners" in "The White People": "The essence of sin really is {i}n the taking of heaven by storm ... it is simply an attempt to penetrate into another and a higher sphere in a forbidden manner." Wizard Whateley was one of Machen's great sinners. It only remains to note that, if you are interested, you may find another treatment by Machen of a key image of "The White People" in his short tale "The Ceremony" in the rare collection Ornaments in Jade *(also in the Penguin paperback collection* Holy Terrors*). If the story title puts you in mind of T. E. D. Klein's novel* The Ceremonies, *that's no accident, since the Machen influence is very great there, too.*

The White People

by Arthur Machen

Prologue

Sorcery and sanctity," said Ambrose, "these are the only realities. Each is an ecstasy, a withdrawal from the common life."

Cotgrave listened, interested. He had been brought by a friend to this mouldering house in a northern suburb, through an old garden to the room where Ambrose the recluse dozed and dreamed over his books.

"Yes," he went on, "magic is justified of her children. There are many, I think, who eat dry crusts and drink water, with a joy infinitely sharper than anything within the experience of the 'practical' epicure."

"You are speaking of the saints?"

"Yes, and of the sinners, too. I think you are falling into the very general error of confining the spiritual world to the supremely good; but the supremely wicked, necessarily, have their portion in it. The merely carnal, sensual man can no more be a great sinner than he can be a great saint. Most of us are just indifferent, mixed-up creatures; we muddle through the world without realizing the meaning and the inner sense of things, and consequently, our wickedness and our goodness are alike second-rate, unimportant."

"And you think the great sinner, then, will be an ascetic, as well as the great saint?"

"Great people of all kinds forsake the imperfect copies and go to the perfect originals. I have no doubt but that many of the very highest among the saints have never done a 'good action' (using the words in their ordinary sense). And, on the other hand, there have been those who have sounded the very depths of sin, who all their lives have never done an 'ill deed.'"

He went out of the room for a moment, and Cotgrave, in high delight, turned to his friend and thanked him for the introduction.

"He's grand," he said. "I never saw that kind of lunatic before."

Ambrose returned with more whisky and helped the two men in a liberal manner. He abused the teetotal sect with ferocity, as he handed the seltzer, and pouring out a glass of water for himself, was about to resume his monologue, when Cotgrave broke in.

"I can't stand it, you know," he said, "your paradoxes are too monstrous. A man may be a great sinner and yet never do anything sinful! Come!"

"You're quite wrong," said Ambrose. "I never make paradoxes; I wish I could. I merely said that a man may have an exquisite taste in Romanee Conti, and it's more like a truism than a paradox, isn't it? Your surprise at my remark is due to the fact that you haven't realized what sin is. Oh, yes, there is a sort of connexion between Sin with the capital letter, and actions which are commonly called sinful: with murder, theft, adultery, and so forth. Much the same connexion that there is between the A, B, C and fine literature. But I believe that the misconception—it is all but universal—arises in great measure from our looking at the matter through social spectacles. We think that a man who does evil to *us* and to his neighbours must be very evil. So he

is, from a social standpoint; but can't you realize that Evil in its essence
is a lonely thing, a passion of the solitary, individual soul? Really, the
average murderer, *qua* murderer, is not by any means a sinner in the
true sense of the word. He is simply a wild beast that we have to get
rid of to save our own necks from his knife. I should class him rather
with tigers than with sinners."

"It seems a little strange."

"I think not. The murderer murders not from positive qualities, but
from negative ones; he lacks something which non-murderers possess.
Evil, of course, is wholly positive—only it is on the wrong side. You
may believe me that sin in its proper sense is very rare; it is probable
that there have been far fewer sinners than saints. Yes, your standpoint
is all very well for practical, social purposes; we are naturally inclined
to think that a person who is very disagreeable to us must be a very
great sinner! It is very disagreeable to have one's pocket picked, and
we pronounce the thief to be a very great sinner. In truth, he is merely
an undeveloped man. He cannot be a saint, of course; but he may be,
and often is, an infinitely better creature than thousands who have
never broken a single commandment. He is a great nuisance to *us*, I
admit, and we very properly lock him up if we catch him; but between
his troublesome and unsocial action and evil—oh, the connexion is
of the weakest."

It was getting very late. The man who had brought Cotgrave had
probably heard all this before, since he assisted with a bland and
judicious smile, but Cotgrave began to think that his "lunatic" was
turning into a sage.

"Do you know," he said, "you interest me immensely? You think,
then, that we do not understand the real nature of evil?"

"No, I don't think we do. We over-estimate it and we under-estimate
it. We take the very numerous infractions of our social 'bye-laws'—the
very necessary and very proper regulations which keep the human
company together—and we get frightened at the prevalence of 'sin'
and 'evil.' But this is really nonsense. Take theft, for example. Have
you any *horror* at the thought of Robin Hood, of the Highland caterans
of the seventeenth century, of the moss-troopers, of the company
promoters of our day?

"Then, on the other hand, we underrate evil. We attach such an
enormous importance to the 'sin' of meddling with our pockets (and
our wives) that we have quite forgotten the awfulness of real sin."

"And what is sin?" said Cotgrave.

"I think I must reply to your question by another. What would your feelings be, seriously, if your cat or your dog began to talk to you, and to dispute with you in human accents? You would be overwhelmed with horror. I am sure of it. And if the roses in your garden sang a weird song, you would go mad. And suppose the stones in the road began to swell and grow before your eyes, and if the pebble that you noticed at night had shot out stony blossoms in the morning?

"Well, these examples may give you some notion of what sin really is."

"Look here," said the third man, hitherto placid, "you two seem pretty well wound up. But I'm going home. I've missed my tram, and I shall have to walk."

Ambrose and Cotgrave seemed to settle down more profoundly when the other had gone out into the early misty mornings and the pale light of the lamps.

"You astonish me," said Cotgrave. "I had never thought of that. If that is really so, one must turn everything upside down. Then the essence of sin really is—"

"In the taking of heaven by storm, it seems to me," said Ambrose. "It appears to me that it is simply an attempt to penetrate into another and higher sphere in a forbidden manner. You can understand why it is so rare. There are few, indeed, who wish to penetrate into other spheres, higher or lower, in ways allowed or forbidden. Men, in the mass, are amply content with life as they find it. Therefore there are few saints, and sinners (in the proper sense) are fewer still, and men of genius who partake sometimes of each character are rare also. Yes; on the whole, it is, perhaps, harder to be a great sinner than a great saint."

"There is something profoundly unnatural about sin? Is that what you mean?"

"Exactly. Holiness requires as great, or almost as great, an effort; but holiness works on lines that *were* natural once; it is an effort to recover the ecstasy that was before the Fall. But sin is an effort to gain the ecstasy and the knowledge that pertain alone to angels, and in making this effort man becomes a demon. I told you that the mere murderer is not *therefore* a sinner; that is true, but the sinner is sometimes a murderer. Gilles de Rais is an instance. So you see that while the good and the evil are unnatural to man as he now is—to man the social, civilized being—evil is unnatural in a much deeper sense than good. The saint endeavours to recover a gift which he has lost; the sinner tries to obtain something which was never his. In brief, he repeats the Fall."

"But are you a Catholic?" said Cotgrave.

"Yes, I am a member of the persecuted Anglican Church."

"Then, how about those texts which seem to reckon as sin that which you would set down as a mere trivial dereliction?"

"Yes, but in one place the word 'sorcerers' comes in the same sentence, doesn't it? That seems to me to give the key-note. Consider: Can you imagine for a moment that a false statement which saves an innocent man's life is a sin? No; very good, then, it is not the mere liar who is excluded by those words; it is, above all, the 'sorcerers' who use the material life, who use the failings incidental to material life as instruments to obtain their infinitely wicked ends. And let me tell you this: Our higher senses are so blunted, we are so drenched with materialism, that we should probably fail to recognize real wickedness if we encountered it."

"But shouldn't we experience a certain horror—a terror such as you hinted we would experience if a rose tree sang—in the mere presence of an evil man?"

"We should if we were natural: Children and women feel this horror you speak of, even animals experience it. But with most of us convention and civilization and education have blinded and deafened and obscured the natural reason. No, sometimes we may recognize evil by its hatred of the good—one doesn't need much penetration to guess at the influence which dictated, quite unconsciously, the 'Blackwood' review of Keats—but this is purely incidental; and, as a rule, I suspect that the Hierarchs of Tophet pass quite unnoticed, or, perhaps, in certain cases, as good but mistaken men."

"But you used the word 'unconscious' just now, of Keats' reviewers. Is wickedness ever unconscious?"

"Always. It must be so. It is like holiness and genius in this as in other points; it is a certain rapture or ecstasy of the soul, a transcendent effort to surpass the ordinary bounds. So, surpassing these, it surpasses also the understanding, the faculty that takes note of that which comes before it. No, a man may be infinitely and horribly wicked and never suspect it. But I tell you, evil in this, its certain and true sense, is rare, and I think it is growing rarer."

"I am trying to get hold of it all," said Cotgrave. "From what you say, I gather that the true evil differs generically from that which we call evil?"

"Quite so. There is, no doubt, an analogy between the two, a resemblance such as enables us to use, quite legitimately, such terms as the 'foot of the mountain' and the 'leg of the table.' And, sometimes, of course, the two speak, as it were, in the same language. The rough

miner, or 'puddler', the untrained, undeveloped 'tiger-man', heated by
a quart or two above his usual measure, comes home and kicks his
irritating and injudicious wife to death. He is a murderer. And Gilles
de Rais was a murderer. But you see the gulf that separates the two?
The 'word', if I may so speak, is accidentally the same in each case, but
the 'meaning' is utterly different. It is flagrant 'Hobson Jobson' to
confuse the two, or rather, it is as if one supposed that Juggernaut and
the Argonauts had something to do etymologically with one another.
And no doubt the same weak likeness, or analogy, runs between all the
'social' sins and the real spiritual sins, and in some cases, perhaps, the
lesser may be 'schoolmaster' to lead one on to the greater—from the
shadow to the reality. If you are anything of a theologian, you will see
the importance of all this."

"I am sorry to say," remarked Cotgrave, "that I have devoted very
little of my time to theology. Indeed, I have often wondered on what
grounds theologians have claimed the title of Science of Sciences for
their favourite study; since the 'theological' books I have looked into
have always seemed to me to be concerned with feeble and obvious
pieties, or with the kings of Israel and Judah. I do not care to hear about
those kings."

Ambrose grinned.

"We must try to avoid theological discussion," he said. "I perceive
that you would be a bitter disputant. But perhaps the 'dates of the
kings' have as much to do with theology as the hobnails of the
murderous puddler with evil."

"Then, to return to our main subject, you think that sin is an esoteric,
occult thing?"

"Yes. It is the infernal miracle as holiness is the supernal. Now and
then it is raised to such a pitch that we entirely fail to suspect its
existence; it is like the note of the great pedal pipes of the organ, which
is so deep that we cannot hear it. In other cases it may lead to the lunatic
asylum, or to still stranger issues. But you must never confuse it with
mere social misdoing. Remember how the Apostle, speaking of the
'other side,' distinguishes between 'charitable' actions and charity. And
as one may give all one's goods to the poor, and yet lack charity, so,
remember, one may avoid every crime and yet be a sinner."

"Your psychology is very strange to me," said Cotgrave, "but I
confess I like it, and I suppose that one might fairly deduce from your
premises the conclusion that the real sinner might very possibly strike
the observer as a harmless personage enough?"

"Certainly, because the true evil has nothing to do with social life or social laws, or if it has, only incidentally and accidentally. It is a lonely passion of the soul—or a passion of the lonely soul—whichever you like. If, by chance, we understand it, and grasp its full significance, then, indeed, it will fill us with horror and with awe. But this emotion is widely distinguished from the fear and the disgust with which we regard the ordinary criminal, since this latter is largely or entirely founded on the regard which we have for our own skins or purses. We hate a murderer, because we know that we should hate to be murdered, or to have any one that we like murdered. So, on the 'other side', we venerate the saints, but we don't 'like' them as we like our friends. Can you persuade yourself that you would have 'enjoyed' St. Paul's company? Do you think that you and I would have 'got on' with Sir Galahad?

"So with the sinners, as with the saints. If you met a very evil man, and recognized his evil, he would, no doubt, fill you with horror and awe; but there is no reason why you should 'dislike' him. On the contrary, it is quite possible that if you could succeed in putting the sin out of your mind you might find the sinner capital company, and in a little while you might have to reason yourself back into horror. Still, how awful it is. If the roses and the lilies suddenly sang on this coming morning, if the furniture began to move in procession, as in De Maupassant's tale!"

"I am glad you have come back to that comparison," said Cotgrave, "because I wanted to ask you what it is that corresponds in humanity to these imaginary feats of inanimate things. In a word—what is sin? You have given me, I know, an abstract definition, but I should like a concrete example."

"I told you it was very rare," said Ambrose, who appeared willing to avoid the giving of a direct answer. "The materialism of the age, which has done a good deal to suppress sanctity, has done perhaps more to suppress evil. We find the earth so very comfortable that we have no inclination either for ascents or descents. It would seem as if the scholar who decided to 'specialize' in Tophet would be reduced to purely antiquarian researches. No palaeontologist could show you a *live* pterodactyl."

"And yet you, I think, have 'specialized', and I believe that your researches have descended to our modern times."

"You are really interested, I see. Well, I confess that I have dabbled a little, and if you like I can show you something that bears on the very curious subject we have been discussing."

Ambrose took the candle and went away to a far, dim corner of the room. Cotgrave saw him open a venerable bureau that stood there, and from some secret recess he drew out a parcel, and came back to the window where they had been sitting.

Ambrose undid a wrapping of paper, and produced a green book.

"You will take care of it?" he said. "Don't leave it lying about. It is one of the choicer pieces in my collection, and I should be very sorry if it were lost."

He fondled the faded binding.

"I knew the girl who wrote this," he said. "When you read it, you will see how it illustrates the talk we have had to-night. There is a sequel, too, but I won't talk of that."

"There was an odd article in one of the reviews some months ago," he began again, with the air of a man who changes the subject. "It was written by a doctor—Dr. Coryn, I think, was the name. He says that a lady, watching her little girl playing at the drawing-room window, suddenly saw the heavy sash give way and fall on the child's fingers. The lady fainted, I think, but at any rate the doctor was summoned, and when he had dressed the child's wounded and maimed fingers he was summoned to the mother. She was groaning with pain, and it was found that three fingers of her hand, corresponding with those that had been injured on the child's hand, were swollen and inflamed, and later, in the doctor's language, purulent sloughing set in."

Ambrose still handled delicately the green volume.

"Well, here it is," he said at last, parting with difficulty, it seemed, from his treasure.

"You will bring it back as soon as you have read it," he said, as they went out into the hall, into the old garden, faint with the odour of white lilies.

There was a broad red band in the east as Cotgrave turned to go, and from the high ground where he stood he saw that awful spectacle of London in a dream.

The Green Book

The morocco binding of the book was faded, and the colour had grown faint, but there were no stains nor bruises nor marks of usage. The book looked as if it had been bought "on a visit to London" some seventy or eighty years ago, and had somehow been forgotten and suffered to lie away out of sight. There was an old, delicate, lingering odour about it, such an odour as sometimes haunts an ancient piece of furniture for a

century or more. The end-papers, inside the binding, were oddly
decorated with coloured patterns and faded gold. It looked small, but
the paper was fine, and there were many leaves, closely covered with
minute, painfully formed characters.

I found this book (the manuscript began) in a drawer in the old
bureau that stands on the landing. It was a very rainy day and I could
not go out, so in the afternoon I got a candle and rummaged in the
bureau. Nearly all the drawers were full of old dresses, but one of the
small ones looked empty, and I found this book hidden right at the
back. I wanted a book like this, so I took it to write in. It is full of
secrets. I have a great many other books of secrets I have written, hidden
in a safe place, and I am going to write here many of the old secrets
and some new ones; but there are some I shall not put down at all. I
must not write down the real names of the days and months which I
found out a year ago, nor the way to make the Aklo letters, or the Chian
language, or the great beautiful Circles, nor the Mao Games, nor the
chief songs. I may write something about all these things but not the
way to do them, for peculiar reasons. And I must not say who the
Nymphs are, or the Dôls, or Jeelo, or what voolas mean. All these are
most secret secrets, and I am glad when I remember what they are, and
how many wonderful languages I know, but there are some things that
I call the secrets of the secrets of the secrets that I dare not think of
unless I am quite alone, and then I shut my eyes, and put my hands
over them and whisper the word, and the Alala comes. I only do this
at night in my room or in certain woods that I know, but I must not
describe them, as they are secret woods. Then there are the Ceremonies,
which are all of them important, but some are more delightful than
others—there are the White Ceremonies, and the Green Ceremonies,
and the Scarlet Ceremonies. The Scarlet Ceremonies are the best, but
there is only one place where they can be performed properly, though
there is a very nice imitation which I have done in other places. Besides
these, I have the dances, and the Comedy, and I have done the Comedy
sometimes when the others were looking, and they didn't understand
anything about it. I was very little when I first knew about these things.

When I was very small, and mother was alive, I can remember
remembering things before that, only it has all got confused. But I
remember when I was five or six I heard them talking about me when
they thought I was not noticing. They were saying how queer I was a
year or two before, and how nurse had called my mother to come and
listen to me talking all to myself, and I was saying words that nobody
could understand. I was speaking the Xu language, but I only remem-

ber a very few of the words, as it was about the little white faces that
used to look at me when I was lying in my cradle. They used to talk
to me, and I learnt their language and talked to them in it about some
great white place where they lived, where the trees and the grass were
all white, and there were white hills as high up as the moon, and a cold
wind. I have often dreamed of it afterwards, but the faces went away
when I was very little. But a wonderful thing happened when I was
about five. My nurse was carrying me on her shoulder; there was a field
of yellow corn, and we went through it, it was very hot. Then we came
to a path through a wood, and a tall man came after us, and went with
us till we came to a place where there was a deep pool, and it was very
dark and shady. Nurse put me down on the soft moss under a tree, and
she said: "She can't get to the pond now." So they left me there, and I
sat quite still and watched, and out of the water and out of the wood
came two wonderful white people, and they began to play and dance
and sing. They were a kind of creamy white like the old ivory figurine
in the drawing-room; one was a beautiful lady with kind dark eyes,
and a grave face, and long black hair, and she smiled such a strange sad
smile at the other, who laughed and came to her. They played together,
and danced round and round the pool, and they sang a song till I fell
asleep. Nurse woke me up when she came back, and she was looking
something like the lady had looked, so I told her all about it, and asked
her why she looked like that. At first she cried, and then she looked
very frightened, and turned quite pale. She put me down on the grass
and stared at me, and I could see she was shaking all over. Then she
said I had been dreaming, but I knew I hadn't. Then she made me
promise not to say a word about it to anybody, and if I did I should be
thrown into the black pit. I was not frightened at all, though nurse
was, and I never forgot about it, because when I shut my eyes and it
was quite quiet, and I was all alone, I could see them again, very faint
and far away, but very splendid; and little bits of the song they sang
came into my head, but I couldn't sing it.

I was thirteen, nearly fourteen, when I had a very singular adventure,
so strange that the day on which it happened is always called the White
Day. My mother had been dead for more than a year, and in the morning
I had lessons, but they let me go out for walks in the afternoon. And
this afternoon I walked a new way, and a little brook led me into a new
country, but I tore my frock getting through many bushes, and beneath
the low branches of trees, and up thorny thickets on the hills, and by
dark woods full of creeping thorns. And it was a long, long way. It
seemed as if I was going on for ever and ever, and I had to creep by a

place like a tunnel where a brook must have been, but all the water
had dried up, and the floor was rocky, and the bushes had grown
overhead till they met, so that it was quite dark. And I went on and
on through that dark place; it was a long, long way. And I came to a
hill that I never saw before. I was in a dismal thicket full of black
twisted boughs that tore me as I went through them, and I cried out
because I was smarting all over, and then I found that I was climbing,
and I went up and up a long way, till at last the thicket stopped and I
came out crying just under the top of a big bare place, where there
were ugly grey stones lying all about on the grass, and here and there
a little twisted, stunted tree came out from under a stone, like a snake.
And I went up, right to the top, a long way. I never saw such big ugly
stones before; they came out of the earth some of them, and some looked
as if they had been rolled to where they were, and they went on and on
as far as I could see, a long, long way. I looked out from them and saw
the country, but it was strange. It was winter time, and there were
black terrible woods hanging from the hills all round; it was like seeing
a large room hung with black curtains, and the shape of the trees
seemed quite different from any I had ever seen before. I was afraid.
Then beyond the woods there were other hills round in a great ring,
but I had never sen any of them; it all looked black, and everything
had a voor over it. It was all still and silent, and the sky was heavy and
grey and sad, like a wicked voorish dome in Deep Dendo. I went on
into the dreadful rocks. There were hundreds and hundreds of them.
Some were like horrid-grinning men; I could see their faces as if they
would jump at me out of the stone, and catch hold of me, and drag me
with them back into the rock, so that I should always be there. And
there were other rocks that were like animals, creeping, horrible
animals, putting out their tongues, and others were like words that I
could not say, and others were like dead people lying on the grass. I
went on among them, though they frightened me, and my heart was
full of wicked songs that they put into it; and I wanted to make faces
and twist myself about in the way they did, and I went on and on a
long way till at last I liked the rocks, and they didn't frighten me
anymore. I sang the songs I thought of; songs full of words that must
not be spoken or written down. Then I made faces like the faces on the
rocks, and I twisted myself about like the twisted ones, and I lay down
flat on the ground like the dead ones, and I went up to one that was
grinning, and put my arms round him and hugged him. And so I went
on and on through the rocks till I came to a round mound in the middle
of them. It was higher than a mound, it was nearly as high as our house,

and it was like a great basin turned upside down, all smooth and round
and green, with one stone, like a post, sticking up at the top. I climbed
up the sides, but they were so steep I had to stop or I should have rolled
all the way down again, and I should have knocked against the stones
at the bottom, and perhaps been killed. But I wanted to get up to the
very top of the big round mound, so I lay down flat on my face, and
took hold of the grass with my hands and drew myself up, bit by bit,
till I was at the top. Then I sat down on the stone in the middle, and
looked all round abut. I felt I had come such a long, long way, just as
if I were a hundred miles from home, or in some other country, or in
one of the strange places I had read about in the *Tales of the Genie* and
the *Arabian Nights,* or as if I had gone across the sea, far away, for years
and I had found another world that nobody had ever seen or heard of
before, or as if I had somehow flown through the sky and fallen on one
of the stars I had read about where everything is dead and cold and
grey, and there is no air, and the wind doesn't blow. I sat on the stone
and looked all round and down and round about me. It was just as if I
was sitting on a tower in the middle of a great empty town, because I
could see nothing all around but the grey rocks on the ground. I
couldn't make out their shapes any more, but I could see them on and
on for a long way, and I looked at them, and they seemed as if they had
been arranged into patterns, and shapes, and figures. I knew they
couldn't be, because I had seen a lot of them coming right out of the
earth, joined to the deep rocks below, so I looked again, but still I saw
nothing but circles, and small circles inside big ones, and pyramids,
and domes, and spires, and they seemed all to go round and round the
place where I was sitting, and the more I looked, the more I saw great
big rings of rocks, getting bigger and bigger, and I stared so long that
it felt as if they were all moving and turning, like a great wheel, and I
was turning, too, in the middle. I got quite dizzy and queer in the
head, and everything began to be hazy and not clear, and I saw little
sparks of blue light, and the stones looked as if they were springing
and dancing and twisting as they went round and round and round. I
was frightened again, and I cried out loud, and jumped up from the
stone I was sitting on, and fell down. When I got up I was so glad they
all looked still, and I sat down on the top and slid down the mound,
and went on again. I danced as I went in the peculiar way the rocks
had danced when I got giddy, and I was so glad I could do it quite well,
and I danced and danced along, and sang extraordinary songs that came
into my head. At last I came to the edge of that great flat hill, and there
were no more rocks, and the way went again through a dark thicket

in a hollow. It was just as bad as the other one I went through climbing up, but I didn't mind this one, because I was so glad I had seen those singular dances and could imitate them. I went down, creeping through the bushes, and a tall nettle stung me on my leg, and made me burn, but I didn't mind it, and I tingled with the boughs and the thorns, but I only laughed and sang. Then I got out of the thicket into a close valley, a little secret place like a dark passage that nobody ever knows of, because it was so narrow and deep and the woods were so thick round it. There is a steep bank with trees hanging over it, and there the ferns keep green all through the winter, when they are dead and brown upon the hill, and the ferns there have a sweet, rich smell like what oozes out of fir trees. There was a little stream of water running down this valley, so small that I could easily step across it. I drank the water with my hand, and it tasted like bright, yellow wine, and it sparkled and bubbled as it ran down over beautiful red and yellow stones, so that it seemed alive and all colours at once. I drank it, and I drank more with my hand, but I couldn't drink enough, so I lay down and bent my head and sucked the water up with my lips. It tasted much better, drinking it that way, and a ripple would come up to my mouth and give me a kiss, and I laughed, and drank again, and pretended there was a nymph, like the one in the old picture at home, who lived in the water and was kissing me. So I bent low down to the water, and put my lips softly to it, and whispered to the nymph that I would come again. I felt sure it would not be common water, I was so glad when I got up and went on; and I danced again and went up and up the valley, under hanging hills. And when I came to the top, the ground rose up in front of me, tall and steep as a wall, and there was nothing but the green wall and the sky. I thought of "for ever and for ever, world without end, Amen"; and I thought I must have really found the end of the world, because it was like the end of everything, as if there could be nothing at all beyond, except the kingdom of Voor, where the light goes when it is put out, and the water goes when the sun takes it away. I began to think of all the long, long way I had journeyed, how I had found a brook and followed it, and followed it on, and gone through bushes and thorny thickets, and dark woods full of creeping thorns. Then I had crept up a tunnel under trees, and climbed a thicket, and seen all the grey rocks, and sat in the middle of them when they turned round, and then I had gone on through the grey rocks and come down the hill through the stinging thicket and up the dark valley, all a long, long way. I wondered how I should get home again, if I could ever find the way, and if my home was there any more, or if it were turned and everybody in it into grey rocks, as in the *Arabian Nights*. So I sat down on the grass and thought what I should do next. I was tired, and my feet were hot with walking, and as I looked about I saw there was a wonderful well just under the high, steep wall of grass. All the ground round it was covered with bright, green, dripping moss; there was every kind of moss there, moss like beautiful little ferns, and like palms and fir trees, and it was all green as jewellery, and drops of water hung on it like diamonds. And in the middle was the great well, deep and shining and beautiful, so clear it looked as if I could touch the red sand at the bottom, but it was far below. I stood by it and looked in, as if I were looking in a glass. At the bottom of the well, in the middle of it, the red grains of sand were moving and stirring all the time, and I saw how the water bubbled up, but at the top it was quite smooth, and full and brimming. It was a great well, large like a bath, and with the shining, glittering green moss about it, it looked like a great white jewel, with green jewels all round. My feet were so hot and tired that I took off my boots and stockings, and let my feet down into the water, and the water was soft and cold, and when I got up I wasn't tired any more, and I felt I must go on, farther and farther, and see what was on the other side of the wall. I climbed up it very slowly, going sideways all the time, and when I got to the top and looked over, I was in the queerest country I had seen, stranger even than the hill of the grey rocks. It looked as if earth-children had been playing there with their spades, as it was all hills and hollows, and castles and walls made of earth and covered with grass. There were two mounds like big beehives, round and great and solemn, and then hollow basins, and then a steep mounting wall like the ones I saw once by the seaside where the big guns and the soldiers were. I nearly fell into one of the round hollows, it went away from under my feet so suddenly, and I ran fast down the side and stood at the bottom and looked up. It was trange and solemn to look up. There was nothing but the grey, heavy sky and the sides of the hollow; everything else had gone away, and the hollow was the whole world, and I thought that at night it must be full of ghosts and moving shadows and pale things when the moon shone down to the bottom at the dead of the night, and the wind wailed up above. It was so strange and solemn and lonely, like a hollow temple of dead heathen gods. It reminded me of a tale my nurse had told me when I was quite little; it was the same nurse that took me into the wood where I saw the beautiful white people. And I remembered how nurse had told me the story one winter night, when the wind was beating the trees against

the wall, and crying and moaning in the nursery chimney. She said
there was, somewhere or other, a hollow pit, just like the one I was
standing in, everybody was afraid to go into it or near it, it was such
a bad place. But once upon a time there was a poor girl who said
she would go into the hollow pit, and everybody tried to stop her,
but she would go. And she went down into the pit and came back
laughing, and said there was nothing there at all, except green grass
and red stones, and white stones and yellow flowers. And soon after
people saw she had most beautiful emerald earrings, and they asked
how she got them, as she and her mother were quite poor. But she
laughed, and said her earrings were not made of emeralds at all, but
only of green grass. Then, one day, she wore on her breast the reddest
ruby that any one had ever seen, and it was as big as a hen's egg,
and glowed and sparkled like a hot burning coal of fire. And they
asked how she got it, as she and her mother were quite poor. But
she laughed, and said it was not a ruby at all, but only a red stone.
Then one day she wore round her neck the loveliest necklace that
any one had ever seen, much finer than the queen's finest, and it was
made of great bright diamonds, hundreds of them, and they shone
like all the stars on a night in June. So they asked her how she got
it, as she and her mother were quite poor. But she laughed, and said
they were not diamonds at all, but only white stones. And one day
she went to the court, and she wore on her head a crown of pure
angel-gold, so nurse said, and it shone like the sun, and it was much
more splendid than the crown the king was wearing himself, and in
her ears she wore the emeralds, and the big ruby was the brooch on
her breast, and the great diamond necklace was sparkling on her
neck. And the king and queen thought she was some great princess
from a long way off, and got down from their thrones and went to
meet her, but somebody told the king and queen who she was, and
that she was quite poor So the king asked why she wore a gold crown,
and how she got it, as she and her mother were so poor. And she
laughed, and said it wasn't a gold crown at all, but only some yellow
flowers she had put in her hair. And the king thought it was very
strange, and said she should stay at the court, and they would see
what would happen next. And she was so lovely that everybody said
that her eyes were greener than the emeralds, that her lips were
redder than the ruby, that her skin was whiter than the diamonds, and
that her hair was brighter than the golden crown. So the king's son said
he would marry her, and the king said he might. And the bishop
married them, and there was a great supper, and afterwards the king's

son went to his wife's room. But just when he had his hand on the
door, he saw a tall, black man, with a dreadful face, standing in front
of the door, and a voice said—
                    Venture not upon your life,
              This is mine own wedded wife.

    Then the king's son fell down on the ground in a fit. And they came
and tried to get into the room, but they couldn't, and they hacked at
the door with hatchets, but the wood had turned hard as iron, and at
last everybody ran away, they were so frightened at the screaming and
laughing and shrieking and crying that came out of the room. But next
day they went in, and found there was nothing in the room but thick
black smoke, because the black man had come and taken her away. And
on the bed there were two knots of faded grass and a red stone, and
some white stones, and some faded yellow flowers. I remembered this
tale of nurse's while I was standing at the bottom of the deep hollow;
it was so strange and solitary there, and I felt afraid. I could not see any
stones or flowers, but I was afraid of bringing them away without
knowing, and I thought I would do a charm that came into my head
to keep the black man away. So I stood right in the very middle of the
hollow, and I made sure that I had none of those things on me, and
then I walked round the place, and touched my eyes, and my lips, and
my hair in a peculiar manner, and whispered some queer words that
nurse taught me to keep bad things away. Then I felt safe and climbed
up out of the hollow, and went on through all those mounds and
hollows and walls, till I came to the end, which was high above all the
rest, and I could see that all the different shapes of the earth were
arranged in patterns, something like the grey rocks, only the pattern
was different. It was getting late, and the air was indistinct, but it
looked from where I was standing something like two great figures of
people lying on the grass. And I went on, and at last I found a certain
wood, which is too secret to be described, and nobody knows of the
passage into it, which I found out in a very curious manner, by seeing
some little animal run into the wood through it. So I went in after the
animal by a very narrow dark way, under thorns and bushes, and it was
almost dark when I came to a kind of ope place in the middle. And
there I saw the most wonderful sight I have ever seen, but it was only
for a minute, as I ran away directly, and crept out of the wood by the
passage I had come by, and ran and ran as fast as ever I could, because
I was afraid, what I had seen was so wonderful and so strange and
beautiful. But I wanted to get home and think of it, and I did not know

what might not happen if I stayed by the wood. I was hot all over and
trembling, and my heart was beating, and strange cries that I could
not help came from me as I ran from the wood. I was glad that a great
white moon came up from over a round hill and showed me the way,
so I went back through the mounds and hollows and down the close
valley, and up through the thicket over the place of the grey rocks, and
so at last I got home again. My father was busy in his study, and the
servants had not told about my not coming home, though they were
frightened, and wondered what they ought to do, so I told them I had
lost my way, but I did not let them find out the real way I had been. I
went to bed and lay awake all through the night, thinking of what I
had seen. When I came out of the narrow way, and it looked all shining,
though the air was dark, it seemed so certain, and all the way home I
was quite sure that I had seen it, and I wanted to be alone in my room,
and be glad over it all to myself, and shut my eyes and pretend it was
there, and do all the things I would have done if I had not been so
afraid. But when I shut my eyes the sight would not come, and I began
to think about my adventures all over again, and I remembered how
dusky and queer it was at the end, and I was afraid it must be all a
mistake, because it seemed impossible it could happen. It seemed like
one of nurse's tales, which I didn't really believe in, though I was
frightened at the bottom of the hollow; and the stories she told me
when I was little came back into my head, and I wondered whether it
was really there what I thought I had seen, or whether any of her tales
could havehappened a long time ago. It was so queer; I lay awake there
in my room at the back of the house, and the moon was shining on the
other side towards the river, so the bright light did not fall upon the
wall. And the house was quite still. I had heard my father come
upstairs, and just after the clock struck twelve, and after the house was
still and empty, as if there was nobody alive in it. And though it was
all dark and indistinct in my room, a pale glimmering kind of light
shone in through the white blind, and once I got up and looked out,
and there was a great black shadow of the house covering the garden,
looking like a prison where men are hanged; and then beyond it was
all white; and the wood shone white with black gulfs between the trees.
It was still and clear, and there were no clouds in the sky. I wanted to
think of what I had seen but I couldn't, and I began to think of all the
tales that nurse had told me so long ago that I thought I had forgotten,
but they all came back, and mixed up with the thickets and the grey
rocks and the hollows in the earth and the secret wood, till I hardly
knew what was new and what was old, or whether it was not all

dreaming. And then I remembered that hot summer afternoon, so long ago, when nurse left me by myself in the shade, and the white people came out of the water and out of the wood, and played, and danced, and sang, and I began to fancy that nurse told me about something like it before I saw them, only I couldn't recollect exactly what she told me. Then I wondered whether she had been the white lady, as I remembered she was just as white and beautiful, and had the same dark eyes and black hair; and sometimes she smiled and looked like the lady had looked, when she was telling me some of her stories, beginning with "Once on a time", or "In the time of the fairies." But I thought she couldn't be the lady, as she seemed to have gone a different way into the wood, and I didn't think the man who came after us could be the other, or I couldn't have seen that wonderful secret in the secret wood. I thought of the moon: But it was afterwards when I was in the middle of the wild land, where the earth was made into the shape of great figures, and it was all walls, and mysterious hollows, and smooth round mounds, that I saw the great white moon come up over a round hill. I was wondering about all these things, till at last I got quite frightened, because I was afraid something had happened to me, and I remembered nurse's tale of the poor girl who went into the hollow pit, and was carried away at last by the black man. I knew I had gone into a hollow pit too, and perhaps it was the same, and I had done something dreadful. So I did the charm over again, and touched my eyes and my lips and my hair in a peculiar manner, and said the old words from the fairy language, so that I might be sure I had not been carried away. I tried again to see the secret wood, and to creep up the passage and see what I had seen there, but somehow I couldn't and I kept on thinking of nurse's stories. There was one I remembered about a young man who once upon a time went hunting, and all the day he and his hounds hunted everywhere, and they crossed the rivers and went into all the woods, and went round the marshes, but they couldn't find anything at all, and they hunted all day till the sun sank down and began to set behind the mountain. And the young man was angry because he couldn't find anything, and he was going to turn back, when just as the sun touched the mountain, he saw come out of a brake in front of him a beautiful white stag. And he cheered to his hounds, but they whined and would not follow, and he cheered to his horse, but it shivered and stood stock still, and the young man jumped off the horse and left the hounds and began to follow the white stag all alone. And soon it was quite dark, nd the sky was black, without a single star shining in it, and the stag went away into the darkness. And though the man had brought his gun with him he never shot at the stag, because he wanted to catch it, and he was afraid he would lose it in the night. But he never lost it once, though the sky was so black and the air was so dark, and the stag went on and on till the young man didn't know a bit where he was. And they went through enormous woods where the air was full of whispers and a pale, dead light came out from the rotten trunks that were lying on the ground, and just as the man thought he had lost the stag, he would see it all white and shining in front of him, and he would run fast to catch it, but the stag always ran faster, so he did not catch it. And they went through the enormous woods, and they swam across rivers, and they waded through black marshes where the ground bubbled, and the air was full of will-o'-the-wisps, and the stag fled away down into rocky narrow valleys, where the air was like the smell of a vault, and the man went after it. And they went over the great mountains, and the man heard the wind come down from the sky, and the stag went on and the man went after. At last the sun rose and the young man found he was in a country that he had never seen before; it was a beautiful valley with a bright stream running through it, and a great, big round hill in the middle. And the stag went down the valley, towards the hill, and it seemed to be getting tired and went slower and slower, and though the man was tired, too, he began to run faster, and he was sure he would catch the stag at last. But just as they got to the bottom of the hill, and the man stretched out his hand to catch the stag, it vanished into the earth, and the man began to cry; he was so sorry that he had lost it after all his long hunting. But as he was crying he saw there was a door in the hill, just in front of him, and he went in, and it was quite dark, but he went on, as he thought he would find the white stag. And all of sudden it got light, and there was the sky, and the sun shining, and birds singing in the trees, and there was a beautiful fountain. And by the fountain a lovely lady was sitting, who was the queen of the fairies, and she told the man that she had changed herself into a stag to bring him there because she loved him so much. Then she brought out a great gold cup, covered with jewels, from her fairy palace, and she offered him wine in the cup to drink. And he drank, and the more he drank the more he longed to drink, because the wine was enchanted. So he kissed the lovely lady, and she became his wife, and he stayed all that day and all that night in the hill where she lived, and when he woke he found he was lying on the ground, close to where he had seen the stag first, and his horse was there and his hounds were there waiting, and he looked up, and the sun sank behind the mountain.

And he went home and lived a long time, but he would never kiss any other lady because he had drunk enchanted wine. And sometimes nurse told me tales that she had heard from her great-grandmother, who was very old, and lived in a cottage on the mountain all alone, and most of these tales were about a hill where people used to meet at night long ago, and they used to play all sorts of strange games and do queer things that nurse told me of, but I couldn't understand, and now, she said, everybody but her great-grandmother had forgotten all about it, and nobody knew where the hill was, not even her great-grandmother. But she told me one very strange story about the hill, and I trembled when I remembered it. She said that people always went there in summer, when it was very hot, and they had to dance a good deal. It would be all dark at first, and there were trees there, which made it much darker, and people would come, one by one, from all directions, by a secret path which nobody else knew, and two persons would keep the gate, and every one as they came up had to give a very curious sign, which nurse showed me as well as she could, but she said she couldn't show me properly. And all kinds of people would come; there would be gentle folks and village folks, and some old people and boys and girls, and quite small children, who sat and watched. And it would be all dark as they came in, except in one corner where some one was burning something that smelt strong and sweet, and made them laugh, and there one would see a glaring of coals, and the smoke mounting up red. So they would all come in, and when the last had come there was no door any more, so that no one else could get in, even if they knew there was anything beyond. And once a gentleman who was a stranger and had ridden a long way, lost his path at night, and his horse took him into the very middle of the wild country, where everything was upside down, and there were dreadful marshes and great stones everywhere, and holes underfoot, and te trees looked like gibbet-posts, because they had great black arms that stretched out across the way. And this strange gentleman was very frightened, and his horse began to shiver all over, and at last it stopped and wouldn't go any farther, and the gentleman got down and tried to lead the horse, but it wouldn't move, and it was all covered with a sweat, like death. So the gentleman went on all alone, going farther and farther into the wild country, till at last he came to a dark place, where he heard shouting and singing and crying, like nothing he had ever heard before. It all sounded quite close to him, but he couldn't get in, and so he began to call, and while he was calling, something came behind him, and in a minute his mouth and arms and legs were all bound up, and he fell into a swoon. And when he came

to himself, he was lying by the roadside, just where he had first lost
his way, under a blasted oak with a black trunk, and his horse was tied
beside him. So he rode on to the town and told the people there what
had happened, and some of them were amazed; but others knew. So
when once everybody had come, there was no door at all for anybody
else to pass in by. And when they were all inside, round in a ring,
touching each other, some one began to sing in the darkness, and some
one else would make a noise like thunder with a thing they had on
purpose, and on still nights people would hear the thundering noise
far, far away beyond the wild land, and some of them, who thought
they knew what it was, used to make a sign on their breasts when they
woke up in their beds at dead of night and heard that terrible deep
noise, like thunder on the mountains. And the noise and the singing
would go on and on for a long time, and the people who were in a ring
swayed a little to and fro; and the song was in an old, old language that
nobody knows now, and the tune was queer. Nurse said her great-
grandmother had known some one who remembered a little of it, when
she was quite a little girl, and nurse tried to sing some of it o me, and
it was so strange a tune that I turned all cold and my flesh crept as if
I had put my hand on something dead. Sometimes it was a man that
sang and sometimes it was a woman, and sometimes the one who sang
it did it so well that two or three of the people who were there fell to
the ground shrieking and tearing with their hands. The singing went
on, and the people in the ring kept swaying to and fro for a long time,
and at last the moon would rise over a place they called the Tole Deol,
and came up and showed them swinging and swaying from side to side,
with the sweet thick smoke curling up from the burning coals, and
floating in circles all around them. Then they had their supper. A boy
and a girl brought it to them; the boy carried a great cup of wine, and
the girl carried a cake of bread, and they passed the bread and the wine
round and round, but they tasted quite different from common bread
and common wine, and changed everybody that tasted them. Then
they all rose up and danced, and secret things were brought out of some
hiding place, and they played extraordinary games, and danced
round and round and round in the moonlight, and sometimes people
would suddenly disappear and never be heard of afterwards, and
nobody knew what had happened to them. And they drank more of
that curious wine, and they made images and worshipped them, and
nurse showed me how the images were made one day when we were
out for a walk, and we passed by a place where there was a lot of wet
clay. So nurse asked me if I would like to know what those things were

like that they made on the hill, and I said yes. Then she asked me if I would promise never to tell a living soul a word about it, and if I did I was to be thrown into the black pit with the dead people, and I said I wouldn't tell anybody, and she said the same thing again and again, and I promised. So she took my wooden spade and dug a big lump of clay and put it in my tin bucket, and told me to say if any one met us that I was going to make pies when I went home. Then we went on a little way till we came to a little brake growing right down into the road, and nurse stopped, and looked up the road and down it, and then peeped through the hedge into the field on the other side, and then she said "Quick!" and we ran into the brake, and crept in and out among the bushes till we had gone a good way from the road. Then we sat down under a bush, and I wanted so much to know what nurse was going to make with the clay, but before she would begin she made me promise again not to say a word about it, and she went again and peeped through the bushes on every side, though the lane was so small and deep that hardly anybody ever went there. So we sat down, and nurse took the clay out of the bucket, and began to knead it with her hands, and do queer things with it, and turn it about. And she hid it under a big dock-leaf for a minute or two and then she brought it out again, and then she stood up and sat down, and walked round the clay in a peculiar manner, and all the time she was softly singing a sort of rhyme, and her face got very red. Then she sat down again, and took the clay in her hands and began to shape it into a doll, but not like the dolls I have at home, and she made the queerest doll I had ever seen, all out of the wet clay, and hid it under a bush to get dry and hard, and all the time she was making it she was singing these rhymes to herself, and her face got redder and redder. So we left the doll there, hidden away in the bushes where nobody would ever find it. And a few days later we went the same walk, and when we came to that narrow, dark part of the lane where the brake runs down to the bank, nurse made me promise all over again, and she looked about, just as she had done before, and we crept into the bushes till we got to the green place where the little clay man was hidden. I remember it all so well, though I was only eight, and it is eight years ago now as I am writing it down, but the sky was a deep violet blue, and in the middle of the brake where we were sitting there was a great elder tree covered with blossoms, and on the other side there was a clump of meadowsweet, and when I think of that day the smell of the meadowsweet and elder blossom seems to fill the room, and if I shut my eyes I can see the glaring sky, with little clouds very white floating across it, and nurse who went away long ago sitting opposite me and looking like the beautiful white lady in the wood. So we sat down and nurse took out the clay doll from the secret place where she had hidden it, and she said we must "pay our respects", and she would show me what to do, and I must watch her all the time. So she did all sorts of queer things with the little clay man, and I noticed she was all streaming with perspiration, though we had walked so slowly, and then told me to "pay my respects", and I did everything she did because I liked her, and it was such an odd game. And she said that if one loved very much, the clay man was very good, if one did certain things with it, and if one hated very much, it was just as good, only one had to do different things, and we played with it a long time, and pretended all sorts of things. Nurse said her great-grandmother had told her all about these images, but what we did was no harm at all, only a game. But she told me a story about these images that frightened me very much, and that was what I remembered that night when I was lying awake in my room in the pale, empty darkness, thinking of what I had seen and the secret wood. Nurse said there was once a young lady of the high gentry, who lived in a great castle. And she was so beautiful that all the gentlemen wanted to marry her, because she was the loveliest lady that anybody had ever seen, and she was kind to everybody, and everybody thought she was very good. But though she was polite to all the gentlemen who wished to marry hr, she put them off, and said she couldn't make up her mind, and she wasn't sure she wanted to marry anybody at all. And her father, who was a very great lord, was angry, though he was so fond of her, and he asked her why she wouldn't choose a bachelor out of all the handsome young men who came to the castle. But she only said she didn't love any of them very much, and she must wait, and if they pestered her, she said she would go and be a nun in a nunnery. So all the gentlemen said they would go away and wait for a year and a day, and when a year and a day were gone, they would come back again and ask her to say which one she would marry. So the day was appointed and they all went away; and the lady had promised that in a year and a day it would be her wedding day with one of them. But the truth was, that she was the queen of the people who danced on the hill on summer nights, and on the proper nights she would lock the door of her room, and she and her maid would steal out of the casle by a secret passage that only they knew of, and go away up to the hill in the wild land. And she knew more of the secret things than any one else, and more than any one knew before or after, because she would not tell anybody the most secret secrets. She knew how to do all the awful things, how to destroy young men, and how to put a curse on people, and other things that I could not understand. And her real name was the Lady Avelin, but the dancing people called her Cassap, which meant somebody very wise, in the old language. And she was whiter than any of them and taller, and her eyes shone in the dark like burning rubies; and she could sing songs that none of the others could sing, and when she sang they all fell down on their faces and worshipped her. And she could do what they called shib-show, which was a very wonderful enchantment. She would tell the great lord, her father, that she wanted to go into the woods to gather flowers, so he let her go, and she and her maid went into the woods where nobody came, and the maid would keep watch. Then the lady would lie down under the trees and begin to sing a particular song, and she stretched out her arms, and from every part of the wood great serpents would come, hissing and gliding in and out among the trees, and shooting out their forked tongues as they crawled up to the lady. And they all came to her, and twisted round her, round her body, and her arms, and her neck, till she was covered with writhing serpents, and there was only her head to be seen. And she whispered to them, and she sang to them, and they writhed round and round, faster and faster, till she told them to go. And they all went away directly, back to their holes, and on the lady's breast there would be a most curious, beautiful stone, shaped something like an egg, and coloured dark blue and yellow, and red, and green, marked like a serpent's scales. It was called a glame stone, and with it one could do all sorts of wonderful things, and nurse said her great-grandmother had seen a glame stone with her own eyes, and it was for all the world shiny and scaly like a snake. And the lady could do a lot of other things as well, but she was quite fixed that she would not be married. And there were a great many gentlemen who wanted to marry her, but therewere five of them who were chief, and their names were Sir Simon, Sir John, Sir Oliver, Sir Richard, and Sir Rowland. All the others believed she spoke the truth, and that she would choose one of them to be her man when a year and a day was done; it was only Sir Simon, who was very crafty, who thought she was deceiving them all, and he vowed he would watch and try if he could find out anything. And though he was very wise he was very young, and he had a smooth, soft face like a girl's, and he pretended, as the rest did, that he would not come to the castle for a year and a day, and he said he was going away beyond the sea to foreign parts. But he really only went a very little way, and came back dressed like a servant girl, and so he got a place in the castle to wash the dishes. And he waited and watched, and he listened and said nothing, and he hid in dark places, and woke up at night and looked out, and he heard things and he saw things that he thought were very strange. And he was so sly that he told the girl that waited on the lady that he was really a young man, and that he had dressed up as a girl because he loved her so very much and wanted to be in the same house with her, and the girl was so pleased that she told him many things, and he was more than ever certain that the Lady Avelin was deceiving him and the others. And he was so clever, and told the servant so many lies, that one night he managed to hide in the Lady Avelin's room behind the curtains. And he stayed quite still and never moved, and at last the lady came. And she bent down under the bed, and raised up a stone, and there was a hollow place underneath, and out of it she took a waxen image, just like the clay one that I and nurse had made in the brake. And all the time her eyes were burning like rubies. And she took the little wax doll up in her arms and held it to her breast, and she whispered and she murmured, and she took it up and she laid it down again, and she held it high, and she held it low, and she laid it down again. And she said, "Happy is he that begat the bishop, that ordered the clerk, that married the man, that had the wife, that fashioned the hive, that harboured the bee, that gathered the wax that my own true love was made of." And she brought out of an aumbry a great golden bowl, and she brought out of a closet a great jar of wine, and she poured some of the wine into the bowl, and she laid her mannikin very gently in the wine, and washed it in the wine all over. Then she went to a cupboard and took a small round cake and laid it on the image's mouth, and then she bore it softly and covered it up. And Sir Simon, who was watching all the time, though he was terribly frightened, saw the lady bend down and stretch out her arms and whisper and sing, and then Sir Simon saw beside her a handsome young man, who kissed her on the lips. And they drank wine out of the golden bowl together, and then ate the cake together. But when the sun rose there was only the little wax doll, and the lady hid it again under the bed in the hollow place. So Sir Simon knew quite well what the lady was, and he waited and watched, till the time she had said was nearly over, and in a week the year and a day would be done. And one night, when he was watching behind the curtains in her room, he saw her making more wax dolls. And she made five, and hid them away. And the next night she took one out, and held it up, and filled the golden bowl with water, and took the doll by the neck and held it under the water. Then she said—

Sir Dickon, Sir Dickon, your day is done,
You shall be drowned in the water wan.

And the next day news came to the castle that Sir Richard had been
drowned at the ford. And at night she took another doll and tied a
violet cord round its neck and hung it up on a nail. Then she said—
Sir Rowland, your life has ended its span,
High on a tree I see you hang.

And the next day news came to the castle that Sir Rowland had been
hanged by robbers in the wood. And at night she took another doll,
and drove her bodkin right into its heart. Then she said—
Sir Noll, Sir Noll, so cease your life,
Your heart pierced with the knife.

And the next day news came to the castle that Sir Oliver had fought
in a tavern, and a stranger had stabbed him to the heart. And at night
she took another doll, and held it to a fire of charcoal till it was melted.
Then she said—
Sir John, return, and turn to clay,
In fire of fever you waste away.

And the next day news came to the castle that Sir John had died in
a burning fever. So then Sir Simon went out of the castle and mounted
his horse and rode away to the bishop and told him everything. And
the bishop sent his men, and they took the Lady Avelin, and everything
she had done was found out. So on the day after the year and a day,
when she was to have been married, they carried her through the town
in her smock, and they tied her to a great stake in the market-place,
and burned her alive before the bishop with her wax image hung round
her neck. And people said the wax man screamed in the burning of the
flames. And I thought of this story again and again as I was lying awake
in my bed, and I seemed to see the Lady Avelin in the market-place,
with the yellow flames eating up her beautiful white body. And I
thought of it so much that I seemed to get into the story myself, and
I fancied I was the lady, and that they were coming to take me to be
burnt with fire, with all the people in the town looking at me. And I
wondered whether she cared, after all the strange things she had done,
and whether it hurt very much to be burned at the stake. I tried again
and again to forget nurse's stories, and to remember the secret I had
seen that afternoon, and what was in the secret wood, but I could only
see the dark and a glimmering in the dark, and then it went away, and

I only saw myself running, and then a great moon came up white over a dark round hill. Then all the old stories came back again, and the queer rhymes that nurse used to sing to me; and there was one beginning "Halsy cumsy Helen musty", that she used to sing very softly when she wanted me to go to sleep. And I began to sing it to myself inside of my head, and I went to sleep.

The next morning I was very tired and sleepy, and could hardly do my lessons, and I was very glad when they were over and I had had my dinner, as I wanted to go out and be alone. It was a warm day, and I went to a nice turfy hill by the river, and sat down on my mother's old shawl that I had brought with me on purpose. The sky was grey, like the day before, but there was a kind of white gleam behind it, and from where I was sitting I could look down on the town, and it was all still and quiet and white, like a picture. I remembered that it was on that hill that nurse taught me to play an old game called "Troy Town", in which one had to dance, and wind in and out on a pattern in the grass, and then when one had danced and turned long enough the other person asks you questions, and you can't help answering whether you want to or not, and whatever you are told to do you feel you have to do it. Nurse said there used to be a lot of games like that that some people knew of, and there was one by which people could be turned into anything you liked, and an old man her great-grandmother had seen had known a girl who had been turned into a large snake. And there was another very ancient game of dancing and winding and turning, by which you could take a person out of himself and hide him away as long as you liked, and his body went walking about quite empty, without any sense in it. But I came to that hill because I wanted to think of what had happened the day before, and of the secret of the wood. From the place where I was sitting I could see beyond the town, into the opening I had found, where a little brook had led me into an unknown country. And I pretended I was following the brook over again, and I went all the way in my mind, and at last I found the wood, and crept into it under the bushes, and then in the dusk I saw something that made me feel as if I were filled with fire, as if I wanted to dance and sing and fly up into the air, because I was changed and wonderful. But what I saw was not changed at all, and had not grown old, and I wondered again and again how such things could happen, and whether nurse's stories were really true, because in the daytime in the open air everything seemed quite different from what it was at night, when I was frightened, and thought I was to be burned alive. I once told my father one of her little tales, which was about a ghost,

and asked him if it was true, and he told me it was not true at all, and
that only common, ignorant people believed in such rubbish. He was
very angry with nurse for telling me the story, and scolded her, and
after that I promised her I would never whisper a word of wat she told
me, and if I did I should be bitten by the great black snake that lived
in the pool in the wood. And all alone on the hill I wondered what was
true. I had seen something very amazing and very lovely, and I knew
a story, and if I had really seen it, and not made it up out of the dark,
and the black bough, and the bright shining that was mounting up to
the sky from over the great round hill, but had really seen it in truth,
then there were all kinds of wonderful and lovely and terrible things
to think of, so I longed and trembled, and I burned and got cold. And
I looked down on the town, so quiet and still, like a little white picture,
and I thought over and over if it could be true. It was a long time before
I could make up my mind to anything; there was such a strange
fluttering at my heart that seemed to whisper to me all the time that
I had not made it up out of my head, and it seemed quite impossible,
and I knew my father and everybody would say it was dreadful rubbish.
I never dreamed of telling him or anybody else a word about it, because
I knew it would be of no use, and I should only get laughed at or
scolded, so for a long time I was very quiet, and went about thinking
and wondering; and at night I used to dream of amazing things, and
sometimes I woke up in the early morning and held out my arms with
a cry. And I was frightened, too, because there were dangers, and some
awful thing would happen to me, unless I took great care, if the story
were true. These old tales were always in my head, night and morning,
and I went over them and told them to myself over and over again, and
went for walks in the places where nurse had told them to me; and
when I sat in the nursery by the fire in the evenings I used to fancy
nurse was sitting in the other chair, and telling me some wonderful
story in a low voice, for fear anybody should be listening. But she used
to like best to tell me about things when we were right out in the
country, far from the house, because she said she was telling me such
secrets, ad walls have ears. And if it was something more than ever
secret, we had to hide in brakes or woods; and I used to think it was
such fun creeping along a hedge, and going very softly, and then we
would get behind the bushes or run into the woods all of a sudden,
when we were sure that none was watching us; so we knew that we had
our secrets quite all to ourselves, and nobody else at all knew anything
about them. Now and then, when we had hidden ourselves as I have
described, she used to show me all sorts of odd things. One day, I

remember, we were in a hazel brake, overlooking the brook, and we were so snug and warm, as though it was April; the sun was quite hot, and the leaves were just coming out. Nurse said she would show me something funny that would make me laugh, and then she showed me, as she said, how one could turn a whole house upside down, without anybody being able to find out, and the pots and pans would jump about, and the china would be broken, and the chairs would tumble over of themselves. I tried it one day in the kitchen, and I found I could do it quite well, and a whole row of plates on the dresser fell off it, and cook's little work-table tilted up and turned right over "before her eyes", as she said, but she was so frightened and turned so white that I didn't do it again, as I liked her. And afterwards, in the hazel copse, when she had shown me how to make things tumble about, she showed me how to make rapping noises, and I learnt how to do that, too. Then she taught me rhymes to say on certain occasions, and peculiar marks to make on other occasions, and other things that her great-grand-mother had taught her when she was a little girl herself. And these were all the things I was thinking about in those days after the strange walk when I thought I had seen a great secret, and I wished nurse were there for me to ask her about it, but she had gone away more than two years before, and nobody seemed to know what had become of her, or where she had gone. But I shall always remember those days if I live to be quite old, because all the time I felt so strange, wondering and doubting, and feeling quite sure at one time, and making up my mind, and then I would feel quite sure that such things couldn't happen really, and it began all over again. But I took great care not to do certain things that might be very dangerous. So I waited and wondered for a long time, and though I was not sure at all, I never dared to try to find out. But one day I became sure that all that nurse said was quite true, and I was all alone when I found it out. I trembled all over with joy and terror, and as fast as I could I ran into one of the old brakes where we used to go—it was the one by the lane, where nurse made the little clay man—and I ran into it, and I crept into it; and when I came to the place where the elder was, I covered up my face with my hands and lay down flat on the grass, and I stayed there for two hours without moving, whispering to myself delicious, terrible things, and saying some words over and over again. It was all true and wonderful and splendid, and when I remembered the story I knew and thought of what I had really seen, I got hot and I got cold, and the air seemed full of scent, and flowers, and singing. And first I wanted to make a little clay man, like the one nurse had made so long ago, and I had to invent plans and stratagems, and to look about, and to think of things beforehand, because nobody must dream of anything that I was doing or going to do, and I was too old to carry clay about in a tin bucket. At last I thought of a plan, and I brought the wet clay to the brake, and did everything that nurse had done, only I made a much finer image than the one she had made; and when it was finished I did everything I could imagine and much more than she did, because it was the likeness of something far better. And a few days later, when I had done my lessons early, I went for the second time by the way of the little brook that had led me into a strange country. And I followed the brook, and went through the bushes, and beneath the low branches of trees, and up thorny thickets on the hill, and by dark woods full of creeping thorns, a long, long way. Then I crept through the dark tunnel where the brook had been and the ground was stony, till at last I came to the thicket that climbed up the hill, and though the leaves were coming out upon the trees, everything looked almost as black as it was on the first day that I went there. And the thicket was just the same, and I went up slowly till I came out on the big bare hill, and began to walk among the wonderful rocks. I saw the terrible voor again on everything, for though the sky was brighter, the ring of wild hills all around was still dark, and the hanging woods looked dark and dreadful, and the strange rocks were as grey as ever; and when I looked down on them from the great mound, sitting on the stone, I saw all their amazing circles and rounds within rounds, and I had to sit quite still and watch them as they began to turn about me, and each stone danced in its place, and they seemed to go round and round in a great whirl, as if one were in the middle of all the stars and heard them rushing through the air. So I went down among the rocks to dance with them and to sing extraordinary songs; and I went down through the other thicket, and drank from the bright tream in the close and secret valley, putting my lips down to the bubbling water; and then I went on till I came to the deep, brimming well among the glittering moss, and I sat down. I looked before me into the secret darkness of the valley, and behind me was the great high wall of grass, and all around me there were the hanging woods that made the valley such a secret place. I knew there was nobody here at all besides myself, and that no one could see me. So I took off my boots and stockings, and let my feet down into the water, saying the words that I knew. And it was not cold at all, as I expected, but warm and very pleasant, and when my feet were in it I felt as if they were in silk, or as if the nymph were kissing them. So when I had done, I said the other words and made the signs, and then I dried my feet with a towel I had brought on purpose, and put on my stockings and boots. Then I climbed up the steep wall, and went into the place where there are the hollows, and the two beautiful mounds, and the round ridges of land, and all the strange shapes. I did not go down into the hollow this time, but I turned at the end, and made out the figures quite plainly, as it was lighter, and I had remembered the story I had quite forgotten before, and in the story the two figures are called Adam and Eve, and only those who know the story understand what they mean. So I went on and on till I came to the secret wood which must not be described, and I crept into it by the way I had found. And when I had gone about halfway I stopped, and turned round, and got ready, and I bound the handkerchief tightly round my eyes, and made quite sure that I could not see at all, not a twig, nor the end of a leaf, nor the light of the sky, as it was an old red silk handkerchief with large yellow spots, that went round twice and covered my eyes, so that I could see nothing. Then I began to go on, step by step, very slowly. My heart beat faster and faster, and something rose in my throat that choked me and made me want to cry out, ut I shut my lips and went on. Boughs caught in my hair as I went, and great thorns tore me; but I went on to the end of the path. Then I stopped, and held out my arms and bowed, and I went round the first time, feeling with my hands, and there was nothing. I went round the second time, feeling with my hands and there was nothing. Then I went round the third time, feeling with my hands, and the story was all true, and I wished that the years were gone by, and that I had not so long a time to wait before I was happy for ever and ever.

Nurse must have been a prophet like those we read of in the Bible. Everything that she said began to come true, and since then other things that she told me of have happened. That was how I came to know that her stories were true and that I had not made up the secret myself out of my own head. But there was another thing that happened that day. I went a second time to the secret place. It was at the deep brimming well, and when I was standing on the moss I bent over and looked in, and then I knew who the white lady was that I had seen come out of the water in the wood long ago when I was quite little. And I trembled all over, because that told me other things. Then I remembered how sometime after I had seen the white people in the wood, nurse asked me more about them, and I told her all over again, and she listened, and said nothing for a long, long time, and at last she said, "You will see her again." So I understood what had happened and what was to happen. And I understood about the nymphs; how I might meet them in all kinds of places, and they would always help me, and I must always look for them, and find them in all sorts of strange shapes and appearances. And without the nymphs I could never have found the secret, and without them none of the other things could happen. Nurse had told me all about them long ago, but she called them by another name, and I did not know what she meant, or what her tales of them were about, only that they were very queer. And there were two kinds, the bright and the dark, and both were very lovely and very wonderful, and some people saw only one kind, and some only the other, but some saw them both. But usually the dark appeared first, and the bright ones came afterwards, and there were extraordinary tales about them. It was a day or two after I had come home from the secret place that I first really knew the nymphs. Nurse had shown me how to call them, and I had tried, but I did not know what she meant, and so I thought it was all nonsense. But I made up my mind I would try again, so I went to the wood where the pool was, where I saw the white people, and I tried again. The dark nymph, Alanna, came, and she turned the pool of water into a pool of fire ...

Epilogue

"That's a very queer story," said Cotgrave, handing back the green book to the recluse, Ambrose. "I see the drift of a good deal, but there are many things that I do not grasp at all. On the last page, for example, what does she mean by 'nymphs'?"

"Well, I think there are references throughout the manuscript to certain 'processes' which have been handed down by tradition from age to age. Some of these processes are just beginning to come within the purview of science, which has arrived at them—or rather at the steps which lead to them—by quite different paths. I have interpreted the reference to 'nymphs' as a reference to one of these processes."

"And you believe that there are such things?"

"Oh, I think so. Yes, I believe I could give you convincing evidence on that point. I am afraid you have neglected the study of alchemy. It is a pity, for the symbolism, at all events, is very beautiful, and moreover if you were acquainted with certain books on the subject, I could recall to your mind phrases which might explain a good deal in the manuscript that you have been reading."

"Yes, but I want to know whether you seriously think that there is any foundation of fact beneath these fancies. Is it not all a department of poetry, a curious dream with which man has indulged himself?"

"I can only say that it is no doubt better for the great mass of people to dismiss it all as a dream. But if you ask my veritable belief—that goes quite the other way. No, I should not say belief, but rather knowledge. I may tell you that I have known cases in which men have stumbled quite by accident on certain of these 'processes', and have been astonished by wholly unexpected results. In the cases I am thinking of there could have been no possibility of 'suggestion' or subconscious action of any kind. One might as well suppose a school-boy 'suggesting' the existence of Aeschylus to himself, while he plods mechanically through the declensions.

"But you have noticed the obscurity," Ambrose went on, "and in this particular case it must have been dictated by instinct, since the writer never thought that her manuscripts would fall into other hands. But the practice is universal, and for most excellent reasons. Powerful and sovereign medicines, which are, of necessity, virulent poisons also, are kept in a locked cabinet. The child may find the key by chance, and drink herself dead, but in most cases the search is educational, and the phials contain precious elixirs for him who has patiently fashioned the key for himself."

"You do not care to go into details?"

"No, frankly, I do not. No, you must remain unconvinced. But you saw how the manuscript illustrates the talk we had last week?"

"Is this girl still alive?"

"No. I was one of those who found her. I knew the father well; he was a lawyer, and had always left her very much to herself. He thought of nothing but deeds and leases, and the news came to him as an awful surprise. She was missing one morning; I suppose it was about a year after she had written what you have read. The servants were called, and they told things, and put the only natural interpretation on them—a perfectly erroneous one.

"They discovered that green book somewhere in her room, and I found her in the place that she described with so much dread, lying on the ground before the image."

"It was an image?"

"Yes; it was hidden by the thorns and the thick undergrowth that had surrounded it. It was a wild, lonely country; but you know what it was like by her description, though of course you will understand that the colours have been heightened. A child's imagination always makes the heights higher and the depths deeper than they really are; and she had, unfortunately for herself, something more than imagination. One might say, perhaps, that the picture in her mind which she succeeded in a measure in putting into words, was the scene as it would have appeared to an imaginative artist. But it is a strange, desolate land."

"And she was dead?"

"Yes. She had poisoned herself—in time. No, there was not a word to be said against her in the ordinary sense. You may recollect a story I told you the other night about a lady who saw her child's fingers crushed by a window?"

"And what was this statue?"

"Well, it was of Roman workmanship of a stone that with the centuries had not blackened, but had become white and luminous. The thicket had grown up about it and concealed it, and in the Middle Ages the followers of a very old tradition had known how to use it for their own purposes. In fact it had been incorporated into the monstrous mythology of the Sabbath. You will have noted that those to whom a sight of that shining whiteness had been vouchsafed by chance, or rather, perhaps, by apparent chance, were required to blindfold themselves on their second approach. That is very significant."

"And is it there still?"

"I sent for tools, and we hammered it into dust and fragments.

"The persistence of tradition never surprises me," Ambrose went on after a pause. "I could name many an English parish where such traditions as that girl had listened to in her childhood are still existent in occult but unabated vigour. No, for me, it is the 'story', not the 'sequel', which is strange and awful, for I have always believed that wonder is of the soul."

D onald R. Burleson has done extensive research on the background of "The Dunwich Horror" in HPL's own travels. What follows is my summary of some of his discoveries, from his article "Humour beneath Horror: Some Sources for 'The Dunwich Horror' and 'The Whisperer in Darkness'" (Lovecraft Studies, vol. 1, no. 2, Spring 1980).

On June 24 H. P. Lovecraft embarked on a visit with his friend W. Paul Cook in Athol, Massachusetts. He had just returned from a visit with Vrest Orton in Vermont, where he picked up various ideas he would use in "The Whisperer in Darkness." From Athol he continued on to visit his amateur journalism colleague and correspondent Edith Miniter and her cousin Evanore Beebe in North Wilbraham, Massachusetts. He resolved to use some details of the rich local folklore in future weird tales. Chief among the items he used was the motif of whippoorwills as psychopomps. The idea that their chirping foretells death is familiar from Huckleberry Finn and elsewhere, but the notion of their bearing away the souls of the dead is a variant of which Lovecraft learned in a story customarily told in the Beebe family.

Much of the physical description of the Dunwich countryside is a faithful sketch of Wilbraham. This description of sights seen on this trip, in a letter to Zealia Bishop, sounds like a passage from "The Dunwich Horror" itself:

When the road dips again there are stretches of marshland that one instinctively dislikes, and indeed almost fears at evening when unseen whippoor-wills chatter and the fireflies come out in abnormal profusion to dance to the raucous, creepily insistent rhythms of stridently piping bullfrogs.

"The Dunwich Horror" also bears the marks of the previous stay with Cook, where Lovecraft picked up several prominent Athol names for use in this story, including Wheeler, Farr, Sawyer, Bishop, Houghton, and Frye. Even Dunwich's Sentinel Hill is derived from Sentinel Elm Farm on West Hill. Rice and Morgan, the pair of Miskatonic professors who accompany Dr. Armitage up Sentinel Hill, are two names well known from an Athol transaction in which H. H. Rice sold the mill power in Ahtol to the Morgan Memorial. Cold Spring Glen seems a reflection of the steep and curiously fissured Bear's Den ravine in nearby North New Salem.

Will Murray ("In Search of Arkham Country", Lovecraft Studies, vol. 5, no. 2, 1986) agrees with Andrew E. Rothovius ("Lovecraft and the New England Mega-liths", in Derleth, ed., The Dark Brotherhood, 1966) that the Dunwich Region is actually based on an area to the north of Wilbraham, near the Quabbin Reservoir (the model for the one in "The Colour Out of Space"), and Murray points to a local town of Greenwich as a possible prototype for Dunwich. Lovecraft's Cold Spring Glen may come from the name of Cold Brook Springs, a town in the same area, near Oakham, Massachusetts, which Murray makes the direct inspiration for Arkham.

The Dunwich Horror

by H. P. Lovecraft

"Gorgons, and Hydras, and Chimaeras—dire stories of Celaeno and the Harpies—may reproduce themselves in the brain of superstition—*but they were there before. They are* transcripts, types—the archetypes are in us, and eternal. How else should the recital of that which we know in a waking sense to be false come to affect us at all? Is it that we naturally conceive terror from such objects, considered in their capacity of being able to inflict upon us bodily injury? O, least of all! *These terrors are of older standing. They date beyond body*—or without the body, they would have been the same. ... That the kind of fear here treated is purely spiritual—that it is strong on proportion as it is objectless on earth, that it predominates in the period of our sinless infancy—are difficulties the solution of which might afford some probable insight into our ante-mundane condition, and a peep at least into the shadowland of preexistence."

— *Charles Lamb,* "Witches and Other Night-Fears"

I.

When a traveller in north central Massachusetts takes the wrong fork at the junction of the Aylesbury pike just beyond Dean's Corners he comes upon a lonely and curious country. The ground gets higher, and the brier-bordered stone walls press closer and closer against the ruts of the dusty, curving road. The trees of the frequent forest belts seem too large, and the wild weeds, brambles, and grasses attain a luxuriance not often found in settled regions. At the same time the planted fields appear singularly few and barren; while the sparsely scattered houses wear a surprisingly uniform aspect of age, squalor, and dilapidation. Without knowing why, one hesitates to ask directions from the gnarled, solitary figures spied now and then on crumbling doorsteps or on the sloping, rock-strown meadows. Those figures are so silent and furtive that one feels somehow confronted by forbidden things, with which it would be better to have nothing to do. When a rise in the road brings the mountains in view above the deep woods, the feeling of strange uneasiness is increased.

The summits are too rounded and symmetrical to give a sense of comfort and naturalness, and sometimes the sky silhouettes with especial clearness the queer circles of tall stone pillars with which most of them are crowned.

Gorges and ravines of problematical depth intersect the way, and the crude wooden bridges always seem of dubious safety. When the road dips again there are stretches of marshland that one instinctively dislikes, and indeed almost fears at evening when unseen whippoor-wills chatter and the fireflies come out in abnormal profusion to dance to the raucous, creepily insistent rhythms of stridently piping bull-frogs. The thin, shining line of the Miskatonic's upper reaches has an oddly serpent-like suggestion as it winds close to the feet of the domed hills among which it rises.

As the hills draw nearer, one heeds their wooded sides more than their stone-crowned tops. Those sides loom up so darkly and precipi-tously that one wishes they would keep their distance, but there is no road by which to escape them. Across a covered bridge one sees a small village huddled between the stream and the vertical slope of Round Mountain, and wonders at the cluster of rotting gambrel roofs bespeak-ing an earlier architectural period than that of the neighbouring region. It is not reassuring to see, on a closer glance, that most of the houses are deserted and falling to ruin, and that the broken-steepled church now harbours the one slovenly mercantile establishment of the hamlet. One dreads to trust the tenebrous tunnel of the bridge, yet there is no way to avoid it. Once across, it is hard to prevent the impression of a faint, malign odour about the village street, as of the massed mould and decay of centuries. It is always a relief to get clear of the place, and to follow the narrow road around the base of the hills and across the level country beyond till it rejoins the Aylesbury pike. Afterward one sometimes learns that one has been through Dunwich.

Outsiders visit Dunwich as seldom as possible, and since a certain season of horror all the signboards pointing toward it have been taken down. The scenery, judged by any ordinary aesthetic canon, is more than commonly beautiful; yet there is no influx of artists or summer tourists. Two centuries ago, when talk of witch-blood, Satan-worship, and strange forest presences was not laughed at, it was the custom to give reasons for avoiding the locality. In our sensible age—since the Dunwich horror of 1928 was hushed up by those who had the town's and the world's welfare at heart—people shun it without knowing exactly why. Perhaps one reason—though it cannot apply to unin-formed strangers—is that the natives are now repellently decadent, having gone far along that path of retrogression so common in many New England backwaters. They have come to form a race by themselves, with the well-defined mental and physical stigmata of degeneracy and inbreeding. The average of their intelligence is woefully low, whilst their annals reek of overt viciousness and of half-hidden murders, incests, and deeds of almost unnameable violence and perversity. The old gentry, representing the two or three armigerous families which came from Salem in 1692, have kept somewhat above the general level of decay; though many branches are sunk into the sordid populace so deeply that only their names remain as a key to the origin they disgrace. Some of the Whateleys and Bishops still send their eldest sons to Harvard and Miskatonic, though those sons seldom return to the mouldering gambrel roofs under which they and their ancestors were born.

No one, even those who have the facts concerning the recent horror, can say just what is the matter with Dunwich; though old legends speak of unhallowed rites and conclaves of the Indians, amidst which they called forbidden shapes of shadow out of the great rounded hills, and made wild orgiastic prayers that were answered by loud crackings and rumblings from the ground below. In 1747 the Reverend Abijah Hoadley, newly come to the Congregational Church at Dunwich Village, preached a memorable sermon on the close presence of Satan and his imps; in which he said:

"It must be allow'd, that these Blasphemies of an infernall Train of Daemons are Matters of too common Knowledge to be deny'd; the cursed Voices of *Azazel* and *Buzrael*, of *Beelzebub* and *Belial,* being heard now from under Ground by above a Score of credible Witnesses now living. I my self did not more than a Fortnight ago catch a very plain Discourse of evill Poers in the Hill behind my House; wherein there were a Rattling and Rolling, Groaning, Screeching, and Hissing, such as no Things of this Earth cou'd raise up, and which must needs have come from those Caves that only black Magick can discover, and only the Divell unlock."

Mr. Hoadley disappeared soon after delivering this sermon; but the text, printed in Springfield, is still extant. Noises in the hills continued to be reported from year to year, and still form a puzzle to geologists and physiographers.

Other traditions tell of foul odours near the hill-crowning circles of stone pillars, and of rushing airy presences to be heard faintly at certain hours from stated points at the bottom of the great ravines; while still others try to explain the Devil's Hop Yard—a bleak, blasted hillside where no tree, shrub, or grass-blade will grow. Then too, the natives are mortally afraid of the numerous whippoorwills which grow vocal on warm nights. It is vowed that the birds are psychopomps lying in wait for the souls of the dying, and that they time their eerie cries in unison with the sufferer's struggling breath. If they can catch the fleeting soul when it leaves the body, they instantly flutter away chittering in daemoniac laughter; but if they fail, they subside gradually into a disappointed silence.

These tales, of course, are obsolete and ridiculous; because they come down from very old times. Dunwich is indeed ridiculously old—older by far than any of the communities within thirty miles of it. South of the village one may still spy the cellar walls and chimney of the ancient Bishop house, which was built before 1700; whilst the ruins of the mill at the falls, built in 1806, form the most modern piece of architecture to be seen. Industry did not flourish here, and the nineteenth-century factory movement proved short-lived. Oldest of all are the great rings of rough-hewn stone columns on the hill-tops, but these are more generally attributed to the Indians than to the settlers. Deposits of skulls and bones, found within these circles and around the sizeable table-like rock on Sentinel Hill, sustain the popular belief that such spots were once the burial-places of the Pocumtucks; even though many ethnologists, disregarding the absurd improbability of such a theory, persist in believing the remains Caucasian.

II.

It was in the township of Dunwich, in a large and partly inhabited farmhouse set against a hillside four miles from the village and a mile and a half from any other dwelling, that Wilbur Whateley was born at 5 a.m. on Sunday, the second of February, 1913. This date was recalled because it was Candlemas, which people in Dunwich curiously observe under another name; and because the noises in the hills had sounded, and all the dogs of the countryside had barked persistently, throughout the night before. Less worthy of notice was the fact that the mother was one of the decadent Whateleys, a somewhat deformed, unattractive albino woman of thirty-five, living with an aged and half-insane father about whom the most frightful tales of wizardry had been whispered in his youth. Lavinia Whateley had no known husband, but according to the custom of the region made no attempt to disavow the child; concerning the other side of whose ancestry the country folk might—and did—speculate as widely as they chose. On the contrary, she seemed strangely proud of the dark, goatish-looking infant who formed such a contrast to her own sickly and pink-eyed albinism, and was heard to mutter many curious prophecies about its unusual powers and tremendous future.

Lavinia was one who would be apt to mutter such things, for she was a lone creature given to wandering amidst thunderstorms in the hills and trying to read the great odorous books which her father had inherited through two centuries of Whateleys, and which were fast falling to pieces with age and worm-holes. She had never been to school, but was filled with disjointed scraps of ancient lore that Old Whateley had taught her. The remote farmhouse had always been feared because of Old Whateley's reputation for black magic, and the unexplained death by violence of Mrs. Whateley when Lavinia was twelve years old had not helped to make the place popular. Isolated among strange influences, Lavinia was fond of wild and grandiose day-dreams and singular occupations; nor was her leisure much taken up by household cares in a home from which all standards of order and cleanliness had long since disappeared.

There was a hideous screaming which echoed above even the hill noises and the dogs' barking on the night Wilbur was born, but no known doctor or midwife presided at his coming. Neighbours knew nothing of him till a week afterward, when Old Whateley drove his sleigh through the snow into Dunwich Village and discoursed incoherently to the group of loungers at Osborn's general store. There seemed to be a change in the old man—an added element of furtiveness in the clouded brain which subtly transformed him from an object to a subject of fear—though he was not one to be perturbed by any common family event. Amidst it all he shewed some trace of the pride later noticed in his daughter, and what he said of the child's paternity was remembered by many of his hearers years afterward.

"I dun't keer what folks think—ef Lavinny's boy looked like his pa, he wouldn't look like nothin' ye expeck. Ye needn't think the only folks is the folks hereabouts. Lavinny's read some, an' has seed some things the most o' ye only tell abaout. I calc'late her man is as good a husban' as ye kin find this side of Aylesbury; an' ef ye knowed as much abaout the hills as I dew, ye wouldn't ast no better church weddin' nor her'n. Let me tell ye suthin'—*some day yew folks'll hear a child o' Lavinny's a-callin' its father's name on the top o' Sentinel Hill!*"

The only persons who saw Wilbur during the first month of his life were old Zechariah Whateley, of the undecayed Whateleys, and Earl Sawyer's common-law wife, Mamie Bishop. Mamie's visit was frankly

one of curiosity, and her subsequent tales did justice to her observa-
tions; but Zechariah came to lead a pair of Alderney cows which Old
Whateley had bought of his son Curtis. This marked the beginning of
a course of cattle-buying on the part of small Wilbur's family which
ended only in 1928, when the Dunwich horror came and went; yet at
no time did the ramshackle Whateley barn seem overcrowded with
livestock. There came a period when people were curious enough to
steal up and count the herd that grazed precariously on the steep
hillside above the old farmhouse, and they could never find more than
ten or twelve anaemic, bloodless-looking specimens. Evidently some
blight or distemper, perhaps sprung from the unwholesome pasturage
or the diseased fungi and timbers of the filthy barn, caused a heavy
mortality amongst the Whateley animals. Odd wounds or sores,
having something of the aspect of incisions, seemed to afflict the visible
cattle; and once or twice during the earlier months certain callers
fancied they could discern similar sores about the throats of the grey,
unshaven old man and his slatternly, crinkly-haired albino daughter.

In the spring after Wilbur's birth Lavinia resumed her customary
rambles in the hills, bearing in her misproportioned arms the swarthy
child. Public interest in the Whateleys subsided after most of the
country folk had seen the baby, and no one bothered to comment on
the swift development which that newcomer seemed every day to
exhibit. Wilbur's growth was indeed phenomenal, for within three
months of his birth he had attained a size and muscular power not
usually found in infants under a full year of age. His motions and even
his vocal sounds shewed a restraint and deliberateness highly peculiar
in an infant, and no one was really unprepared when, at seven months,
he began to walk unassisted, with falterings which another month was
sufficient to remove.

It was somewhat after this time—on Hallowe'en—that a great blaze
was seen at midnight on the top of Sentinel Hill where the old
table-like stone stands amidst its tumulus of ancient bones. Considerable talk was started when Silas Bishop—of the undecayed
Bishops—mentioned having seen the boy running sturdily up that hill
ahead of his mother about an hour before the blaze was remarked. Silas
was rounding up a stray heifer, but he nearly forgot his mission when
he fleetingly spied the two figures in the dim light of his lantern. They
darted almost noiselessly through the underbrush, and the astonished
watcher seemed to think they were entirely unclothed. Afterward he
could not be sure about the boy, who may have had some kind of a
fringed belt and a pair of dark trunks or trousers on. Wilbur was never

subsequently seen alive and conscious without complete and tightly buttoned attire, the disarrangement or threatened disarrangement of which always seemed to fill him with anger and alarm. His contrast with his squalid mother and grandfather in this respect was thought very notable until the horror of 1928 suggested the most valid of reasons.

The next January gossips were mildly interested in the fact that "Lavinny's black brat" had commenced to talk, and at the age of only eleven months. His speech was somewhat remarkable both because of its difference from the ordinary accents of the region, and because it displayed a freedom from infantile lisping of which many children of three or four might well be proud. The boy was not talkative, yet when he spoke he seemed to reflect some elusive element wholly unpossessed by Dunwich and its denizens. The strangeness did not reside in what he said, or even in the simple idioms he used; but seemed vaguely linked with his intonation or with the internal organs that produced the spoken sounds. His facial aspect, too, was remarkable for its maturity; for though he shared his mother's and grandfather's chinless-ness, his firm and precociously shaped nose united with the expression of his large, dark, almost Latin eyes to give him an air of quasi-adult-hood and well-nigh preternatural intelligence. He was, however, exceedingly ugly despite his appearance of brilliancy; there being something almost goatish or animalistic about his thick lips, large-pored, yellowish skin, coarse crinkly hair, and oddly elongated ears. He was soon disliked even more decidedly than his mother and grandsire, and all conjectures about him were spiced with references to the bygone magic of Old Whateley, and how the hills once shook when he shrieked the dreadful name of *Yog-Sothoth* in the midst of a circle of stones with a great book open in his arms before him. Dogs abhorred the boy, and he was always obliged to take various defensive measures against their barking menace.

III.

Meanwhile Old Whateley continued to buy cattle without measurably increasing the size of his herd. He also cut timber and began to repair the unused parts of his house—a spacious, peaked-roofed affair whose rear end was buried entirely in the rocky hillside, and whose three least-ruined ground-floor rooms had always been sufficient for himself and his daughter. There must have been prodigious reserves of strength in the old man to enable him to accomplish so much hard labour; and though he still babbled dementedly at times, his carpentry seemed to shew the effects of sound calculation. It had already begun as soon as Wilbur was born, when one of the many tool-sheds had been put suddenly in order, clapboarded, and fitted with a stout fresh lock. Now, in restoring the abandoned upper story of the house, he was a no less thorough craftsman. His mania shewed itself only in his tight boarding-up of all the windows in the reclaimed section—though many declared that it was a crazy thing to bother with the reclamation at all. Less inexplicable was his fitting up of another downstairs room for his new grandson—a room which several callers saw, though no one was ever admitted to the closely boarded upper story. This chamber he lined with tall, firm shelving; along which he began gradually to arrange, in apparently careful order, all the rotting ancient books and parts of books which during his own day had been heaped promiscuously in odd corners of the various rooms.

"I made some use of 'em," he would say as he tried to mend a torn black-letter page with paste prepared on the rusty kitchen stove, "but the boy's fitten to make better use of 'em. He'd orter hev 'em as well sot as he kin, for they're goin' to be all of his larnin'."

When Wilbur was a year and seven months old—in September of 1914—his size and accomplishments were almost alarming. He had grown as large as a child of four, and was a fluent and incredibly intelligent talker. He ran freely about the fields and hills, and accompanied his mother on all her wanderings. At home he would pore diligently over the queer pictures and charts in his grandfather's books, while Old Whateley would instruct and catechise him through long, hushed afternoons. By this time the restoration of the house was finished, and those who watched it wondered why one of the upper windows had been made into a solid plank door. It was a window in the rear of the east gable end, close against the hill; and no one could imagine why a cleated wooden runway was built up to it from the ground. About the period of this work's completion people noticed that the old tool-house, tightly locked and windowlessly clapboarded since Wilbur's birth, had been abandoned again. The door swung listlessly open, and when Earl Sawyer once stepped within after a cattle-selling call on Old Whateley he was quite discomposed by the singular odour he encountered—such a stench, he averred, as he had never before smelt in all his life except near the Indian circles on the hills, and which could not come from anything sane or of this earth. But then, the homes and sheds of Dunwich folk have never been remarkable for olfactory immaculateness.

The following months were void of visible events, save that everyone
swore to a slow but steady increase in the mysterious hill noises. On
May Eve of 1915 there were tremors which even the Aylesbury people
felt, whilst the following Hallowe'en produced an underground rumbling queerly synchronised with bursts of flame—"them witch
Whateleys' doin's"—from the summit of Sentinel Hill. Wilbur was
growing up uncannily, so that he looked like a boy of ten as he entered
his fourth year. He read avidly by himself now; but talked much less
than formerly. A settled taciturnity was absorbing him, and for the
first time people began to speak specifically of the dawning look of evil
in his goatish face. He would sometimes mutter an unfamiliar jargon,
and chant in bizarre rhythms which chilled the listener with a sense of
unexplainable terror. The aversion displayed toward him by dogs had
now become a matter of wide remark, and he was obliged to carry a
pistol in order to traverse the countryside in safety. His occasional use
of the weapon did not enhance his popularity amongst the owners of
canine guardians.

The few callers at the house would often find Lavinia alone on the
ground floor, while odd cries and footsteps resounded in the boarded-
up second story. She would never tell what her father and the boy were
doing up there, though once she turned pale and displayed an abnormal
degree of fear when a jocose fish-peddler tried the locked door leading
to the stairway. That peddler told the store loungers at Dunwich
Village that he thought he heard a horse stamping on that floor above.
The loungers reflected, thinking of the door and runway, and of the
cattle that so swiftly disappeared. Then they shuddered as they recalled
tales of Old Whateley's youth, and of the strange things that are called
out of the earth when a bullock is sacrificed at the proper time to certain
heathen gods. It had for some time been noticed that dogs had begun
to hate and fear the whole Whateley place as violently as they hated
and feared young Wilbur personally.

In 1917 the war came, and Squire Sawyer Whateley, as chairman of
the local draft board, had hard work finding a quota of young Dunwich
men fit even to be sent to a development camp. The government,
alarmed at such signs of wholesale regional decadence, sent several
officers and medical experts to investigate; conducting a survey which
New England readers may still recall. It was the publicity attending
this investigation which set reporters on the track of the Whateleys,
and caused the *Boston Globe* and *Arkham Advertiser* to print flamboyant
Sunday stories of young Wilbur's precociousness, Old Whateley's black
magic, the shelves of strange books, the sealed second story of the

ancient farmhouse, and the weirdness of the whole region and its hill noises. Wilbur was four and a half then, and looked like a lad of fifteen. His lips and cheeks were fuzzy with a coarse dark down, and his voice had begun to break.

Earl Sawyer went out to the Whateley place with both sets of reporters and camera men, and called their attention to the queer stench which now seemed to trickle down from the sealed upper spaces. It was, he said, exactly like a smell he had found in the tool-shed abandoned when the house was finally repaired; and like the faint odours which he sometimes thought he caught near the stone circles on the mountains. Dunwich folk read the stories when they appeared, and grinned over the obvious mistakes. They wondered, too, why the writers made so much of the fact that Old Whateley always paid for his cattle in gold pieces of extremely ancient date. The Whateleys had received their visitors with ill-concealed distaste, though they did not dare court further publicity by a violent resistance or refusal to talk.

IV.

For a decade the annals of the Whateleys sink indistinguishably into the general life of a morbid community used to their queer ways and hardened to their May-Eve and All-Hallows orgies. Twice a year they would light fires on the top of Sentinel Hill, at which times the mountain rumblings would recur with greater and greater violence; while at all seasons there were strange and portentous doings at the lonely farmhouse. In the course of time callers professed to hear sounds in the sealed upper story even when all the family were downstairs, and they wondered how swiftly or how lingeringly a cow or bullock was usually sacrificed. There was talk of a complaint to the Society for the Prevention of Cruelty to Animals; but nothing ever came of it, since Dunwich folk are never anxious to call the outside world's attention to themselves.

About 1923, when Wilbur was a boy of ten whose mind, voice, stature, and bearded face gave all the impressions of maturity, a second great siege of carpentry went on at the old house. It was all inside the sealed upper part, and from bits of discarded lumber people concluded that the youth and his grandfather had knocked out all the partitions and even removed the attic floor, leaving only one vast open void between the ground story and the peaked roof. They had torn down the great central chimney, too, and fitted the rusty range with a flimsy outside tin stovepipe.

In the spring after this event Old Whateley noticed the growing
number of whippoorwills that would come out of Cold Spring Glen to
chirp under his window at night. He seemed to regard the circumstance as one of great significance, and told the loungers at Osborn's
that he thought his time had almost come.

"They whistle jest in tune with my breathin' naow," he said, "an' I
guess they're gittin' ready to ketch my soul. They know it's a-goin'
aout, an' dun't calc'late to miss it. Yew'll know, boys, arter I'm gone,
whether they git me er not. Ef they dew, they'll keep up a-singin'
an' laffin' till break o' day. Ef they dun't they'll kinder quiet daown
like. I expeck them an' the souls they hunts fer hev some pretty tough
tussles sometimes."

On Lammas Night, 1924, Dr. Houghton of Aylesbury was hastily
summoned by Wilbur Whateley, who had lashed his one remaining
horse through the darkness and telephoned from Osborn's in the
village. He found Old Whateley in a very grave state, with a cardiac
action and stertorous breathing that told of an end not far off. The
shapeless albino daughter and oddly bearded grandson stood by the
bedside, whilst from the vacant abyss overhead there came a disquieting suggestion of rhythmical surging or lapping, as of the waves on
some level beach. The doctor, though, was chiefly disturbed by the
chattering night birds outside; a seemingly limitless legion of whippoorwills that cried their endless message in repetitions timed
diabolically to the wheezing gasps of the dying man. It was uncanny
and unnatural—too much, thought Dr. Houghton, like the whole of
the region he had entered so reluctantly in response to the urgent call.

Toward one o'clock Old Whateley gained consciousness, and interrupted his wheezing to choke out a few words to his grandson.

"More space, Willy, more space soon. Yew grows—an' *that* grows
faster. It'll be ready to sarve ye soon, boy. Open up the gates to
Yog-Sothoth with the long chant that ye'll find on page 751 *of the
complete edition,* an' *then* put a match to the prison. Fire from airth can't
burn it nohaow."

He was obviously quite mad. After a pause, during which the flock
of whippoorwills outside adjusted their cries to the altered tempo while
some indications of the strange hill noises came from afar off, he added
another sentence or two.

"Feed it reg'lar, Willy, an' mind the quantity; but dun't let it
grow too fast fer the place, fer ef it busts quarters or gits aout afore ye
opens to Yog-Sothoth, it's all over an' no use. Only them from beyont

kin make it multiply an' work .... Only them, the old uns as wants to
come back ...."

But speech gave place to gasps again, and Lavinia screamed at the
way the whippoorwills followed the change. It was the same for more
than an hour, when the final throaty rattle came. Dr. Houghton drew
shrunken lids over the glazing grey eyes as the tumult of birds faded
imperceptibly to silence. Lavinia sobbed, but Wilbur only chuckled
whilst the hill noises rumbled faintly.

"They didn't git him," he muttered in his heavy bass voice.

Wilbur was by this time a scholar of really tremendous erudition in
his one-sided way, and was quietly known by correspondence to many
librarians in distant places where rare and forbidden books of old days
are kept. He was more and more hated and dreaded around Dunwich
because of certain youthful disappearances which suspicion laid
vaguely at his door; but was always able to silence inquiry through fear
or through use of that fund of old-time gold which still, as in his
grandfather's time, went forth regularly and increasingly for cattle-
buying. He was now tremendously mature of aspect, and his height,
having reached the normal adult limit, seemed inclined to wax beyond
that figure. In 1925, when a scholarly correspondent from Miskatonic
University called upon him one day and departed pale and puzzled, he
was fully six and three-quarters feet tall.

Through all the years Wilbur had treated his half-deformed albino
mother with a growing contempt, finally forbidding her to go to the
hills with him on May-Eve and Hallowmass; and in 1926 the poor
creature complained to Mamie Bishop of being afraid of him.

"They's more abaout him as I knows than I kin tell ye, Mamie," she
said, "an' naowadays they's more nor what I know myself. I vaow afur
Gawd, I dun't know what he wants nor what he's a-tryin' to dew."

That Hallowe'en the hill noises sounded louder than ever, and fire
burned on Sentinel Hill as usual; but people paid more attention to
the rhythmical screaming of vast flocks of unnaturally belated whippoorwills which seemed to be assembled near the unlighted Whateley
farmhouse. After midnight their shrill notes burst into a kind of
pandaemoniac cachinnation which filled all the countryside, and not
until dawn did they finally quiet down. Then they vanished, hurrying
southward where they were fully a month overdue. What this meant,
no one could be quite certain till later. None of the country folk seemed
to have died—but poor Lavinia Whateley, the twisted albino, was
never seen again.

In the summer of 1927 Wilbur repaired two sheds in the farmyard and began moving his books and effects out to them. Soon afterward Earl Sawyer told the loungers at Osborn's that more carpentry was going on in the Whateley farmhouse. Wilbur was closing all the doors and windows on the ground floor, and seemed to be taking out partitions as he and his grandfather had done upstairs four years before. He was living in one of the sheds, and Sawyer thought he seemed unusually worried and tremulous. People generally suspected him of knowing something about his mother's disappearance, and very few ever approached his neighbourhood now. His height had increased to more than seven feet, and shewed no signs of ceasing its development.

V.

The following winter brought an event no less strange than Wilbur's first trip outside the Dunwich region. Correspondence with the Widener Library at Harvard, the Bibliothèque Nationale in Paris, the British Museum, the University of Buenos Aires, and the Library of Miskatonic University of Arkham had failed to get him the loan of a book he desperately wanted; so at length he set out in person, shabby, dirty, bearded, and uncouth of dialect, to consult the copy at Miskatonic, which was the nearest to him geographically. Almost eight feet tall, and carrying a cheap new valise from Osborn's general store, this dark and goatish gargoyle appeared one day in Arkham in quest of the dreaded volume kept under lock and key at the college library—the hideous *Necronomicon* of the mad Arab Abdul Alhazred in Olaus Wormius' Latin version, as printed in Spain in the seventeenth century. He had never seen a city before, but had no thought save to find his way to the university grounds; where, indeed, he passed heedlessly by the great white-fanged watchdog that barked with unnatural fury and enmity, and tugged frantically at its stout chain.

Wilbur had with him the priceless but imperfect copy of Dr. Dee's English version which his grandfather had bequeathed him, and upon receiving access to the Latin copy he at once began to collate the two texts with the aim of discovering a certain passage which would have come on the 751st page of his own defective volume. This much he could not civilly refrain from telling the librarian—the same erudite Henry Armitage (A.M. Miskatonic, Ph.D. Princeton, Litt.D. Johns Hopkins) who had once called at the farm, and who now politely plied him with questions. He was looking, he had to admit, for a kind of formula or incantation containing the frightful name *Yog-Sothoth*, and it puzzled him to find discrepancies, duplications, and ambiguities which made the matter of determination far from easy. As he copied the formula he finally chose, Dr. Armitage looked involuntarily over his shoulder at the open pages; the left-hand one of which, in the Latin version, contained such monstrous threats to the peace and sanity of the world.

"Nor is it to be thought," ran the text as Armitage mentally translated it, "that man is either the oldest or the last of earth's masters, or that the common bulk of life and substance walks alone. The Old Ones were, the Old Ones are, and the Old Ones shall be. Not in the spaces we know, but *between* them, They walk serene and primal, undimensioned and to us unseen. *Yog-So-thoth* knows the gate. *Yog-So-thoth* is the gate. *Yog-So-thoth* is the key and the guardian of the gate. Past, present, future, all are one in *Yog-So-thoth.* He knows where the Old Ones broke through of old, and where They shall break through again. He knows where They have trod earth's fields, and where They still tread them, and why no one can behold Them as They tread. By Their smell can men sometimes know Them near, but of Their semblance can no man know, *saving only in the features of those They have begotten on mankind;* and of those are there many sorts, differing in likeness from man's truest eidolon to that shape without sight or substance which is *Them.* They walk unseen and foul in lonely places where the Words have been spoken and the Rites howled through at their Seasons. The wind gibbers with Their voices, and the earth mutters with Their consciousness. They bend the forest and crush the city, yet may not forest or city behold the hand that smites. Kadath in the cold waste hath known Them, and what man knows Kadath? The ice desert of the South and the sunken isles of Ocean hold stones whereon Their seal is engraven, but who hath seen the deep frozen city or the sealed tower long garlanded with seaweed and barnacles? Great Cthulhu is Their cousin, yet can he spy Them only dimly. *Iä! Shub-Niggurath!* As a foulness shall ye know Them. Their hand is at your throats, yet ye see Them not; and Their habitation is even one with your guarded threshold. *Yog-So-thoth* is the key to the gate, whereby the spheres meet. Man rules now where They ruled once; They shall soon rule where man rules now. After summer is winter, and after winter summer. They wait patient and potent, for here shall They reign again."

Dr. Armitage, associating what he was reading with what he had heard of Dunwich, and its brooding presences, and of Wilbur Whateley and his dim, hideous aura that stretched from a dubious birth to a cloud of probable matricide, felt a wave of fright as tangible as a draught of the tomb's cold clamminess. The bent, goatish giant before him seemed like the spawn of another planet or dimension; like something only partly of mankind, and linked to black gulfs of essence and entity that stretch like titan phantasms beyond all spheres of force and matter, space and time. Presently Wilbur raised his head and began speaking in that strange, resonant fashion which hinted at sound-producing organs unlike the run of mankind's.

"Mr. Armitage," he said, "I calc'late I've got to take that book home. They's things in it I've got to try under sarten conditions that I can't git here, an' it 'ud be a mortal sin to let a red-tape rule hold me up. Let me take it along, Sir, an' I'll swar they wun't nobody know the difference. I dun't need to tell ye I'll take good keer of it. It wa'n't me that put this Dee copy in the shape it is ...."

He stopped as he saw firm denial on the librarian's face, and his own goatish features grew crafty. Armitage, half-ready to tell him he might make a copy of what parts he needed, thought suddenly of the possible consequences and checked himself. There was too much responsibility in giving such a being the key to such blasphemous outer spheres. Whateley saw how things stood, and tried to answer lightly.

"Wal, all right, ef ye feel that way abaout it. Maybe Harvard wun't be so fussy as yew be." And without saying more he rose and strode out of the building, stooping at each doorway.

Armitage heard the savage yelping of the great watchdog, and studied Whateley's gorilla-like lope as he crossed the bit of campus visible from the window. He thought of the wild tales he had heard, and recalled the old Sunday stories in the *Advertiser;* these things, and the lore he had picked up from Dunwich rustics and villagers during his one visit there. Unseen things not of earth—or at least not of tri-dimensional earth—rushed foetid and horrible through New England's glens, and brooded obscenely on the mountain-tops. Of this he had long felt certain. Now he seemed to sense the close presence of some terrible part of the intruding horror, and to glimpse a hellish advance in the black dominion of the ancient and once passive nightmare. He locked away the *Necronomicon* with a shudder of disgust, but the room still reeked with an unholy and unidentifiable stench. "As a foulness shall ye know them," he quoted. Yes—the odour was the same as that which had sickened him at the Whateley farmhouse less than three years before. He thought of Wilbur, goatish and ominous, once again, and laughed mockingly at the village rumours of his parentage.

"Inbreeding?" Armitage muttered half-aloud to himself. "Great God, what simpletons! Shew them Arthur Machen's Great God Pan

and they'll think it a common Dunwich scandal! But what thing—
what cursed shapeless influence on or off this three-dimensioned
earth—was Wilbur Whateley's father? Born on Candlemas—nine
months after May-Eve of 1912, when the talk about the queer earth
noises reached clear to Arkham—what walked on the mountains that
May-Night? What Roodmas horror fastened itself on the world in
half-human flesh and blood?"

During the ensuing weeks, Dr. Armitage set about to collect all
possible data on Wilbur Whateley and the formless presences around
Dunwich. He got in communication with Dr. Houghton of Aylesbury,
who had attended Old Whateley in his last illness, and found much to
ponder over in the grandfather's last words as quoted by the physician.
A visit to Dunwich Village failed to bring out much that was new; but
a close survey of the *Necronomicon,* in those parts which Wilbur sought
so avidly, seemed to supply new and terrible clues to the nature,
methods, and desires of the strange evil so vaguely threatening this
planet. Talks with several students of archaic lore in Boston, and letters
to many others elsewhere, gave him a growing amazement which
passed slowly through varied degrees of alarm to a state of really acute
spiritual fear. As the summer drew on he felt dimly that something
ought to be done about the lurking terrors of the upper Miskatonic
valley, and about the monstrous being known to the human world as
Wilbur Whateley.

VI.

The Dunwich horror itself came between Lammas and the equinox of
1928, and Dr. Armitage was among those who witnessed its monstrous
prologue. He had heard, meanwhile, of Whateley's grotesque trip to
Cambridge, and of his frantic efforts to borrow or copy from the
Necronomicon at the Widener Library. Those efforts had been in vain,
since Armitage had issued warnings of the keenest intensity to all
librarians having charge of the dreaded volume. Wilbur had been
shockingly nervous at Cambridge; anxious for the book, yet almost
equally anxious to get home again, as if he feared the results of being
away long.

Early in August the half-expected outcome developed, and in the
small hours of the 3rd Dr. Armitage was awakened suddenly by the
wild, fierce cries of the savage watchdog on the college campus. Deep
and terrible, the snarling, half-mad growls and barks continued; always
in mounting volume, but with hideously significant pauses. Then

there rang out a scream from a wholly different throat—such a scream
as roused half the sleepers of Arkham and haunted their dreams ever
afterward—such a scream as could come from no being born of earth,
or wholly of earth.

Armitage, hastening into some clothing and rushing across the
street and lawn to the college buildings, saw that others were ahead of
him; and heard the echoes of a burglar-alarm still shrilling from the
library. An open window shewed black and gaping in the moonlight.
What had come had indeed completed its entrance; for the barking
and the screaming, now fast fading into a mixed low growling and
moaning, proceeded unmistakably from within. Some instinct warned
Armitage that what was taking place was not a thing for unfortified
eyes to see, so he brushed back the crowd with authority as he unlocked
the vestibule door. Among the others he saw Professor Warren Rice
and Dr. Francis Morgan, men to whom he had told some of his
conjectures and misgivings; and these two he motioned to accompany
him inside. The inward sounds, except for a watchful, droning whine
from the dog, had by this time quite subsided; but Armitage now
perceived with a sudden start that a loud chorus of whippoorwills
among the shrubbery had commenced a damnably rhythmical piping,
as if in unison with the last breaths of a dying man.

The building was full of a frightful stench which Dr. Armitage knew
too well, and the three men rushed across the hall to the small
genealogical reading-room whence the low whining came. For a second
nobody dared to turn on the light, then Armitage summoned up his
courage and snapped the switch. One of the three—it is not certain
which—shrieked aloud at what sprawled before them among disor-
dered tables and overturned chairs. Professor Rice declares that he
wholly lost consciousness for an instant, though he did not stumble
or fall.

The thing that lay half-bent on its side in a foetid pool of greenish-
yellow ichor and tarry stickiness was almost nine feet tall, and the dog
had torn off all the clothing and some of the skin. It was not quite dead,
but twitched silently and spasmodically while its chest heaved in
monstrous unison with the mad piping of the expectant whippoorwills
outside. Bits of shoe-leather and fragments of apparel were scattered
about the room, and just inside the window an empty canvas sack lay
where it had evidently been thrown. Near the central desk a revolver
had fallen, a dented but undischarged cartridge later explaining why
it had not been fired. The thing itself, however, crowded out all other
images at the time. It would be trite and not wholly accurate to say

that no human pen could describe it, but one may properly say that it
could not be vividly visualised by anyone whose ideas of aspect and
contour are too closely bound up with the common life-forms of this
planet and of the three known dimensions. It was partly human,
beyond a doubt, with very man-like hands and head, and the goatish,
chinless face had the stamp of the Whateleys upon it. But the torso
and lower parts of the body were teratologically fabulous, so that only
generous clothing could ever have enabled it to walk on earth unchal-
lenged or uneradicated.

Above the waist it was semi-anthropomorphic; though its chest,
where the dog's rending paws still rested watchfully, had the leathery,
reticulated hide of a crocodile or alligator. The back was piebald with
yellow and black, and dimly suggested the squamous covering of
certain snakes. Below the waist, though, it was the worst; for here all
human resemblance left off and sheer phantasy began. The skin was
thickly covered with coarse black fur, and from the abdomen a score of
long greenish-gray tentacles with red sucking mouths protruded
limply. Their arrangement was odd, and seemed to follow the symme-
tries of some cosmic geometry unknown to earth or the solar system.
On each of the hips, deep set in a kind of pinkish, ciliated orbit, was
what seemed to be a rudimentary eye; whilst in lieu of a tail there
depended a kind of trunk or feeler with purple annular markings, and
with many evidences of being an undeveloped mouth or throat. The
limbs, save for their black fur, roughly resembled the hind legs of
prehistoric earth's giant saurians; and terminated in ridgy-veined pads
that were neither hooves nor claws. When the thing breathed, its tail
and tentacles rhythmically changed colour, as if from some circulatory
cause normal to the non-human side of its ancestry. In the tentacles
this was observable as a deepening of the greenish tinge, whilst in the
tail it was manifest as a yellowish appearance which alternated with a
sickly greyish-white in the spaces between the purple rings. Of genuine
blood there was none; only the foetid greenish-yellow ichor which
trickled along the painted floor beyond the radius of the stickiness, and
left a curious discolouration behind it.

As the presence of the three men seemed to rouse the dying thing,
it began to mumble without turning or raising its head. Dr. Armitage
made no written record of its mouthings, but asserts confidently that
nothing in English was uttered. At first the syllables defied all corre-
lation with any speech of earth, but toward the last there came some
disjointed fragments evidently taken from the *Necronomicon,* that monstrous blasphemy in quest of which the thing had perished. These

fragments, as Armitage recalls them, ran something like *"N'gai, n'gha'ghaa, bugg-shoggog, y'hah; Yog-Sothoth, Yog-Sothoth ...."* They trailed off into nothingness as the whippoorwills shrieked in rhythmical crescendoes of unholy anticipation.

Then came a halt in the gasping, and the dog raised its head in a long, lugubrious howl. A change came over the yellow, goatish face of the prostrate thing, and the great black eyes fell in appallingly. Outside the window the shrilling of the whippoorwills had suddenly ceased, and above the murmurs of the gathering crowd there came the sound of a panic-struck whirring and fluttering. Against the moon vast clouds of feathery watchers rose and raced from sight, frantic at that which they had sought for prey.

All at once the dog started up abruptly, gave a frightened bark, and leaped nervously out of the window by which it had entered. A cry rose from the crowd, and Dr. Armitage shouted to the men outside that no one must be admitted till the police or medical examiner came. He was thankful that the windows were just too high to permit of peering in, and drew the dark curtains carefully down over each one. By this time two policemen had arrived; and Dr. Morgan, meeting them in the vestibule, was urging them for their own sakes to postpone entrance to the stench-filled reading-room till the examiner came and the prostrate thing could be covered up.

Meanwhile frightful changes were taking place on the floor. One need not describe the *kind* and *rate* of shrinkage and disintegration that occurred before the eyes of Dr. Armitage and Professor Rice; but it is permissible to say that, aside from the external appearance of face and hands, the really human element in Wilbur Whateley must have been very small. When the medical examiner came, there was only a sticky whitish mass on the painted boards, and the monstrous odour had nearly disappeared. Apparently Whateley had no skull or bony skeleton; at least, in any true or stable sense. He had taken somewhat after his unknown father.

VII.

Yet all this was only the prologue of the actual Dunwich horror. Formalities were gone through by bewildered officials, abnormal details were duly kept from press and public, and men were sent to Dunwich and Aylesbury to look up property and notify any who might be heirs of the late Wilbur Whateley. They found the countryside in great agitation, both because of the growing rumblings beneath the domed hills, and because of the unwonted stench and the surging, lapping sounds which came increasingly from the great empty shell formed by Whateley's boarded-up farmhouse. Earl Sawyer, who tended the horse and cattle during Wilbur's absence, had developed a woefully acute case of nerves. The officials devised excuses not to enter the noisome boarded place; and were glad to confine their survey of the deceased's living quarters, the newly mended sheds, to a single visit. They filed a ponderous report at the court-house in Aylesbury, and litigations concerning heirship are said to be still in progress amongst the innumerable Whateleys, decayed and undecayed, of the upper Miskatonic Valley.

An almost interminable manuscript in strange characters, written in a huge ledger and adjudged a sort of diary because of the spacing and the variations in ink and penmanship, presented a baffling puzzle to those who found it on the old bureau which served as its owner's desk. After a week of debate it was sent to Miskatonic University, together with the deceased's collection of strange books, for study and possible translation; but even the best linguists soon saw that it was not likely to be unriddled with ease. No trace of the ancient gold with which Wilbur and Old Whateley always paid their debts has yet been discovered.

It was in the dark of September 9th that the horror broke loose. The hill noises had been very pronounced during the evening, and dogs barked frantically all night. Early risers on the 10th noticed a peculiar stench in the air. About seven o'clock Luther Brown, the hired boy at George Corey's, between Cold Spring Glen and the village, rushed frenziedly back from his morning trip to Ten-Acre Meadow with the cows. He was almost convulsed with fright as he stumbled into the kitchen; and in the yard outside the no less frightened herd were pawing and lowing pitifully, having followed the boy back in the panic they shared with him. Between gasps Luther tried to stammer out his tale to Mrs. Corey.

"Up thar in the rud beyont the glen, Mis' Corey—they's suthin' ben thar! It smells like thunder, an' all the bushes an' little trees is pushed back from the rud like they'd a haouse ben moved along of it. An' that ain't the wust, nuther. They's *prints* in the rud, Mis' Corey—great raound prints as big as barrel-heads, all sunk daown deep like a elephant had ben along, *only they's a sight more nor four feet could make!* I looked at one or two afore I run, an' I see every one was covered with lines spreadin' aout from one place, like as if big palm-leaf fans—twict or three times as big as any they is—hed of ben paounded daown into the rud. An' the smell was awful, like what it is araound Wizard Whateley's old haouse ...."

Here he faltered, and seemed to shiver afresh with the fright that had sent him flying home. Mrs. Corey, unable to extract more information, began telephoning the neighbours; thus starting on its rounds the overture of panic that heralded the major terrors. When she got Sally Sawyer, housekeeper at Seth Bishop's, the nearest place to Whateley's, it became her turn to listen instead of transmit; for Sally's boy Chauncey, who slept poorly, had been up on the hill toward Whateley's, and had dashed back in terror after one look at the place, and at the pasturage where Mr. Bishop's cows had been left out all night.

"Yes, Mis' Corey," came Sally's tremulous voice over the party wire, "Cha'ncey he just come back a-postin', and couldn't haff talk fer bein' scairt! He says Ol' Whateley's haouse is all blowed up, with the timbers scattered raound like they'd ben dynamite inside; only the bottom floor ain't through, but is all covered with a kind o' tar-like stuff that smells awful an' drips daown offen the aidges onto the graoun' whar the side timbers is blowed away. An' they's awful kinder marks in the yard, tew—great raound marks bigger raound than a hogshead, an' all sticky with stuff like is on the blowed-up haouse. Cha'ncey he says they leads off into the medders, whar a great swath wider'n a barn is matted daown, an' all the stun walls tumbled every whichway wherever it goes.

"An' he says, says he, Mis' Corey, as haow he sot to look fer Seth's caows, frighted ez he was; an' faound 'em in the upper pasture nigh the Devil's Hop Yard in an awful shape. Haff on 'em's clean gone, an' nigh haff o' them that's left is sucked most dry o' blood, with sores on 'em like they's ben on Whateley's cattle ever senct Lavinny's black brat was born. Seth he's gone aout naow to look at 'em, though I'll vaow he wun't keer ter git very nigh Wizard Whateley's! Cha'ncey didn't look keerful ter see whar the big matted-daown swath led arter it leff the pasturage, but he says he thinks it p'inted towards the glen rud to the village.

"I tell ye, Mis' Corey, they's suthin' abroad as hadn't orter be abroad, an' I for one think that black Wilbur Whateley, as come to the bad eend he desarved, is at the bottom of the breedin' of it. He wa'n't all human hisself, I allus says to everybody; an' I think he an' Ol' Whateley must a raised suthin' in that there nailed-up haouse as ain't even so human as he was. They's allus ben unseen things araound Dunwich—livin' things—as ain't human an' ain't good fer human folks.

"The graoun' was a-talkin' lass night, an' towards mornin' Cha'ncey he heerd the whippoorwills so laoud in Col' Spring Glen he couldn't sleep nun. Then he thought he heerd another faint-like saound over towards Wizard Whateley's—a kinder rippin' or tearin' o' wood, like some big box er crate was bein' opened fur off. What with this an' that, he didn't git to sleep at all till sunup, an' no sooner was he up this mornin', but he's got to go over to Whateley's an' see what's the matter. He see enough, I tell ye, Mis' Corey! This dun't mean no good, an' I think as all the men-folks ought to git up a party an' do suthin'. I know suthin' awful's abaout, an' feel my time is nigh, though only Gawd knows jest what it is.

"Did your Luther take accaount o' whar them big tracks led tew? No? Wal, Mis' Corey, ef they was on the glen rud this side o' the glen, an' ain't got to your haouse yet, I calc'late they must go into the glen itself. They would do that. I allus says Col' Spring Glen ain't no healthy nor decent place. The whippoorwills an' fireflies there never did act like they was creaters o' Gawd, an' they's them as says ye kin hear strange things a-rushin' an' a-talkin' in the air daown thar ef ye stand in the right place, atween the rock falls an' Bear's Den."

By that noon fully three-quarters of the men and boys of Dunwich were trooping over the roads and meadows between the new-made Whateley ruins and Cold Spring Glen, examining in horror the vast, monstrous prints, the maimed Bishop cattle, the strange, noisome wreck of the farmhouse, and the bruised, matted vegetation of the fields and roadsides. Whatever had burst loose upon the world had assuredly gone down into the great sinister ravine; for all the trees on the banks were bent and broken, and a great avenue had been gouged in the precipice-hanging underbrush. It was as though a house, launched by an avalanche, had slid down through the tangled growths of the almost vertical slope. From below no sound came, but only a distant, undefinable foetor; and it is not to be wondered at that the men preferred to stay on the edge and argue, rather than descend and beard the unknown Cyclopean horror in its lair. Three dogs that were with the party had barked furiously at first, but seemed cowed and reluctant when near the glen. Someone telephoned the news to the *Aylesbury Transcript;* but the editor, accustomed to wild tales from Dunwich, did no more than concoct a humorous paragraph about it; an item soon afterward reproduced by the Associated Press.

That night everyone went home, and every house and barn was barricaded as stoutly as possible. Needless to say, no cattle were allowed to remain in open pasturage. About two in the morning a frightful

stench and the savage barking of the dogs awakened the household at
Elmer Frye's, on the eastern edge of Cold Spring Glen, and all agreed
that they could hear a sort of muffled swishing or lapping sound from
somewhere outside. Mrs. Frye proposed telephoning the neighbours,
and Elmer was about to agree when the noise of splintering wood burst
in upon their deliberations. It came, apparently, from the barn; and
was quickly followed by a hideous screaming and stamping amongst
the cattle. The dogs slavered and crouched close to the feet of the
fear-numbed family. Frye lit a lantern through force of habit, but knew
it would be death to go out into that black farmyard. The children and
the womenfolk whimpered, kept from screaming by some obscure,
vestigial instinct of defence which told them their lives depended on
silence. At last the noise of the cattle subsided to a pitiful moaning,
and a great snapping, crashing, and crackling ensued. The Fryes,
huddled together in the sitting-room, did not dare to move until the
last echoes died away far down in Cold Spring Glen. Then, amidst the
dismal moans from the stable and the daemoniac piping of late
whippoorwills in the glen, Selina Frye tottered to the telephone and
spread what news she could of the second phase of the horror.

The next day all the countryside was in a panic; and cowed,
uncommunicative groups came and went where the fiendish thing had
occurred. Two titan swaths of destruction stretched from the glen to
the Frye farmyard, monstrous prints covered the bare patches of
ground, and one side of the old red barn had completely caved in. Of
the cattle, only a quarter could be found and identified. Some of these
were in curious fragments, and all that survived had to be shot. Earl
Sawyer suggested that help be asked from Aylesbury or Arkham, but
others maintained that it would be of no use. Old Zebulon Whateley,
of a branch that hovered about half way between soundness and
decadence, made darkly wild suggestions about rites that ought to be
practiced on the hill-tops. He came of a line where tradition ran strong,
and his memories of chantings in the great stone circles were not
altogether connected with Wilbur and his grandfather.

Darkness fell upon a stricken countryside too passive to organise for
real defence. In a few cases closely related families would band together
and watch in the gloom under one roof; but in general there was only
a repetition of the barricading of the night before, and a futile,
ineffective gesture of loading muskets and setting pitchforks handily
about. Nothing, however, occurred except some hill noises; and when
the day came there were many who hoped that the new horror had gone
as swiftly as it had come. There were even bold souls who proposed an

offensive expedition down in the glen, though they did not venture to set an actual example to the still reluctant majority.

When night came again the barricading was repeated, though there was less huddling together of families. In the morning both the Frye and the Seth Bishop households reported excitement among the dogs and vague sounds and stenches from afar, while early explorers noted with horror a fresh set of the monstrous tracks in the road skirting Sentinel Hill. As before, the sides of the road shewed a bruising indicative of the blasphemously stupendous bulk of the horror; whilst the conformation of the tracks seemed to argue a passage in two directions, as if the moving mountain had come from Cold Spring Glen and returned to it along the same path. At the base of the hill a thirty-foot swath of crushed shrubbery saplings led steeply upward, and the seekers gasped when they saw that even the most perpendicular places did not deflect the inexorable trail. Whatever the horror was, it could scale a sheer stony cliff of almost complete verticality; and as the investigators climbed around to the hill's summit by safer routes they saw that the trail ended—or rather, reversed—there.

It was here that the Whateleys used to build their hellish fires and chant their hellish rituals by the table-like stone on May-Eve and Hallowmass. Now that very stone formed the centre of a vast space thrashed around by the mountainous horror, whilst upon its slightly concave surface was a thick and foetid deposit of the same tarry stickiness observed on the floor of the ruined Whateley farmhouse when the horror escaped. Men looked at one another and muttered. Then they looked down the hill. Apparently the horror had descended by a route much the same as that of its ascent. To speculate was futile. Reason, logic, and normal ideas of motivation stood confounded. Only old Zebulon, who was not with the group, could have done justice to the situation or suggested a plausible explanation.

Thursday night began much like the others, but it ended less happily. The whippoorwills in the glen had screamed with such unusual persistence that many could not sleep, and about 3 a.m. all the party telephones rang tremendously. Those who took down their receivers heard a fright-mad voice shriek out, "Help, oh, my Gawd!..." and some thought a crashing sound followed the breaking off of the exclamation. There was nothing more. No one dared do anything, and no one knew till morning whence the call came. Then those who had heard it called everyone on the line, and found that only the Fryes did not reply. The truth appeared an hour later, when a hastily assembled group of armed men trudged out to the Frye place at the head of the glen. It was horrible, yet hardly a surprise. There were more swaths and monstrous prints, but there was no longer any house. It had caved in like an egg-shell, and amongst the ruins nothing living or dead could be discovered. Only a stench and a tarry stickiness. The Elmer Fryes had been erased from Dunwich.

VIII.

In the meantime a quieter yet even more spiritually poignant phase of the horror had been blackly unwinding itself behind the closed door of a shelf-lined room in Arkham. The curious manuscript record or diary of Wilbur Whateley, delivered to Miskatonic University for translation, had caused much worry and bafflement among the experts in languages both ancient and modern; its very alphabet, notwith-standing a general resemblance to the heavily shaded Arabic used in Mesopotamia, being absolutely unknown to any available authority. The final conclusion of the linguists was that the text represented an artificial alphabet, giving the effect of a cipher; though none of the usual methods of cryptographic solution seemed to furnish any clue, even when applied on the basis of every tongue the writer might conceivably have used. The ancient books taken from Whateley's quarters, while absorbingly interesting and in several cases promising to open up new and terrible lines of research among philosophers and men of science, were of no assistance whatever in this matter. One of them, a heavy tome with an iron clasp, was in another unknown alphabet—this one of a very different cast, and resembling Sanscrit more than anything else. The old ledger was at length given wholly into the charge of Dr. Armitage, both because of his peculiar interest in the Whateley matter, and because of his wide linguistic learning and skill in the mystical formulae of antiquity and the Middle Ages.

Armitage had an idea that the alphabet might be something esoteri-cally used by certain forbidden cults which have come down from old times, and which have inherited many forms and traditions from the wizards of the Saracenic world. That question, however, he did not deem vital; since it would be unnecessary to know the origin of the symbols if, as he suspected, they were used as a cipher in a modern language. It was his belief that, considering the great amount of text involved, the writer would scarcely have wished the trouble of using another speech than his own, save perhaps in certain special formulae and incantations. Accordingly he attacked the manuscript with the preliminary assumption that the bulk of it was English.

Dr. Armitage knew, from the repeated failures of his colleagues, that the riddle was a deep and complex one; and that no simple mode of solution could merit even a trial. All through late August he fortified himself with the massed lore of cryptography; drawing upon the fullest resources of his own library, and wading night after night amidst the arcana of Trithemius' *Poligraphia*, Giambattista Porta's *De Furtivis Literarum Notis*, De Vigénère's *Traité des Chiffres*, Falconer's *Cryptomenysis Patefacta*, Davys' and Thicknesse's eighteenth-century treatises, and such fairly modern authorities as Blair, von Marten, and Klüber's *Kryptographik*. He interspersed his study of the books with attacks on the manuscript itself, and in time became convinced that he had to deal with one of those subtlest and most ingenious of cryptograms, in which many separate lists of corresponding letters are arranged like the multiplication table, and the message built up with arbitrary key-words known only to the initiated. The older authorities seemed rather more helpful than the newer ones, and Armitage concluded that the code of the manuscript was one of great antiquity, no doubt handed down through a long line of mystical experimenters. Several times he seemed near daylight, only to be set back by some unforeseen obstacle. Then, as September approached, the clouds began to clear. Certain letters, as used in certain parts of the manuscript, emerged definitely and unmistakably; and it became obvious that the text was indeed in English.

On the evening of September 2nd the last major barrier gave way, and Dr. Armitage read for the first time a continuous passage of Wilbur Whateley's annals. It was in truth a diary, as all had thought; and it was couched in a style clearly shewing the mixed occult erudition and general illiteracy of the strange being who wrote it. Almost the first long passage that Armitage deciphered, an entry dated November 26, 1916, proved highly startling and disquieting. It was written, he remembered, by a child of three and a half who looked like a lad of twelve or thirteen.

"Today learned the Aklo for the Sabaoth," it ran, "which did not like, it being answerable from the hill and not from the air. That upstairs more ahead of me than I had thought it would be, and is not like to have much earth brain. Shot Elam Hutchins' collie Jack when he went to bite me, and Elam says he would kill me if he dast. I guess he won't. Grandfather kept me saying the Dho formula last night, and I think I saw the inner city at the 2 magnetic poles. I shall go to those poles when the earth is cleared off, if I can't break through with the Dho-Hna formula when I commit it. They from the air told me at

Sabbat that it will be years before I can clear off the earth, and I guess grandfather will be dead then, so I shall have to learn all the angles of the planes and all the formulas between the Yr and the Nhhngr. They from outside will help, but they cannot take body without human blood. That upstairs looks it will have the right cast. I can see it a little when I make the Voorish sign or blow the powder of Ibn Ghazi at it, and it is near like them at May-Eve on the Hill. The other face may wear off some. I wonder how I shall look when the earth is cleared and there are no earth beings on it. He that came with the Aklo Sabaoth said I may be transfigured, there being much of outside to work on."

Morning found Dr. Armitage in a cold sweat of terror and a frenzy of wakeful concentration. He had not left the manuscript all night, but sat at his table under the electric light turning page after page with shaking hands as fast as he could decipher the cryptic text. He had nervously telephoned his wife he would not be home, and when she brought him a breakfast from the house he could scarcely dispose of a mouthful. All that day he read on, now and then halted maddeningly as a reapplication of the complex key became necessary. Lunch and dinner were brought him, but he ate only the smallest fraction of either. Toward the middle of the next night he drowsed off in his chair, but soon woke out of a tangle of nightmares almost as hideous as the truths and menaces to man's existence he had uncovered.

On the morning of September 4th Professor Rice and Dr. Morgan insisted on seeing him for a while, and departed trembling and ashen-grey. That evening he went to bed, but slept only fitfully. Wednesday—the next day—he was back at the manuscript, and began to take copious notes both from the current sections and from those he had already deciphered. In the small hours of that night he slept a little in an easy-chair in his office, but was at the manuscript again before dawn. Sometime before noon his physician, Dr. Hartwell, called to see him and insisted that he cease work. He refused; intimating that it was of the most vital importance for him to complete the reading of the diary, and promising an explanation in due course of time.

That evening, just as twilight fell, he finished his terrible perusal and sank back exhausted. His wife, bringing his dinner, found him in a half-comatose state; but he was conscious enough to warn her off with a sharp cry when he saw her eyes wander toward the notes he had taken. Weakly rising, he gathered up the scribbled papers and sealed them all in a great envelope, which he immediately placed in his inside coat pocket. He had sufficient strength to get home, but was so clearly in need of medical aid that Dr. Hartwell was summoned at once. As the doctor put him to bed he could only mutter over and over again, *"But what, in God's name, can we do?"*

Dr. Armitage slept, but was partly delirious the next day. He made no explanations to Hartwell, but in his calmer moments spoke of the imperative need of a long conference with Rice and Morgan. His wilder wanderings were very startling indeed, including frantic appeals that something in a boarded-up farmhouse be destroyed, and fantastic references to some plan for the extirpation of the entire human race and all animal and vegetable life from the earth by some terrible elder race of beings from another dimension. He would shout that the world was in danger, since the Elder Things wished to strip it and drag it away from the solar system and cosmos of matter into some other plane or phase of entity from which it had once fallen, vigintillions of aeons ago. At other times he would call for the dreaded *Necronomicon* and the *Daemonolatreia* of Remigius, in which he seemed hopeful of finding some formula to check the peril he conjured up.

"Stop them, stop them!" he would shout. "Those Whateleys meant to let them in, and the worst of all is left! Tell Rice and Morgan we must do something—it's a blind business, but I know how to make the powder .... It hasn't been fed since the second of August, when Wilbur came here to his death, and at that rate ...."

But Armitage had a sound physique despite his seventy-three years, and slept off his disorder that night without developing any real fever. He woke late Friday, clear of head, though sober with a gnawing fear and tremendous sense of responsibility. Saturday afternoon he felt able to go over to the library and summon Rice and Morgan for a conference, and the rest of that day and evening the three men tortured their brains in the wildest speculation and the most desperate debate. Strange and terrible books were drawn voluminously from the stack shelves and from secure places of storage; and diagrams and formulae were copied with feverish haste and in bewildering abundance. Of scepticism there was none. All three had seen the body of Wilbur Whateley as it lay on the floor in a room of that very building, and after that not one of them could feel even slightly inclined to treat the diary as a madman's raving.

Opinions were divided as to notifying the Massachusetts State Police, and the negative finally won. There were things involved which simply could not be believed by those who had not seen a sample, as indeed was made clear during certain subsequent investigations. Late at night the conference disbanded without having developed a definite plan, but all day Sunday Armitage was busy comparing formulae and mixing chemicals obtained from the college laboratory. The more he reflected on the hellish diary, the more he was inclined to doubt the efficacy of any material agent in stamping out the entity which Wilbur Whateley had left behind him—the earth-threatening entity which, unknown to him, was to burst forth in a few hours and become the memorable Dunwich horror.

Monday was a repetition of Sunday with Dr. Armitage, for the task in hand required an infinity of research and experiment. Further consultations of the monstrous diary brought about various changes of plan, and he knew that even in the end a large amount of uncertainty must remain. By Tuesday he had a definite line of action mapped out, and believed he would try a trip to Dunwich within a week. Then, on Wednesday, the great shock came. Tucked obscurely away in a corner of the *Arkham Advertiser* was a facetious little item from the Associated Press, telling what a record-breaking monster the bootleg whiskey of Dunwich had raised up. Armitage, half stunned, could only telephone for Rice and Morgan. Far into the night they discussed, and the next day was a whirlwind of preparation on the part of them all. Armitage knew he would be meddling with terrible powers, yet saw that there was no other way to annul the deeper and more malign meddling which others had done before him.

IX.

Friday morning Armitage, Rice, and Morgan set out by motor for Dunwich, arriving at the village about one in the afternoon. The day was pleasant, but even in the brightest sunlight a kind of quiet dread and portent seemed to hover about the strangely domed hills and the deep, shadowy ravines of the stricken region. Now and then on some mountain-top a gaunt circle of stones could be glimpsed against the sky. From the air of hushed fright at Osborn's store they knew something hideous had happened, and soon learned of the annihilation of the Elmer Frye house and family. Throughout that afternoon they rode around Dunwich; questioning the natives concerning all that had occurred, and seeing for themselves with rising pangs of horror the drear Frye ruins with their lingering traces of the tarry stickiness, the blasphemous tracks in the Frye yard, the wounded Seth Bishop cattle, and the enormous swaths of disturbed vegetation in various places. The trail up and down Sentinel Hill seemed to Armitage of almost cataclysmic significance, and he looked long at the sinister altar-like stone on the summit.

At length the visitors, apprised of a party of State Police which had come from Aylesbury that morning in response to the first telephone reports of the Frye tragedy, decided to seek out the officers and compare notes as far as practicable. This, however, they found more easily planned than performed; since no sign of the party could be found in any direction. There had been five of them in the car, but now the car stood empty near the ruins of the Frye yard. The natives, all of whom had talked with the policemen, seemed at first as perplexed as Armitage and his companions. Then old Sam Hutchins thought of something and turned pale, nudging Fred Farr and pointing to the dank, deep hollow that yawned close by.

"Gawd," he gasped, "I telled 'em not ter go daown into the glen, an' I never thought nobody'd dew it with them tracks an' that smell an' the whippoorwills a-screechin' daown thar in the dark o' noon-day ...."

A cold shudder ran through natives and visitors alike, and every ear seemed strained in a kind of instinctive, unconscious listening. Armitage, now that he had actually come upon the horror and its monstrous work, trembled with the responsibility he felt to be his. Night would soon fall, and it was then that the mountainous blasphemy lumbered upon its eldritch course. *Negotium perambulans in tenebris ....* The old librarian rehearsed the formulae he had memorised. He saw that his electric flashlight was in working order. Rice, beside him, took from a valise a metal sprayer of the sort used in combating insects; whilst Morgan uncased the big-game rifle on which he relied despite his colleague's warnings that no material weapon would be of help.

Armitage, having read the hideous diary, knew painfully well what kind of a manifestation to expect; but he did not add to the fright of the Dunwich people by giving any hints or clues. He hoped that it might be conquered without any revelation to the world of the monstrous thing that had escaped. As the shadows gathered, the natives commenced to disperse homeward, anxious to bar themselves indoors despite the present evidence that all human locks and bolts were useless before a force that could bend trees and crush houses when it chose. They shook their heads at the visitors' plan to stand guard at the Frye ruins near the glen; and as they left, had little expectancy of ever seeing the watchers again.

There were rumblings under the hills that night, and the whippoor-wills piped threateningly. Once in a while a wind, sweeping up out of Cold Sprins Glen, would bring a touch of ineffable foetor to the heavy night air; such a foetor as all three of the watchers had smelled once before, when they stood above a dying thing that had passed for fifteen years and a half as a human being. But the looked-for terror did not appear. Whatever was down there in the glen was biding its time, and Armitage told his colleagues it would be suicidal to try to attack it in the dark.

Morning came wanly, and the night-sounds ceased. It was a grey, bleak day, with now and then a drizzle of rain; and heavier and heavier clouds seemed to be piling themselves up beyond the hills to the northwest. The men from Arkham were undecided what to do. Seeking shelter from the increasing rainfall beneath one of the few undestroyed Frye outbuildings, they debated the wisdom of waiting, or of taking the aggressive and going down into the glen in quest of their nameless, monstrous quarry. The downpour waxed in heaviness, and distant peals of thunder sounded from far horizons. Sheet lightning shimmered, and then a forky bolt flashed near at hand, as if descending into the accursed glen itself. The sky grew very dark, and the watchers hoped that the storm would prove a short, sharp one followed by clear weather.

It was still gruesomely dark when, not much over an hour later, a confused babel of voices sounded down the road. Another moment brought into view a frightened group of more than a dozen men, running, shouting, and even whimpering hysterically. Someone in the lead began sobbing out words, and the Arkham men started violently when those words developed a coherent form.

"Oh, my Gawd, my Gawd," the voice choked out. "It's a-goin' agin, *an' this time by day!* It's aout—it's aout an' a-movin' this very minute, an' only the Lord knows when it'll be on us all!"

The speaker panted into silence, but another took up his message.

"Nigh on a haour ago Zeb Whateley here heered the 'phone a-ringin', an' it was Mis' Corey, George's wife, that lives daown by the junction. She says the hired boy Luther was aout drivin' in the caows from the storm arter the big bolt, when he see all the trees a-bendin' at the maouth o' the glen—opposite side ter this—an' smelt the same awful smell like he smelt when he faound the big tracks las' Monday mornin'. An' she says he says they was a swishin', lappin' saound, more nor what the bendin' trees an' bushes could make, an' all on a suddent the trees along the rud begun ter git pushed one side, an' they was a awful stompin' an' splashin' in the mud. But mind ye, Luther he didn't see nothin' at all, only just the bendin' trees an' underbrush.

"Then fur ahead where Bishop's Brook goes under the rud he heerd a awful creakin' an' strainin' on the bridge, an' says he could tell the saound o' wood a-startin' to crack an' split. An' all the whiles he never see a thing, only them trees an' bushes a-bendin'. An' when the swishin'

saound got very fur off—on the rud towards Wizard Whateley's an'
Sentinel Hill—Luther he had the guts ter step up whar he'd heerd it
furst an' look at the graound. It was all mud an' water, an' the sky was
dark, an' the rain was wipin' aout all tracks about as fast as could be;
but beginnin' at the glen maouth, whar the trees had moved, they was
still some o' them awful prints big as bar'ls like he seen Monday."

At this point the first excited speaker interrupted.

"But *that* ain't the trouble naow—that was only the start. Zeb here
was callin' folks up an' everybody was a-listenin' in when a call from
Seth Bishop cut in. His haousekeeper Sally was carryin' on fit ter
kill—she'd jest seed the trees a-bendin' beside the rud, an' says they
was a kind o' mushy saound, like a elephant puffin' an' treadin',
a-headin' fer the haouse. Then she up an' spoke suddent of a fearful
smell, an' says her boy Cha'ncey was a-screamin' as haow it was jest
like what he smelt up to the Whateley rewins Monday mornin'. An'
the dogs was all barkin' an' whinin' awful.

"An' then she let aout a turrible yell, an' says the shed daown the
rud had jest caved in like the storm hed blowed it over, only the wind
wa'n't strong enough to dew that. Everybody was a-listenen', an' we
could hear lots o' folks on the wire a-gaspin'. All to onct Sally she yelled
agin, an' says the front yard picket fence hed just crumbled up, though
they wa'n't no sign o' what done it. Then everybody on the line could
hear Cha'ncey an' ol' Seth Bishop a-yellin' tew, an' Sally was shriekin'
aout that suthin' heavy hed struck the haouse—not lightnin' nor
nothin', but suthin' heavy agin' the front, that kep' a-launchin' itself
agin an' agin, though ye couldn't see nothin' aout the front winders.
An' then ... an' then ...."

Lines of fright deepened on every face; and Armitage, shaken as he
was, had barely poise enough to prompt the speaker.

"An' then ... Sally she yelled aout, 'O help, the haouse is a-cavin'
in' ... an' on the wire we could hear a turrible crashin', an' a hull flock
o' screamin' ... jest like when Elmer Frye's place was took, only wuss ...."

The man paused, and another of the crowd spoke.

"That's all—not a saound nor squeak over the 'phone arter that. Jest
still-like. We that heerd it got aout Fords an' wagons an' raounded up
as many able-bodied menfolks as we could git, at Corey's place, an'
come up here ter see what yew thought best ter dew. Not but what I
think it's the Lord's jedgment fer our iniquities, that no mortal kin
ever set aside."

Armitage saw that the time for positive action had come, and spoke
decisively to the faltering group of frightened rustics.

"We must follow it, boys." He made his voice as reassuring as possible. "I believe there's a chance of putting it out of business. You men know that those Whateleys were wizards—well, this thing is a thing of wizardry, and must be put down by the same means. I've seen Wilbur Whateley's diary and read some of the strange old books he used to read; and I think I know the right kind of spell to recite to make the thing fade away. Of course, one can't be sure, but we can always take a chance. It's invisible—I knew it would be—but there's a powder in this long-distance sprayer that might make it shew up for a second. Later on we'll try it. It's a frightful thing to have alive, but it isn't as bad as what Wilbur would have let in if he'd lived longer. You'll never know what the world has escaped. Now we've only this one thing to fight, and it can't multiply. It can, though, do a lot of harm; so we mustn't hesitate to rid the community of it.

"We must follow it—and the way to begin is to go to the place that has just been wrecked. Let somebody lead the way—I don't know your roads very well, but I've an idea there might be a shorter cut across lots. How about it?"

The men shuffled about a moment, and then Earl Sawyer spoke softly, pointing with a grimy finger through the steadily lessening rain.

"I guess ye kin git to Seth Bishop's quickest by cuttin' acrost the lower medder here, wadin' the brook at the low place, an' climbin' through Carrier's mowin' and the timber-lot beyont. That comes aout on the upper rud mighty nigh Seth's—a leetle t'other side."

Armitage, with Rice and Morgan, started to walk in the direction indicated; and most of the natives followed slowly. The sky was growing lighter, and there were signs that the storm had worn itself away. When Armitage inadvertently took the wrong direction, Joe Osborn warned him and walked ahead to shew the right one. Courage and confidence were mounting; though the twilight of the almost perpendicular wooded hill which lay toward the end of their short cut, and among whose fantastic ancient trees they had to scramble as if up a ladder, put these qualities to a severe test.

At length they emerged on a muddy road to find the sun coming out. They were a little beyond the Seth Bishop place, but bent trees and hideously unmistakable tracks shewed what had passed by. Only a few moments were consumed in surveying the ruins just around the bend. It was the Frye incident all over again, and nothing dead or living was found in either of the collapsed shells which had been the Bishop house and barn. No one cared to remain there amidst the stench and tarry stickiness, but all turned instinctively to the line of horrible prints leading on toward the wrecked Whateley farmhouse and the altar-crowned slopes of Sentinel Hill.

As the men passed the site of Wilbur Whateley's abode they shuddered visibly, and seemed again to mix hesitancy with their zeal. It was no joke tracking down something as big as a house that one could not see, but that had all the vicious malevolence of a daemon. Opposite the base of Sentinel Hill the tracks left the road, and there was a fresh bending and matting visible along the broad swath marking the monster's former route to and from the summit.

Armitage produced a pocket telescope of considerable power and scanned the steep green side of the hill. Then he handed the instrument to Morgan, whose sight was keener. After a moment of gazing Morgan cried out sharply, passing the glass to Earl Sawyer and indicating a certain spot on the slope with his finger. Sawyer, as clumsy as most non-users of optical devices are, fumbled a while; but eventually focussed the lenses with Armitage's aid. When he did so his cry was less restrained than Morgan's had been.

"Gawd almighty, the grass an' bushes is a-movin'! It's a-goin' up—slow-like—creepin' up ter the top this minute, heaven only knows what fur!"

Then the germ of panic seemed to spread among the seekers. It was one thing to chase the nameless entity, but quite another to find it. Spells might be all right—but suppose they weren't? Voices began questioning Armitage about what he knew of this thing, and no reply seemed quite to satisfy. Everyone seemed to feel himself in close proximity to phases of Nature and of being utterly forbidden, and wholly outside the sane experience of mankind.

X.

In the end the three men from Arkham—old, white-bearded Dr. Armitage, stocky, iron-grey Professor Rice, and lean, youngish Dr. Morgan—ascended the mountain alone. After much patient instruction regarding its focussing and use, they left the telescope with the frightened group that remained in the road; and as they climbed they were watched closely by those among whom the glass was passed around. It was hard going, and Armitage had to be helped more than once. High above the toiling group the great swath trembled as its hellish maker re-passed with snail-like deliberateness. Then it was obvious the pursuers were gaining.

Curtis Whateley—of the undecayed branch—was holding the telescope when the Arkham party detoured radically from the swath. He
told the crowd that the men were evidently trying to get to a subordinate peak which overlooked the swath at a point considerably ahead
of where the shrubbery was now bending. This, indeed, proved to be
true; and the party were seen to gain the minor elevation only a short
time after the invisible blasphemy had passed it.

Then Wesley Corey, who had taken the glass, cried out that Armitage was adjusting the sprayer which Rice held, and that something
must be about to happen. The crowd stirred uneasily, recalling that
this sprayer was expected to give the unseen horror a moment of
visibility. Two or three men shut their eyes, but Curtis Whateley
snatched back the telescope and strained his vision to the utmost. He
saw that Rice, from the party's point of vantage above and behind the
entity, had an excellent chance of spreading the potent power with
marvellous effect.

Those without the telescope saw only an instant's flash of grey
cloud—a cloud about the size of a moderately large building—near
the top of the mountain. Curtis, who had held the instrument, dropped
it with a piercing shriek into the ankle-deep mud of the road. He
reeled, and would have crumpled to the ground had not two or three
others seized and steadied him. All he could do was moan
half-inaudibly, "Oh, oh, great Gawd ... *that* ... *that* ...."

There was a pandemonium of questioning, and only Henry Wheeler
thought to rescue the fallen telescope and wipe it clean of mud. Curtis
was past all coherence, and even isolated replies were almost too much
for him.

"Bigger'n a barn ... all made o' squirmin' ropes ... hull thing sort
o' shaped like a hen's egg bigger'n anything, with dozens o' legs like
hogsheads that haff shut up when they step ... nothin' solid abaout
it—all like jelly, an' made o' sep'rit wrigglin' ropes pushed clost
together ... great bulgin' eyes all over it ... ten or twenty maouths or
trunks a-stickin' aout all along the sides, big as stove-pipes, an' all
a-tossin' an' openin' an' shuttin' ... all grey, with kinder blue or purple
rings ... *an' Gawd in heaven—that haff face on top!* ..."

This final memory, whatever it was, proved too much for poor
Curtis; and he collapsed completely before he could say more. Fred Farr
and Will Hutchins carried him to the roadside and laid him on the
damp grass. Henry Wheeler, trembling, turned the rescued telescope
on the mountain to see what he might. Through the lenses were
discernible three tiny figures, apparently running toward the summit

as fast as the steep incline allowed. Only these—nothing more. Then everyone noticed a strangely unseasonable noise in the deep valley behind, and even in the underbrush of Sentinel Hill itself. It was the piping of unnumbered whippoorwills, and in their shrill chorus there seemed to lurk a note of tense and evil expectancy.

Earl Sawyer now took the telescope and reported the three figures as standing on the topmost ridge, virtually level with the altar-stone but at a considerable distance from it. One figure, he said, seemed to be raising its hands above its head at rhythmic intervals; and as Sawyer mentioned the circumstance the crowd seemed to hear a faint, half-musical sound from the distance, as if a loud chant were accompanying the gestures. The weird silhouette on that remote peak must have been a spectacle of infinite grotesqueness and impressiveness, but no ob-server was in a mood for aesthetic appreciation. "I guess he's sayin' the spell," whispered Wheeler as he snatched back the telescope. The whippoorwills were piping wildly, and in a singularly curious irregular rhythm quite unlike that of the visible ritual.

Suddenly the sunshine seemed to lessen without the intervention of any discernible cloud. It was a very peculiar phenomenon, and was plainly marked by all. A rumbling sound seemed brewing beneath the hills, mixed strangely with a concordant rumbling which clearly came from the sky. Lightning flashed aloft, and the wondering crowd looked in vain for the portents of storm. The chanting of the men from Arkham now became unmistakable, and Wheeler saw through the glass that they were all raising their arms in the rhythmic incantation. From some farmhouse far away came the frantic barking of dogs.

The change in the quality of the daylight increased, and the crowd gazed about the horizon in wonder. A purplish darkness, born of nothing more than a spectral deepening of the sky's blue, pressed down upon the rumbling hills. Then the lightning flashed again, somewhat brighter than before, and the crowd fancied that it had shewed a certain mistiness around the altar-stone on the distant height. No one, how-ever, had been using the telescope at that instant. The whippoorwills continued their irregular pulsation, and the men of Dunwich braced themselves tensely against some imponderable menace with which the atmosphere seemed surcharged.

Without warning came those deep, cracked, raucous vocal sounds which will never leave the memory of the stricken group who heard them. Not from any human throat were they born, for the organs of man can yield no such acoustic perversions. Rather would one have said they came from the pit itself, had not their source been so unmistakably the altar-stone on the peak. It is almost erroneous to call them *sounds* at all, since so much of their ghastly, infra-bass timbre spoke to dim seats of consciousness and terror far subtler than the ear; yet one must do so, since their form was indisputably though vaguely that of half-articulate *words*. They were loud—loud as the rumblings and the thunder above which they echoed—yet did they come from no visible being. And because imagination might suggest a conjectural source in the world of non-visible beings, the huddled crowd at the mountain's base huddled still closer, and winced as if in expectation of a blow.

"*Ygnaiih ... ygnaiih ... thflthkh'ngha ... Yog-Sothoth ...,*" rang the hideous croaking out of space. "*Y'bthnk ... h'ehye—n'grkdl'lh ....*"

The speaking impulse seemed to falter here, as if some frightful psychic struggle were going on. Henry Wheeler strained his eye at the telescope, but saw only the three grotesquely silhouetted human figures on the peak, all moving their arms furiously in strange gestures as their incantation drew near its culmination. From what black wells of Acherontic fear or feeling, from what unplumbed gulfs of extra-cosmic consciousness or obscure, long-latent heredity, were those half-articulate thunder-croakings drawn? Presently they began to gather renewed force and coherence as they grew in stark, utter, ultimate frenzy.

"*Eh-ya-ya-ya-yahaah—e'yayayayaaaa ... ngh'aaaaa ... ngh'aaaa ... h'yuh ... h'yuh ... HELP! HELP! ...ff—ff—ff—FATHER! FATHER! YOG-SOTHOTH! ...*"

But that was all. The pallid group in the road, still reeling at the *indisputably English* syllables that had poured thickly and thunderously down from the frantic vacancy beside that shocking altar-stone, were never to hear such syllables again. Instead, they jumped violently at the terrific report which seemed to rend the hills; the deafening, cataclysmic peal whose source, be it inner earth or sky, no hearer was ever able to place. A single lightning-bolt shot from the purple zenith to the altar-stone, and a great tidal wave of viewless force and indescribable stench swept down from the hill to all the countryside. Trees, grass, and underbrush were whipped into a fury; and the frightened crowd at the mountain's base, weakened by the lethal foetor that seemed about to asphyxiate them, were almost hurled off their feet. Dogs howled in the distance, green grass and foliage wilted to a curious, sickly yellow-grey, and over field and forest were scattered the bodies of dead whippoorwills.

The stench left quickly, but the vegetation never came right again. To this day there is something queer and unholy about the growths on and around that fearsome hill. Curtis Whateley was only just regaining consciousness when the Arkham men came slowly down the mountain in the beams of a sunlight once more brilliant and untainted. They were grave and quiet, and seemed shaken by memories and reflections even more terrible than those which had reduced the group of natives to a state of cowed quivering. In reply to a jumble of questions they only shook their heads and reaffirmed one vital fact.

"The thing has gone forever," Armitage said. "It has been split up into what it was originally made of, and can never exist again. It was an impossibility in a normal world. Only the least fraction was really matter in any sense we know. It was like its father—and most of it has gone back to him in some vague realm or dimension outside our material universe; some vague abyss out of which only the most accursed rites of human blasphemy could ever have called him for a moment on the hills."

There was a brief silence, and in that pause the scattered senses of poor Curtis Whateley began to knit back into a sort of continuity; so that he put his hands to his head with a moan. Memory seemed to pick itself up where it had left off, and the horror of the sight that had prostrated him burst in upon him again.

"Oh, oh, my Gawd, that haff face—that haff face on top of it ... that face with the red eyes an' crinkly albino hair, an' no chin, like the Whateleys .... It was a octopus, centipede, spider kind o' thing, but they was a haff-shaped man's face on top of it, an' it looked like Wizard Whateley's, only it was yards an' yards acrost ...."

He paused exhausted, as the whole group of natives stared in a bewilderment not quite crystallised into fresh terror. Only old Zebulon Whateley, who wanderingly remembered ancient things but who had been silent heretofore, spoke aloud.

"Fifteen year' gone," he rambled, "I heerd Ol' Whateley say as haow some day we'd hear a child o' Lavinny's a-callin' its father's name on the top o' Sentinel Hill...."

But Joe Osborn interrupted him to question the Arkham men anew.

"What was it, anyhaow, an' haowever did young Wizard Whateley call it aout o' the air it come from?"

Armitage chose his words very carefully.

"It was—well, it was mostly a kind of force that doesn't belong in our part of space; a kind of force that acts and grows and shapes itself by other laws than those of our sort of Nature. We have no business

calling in such things from outside, and only very wicked people and
very wicked cults ever try to. There was some of it in Wilbur Whateley
himself—enough to make a devil and a precocious monster of him,
and to make his passing out a pretty terrible sight. I'm going to burn
his accursed diary, and if you men are wise you'll dynamite that
altar-stone up there, and pull down all the rings of standing stones on
the other hills. Things like that brought down the beings those
Whateleys were so fond of—the beings they were going to let in
tangibly to wipe out the human race and drag the earth off to some
nameless place for some nameless purpose.

"But as to this thing we've just sent back—the Whateleys raised it
for a terrible part in the doings that were to come. It grew fast and big
from the same reason that Wilbur grew fast and big—but it beat him
because it had a greater share of the *outsideness* in it. You needn't ask
how Wilbur called it out of the air. He didn't call it out. *It was his twin
brother, but it looked more like the father than he did.*"

This sequel to "The Dunwich Horror" derives its protagonist from the following passage in "The Dunwich Horror": "Some of the Whateleys and Bishops still send their eldest sons to Harvard and Miskatonic, though those sons seldom return to the mouldering gambrel roofs under which they and their ancestors were born." Derleth, as always, with a sharp eye for neglected and intriguing details of Lovecraft's stories, got to wondering just what happened when the rare Dunwich scion did return home. In "The Shuttered Room" we find out. In fact, I imagine it was this passage from "The Dunwich Horror" that formed the sole Lovecraftian basis for "The Shuttered Room," not any entry from the Commonplace Book, as was usually the case in Derleth's "posthumous collaborations." Here is the only jotted entry that David E. Schultz, the leading student of the Commonplace Book, can even guess might have suggested the tale to Derleth: "Ultimate Horror – grand-father returns from strange trip – mystery in house – wind & darkness – grandf. & mother engulfed – questions forbidden – somnolence – investigation – cataclysm – screams overheard." Not very close, I'd say. The story of "The Shuttered Room" does not end here. A 1966 movie adaptation starring Gig Young, Oliver Reed, and Carol Lynley eliminated all the supernatural, but, set on Dunwich Island, it does quite a good job of depicting the repellant backwater decadence that Lovecraft and Derleth mythologized in their Dunwich horrors. The film was then novelized as The Shuttered Room by Julia Withers (Dell Books, 1971).

The Shuttered Room

by August W. Derleth

At dusk, the wild, lonely country guarding the approaches to the village of Dunwich in north central Massachusetts seems more desolate and forbidding than it ever does by day. Twilight lends the barren fields and domed hills a strangeness that sets them apart from the country around that area; it brings to everything a kind of sentient, watchful animosity—to the ancient trees, to the brier-bordered stone walls pressing close upon the dusty road, to the low marshes with their myriads of fireflies and their incessantly calling whippoorwills vying with the muttering of frogs and the shrill songs of toads, to the sinuous windings of the upper reaches of the Miskatonic flowing among the dark hills seaward, all of which seem to close in upon the traveller as if intent upon holding him fast, beyond all escape.

On his way to Dunwich, Abner Whateley felt all this again, as once in childhood he had felt it and run screaming in terror to beg his mother to take him away from Dunwich and Grandfather Luther Whateley.

So many years ago! He had lost count of them. It was curious that the country should affect him so, pushing through all the years he had lived since then—the years at the Sorbonne, in Cairo, in London—pushing through all the learning he had assimilated since those early visits to grim old Grandfather Whateley in his ancient house attached to the mill along the Miskatonic, the country of his childhood, coming back now out of the mists of time as were it but yesterday that he had visited his kinfolk.

They were all gone now—Mother, Grandfather Whateley, Aunt Sarey, whom he had never seen but only knew to be living somewhere in that old house—the loathsome cousin Wilbur and his terrible twin brother few had ever known before his frightful death on top of Sentinel Hill. But Dunwich, he saw as he drove through the cavernous covered bridge, had not changed; its main street lay under the looming mound of Round Mountain, its gambrel roofs as rotting as ever, its houses deserted, the only store still in the broken-steepled church, over everything the unmistakable aura of decay.

He turned off the main street and followed a rutted road up along the river, until he came within sight of the great old house with the mill wheel on the river-side. It was his property now, by the will of Grandfather Whateley, who had stipulated that he must settle the estate and "take such steps as may be necessary to bring about that dissolution I myself was not able to take." A curious proviso, Abner thought. But then, everything about Grandfather Whateley had been strange, as if the decadence of Dunwich had infected him irrevocably.

And nothing was stranger than that Abner Whateley should come back from his cosmopolitan way of life to heed his grandfather's adjurations for property which was scarcely worth the time and trouble it would take to dispose of it. He reflected ruefully that such relatives as still lived in or near Dunwich might well resent his return in their curious inward growing and isolated rustication which had kept most of the Whateleys in this immediate region, particularly since the shocking events which had overtaken the country branch of the family on Sentinel Hill.

The house appeared to be unchanged. The river-side of the house was given over to the mill, which had long ago ceased to function, as more and more of the fields around Dunwich had grown barren; except for one room above the mill-wheel—Aunt Sarey's room—the entire side of the structure bordering the Miskatonic had been abandoned even in the time of his boyhood, when Abner Whateley had last visited his grandfather, then living alone in the house except for the never seen

Aunt Sarey who abode in her shuttered room with her door locked, never to move about the house under prohibition of such movement by her father, from whose domination only death at last had freed her.

A verandah, fallen in at the corner of the house, circled that part of the structure used as a dwelling; from the lattice-work under the eaves great cobwebs hung, undisturbed by anything save the wind for years. And dust lay over everything, inside as well as out, as Abner discovered when he had found the right key among the lot the lawyer had sent him. He found a lamp and lit it, for Grandfather Whateley had scorned electricity. In the yellow glow of light, the familiarity of the old kitchen with its nineteenth-century appointments smote him like a blow. Its spareness, the hand-hewn table and chairs, the century-old clock on the mantel, the worn broom—all were tangible reminders of his fear-haunted childhood visits to this formidable house and its even more formidable occupant, his mother's aged father.

The lamplight disclosed something more. On the kitchen table lay an envelope addressed to him in handwriting so crabbed that it could only be that of a very old or infirm man—his grandfather. Without troubling to bring the rest of his things from the car, Abner sat down to the table, blowing the dust off the chair and sufficiently from the table to allow him a resting place for his elbows, and opened the envelope.

The spidery script leapt out at him. The words were as severe as he remembered his grandfather to have been. And abrupt, with no term of endearment, not even the prosaic form of greeting.

Grandson:

When you read this, I will be some months dead. Perhaps more, unless they find you sooner than I believe they will. I have left you a sum of money—all I have and die possessed of—which is in the bank at Arkham under your name now. I do this not alone because you are my own and only grandson but because among all the Whateleys—we are an accursed clan, my boy—you have gone forth into the world and gathered to yourself learning sufficient to permit you to look upon all things with an inquiring mind ridden neither by the superstition of ignorance nor the superstition of science. You will understand my meaning.

It is my wish that at least the mill section of this house be destroyed. Let it be taken apart, board by board. *If anything in it lives, I adjure you solemnly to kill it. No matter how small it may be. No matter what form it may have, for if it seems to you human it will beguile you and endanger your life and God knows how many others.*

Heed me in this.

If I seem to have the sound of madness, pray recall that worse than madness has spawned among the Whateleys. I have stood free of it. It has not been so of all that is mine. There is more stubborn madness in those who are unwilling to believe in what they know not of and deny that such exists, than in those of our blood who have been guilty of terrible practices, and blasphemy against God, and worse.

Your Grandfather, Luther S. Whateley.

How like Grandfather! thought Abner. He remembered, spurred into memory by this enigmatic, self-righteous communication, how on one occasion when his mother had mentioned her sister Sarah, and clapped her fingers across her mouth in dismay, he had run to his grandfather to ask, "Grandpa, where's Aunt Sarey?"

The old man had looked at him out of eyes that were basilisk and answered, "Boy, we do not speak of Sarah here."

Aunt Sarey had offended the old man in some dreadful way—dreadful, at least, to that firm disciplinarian—for from that time beyond even Abner Whateley's memory, his aunt had been only the name of a woman, who was his mother's older sister, and who was locked in the big room over the mill and kept for ever invisible within those walls, behind the shutters nailed to her windows. It had been forbidden both Abner and his mother even to linger before the door of that shuttered room, though on one occasion Abner had crept up to the door and put his ear against it to listen to the snuffling and whimpering sounds that went on inside, as from some large person, and Aunt Sarey, he had decided, must be as large as a circus fat lady, for she devoured so much, judging by the great platters of food—chiefly meat, which she must have prepared herself, since so much of it was raw—carried to the room twice daily by old Luther Whateley himself, for there were no servants in that house, and had not been since the time Abner's mother had married, after Aunt Sarey had come back, strange and mazed, from a visit to distant kin in Innsmouth.

He refolded the letter and put it back into the envelope. He would think of its contents another day. His first need now was to make sure of a place to sleep. He went out and got his two remaining bags from the car and brought them to the kitchen. Then he picked up the lamp and went into the interior of the house. The old-fashioned parlour, which was always kept closed against that day when visitors came— and none save Whateleys called upon Whateleys in Dunwich—he ignored. He made his way instead to his grandfather's bedroom; it was fitting that he should occupy the old man's bed now that he, and not Luther Whateley, was master here.

The large, double bed was covered with faded copies of the *Arkham Advertiser,* carefully arranged to protect the fine cloth of the spread, which had been embossed with an armigerous design, doubtless a legitimate Whateley heritage. He set down the lamp and cleared away the newspapers. When he turned down the bed, he saw that it was clean and fresh, ready for occupation; some cousin of his grandfather's had doubtless seen to this, against his arrival, after the obsequies.

Then he got his bags and transferred them to the bedroom, which was in that corner of the house away from the village; its windows looked along the river, though they were more than the width of the mill from the bank of the stream. He opened the only one of them which had a screen across its lower half, then sat down on the edge of the bed, bemused, pondering the circumstances which had brought him back to Dunwich after all these years.

He was tired now. The heavy traffic around Boston had tired him. The contrast between the Boston region and this desolate Dunwich country depressed and troubled him. Moreover, he was conscious of an intangible uneasiness. If he had not had need of his legacy to continue his research abroad into the ancient civilizations of the South Pacific, he would never have come here. Yet family ties existed, for all that he would deny them. Grim and forbidding as old Luther Whateley had always been, he was his mother's father, and to him his grandson owed the allegiance of common blood.

Round Mountain loomed close outside the bedroom; he felt its presence as he had when a boy, sleeping in the room above. Trees, for long untended, pressed upon the house, and from one of them at this hour of deep dusk, a screech owl's bell-like notes dropped into the still summer air. He lay back for a moment, strangely lulled by the owl's pleasant song. A thousand thoughts crowded upon him, a myriad of memories. He saw himself again as the little boy he was, always half-fearful of enjoying himself in these foreboding surroundings, always happy to come and happier to leave.

But he could not lie here, however relaxing it was. There was so much to be done before he could hope to take his departure that he could ill afford to indulge himself in rest and make a poor beginning of his nebulous obligation. He swung himself off the bed, picked up the lamp again, and began a tour of the house.

He went from the bedroom to the dining room, which was situated between it and the kitchen—a room of stiff, uncomfortable furniture, also handmade—and from there across to the parlour, the door of which opened upon a world far closer in its furniture and decorations to the eighteenth century than to the nineteenth, and far removed from the twentieth. The absence of dust testified to the tightness of the doors closing the room off from the rest of the house. He went up the open stairs to the floor above, from bedroom to bedroom—all dusty, with faded curtains, and showing every sign of having remained unoccupied for many years even before old Luther Whateley died.

Then he came to the passage which led to the shuttered room—Aunt Sarey's hideaway—or prison—he could now never learn what it might have been, and, on impulse, he went down and stood before that forbidden door. No snuffling, no whimpering greeted him now— nothing at all, as he stood before it, remembering, still caught in the spell of the prohibition laid upon him by his grandfather.

But there was no longer any reason to remain under that adjuration. He pulled out the ring of keys, and patiently tried one after another in the lock, until he found the right one. He unlocked the door and pushed; it swung protestingly open. He held the lamp high.

He had expected to find a lady's boudoir, but the shuttered room was startling in its condition—bedding scattered about, pillows on the floor, the remains of food dried on a huge platter hidden behind a bureau. An odd, ichthic smell pervaded the room, rushing at him with such musty strength that he could hardly repress a gasp of disgust. The room was in a shambles; moreover, it wore the aspect of having been in such wild disorder for a long, long time.

Abner put the lamp on a bureau drawn away from the wall, crossed to the window above the mill wheel, unlocked it, and raised it. He strove to open the shutters before he remembered that they had been nailed shut. Then he stood back, raised his foot, and kicked the shutters out to let a welcome blast of fresh, damp air into the room.

He went around to the adjoining outer wall and broke away the shutters from the single window in that wall, as well. It was not until he stood back to survey his work that he noticed he had broken a small corner out of the pane of the window above the mill wheel. His quick regret was quickly repressed in the memory of his grandfather's insistence that the mill and this room above it be torn down or otherwise destroyed. What mattered a broken pane!

He returned to take up the lamp again. As he did so, he gave the bureau a shove to push it back against the wall once more. At the same moment he heard a small, rustling sound along the baseboard, and, looking down, caught sight of a long-legged frog or toad—he could not make out which—vanishing under the bureau. He was tempted to rout the creature out, but he reflected that its presence could not matter—if it had existed in these locked quarters for so long on such cockroaches and other insects as it had managed to uncover, it merited being left alone.

He went out of the room, locked the door again, and returned to the master bedroom downstairs. He felt, obscurely, that he had made a beginning, however trivial; he had scouted the ground, so to speak. And he was twice as tired for his brief look around as he had been before. Though the hour was not yet late, he decided to go to bed and get an early start in the morning. There was the old mill yet to be gone through—perhaps some of the machinery could be sold, if any remained—and the mill wheel was now a curiosity, having continued to exist beyond its time.

He stood for a few minutes on the verandah, marking with surprise the welling stridulation of the crickets and katydids, and the almost overwhelming choir of the whippoorwills and frogs, which rose on all sides to assault him with a deafening insistence of such proportion as to drown out all other sounds, even such as might have risen from Dunwich. He stood there until he could tolerate the voices of the night no longer; then he retreated, locking the door, and made his way to the bedroom.

He undressed and got into bed, but he did not sleep for almost an hour, bedeviled by the chorus of natural sounds outside the house and from within himself by a rising confusion about what his grandfather had meant by the "dissolution" he himself had not been able to make. But at last he drifted into a troubled sleep.

II.

He woke with the dawn, little rested. All night he had dreamed of strange places and beings that filled him with beauty and wonder and dread—of swimming in the ocean's depths and up the Miskatonic among fish and amphibia and strange men, half batrachian in aspect— of monstrous entities that lay sleeping in an eerie stone city at the bottom of the sea—of utterly *outré* music as of flutes accompanied by weird ululations from throats far, far from human—of Grandfather Luther Whateley standing accusingly before him and thundering forth his wrath at him for having dared to enter Aunt Sarey's shuttered room.

He was troubled, but he shrugged his unease away before the necessity of walking into Dunwich for the provisions he had neglected to bring with him in his haste. The morning was bright and sunny; peewees and thrushes sang, and dew pearled on leaf and blade reflected the sunlight in a thousand jewels along the winding path that led to the main street of the village. As he went along, his spirits rose; he whistled happily, and contemplated the early fulfillment of his obligation, upon which his escape from this desolate, forgotten pocket of ingrown humanity was predicated.

But the main street of Dunwich was no more reassuring under the light of the sun than it had been in the dusk of the past evening. The village huddled between the Miskatonic and the almost vertical slope of Round Mountain, a dark and brooding settlement which seemed somehow never to have passed 1900, as if time had ground to a stop before the turn of the last century. His whistle faltered and died away; he averted his eyes from the buildings falling into ruin; he avoided the curiously expressionless faces of passers-by, and went directly to the old church with its general store, which he knew he would find slovenly and ill-kept, in keeping with the village itself.

A gaunt-faced storekeeper watched his advance down the aisle, searching his features for any familiar lineament.

Abner strode up to him and asked for bacon, coffee, eggs, and milk.

The storekeeper peered at him. He made no move. "Ye'll be a Whateley," he said at last. "I dun't expeck ye know me. I'm yer cousin Tobias. Which one uv 'em are ye?"

"I'm Abner—Luther's grandson." He spoke reluctantly.

Tobias Whateley's face froze. "Libby's boy—Libby, that married cousin Jeremiah. Yew folks ain't back—back at Luther's? Yew folks ain't a-goin' to start things again?"

"There's no one but me," said Abner shortly. "What things are you talking about?"

"If ye dun't know, taint fer me to say."

Nor would Tobias Whateley speak again. He put together what Abner wanted, took his money sullenly, and watched him out of the store with ill-concealed animosity.

Abner was disagreeably affected. The brightness of the morning had dimmed for him, though the sun shone from the same unclouded heaven. He hastened away from the store and main street, and hurried along the lane towards the house he had but recently quitted.

He was even more disturbed to discover, standing before the house, an ancient rig drawn by an old work-horse. Beside it stood a boy, and inside it sat an old, white-bearded man, who, at sight of Abner's approach, signalled to the boy for assistance, and by the lad's aid, laboriously descended to the ground and stood to await Abner.

As Abner came up, the boy spoke, unsmiling. "Great-grampa'll talk to yew."

"Abner," said the old man quaveringly, and Abner saw for the first time how very old he was.

"This here's Great-grampa Zebulon Whateley," said the boy.

Grandfather Luther Whateley's brother—the only living Whateley of his generation. "Come in, sir," said Abner, offering the old man his arm.

Zebulon Whateley took it.

The three of them made slow progress towards the verandah, where the old man halted at the foot of the steps, turning his dark eyes upon Abner from under their bushy white brows, and shaking his head gently.

"Naow, if ye'll fetch me a cheer, I'll set."

"Bring a chair from the kitchen, boy," said Abner.

The boy sped up the steps and into the house. He was out as fast with a chair for the old man, and helped to lower him to it, and stood beside him while Zebulon Whateley caught his breath.

Presently he turned his eyes full upon Abner and contemplated him, taking in every detail of his clothes, which, unlike his own, were not made by hand.

"Why have ye come, Abner?" he asked, his voice firmer now.

Abner told him, as simply and directly as he could.

Zebulon Whateley shook his head. "Ye know no more'n the rest, and less'n some," he said. "What Luther was abaout, only God knowed. Naow Luther's gone, and ye'll have it to dew. I kin tell ye, Abner, I vaow afur God, I dun't know why Luther took on so and locked hisself up and Sarey that time she come back from Innsmouth—but I kin say it was suthin' turrible, turrible—and the things what happened was turrible. Ain't nobody left to say Luther was to blame, nor poor Sarey—but take care, take care, Abner."

"I expect to follow my grandfather's wishes," said Abner.

The old man nodded. But his eyes were troubled, and it was plain that he had little faith in Abner.

"How'd you find out I was here, Uncle Zebulon?" Abner asked.

"I had the word ye'd come. It was my bounden duty to talk to ye. The Whateleys has a curse on 'em. Thar's been them naow gone to graoun' has had to dew with the devil, and thar's some what whistled turrible things aout o' the air, and thar's some what had to dew with things that wasn't all human nor all fish but lived in the water and swum aout—way aout—to sea, and thar's some what growed in on themselves and got all mazed and queer—and that's what happened on Sentinel Hill that time—Lavinny's Wilbur—and that other one by the Sentinel Stone—Gawd, I shake when I think on it ...."

"Now, Grandpa—don't ye git yer dander up," chided the boy.

"I wun't, I wun't," said the old man tremulously. "It's all died away naow. It's forgot—by all but me and them what took the signs daown—the signs that pointed to Dunwich, sayin, it was too turrible a place to know about ...." He shook his head and was silent.

"Uncle Zebulon," said Abner. "I never saw my Aunt Sarah."

"No, no, boy—she was locked up that time. Afore you was borned, I think it was."

"Why?"

"Only Luther knowed—and Gawd. Now Luther's gone, and Gawd dun't seem like He knowed Dunwich was still here."

"What was Aunt Sarah doing in Innsmouth?"

"Visitin' kin."

"Are there Whateleys there, too?"

"Not Whateleys. Marshes. Old Obed Marsh that was Pa's cousin. Him and his wife that he faound in the trade—at Ponape, if ye know whar that is."

"I do."

"Ye dew? I never knowed. They say Sarey was visitin' Marsh kin—Obed's son or grandson—I never knowed which. Never heered. Dun't care. She was thar quite a spell. They say when she come back she was different. Flighty. Unsettled. Sassed her pa. And then, not long after, he locked her up in that room till she died."

"How long after?"

"Three, four months. And Luther never said what fer. Nobody saw her again after that till the day she wuz laid aout in her coffin. Two year, might be three year ago. Thar was that time nigh on to a year after she come back from Innsmouth thar was sech goins-on here at this house—a-fightin' and a-screamin' and a-screechin'—most everyone in Dunwich heerd it, but no one went to see whut it was, and next day Luther he said it was only Sarey took with a spell. Might be it was. Might be it was suthin' else ...."

"What else, Uncle Zebulon?"

"Devil's work," said the old man instantly. "But I fergit—ye're the eddicated one. Ain't many Whateleys ever bin eddicated. Thar was Lavinny—she read them turrible books what was no good for her. And Sarey—she read some. Them as has only a little learnin' might's well

have none—they ain't fit to handle life with only a little learnin',
they're fitter with none a-tall."

Abner smiled.

"Dun't ye laugh, boy!"

"I'm not laughing, Uncle Zebulon. I agree with you."

"Then ef ye come face to face with it, ye'll know what to dew. Ye
wun't stop and think—ye'll jest dew."

"With what?"

"I wisht I knowed, Abner. I dun't. Gawd knows. Luther knowed.
Luther's dead. It comes on me Sarey knowed, too. Sarey's dead. Now
nobody knows whut turrible thing it was. Ef I was a prayin' man, I'd
pray you dun't find aout—but if ye dew, dun't stop to figger it aout
by eddication, jest dew whut ye have to dew. Yer Grandpa kep' a
record—look fer it. Ye might learn whut kind a people the Marshes
was—they wasn't like us—suthin' turrible happened to 'em—and
might be it reached aout and tetched Sarey ...."

Something stood between the old man and Abner Whateley—
something unvoiced, perhaps unknown; but it was something that cast
a chill about Abner for all his conscious attempt to belittle what
he felt.

"I'll learn what I can, Uncle Zebulon," he promised.

The old man nodded and beckoned to the boy. He signified that he
wished to rise, to return to the buggy. The boy came running.

"Ef ye need me, Abner, send word to Tobias," said Zebulon
Whateley. "I'll come—ef I can."

"Thank you."

Abner and the boy helped the old man back into the buggy. Zebulon
Whateley raised his forearm in a gesture of farewell, the boy whipped
up the horse, and the buggy drew away.

Abner stood for a moment looking after the departing vehicle. He
was both troubled and irritated—troubled at the suggestion of something dreadful which lurked beneath Zebulon Whateley's words of
warning, irritated because his grandfather, despite all his adjurations,
had left him so little to act upon. Yet this must have been because his
grandfather evidently believed there might be nothing untoward to
greet his grandson when at last Abner Whateley arrived at the old
house. It could be nothing other by way of explanation.

Yet Abner was not entirely convinced. Was the matter one of such
horror that Abner should not know of it unless he had to? Or had Luther
Whateley laid down a key to the riddle elsewhere in the house? He

doubted it. It would not be grandfather's way to seek the devious when he had always been so blunt and direct.

He went into the house with his groceries, put them away, and sat down to map out a plan of action. The very first thing to be accomplished was a survey of the mill part of the structure, to determine whether any machinery could be salvaged. Next he must find someone who would undertake to tear down the mill and the room above it. Thereafter he must dispose of the house and adjoining property, though he had a sinking feeling of futility at the conviction that he would never find anyone who would want to settle in so forlorn a corner of Massachusetts as Dunwich.

He began at once to carry out his obligations.

His search of the mill, however, disclosed that the machinery which had been in it—save for such pieces as were fixed to the running of the wheel—had been removed, and presumably sold. Perhaps the increment from the sale was part of that very legacy Luther Whateley had deposited in the bank at Arkham for his grandson. Abner was thus spared the necessity of removing the machinery before beginning the planned demolition. The dust in the old mill almost suffocated him; it lay an inch thick over everything, and it rose in great gusts to cloud about him when he walked through the empty, cobwebbed rooms. Dust muffled his footsteps and he was glad to leave the mill to go around and look at the wheel.

He worked his way around the wooden ledge to the frame of the wheel, somewhat uncertain, lest the wood give way and plunge him into the water beneath; but the construction was firm, the wood did not give, and he was soon at the wheel. It appeared to be a splendid example of middle nineteenth-century work. It would be a shame to tear it apart, thought Abner. Perhaps the wheel could be removed, and a place could be found for it either in some museum or in some one of those buildings which were for ever being reconstructed by wealthy persons interested in the preservation of American heritage.

He was about to turn away from the wheel, when his eye was caught by a series of small wet prints on the paddles. He bent closer to examine them, but, apart from ascertaining that they were already in part dried, he could not see in them more than marks left by some small animal, probably batrachian—a frog or a toad—which had apparently mounted the wheel in the early hours before the rising of the sun. His eyes, raising, followed the line of the wheel to the broken out shutters of the room above.

He stood for a moment, thinking. He recalled the batrachian creature he had glimpsed along the baseboard of the shuttered room. Perhaps it had escaped through the broken pane? Or, more likely, perhaps another of its kind had discovered its presence and gone up to it. A faint apprehension stirred in him, but he brushed it away in irritation that a man of his intelligence should have been sufficiently stirred by the aura of ignorant, superstitious mystery clinging to his grandfather's memory to respond to it.

Nevertheless, he went around and mounted the stairs to the shuttered room. He half expected, when he unlocked the door, to find some significant change in the aspect of the room as he remembered it from last night, but, apart from the unaccustomed daylight streaming into the room, there was no alteration.

He crossed to the window.

There were prints on the sill. There were two sets of them. One appeared to be leading out, the other entering. They were not the same size. The prints leading outward were tiny, only half an inch across. Those leading in were double that size. Abner bent close and stared at them in fixed fascination.

He was not a zoologist, but he was by no means ignorant of zoology. The prints on the sill were like nothing he had ever seen before, not even in a dream. Save for being or seeming to be webbed, they were perfect prints in miniature of human hands and feet.

Though he made a cursory search for the creature, he saw no sign of it, and finally, somewhat shaken, he retreated from the room and locked the door behind him, already regretting the impulse which had led him to it in the first place and which had caused him to burst open the shutters which for so long had walled the room away from the outer world.

III.

He was not entirely surprised to learn that no one in Dunwich could be found to undertake the demolition of the mill. Even such carpenters as those who had not worked for a long time were reluctant to undertake the task, pleading a variety of excuses, which Abner easily recognized as a disguise for the superstitious fear of the place under which one and all laboured. He found it necessary to drive into Aylesbury, but, though he encountered no difficulty in engaging a trio of husky young men who had formed a partnership to tear down the mill, he was forced to wait upon their previous commitments and had to return to Dunwich with the promise that they would come "in a week or ten days."

Thereupon he set about at once to examine into all the effects of Luther Whateley which still remained in the house. There were stacks of newspapers—chiefly the *Arkham Advertiser* and the *Aylesbury Transcript*—now yellowing with age and mouldering with dust, which he set aside for burning. There were books which he determined to go over individually in order that he might not destroy anything of value. And there were letters which he would have burned at once had he not happened to glance into one of them and caught sight of the name "Marsh", at which he read on.

Luther, what happened to cousin Obed is a singular thing. I do not know how to tell it to you. I do not know how to make it credible. I am not sure I have all the facts in this matter. I cannot believe but that it is a rigmarole deliberately invented to conceal something of a scandalous nature, for you know the Marshes have always been given to exaggeration and had a pronounced flair for deception. Their ways are devious. They have always been.

But the story, as I have it from cousin Alizah, is that when he was a young man Obed and some others from Innsmouth, sailing their trading ships into the Polynesian Islands, encountered there a strange people who called themselves the 'Deep Ones' and who had the ability to live either in the water or on the earth. Amphibians, they would then be. Does this sound credible to you? It does not to me. What is most astonishing is that Obed and some others married women of these people and brought them home to live with them.

Now that is the *legend.* Here are the *facts.* Ever since that time, the Marshes have prospered mightily in the trade. Mrs. Marsh is never seen abroad, save on such occasions as she goes to certain closed affairs of the Order of Dagon Hall. 'Dagon' is said to be a sea god. I know nothing of these pagan religions, and wish to know nothing. The Marsh children have *a very strange* look. I do not exaggerate, Luther, when I tell you that they have such wide mouths and such chinless faces and such large staring eyes that I swear they sometimes look more like frogs than human beings! They are not, at least as far as I can see, *gilled.* The 'Deep Ones' are said to be possessed of gills, and to belong to Dagon or to some other deity of the sea whose name I cannot even pronounce, far less set down. No matter. It is such a rigmarole as the Marshes might well invent to serve their purposes, but by God, Luther, judging by the way the ships Captain Marsh has in the East India trade keep afloat without a smitchin of damage done to them by storm or wear—the brigantine *Columbia,* the barque *Sumatra Queen,* the brig *Hetty* and some others—it might also seem that he has made some sort of bargain with Neptune himself!

Then there are all the doings off the coast where the Marshes live.
Night swimming. They swim way out off Devil Reef, which, as you
know, is a mile and a half out from the harbour here at Innsmouth.
People keep away from the Marshes——except the Martins and some
such others among them who were also in the East India trade. Now
that Obed is gone—and I suppose Mrs. Marsh may be also, since she
is no longer seen anywhere—the children and the grandchildren of
old Captain Obed follow in his strange ways.

The letter dwindled down to commonplaces about prices—ridiculously low figures seen from this vantage of over half a century later,
for Luther Whateley must have been a young man, unmarried, at the
time this letter had been written to him by Ariah, a cousin of whom
Abner had never heard. What it had to say of the Marshes was
nothing—or all, perhaps, if Abner had had the key to the puzzle of
which, he began to believe with mounting irritation, he held only
certain disassociated parts.

But if Luther Whateley had believed this rigmarole, would he, years
later, have permitted his daughter to visit the Marsh cousins? Abner
doubted it.

He went through other letters—bills, receipts, trivial accounts of
journeys made to Boston, Newburyport, Kingsport—post-cards, and
came at last to another letter from Cousin Ariah, written, if a comparison of dates was sufficient evidence, immediately after the one Abner
had just read. They were ten days apart, and Luther would have had
time to reply to that first.

Abner opened it eagerly.

The first page was an account of certain small family matters
pertinent to the marriage of another cousin, evidently a sister of Ariah's;
the second a speculation about the future of the East India trade, with
a paragraph about a new book by Whitman—evidently Walt; but the
third was manifestly in answer to something Grandfather Whateley
had evidently written concerning the Marsh branch of the family.

Well, Luther, you may be right in this matter of race prejudice as responsible for the feeling against the Marshes. I know how people
here feel about other races. It is unfortunate, perhaps, but such is
their lack of education that they find much room for such preju-
dices. But I am not convinced that it is *all* due to race prejudice. I
don't know what kind of race it is that would give the Marshes after
Obed that strange *look*. The East India people—such as I have seen
and recall from my early days in the trade—have features much like
our own, and only a different colour to the skin—copper, I would

call it. Once I did see a native who had a similar appearance, but he was evidently not typical, for he was shunned by all the workers around the ships in the harbour where I saw him. I've forgotten now where it was, but I think Ponape.

To give them their due, the Marshes keep pretty much to themselves—or to those families living here under the same cloud. And they more or less run the town. It may be significant—it may have been accident—that one selectman who spoke out against them was found drowned soon after. I am the first to admit that coincidences more startling than this frequently occur, but you may be sure that people who disliked the Marshes made the most of this.

But I know how your analytical mind is cold to such talk; I will spare you more of it.

Thereafter not a word. Abner went through bundles of letters in vain. What Ariah wrote in subsequent letters dealt scrupulously with family matters of the utmost triviality. Luther Whateley had evidently made his displeasure with mere gossip clear; even as a young man, Luther must have been strictly self-disciplined. Abner found but one further reference to any mystery at Innsmouth—that was a newspaper clipping dealing in very vague terms, suggesting that the reporter who sent in the story did not really know what had taken place, with certain Federal activity in and near Innsmouth in 1928—the attempted destruction of Devil Reef, and the blowing up of large sections of the waterfront, together with wholesale arrests of Marshes and Martins and some others. But this event was decades removed from Ariah's early letters.

Abner put the letters dealing with the Marshes into his pocket, and summarily burned the rest, taking the mass of material he had gone through out along the riverbank and setting fire to it. He stood guarding it, lest a chance wind carry a spark to surrounding grass, which was unseasonably dry. He welcomed the smell of the smoke, however, for a certain dead odour lingered along the riverbank, rising from the remains of fish upon which some animal had feasted—an otter, he thought.

As he stood beside the fire, his eyes roved over the old Whateley building, and he saw with a rueful reflection that it was high time the mill was coming down, that several panes of the window he had broken in the room that had been Aunt Sarey's, together with a portion of the frame, had fallen out. Fragments of the window were scattered on the paddles of the mill wheel.

By the time the fire was sufficiently low to permit his leaving it, the day was drawing to a close. He ate a meagre supper, and, having had his fill of reading for the day, decided against attempting to turn up his grandfather's "record" of which Uncle Zebulon Whateley had spoken, and went out to watch the dusk and the night from the verandah, hearing again the rising chorus of the frogs and whippoorwills.

He retired early, unwontedly weary.

Sleep, however, would not come. For one thing, the summer night was warm; hardly a breath of air stirred. For another, even above the ululation of the frogs and the demoniac insistence of the whippoor-wills, sounds from within the house invaded his consciousness—the creaks and groans of a many-timbered house settling in for the night; a peculiar scuffling or shuffling sound, half-drag, half-hop, which Abner laid to rats, which must abound in the mill section of the structure—and indeed, the noises were muffled, and seemed to reach him as from some distance; and, at one time, the cracking of wood and the tinkle of glass, which, Abner guessed, very probably came from the window above the mill wheel. The house was virtually falling to pieces about him; it was as if he served as a catalytic agent to bring about the final dissolution of the old structure.

This concept amused him because it struck him that, willy-nilly, he was carrying out his grandfather's adjuration. And, so bemused, he fell asleep.

He was awakened early in the morning by the ringing of the telephone, which he had had the foresight to have connected for the duration of his visit to Dunwich. He had already taken down the receiver from the ancient instrument attached to the wall before he realized that the call was on a party line and not intended for him. Nevertheless, the woman's voice that leapt out at him, burst open his ear with such screaming insistence that he remained frozen to the telephone.

"I tell ye, Mis' Corey, I heard things las' night—the graoun' was a-talkin' agen, and along abaout midnight, I heerd that scream—I never figgered a caow'd scream that way—jest like a rabbit, only deeper. That was Lutey Sawyer's cow—they faoun' her this morning—more 'n haff et by animals ...."

"Mis' Bishop, you dun't s'pose ... it's come back?"

"I dun't know. I hope t'Gawd it ain't. But it's the same as the las' time."

"Was it jest that one caow took?"

"Jes the one. I ain't heered abaout no more. But that's how it begun the las' time, Mis' Corey."

Quietly, Abner replaced the receiver. He smiled grimly at this evidence of the rampant superstitions of the Dunwich natives. He had never really known the depths of ignorance and superstition in which dwellers in such out-of-the-way places as Dunwich lived, and this manifestation of it was, he was convinced, but a mild sample.

He had little time, however, to dwell upon the subject, for he had to go into town for fresh milk, and he strode into the morning of sun and clouds with a certain feeling of relief at such brief escape from the house.

Tobias Whateley was uncommonly sullen and silent at Abner's entrance. Abner sensed not only resentment, but a certain tangible fear. He was astonished. To all Abner's comments Tobias replied in muttered monosyllables. Thinking to make conversation, he began to tell Tobias what he had overheard on the party line.

"I know it," said Tobias, curtly, for the first time gazing at Abner's face with naked terror.

Abner was stunned into silence. Terror vied with animosity in Tobias's eyes. His feelings were plain to Abner before he dropped his gaze and took the money Abner offered in payment.

"Yew seen Zebulon?" he asked in a low voice.

"He was at the house," said Abner.

"Yew talk to him?"

"We talked."

It seemed as if Tobias expected that certain matters had passed between them, but there was that in his attitude that suggested he was puzzled by subsequent events, which seemed to indicate that Zebulon had not told him what Tobias had expected the old man to tell him, or else that Abner had disregarded some of his Uncle's advice. Abner began to feel completely mystified; added to the superstitious talk of the natives on the telephone, to the strange hints Uncle Zebulon had dropped, this attitude of his cousin Tobias filled him with utter perplexity. Tobias, no more than Zebulon, seemed inclined to come out frankly and put into words what lay behind his sullen features—each acted as if Abner, as a matter of course, should know.

In his bafflement, he left the store, and walked back to the Whateley house determined to hasten his tasks as much as he could so that he might get away from this forgotten hamlet with its queer, superstition-ridden people, for all that many of them were his relatives.

To that end, he returned to the task of sorting his grandfather's things as soon as he had had his breakfast, of which he ate very little, for his disagreeable visit to the store had dulled the appetite which he had felt when he had set out for the store earlier.

It was not until late afternoon that he found the record he sought—an old ledger, in which Luther Whateley had made certain entries in his crabbed hand.

IV.

By the light of the lamp, Abner sat down at the kitchen table after he had had a small repast, and opened Luther Whateley's ledger. The opening pages had been torn out, but from an examination of the fragments of sheets still attached to the threads of the sewing, Abner concluded that these pages were purely of accounts, as if his grandfather had taken up an old, not completely used account book for a purpose other than keeping accounts, and had removed such sheets as had been more prosaically utilized.

From the beginning, the entries were cryptic. They were undated, except for the day of the week.

"This Saturday Ariah answered my inquiry. S. was seen sev times with Ralsa Marsh. Obed's great-grandson. *Swam* together by night."

Such was the first entry, clearly pertaining to Aunt Sarey's visit to Innsmouth, about which Grandfather had plainly inquired of Ariah. Something had impelled Luther to make such inquiry. From what he knew of his grandfather's character, Abner concluded that the inquiry had been made after Sarey had returned to Dunwich.

Why?

The next entry was pasted in, and was clearly a part of a typewritten letter received by Luther Whateley.

Ralsa Marsh is probably the most repellent of all the family. He is al-most *degenerate* in his looks. I know you have said that it was Libby of your daughters who was the fairest; even so, we cannot imagine how Sarah came to take up with someone who is so repulsive as Ralsa, in whom all those recessive characteristics which have been seen in the Marsh family after Obed's strange marriage to that Poly-nesian woman—(the Marshes have denied that Obed's wife was Poly-nesian, but of course, he was trading there at that time, and I don't credit those stories about that uncharted island where he was sup-posed to have dallied)—seem to have come to fullest fruit.

As far as I can now ascertain—after all, it is over two months—close
to four, I think—since her return to Dunwich—they were constantly
together. I am surprised that Ariah did not inform you of this. None
of us here had any mandate to halt Sarah's seeing Ralsa, and, after
all, they are cousins and she was visiting at Marshes—not here.

Abner judged that this letter had been written by a woman, also a
cousin, who bore Luther some resentment for Sarah's not having been
sent to stay with her branch of the family. Luther had evidently made
enquiry of her regarding Ralsa.

The third entry was once again in Luther's hand, summarizing a
letter from Ariah.

"Saturday. Ariah maintains Deep Ones a sect or quasi-religious
group. Sub-human. Said to live in the sea and worship Dagon. Another
God named Cthulhu. Gilled people. Resembling frogs or toads more
than fish, but eyes ichthic. Claims Obed's late wife was one. Holds that
Obed's children all bore the marks. Marshes gilled? How else could
they swim a mile and a half to Devil Reef, and back? Marshes eat
sparingly, can go without food and drink a long time, diminish or
expand in size rapidly." (To this Luther had appended four scornful
exclamation marks.)

"Zadok Allen swears he saw Sarah swimming out to Devil Reef.
Marshes carrying her along. All *naked*. Swears he saw Marshes with
tough, warty skin. Some with *scales,* like fish! Swears he saw them chase
and eat fish! Tear them apart like animals."

The next entry was again a portion of a letter, patently a reply to one
from Grandfather Whateley.

You ask who is responsible for those *ridiculous* tales about the
Marshes. Well, Luther, it would be impossible to single out any one
or a dozen people over several generations. I agree that old Zadok Allen talks too much, drinks, and may be romancing. But he is only
one. The fact is this legendry—or *rigmarole,* as you call it—has
grown up from one generation to the next. Through three generations. You have only to look at some of the descendants of Captain
Obed to understand why this could have come about. There are
some Marsh offspring said to have been too horrible to look upon.
Old wives' tales? Well, Dr. Rowley Marsh was too ill to attend one
of the Marsh women one time; so they had to call Dr. Gilman, and
Gilman always said that what he delivered was less than human.
And nobody ever saw that particular Marsh, though there were people later who claimed to have seen *things moving on two legs that
weren't human.*

Following this there was but a brief but revealing entry in two words: "Punished Sarah."

This must then mark the date of Sarah Whateley's confinement to the room above the mill. For some time after this entry, there was no mention of his daughter in Luther's script. Instead, his jottings were not dated in any way, and, judging by the difference in the colour of the ink, were made at different times, though run together.

"Many frogs. Seem to bear in on the mill. Seem to be more than in the marshes across the Miskatonic. Sleeping difficult. Are whippoorwills on the increase, too, or is this imagination? ... Counted thirty-seven frogs at the porch steps tonight."

There were more entries of this nature. Abner read them all, but there was no clue in them to what the old man had been getting at. Luther Whateley had thereafter kept book on frogs, fog, fish and their movements in the Miskatonic—when they rose and leaped from the water, and so on. This seemed to be unrelated data, and was not in any way connected to the problem of Sarah.

There was another hiatus after this series of notes, and then came a single, underscored entry.

"Ariah was right!"

But about what had Ariah been right? Abner wondered. And how had Luther Whateley learned that Ariah had been right? There was no evidence that Ariah and Luther had continued their correspondence, or even that Ariah desired to write to the crotchety Luther without a letter of direct inquiry from Luther.

There followed a section of the record to which newspaper clippings had been pasted. These were clearly unrelated, but they did establish for Abner the fact that somewhat better than a year had passed before Luther's next entry, one of the most puzzling Abner found. Indeed, the time hiatus seemed to be closer to two years.

"R. out again."

If Luther and Sarah were the only people in the house, who was "R."? Could it have been Ralsa Marsh come to visit? Abner doubted it, for there was nothing to show that Ralsa Marsh harboured any affection for his distant cousin, or certainly he would have pursued her before this.

The next notation seemed to be unrelated.

"Two turtles, one dog, remains of woodchuck. Bishop's—two cows, found on the Miskatonic end of the pasture."

A little further along, Luther had set down further such data.

"After one month a total of 17 cattle, 6 sheep. Hideous alterations; size commensurate with amt. of food. Z. over. Anxious about talk going around."

Could Z. stand for Zebulon? Abner thought it did. Evidently then Zebulon had come in vain, for he had left him, Abner, with only vague and uncertain hints about the situation at the house when Aunt Sarey was confined to the shuttered room. Zebulon, on the evidence of such conversation as he had shared with Abner, knew less than Abner himself did after reading his grandfather's record. But he did know of Luther's record; so Luther must have told him he had set down certain facts.

These notations, however, were more in the nature of notes for something to be completed later; they were unaccountably cryptic, unless one had the key of basic knowledge which belonged to Luther Whateley. But a growing sense of urgency was clearly manifest in the old man's further entries.

"Ada Wilkerson gone. Trace of scuffle. Strong feeling in Dunwich. John Sawyer shook his fist at me—safely across the street, where I couldn't reach him."

"Monday. Howard Willie this time. They found one shoe, with the foot still in it!"

The record was now near its end. Many pages, unfortunately, had been detached from it—some with violence—but no clue remained as to why this violence had been done to Grandfather Whateley's account. It could not have been done by anyone but Luther himself; perhaps, thought Abner, Luther felt he had told too much, and intended to destroy anything which might put a later reader on the track of the true facts regarding Aunt Sarey's confinement for the rest of her life. He had certainly succeeded.

The next entry once again referred to the elusive "R."

"R. back at last."

Then, "Nailed the shutters to the windows of Sarah's room."

And at last: "Once he has lost weight, he must be kept on a careful diet and to a controllable size."

In a way, this was the most enigmatic entry of them all. Was "he" also "R."? If so, why must he be kept on a careful diet, and what did Luther Whateley mean by controlling his size? There was no ready answer to these questions in such material as Abner had read thus far, either in this record—or the fragmentary account still left in the record—or in letters previously perused.

He pushed away the record-book, resisting an impulse to burn it. He was exasperated, all the more so because he was uneasily aware of an urgent need to learn the secret embalmed within this old building.

The hour was now late; darkness had fallen some time ago, and the ever-present clamour of the frogs and the whippoorwills had begun once more, rising all around the house. Pushing from his thoughts briefly the apparently unconnected jottings he had been reading, he called from his memory the superstitions of the family, representing those prevalent in the countryside—associating frogs and the calling of whippoorwills and owls with death, and from this meditation progressed readily to the amphibian link which presented itself—the presence of the frogs brought before his mind's eye a grotesque caricature of one of the Marsh clan of Innsmouth, as described in the letters Luther Whateley had saved for so many years.

Oddly, this very thought, for all that it was so casual, startled him. The insistence of the frogs and toads on singing and calling in the vicinity was truly remarkable. Yet, batrachia had always been plentiful in the Dunwich vicinity, and he had no way of knowing for how long a period before his arrival they had been calling about the old Whateley house. He discounted the suggestion that his arrival had anything at all to do with it; more than likely, the proximity of the Miskatonic and a low, swampy area immediately across the river on the edge of Dunwich, accounted for the presence of so many frogs.

His exasperation faded away; his concern about the frogs did likewise. He was weary. He got up and put the record left by Luther Whateley carefully into one of his bags, intending to carry it away with him, and to puzzle over it until some sort of meaning came out of it. Somewhere there must exist a clue. If certain horrible events had taken place in the vicinity, something more in the way of a record must exist than Luther Whateley's spare notes. It would do no good to inquire of Dunwich people; Abner knew they would maintain a close-mouthed silence before an "outsider" like himself, for all that he was related to many of them.

It was then that he thought of the stacks of newspapers, still set aside to be burned. Despite his weariness, he began to go through packs of the *Aylesbury Transcript,* which carried, from time to time, a Dunwich department.

After an hour's hasty search, he found three vague articles, none of them in the regular Dunwich columns, which corroborated entries in Luther Whateley's ledger. The first appeared under the heading: WILD ANIMAL SLAYS STOCK NEAR DUNWICH—

"Several cows and sheep have been slain on farms just outside Dunwich by what appears to be a wild animal of some kind. Traces left at the scenes of the slaughter suggest some large beast, but Professor Bethnall of Miskatonic University's anthropology department points out that it is not inconceivable that packs of wolves could lurk in the wild hill country around Dunwich. No beast of the size suggested by the traces reported was ever known to inhabit the eastern seaboard within the memory of man. County officials are investigating."

Search as he might, Abner could find no follow-up story. He did, however, come upon the story of Ada Wilkerson.

"A widow-lady, Ada Wilkerson, 57, living along the Miskatonic out of Dunwich, may have been the victim of foul play three nights ago. When she failed to visit a friend by appointment in Dunwich, her home was visited. No trace of her was found. However, the door of her house had been broken in, and the furniture had been wildly thrown about, as if a violent struggle had taken place. A very strong musk is said to have pervaded the entire area. Up to press time today, Mrs. Wilkerson has not been heard from."

Two subsequent paragraphs reported briefly that authorities had not found any clue to Mrs. Wilkerson's disappearance. The account of a "large animal" was resurrected, lamely, and Professor Bethnall's beliefs on the possible existence of a wolf-pack, but nothing further, for investigation had disclosed that the missing lady had neither money nor enemies, and no one would have had any motive for killing her.

Finally, there was the account of Howard Willie's death, headed, SHOCKING CRIME AT DUNWICH.

"Some time during the night of the twenty-first Howard Willie, 37, a native of Dunwich, was brutally slain as he was on his way home from a fishing trip along the upper reaches of the Miskatonic. Mr. Willie was attacked about half a mile past the Luther Whateley property, as he walked through an arboured lane. He evidently put up a fierce fight, for the ground is badly torn up in all directions. The poor fellow was overcome, and must have been literally torn limb from limb, for the only physical remains of the victim consisted of his right foot, still encased in its shoe. It had evidently been cruelly torn from his leg by great force.

"Our correspondent in Dunwich advises us that people there are very sullen and in a great rage of anger and fear. They suspect many of their number of being at least partly to blame, though they stoutly deny that anyone in Dunwich murdered either Willie or Mrs. Wilkerson, who disappeared a fortnight ago, and of whom no word had since been heard."

The account concluded with some data about Willie's family connections. Thereafter, subsequent editions of the *Transcript* were distinguished only for the lack of information about the events which had taken place in Dunwich, where authorities and reporters alike apparently ran up against blank walls in the stolid refusal of the natives to talk or even speculate about what had happened. There was, however, one insistent note which recurred in the comments of investigators, relayed to the press, and that was that such trail or track as could be seen appeared to have disappeared into the waters of the Miskatonic, suggesting that if an animal were responsible for the orgy of slaughter which had occurred at Dunwich, it may have come from and returned to the river.

Though it was now close to midnight, Abner massed the discarded newspapers together and took them out to the riverbank, where he set them on fire, having saved only torn pages relative to the occurrences at Dunwich. The air being still, he did not feel obliged to watch the fire, since he had already burned a considerable area, and the grass was not likely to catch on fire. As he started away, he heard suddenly above the ululation of the whippoorwills and frogs, now at a frenzied crescendo, the tearing and breaking sound of wood. He thought at once of the window of the shuttered room, and retraced his steps.

In the very dim light flickering towards the house from the burning newspapers, it seemed to Abner that the window gaped wider than before. Could it be that the entire mill part of the house was about to collapse? Then, out of the corner of his eye, he caught sight of a singularly formless moving shadow just beyond the mill wheel, and a moment later heard a churning sound in the water. The voices of the frogs had now risen to such a volume that he could hear nothing more.

He was inclined to dismiss the shadow as the creation of the wild flames leaping upward from the fire. The sound in the water might well have been that of the movement made by a school of fish, darting forward in concert. Nevertheless, he thought, it would do no harm to have another look at Aunt Sarey's room.

He returned to the kitchen, took the lamp, and mounted the stairs. He unlocked the door of the shuttered room, threw open the door, and was almost felled by the powerful musk which pushed hallward. The smell of the Miskatonic, of the marshes, the odour of that slimy deposit left on the stones and sunken debris when the Miskatonic receded to

its low water stage, the cloying pungence of some animal lairs—all
these were combined in the shuttered room.

Abner stood for a moment, wavering on the threshold. True, the
odour of the room could have come in through the open window. He
raised the lamp so that more of its light fell upon the wall above the
mill wheel. Even from where he stood, it was possible to see that
not only was all the window itself now gone, but so was the frame.
Even at this distance it was manifest that the frame had been broken
out *from inside!*

He fell back, slammed the door shut, locked it, and fled downstairs
with the shell of his rationalizations tumbling about him.

V.

Downstairs, he fought for self control. What he had seen was but one
more detail added to the proliferating accumulation of seemingly
unrelated data upon which he had stumbled ever since his coming to
his grandfather's home. He was convinced now that however unlikely
it had at first seemed to him, all these data must be related. What
he needed to learn was the one basic fact or element which bound
them together.

He was badly shaken, particularly because he had the uneasy conviction that he did indeed have all the facts he needed to know, that it
was his scientific training which made it impossible for him to make
the primary assumption, to state the premise which the facts before
him would inevitably prove. The evidence of his senses told him that
something laired in that room—some bestial creature; it was folly to
assume that odours from outside could so permeate Aunt Sarey's old
room and not be noticeable outside the kitchen and at the windows of
his own bedroom.

The habit of rational thinking was strong in him. He took out Luther
Whateley's final letter to him once more and read it again. That was
what his grandfather had meant when he had written, "You have
gone forth into the world and gathered to yourself learning sufficient to permit you to look upon all things with an inquiring mind
ridden neither by the superstition of ignorance nor the superstition
of science." Was this puzzle, with all its horrible connotations,
beyond rationalization?

The wild ringing of the telephone broke in upon his confused
thoughts. Slipping the letter back into his pocket, he strode rapidly to
the wall and took the receiver off the hook.

A man's voice screamed over the wire, amid a chaos of inquiring voices as everyone on the line picked up his receiver as if they waited, like Abner Whateley himself, for word of another tragedy. One of the voices—all were disembodied and unidentifiable for Abner—identified the caller.

"It's Luke Lang!"

"Git a posse up an' come quick," Luke shouted hoarsely over the wire. "It's jest aoutside my door, snufflin' araoun'. Tryin' the door. Feelin' at the winders."

"Luke, what is it?" asked a woman's voice.

"Oh, Gawd! It's some unairthly thing. It's a-hoppin' raoun' like it was too big to move right—like jelly. Oh, hurry, hurry, afore it's too late. It got my dog ...."

"Git off the wire so's we can call fer help," interrupted another subscriber.

But Luke never heard in his extremity. "It's a-pushin' at the door—it's a-bowin' the door in ...."

"Luke! Luke! Git off'n the wire!"

"It's a-trying the winder naow." Luke Lang's voice rose in a scream of terror. "There goes the glass. Gawd! Gawd! Hain't yew comin'? Oh, that hand! That turr'ble arm! Gawd! That face ...!"

Luke's voice died away in a frightful screech. There was the sound of breaking glass and rending wood—then all was still at Luke Lang's, and for a moment all was still along the wire. Then the voices burst forth again in a fury of excitement and fear.

"Git help!"

"We'll meet at Bishop's place."

And someone put in, "It's Abner Whateley done it!"

Sick with shock and half-paralysed with a growing awareness, Abner struggled to tear the receiver from his ear, to shut off the half-crazed bedlam on the party line. He managed it with an effort. Confused, upset, frightened himself, he stood for a moment with his head leaning against the wall. His thoughts seethed around but one central point—the fact that the Dunwich rustics considered him somehow responsible for what was happening. And their conviction, he knew intuitively, was based on more than the countryman's conventional distrust of the stranger.

He did not want to think of what had happened to Luke Lang—and to those others. Luke's frightened, agonized voice rang in his ears. He pulled himself away from the wall, almost stumbling over one of the kitchen chairs. He stood for a moment beside the table, not knowing what to do, but as his mind cleared a little, he thought only of escape. Yet he was caught between the desire to get away, and the obligation to Luther Whateley he had not yet fulfilled.

But he had come, he had gone through the old man's things—all save the books—he had made arrangements to tear down the mill part of the house—he could manage its sale through some agency; there was no need for him to be present. Impulsively, he hastened to the bedroom, threw such things as he had unpacked, together with Luther Whateley's note-filled ledger, into his bags, and carried them out to his car.

Having done this, however, he had second thoughts. Why should he take flight? He had done nothing. No guilt of any kind rested upon him. He returned to the house. All was still, save for the unending chorus of frogs and whippoorwills. He stood briefly undecided; then he sat down at the table and took out Grandfather Whateley's final letter to read it once more.

He read it over carefully, thoughtfully. What had the old man meant when, in referring to the madness that had spawned among the Whateleys, he had said, "It has not been so of all that is mine," though he himself had kept free of that madness? Grandmother Whateley had died long before Abner's birth; his Aunt Julia had died as a young girl; his mother had led a blameless life. There remained Aunt Sarey. What had been her madness then? Luther Whateley could have meant none other. Only Sarey remained. What had she done to bring about her imprisonment unto death?

And what had he intended to hint at when he adjured Abner to kill anything in the mill section of the house, anything that lived? *No matter how small it may be. No matter what form it may have ....* Even something so small as an inoffensive toad? A spider? A fly? Luther Whateley wrote in riddles, which in itself was an affront to an intelligent man. Or did his grandfather think Abner a victim to the superstition of science? Ants, spiders, flies, various kinds of bugs, millers, centipedes, daddy long-legs—all occupied the old mill; and doubtless in its walls were mice as well. Did Luther Whateley expect his grandson to go about exterminating all these?

Behind him suddenly something struck the window. Glass fragmented to the floor, together with something heavy. Abner sprang to his feet and whirled around. From outside came the sound of running footsteps.

A rock lay on the floor amid the shattered glass. There was a piece of "store paper" tied to it by common store string. Abner picked it up, broke the string, and unfolded the paper.

Crude lettering stared up at him. "Git out before ye git kilt!" Store paper and string. It was not meant so much as a threat as a well-intentioned warning. And it was clearly the work of Tobias Whateley, thought Abner. He tossed it contemptuously to the table.

His thoughts were still in turmoil, but he had decided that precipitate flight was not necessary. He would stay, not only to learn if his suspicions about Luke Lang were true—as if the evidence of the telephone left room for doubt—but also to make a final attempt to fathom the riddle Luther Whateley had left behind.

He put out the light and went in darkness to the bedroom where he stretched out fully clothed, upon the bed.

Sleep, however, would not come. He lay probing the maze of his thoughts, trying to make sense out of the mass of data he had accumulated, seeking always that basic fact which was the key to all the others. He felt sure it existed; worse, he was positive that it lay before his eyes—he had but failed to interpret it or to recognize it.

He had been lying there scarcely half an hour, when he heard, rising above the pulsating choir of the frogs and whippoorwills, a splashing from the direction of the Miskatonic—an approaching sound, as if a large wave were washing up the banks on its seaward way. He sat up, listening. But even as he did so, the sound stopped and another took its place—one he was loath to identify, and yet could define as no other than that of someone trying to climb the mill wheel.

He slid off the bed and went out of the room.

From the direction of the shuttered room came a muffled, heavy falling sound—then a curious, choking whimpering that sounded, horribly, like a child at a great distance trying to call out—then all was still, and it seemed that even the noise and clamour of the frogs diminished and fell away.

He returned to the kitchen and lit the lamp.

Pooled in the yellow glow of light, Abner made his way slowly up the stairs towards the shuttered room. He walked softly, carefully to make no sound.

Arriving at the door, he listened. At first he heard nothing—then a susurration smote his ears.

Something in that room—*breathed!*

Fighting back his fear, Abner put the key in the lock and turned it. He flung open the door and held the lamp high.

Shock and horror paralyzed him.

There, squatting in the midst of the tumbled bedding from that long-abandoned bed, sat a monstrous, leathery-skinned creature that was neither frog nor man, one gorged with food, with blood still slavering from its batrachian jaws and upon its webbed fingers—a monstrous entity that had strong, powerfully long arms, grown from its bestial body like those of a frog, and tapering off into a man's hands, save for the webbing between the fingers ....

The tableau held for only a moment.

Then with a frenzied growling sound—"*Eh-ya-ya-ya-yaa-haah—ngh'aaa—h'yuh, h'yuh*"— it rose up, towering, and launched itself at Abner.

His reaction was instantaneous, born of terrible, shattering knowledge. He flung the kerosene-filled lamp with all his might straight at the thing reaching towards him.

Fire enveloped the thing. It halted and began to tear frantically at its burning body, unmindful of the flames rising from the bedding behind it and the floor of the room, and at the same instant the calibre of its voice changed from a deep growling to a shrill, high wailing—"*Mama-mama—ma-aa-ma-aa-ma-aah!*"

Abner pulled the door shut and fled.

Down the stairs, half falling, through the rooms below, with his heart pounding madly, and out of the house. He tumbled into the car, almost bereft of his senses, half-blinded by the perspiration of his fear, turned the key in the ignition, and roared away from that accursed place from which the smoke already poured, while spreading flames in that tinder-dry building began to cast a red glow into the sky.

He drove like one possessed—though Dunwich—through the covered bridge—his eyes half-closed, as if to shut out for ever the sight of that which he had seen, while the dark, brooding hills seemed to reach for him and the chanting whippoorwills and frogs mocked him.

But nothing could erase that final, cataclysmic knowledge seared into his mind—the key to which he had had all along and not known it—the knowledge implicit in his own memories as well as in the notes Luther Whateley had left—the chunks of raw meat he had childishly supposed were going to be prepared in Aunt Sarey's room instead of to be *eaten raw,* the reference to "R." who had come "back at last" after having escaped, back to the only home "R." knew—the seemingly unrelated references also in his grandfather's hand to missing cows, sheep, and the remains of other animals—the hideous suggestion clearly defined now in those entries of Luther Whateley's about R.'s "size commensurate with amt. of food," and "he must be kept on a careful diet and to a controllable size"—like the Innsmouth people!—controlled to nothingness after Sarah's death, with Luther hoping that foodless confinement might shrivel the thing in the shuttered room and kill it beyond revival, despite the doubt that had led him to adjure Abner to kill "anything in it that lives"—*the thing Abner had unwittingly liberated when he broke the pane and kicked out the shutters, liberated to seek its own food and its hellish growth again, at first with fish from the Miskatonic, then with small animals, then cattle, and at last human beings—the thing that was half-batrachian, half-human, but human enough to come back to the only home it had ever known and to cry out in terror for its Mother in the face of the fatal holocaust—the thing that had been born to the unblessed union of Sarah Whateley and Ralsa Marsh, spawn of tainted and degenerate blood, the monster that would loom for ever on the perimeter of Abner Whateley's awareness—his cousin Ralsa, doomed by his grandfather's iron will, instead of being released long ago into the sea to join the Deep Ones amongst the minions of Dagon and great Cthulhu!*

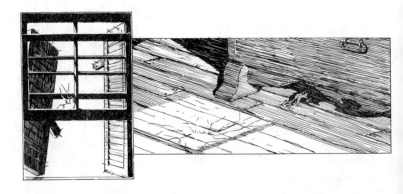

Perhaps the greatest sequel to "The Dunwich Horror" is August Derleth's The Lurker at the Threshold, which transpires in Billington's Wood, just beyond Dunwich. Loosely inspired by a few manuscript notes left by Lovecraft, this novella is composed of three linked episodes, "Billington's Wood", "Manuscript of Stephen Bates", and "Narrative of Winfield Phillips." At first glance we seem to have a serial novel composed of separate stories, like those constituting The Trail of Cthulhu, each standing quite well alone and all published first in various issues of Weird Tales. In fact, The Lurker at the Threshold was written and published as a single work. This makes the discontinuity of the book much more pronounced. The third section, the "Narrative of Winfield Phillips", does not fit the other two at all. Plot threads are severed, intriguing characters of whom we cannot believe we have heard the last are rudely dropped, Yog-Sothoth replaces Ossadogowah, and indeed the entire premise of the first two stories is discarded. The "Narrative of Winfield Phillips", a psychic sleuth story, would fit much better as a chapter of The Trail of Cthulhu. The abrupt genre jump is accompanied by Derleth's inexplicable abandonment of any suggestive restraint; all is cold, explicit, and cut and dried. The superfluous Dr. Lapham and his Watsonian scribe Phillips are forced upon us. Lapham's prolix pontifications and his Gordian "resolution" of the mystery of Billington's Wood make us wonder whether the author of the previous two chapters had been psychically supplanted, like Ambrose Dewart, by some malign intelligence intent on ruining a good story.

Instead it is apparent from clues left in the first and second tales that Derleth must first have intended to make Dunwich into a center, à la Innsmouth, of miscegenation between humans and the spawn of one of the Old Ones, just as in "The Shuttered Room." Only this time it would have been not Cthulhu or Dagon, but rather Tsathoggua, whom Clark Ashton Smith had endowed with the traits of both bat and toad. The stigmata of inbreeding among the retrograde Dunwich folk would have been revealed as the marks of Tsathoggua. The whole notion Derleth must have derived from the fragmentary episode of Goodwife Doten (a Lovecraft snippet, incorporated by Derleth into his pastiche), in which a human bat is born. (A very different attempt to flesh out the Lovecraft fragment is my own brief tale "Young Goodwife Doten" in the anthology 100 Wicked Little Witch Stories from Barnes & Noble Books.) Derleth must have linked the Doten bat-baby with Ossadogowah, the Son of Tsathoggua, in one of the other Lovecraft notes he incorporated into the book. Hadn't Lovecraft himself intimated that Wilbur Whateley's spawning might be taken for granted in the town as "a common Dunwich scandal?" Perhaps the town swarmed with Wilburs, only begotten by Tsathoggua rather than Yog-Sothoth. With unprecedented hubris, I have here attempted a "posthumous collaboration" with August Derleth: Whereas he sought to finish what Lovecraft left in fragments, I have dared to try to improve upon what Derleth left complete. I have chosen to disregard the ill-fitting "Narrative of Winfield Phillips" and to write the conclusion to which I believe Derleth's splendid beginning properly led. Any readers who have been similarly disappointed by the conclusion of The Lurker at the Threshold are hereby invited to reread the first and second sections, then lay the book aside and begin reading what follows. (This story first appeared in Vollmond # 3, Autumn 1990.)

The Round Tower

(Being the Narrative of Armitage Harper)

by Robert M. Price

On the seventh of April, 1922, I received a visitor, unheralded by telephone, in my upper-story office at the Abner Hoag Library of Miskatonic University. The unannounced visitor was my acquaintance Mr. Stephen Bates, a colleague from nearby Boston and a fellow specialist in matters of Commonwealth history, though it was not from Boston that he had now arrived. I had last seen Mr. Bates during his prolonged stay with his troubled cousin Ambrose Dewart at the latter's secluded property the previous autumn. Bates had returned there with his cousin, whom he had persuaded, at my own suggestion, to winter with him in Boston, a healthy distance away from Dewart's recently repossessed ancestral home at Billington's Wood. Now both men had returned, and though I had laid eyes upon Stephen Bates but a few months previously, I was now startled, I hoped not visibly, at the subtle alteration of his appearance. The slanting rays of the afternoon sun through my study skylight revealed new lines in his hardy, forty-odd year old face, and where his still-fulsome hair had before evinced but the merest shadings of encroaching gray, now that process seemed well advanced. I had neither to ask nor to wait long for the explanation of these developments, nor for the reason of his visit.

Last fall, Bates had come asking my advice about his cousin, the enigmatic Dewart, whom Bates feared was manifesting early signs of incipient paranoid schizophrenia, namely puzzling shifts of personality, surly and evasive one moment, accommodating and friendly the next. Connected with these untoward alterations, Bates had noted, was a near-obsession with the matter of his ancestors Richard and Alijah Billington, whom local legend made the veriest warlocks and rogues. Dewart's own genealogical delvings in the study of his inherited family seat lent seeming confirmation, however evocative of deeper mysteries, to these rumors, and it was this historical aspect of the trouble that had led his cousin Bates to seek my advice in the first instance rather than that of an alienist.

On the occasion of that first visit, I sought to assure Bates that while it was altogether possible that the Billingtons had taken to themselves the shunned practices of certain ancient cults still surviving in remote areas of the countryside, and that Dewart's fixation might be no more than the fascination exerted upon the antiquarian mind by such, in this case morbid, matters, I suspected that Dewart might have fallen victim to some lingering psychic malaise, an ectoplasmic residue of the perversions once practiced at Billington House by the former residents. Only so far was I then willing to venture beyond the vagaries of conventional psychology.

Now, seeing Bates' singularly agitated state, I had to wonder whether he, too, had exposed himself too long to the unwholesome atmosphere of Billington's Wood. It was a suspicion he shared, and in fact he was the first to voice it. What made poor Bates begin to question his own sanity was the sudden and nocturnal acquisition by his strangely transformed cousin of a very remarkable servant, a Narragan-sett Indian factotum named, of all things, Quamis. Of course, as Dewart knew he would, Bates instantly recognized the name as that of the Indian servant of old Alijah Billington, recorded in his son Laban's daybook. Given the scarcity of Indians in present-day Massa-chusetts, it was too much to believe that Dewart's new companion happened simply to bear the same name. Yet the implication, which Bates seemed reticent to vocalize, was too much for a sane mind to entertain. Bates had now resolved that the preservation or, as it might be, recovery of his own mental balance necessitated the abandonment, at least for the present, of his efforts to reclaim Ambrose Dewart from the latter's increasingly serious delusions. If nothing else, the trouble taken to secure an Indian for employment, and the forcing upon him of the pseudonym Quamis (if, as I suggested, that alone had happened), indicated that Dewart had come to view himself as Alijah Billington *redivivus*. But Stephen Bates would be of no use to poor Dewart if he found his own sanity threatened. Better to beat a tactful retreat.

Bates hardly needed my counsel on that point: He had in the early hours of dawn packed his valise and upon some flimsy pretext an-nounced his departure to Dewart and his new, impassive companion. Dewart seemed glad enough to hear the news, not even bothering to see his once-beloved cousin to his automobile. Instead he sent Quamis to whistle up yet another new servant, one whose employment, like his identity, was a surprise to poor Bates, for it proved to be a young Dunwich local whom Bates had chanced to apprehend spying from concealment only days before, one Lem Whateley. The youth seemed

cowed, obsequious, truly afraid of his employer, as if the employer-em-
ployee relation were not the true nature of the bond between them.
This lad Dewart dispatched to drive Bates to the Arkham train depot.
With scarcely a word of farewell, Dewart and the Indian turned away
and began to walk in the direction of the ancient tower and circle of
stones about which the great mystery seemed somehow to revolve.

Young Lem loaded Bates' few belongings into his master's Packard
and climbed into the driver's seat. Given his low estimate of the mental
level of the natives of nearby Dunwich, Bates was not sure he trusted
his driver's motoring skills, but greater was his fear of the man, now
the men, he was leaving behind. Attempts at interrogating the tight-
lipped boy proved fruitless. If possible, young Whateley seemed more
frightened, even terrified, than his passenger. Bates could only guess
that he had been caught spying again, this time by Dewart or his
mysterious Indian companion. Perhaps threats of unguessable punish-
ments had bent the lad to Dewart's service. But Bates recalled how all
the degenerate folk of Dunwich seemed to hold the heir of the
Billingtons in a kind of near-religious veneration, even as they seemed
to hate and fear him. It was possible, then, that Lem Whateley had
simply been pressed into service and dared not decline. At any rate, as
no information seemed to be forthcoming, Bates settled down to
endure the drive on the yet-unpaved road his cousin had caused to be
run from Arkham to his property some months before. His occasional
glances at the driver beside him revealed little more than the latter's
hands, white-knuckled, clenching the steering wheel. And though it
was difficult to be sure, with the youth's fingers thus wrapped around
the wheel, Bates felt sure that the fingers were webbed together for an
inch's width, another of the repugnant marks of degeneracy among the
isolated and inbred Dunwich population.

Gladly leaving his companion at the station, Bates waited until the
automobile was out of sight and hailed a taxicab for the Miskatonic
University campus. Thus he came to me. After relating the most recent
episodes of his adventure much as I have related them to you, Bates
deposited with me a sheaf of manuscript pages chronicling his involve-
ment in the Ambrose Dewart business, together with copies of some
of his cousin's documents and clippings. He said he felt a strange
foreboding, that Ambrose, or Alijah, or whatever name now seemed
most appropriate, had let him go rather too easily, given how much he
already knew. In the event anything should happen to him, he wanted
me to have his papers. I tried my best to reassure him, insisting that
once beyond the sinister radius of Billington's Wood, back home safe

in Boston, the shadow would be lifted from his spirits. He seemed mildly heartened by my words of bland optimism. In the meantime, I suggested, since the day was far spent, why not avail himself of such modest accommodations as I could offer? I would return to my small apartment a few blocks from the campus, and he was welcome to make use of the comfortable cot and toiletries I maintained here in my office rooms for those occasions when my research so absorbed me that I did not bother leaving the campus for the night. And if he still felt too agitated for sleep, he might compose his nerves by writing up an account of his cousin's delvings before summoning Bates to join him. Bates had said that during the periods when his cousin seemed to be "his old self" he confided these matters in great detail, and that time constraints had forbidden him to relate more than the highlights to me during our previous interview last autumn. But if I were now to try to take up Bates' efforts toward the reclamation of Ambrose Dewart where Bates had been forced to leave them off, I had best be as near fully informed as possible. Bates thought this advisable, and judging by the length of his report, which I have given the heading "Billington's Wood" and appended, along with his own first-person account, to the present narrative, I imagine he must have slept very little that night after all. Yet he did seem calmer, relieved or perhaps resigned, the next morning when I called upon him again. Promising to telephone him with any new developments or theories, I drove him to meet his train and saw him off to Boston. I was never to see him alive again.

That afternoon I began to work my way through the pile of manuscripts, cross-referring to the various copied documents. As I read, the feeling took hold of me that the mystery was far greater, much more enigmatic and all-encompassing than even the perceptive Bates had come to realize. Strangest of all, I began to think that somehow the danger was not confined to the mad Ambrose Dewart, nor even to any threat he might pose his cousin, nor yet even to me as Bates's successor in the investigation. Perhaps I thought vaguely of the repeated cases of mysterious disappearances and the subsequent discoveries of unaccountably mutilated bodies. Or was there something *more*, on a vaster, even cosmic scale?

Most intriguing from a purely scholarly standpoint were the frequent references in Bates' manuscripts to certain arcane formulae, tongue-twisting names, and ancient forbidden books. It was of course such details that had caused our first conversation to turn to the subject of obsolete regions and suppressed, though still-surviving, cults. Then I thought them merely the accoutrements of Ambrose Dewart's delusions: Now I was not so sure. Possibly these peculiar references might prove more central to the puzzle and its solution. And here I had a considerable advantage over Stephen Bates, namely free access to the volumes in question. Where the Billington study contained fragmentary and in some cases unreadable copies of some of the books, I now quite literally sat on top of one of the fullest collections of such *outré* literature in the Western Hemisphere. And while Dewart's encroaching madness had more and more restricted the prying Bates' access to the Billington collection, I had full authorization to make such use of Miskatonic's locked stacks as I chose.

Taking only a notepad marked with a few bibliographical citations derived from Bates' manuscript, I made my way downstairs and to the Rare Books room, where a few words passed between the circulation clerk and myself ushered me into the otherwise empty room. I paused to glance with some pride over the authentic Shakespeare folio and the little-known fourth century vellum biblical manuscript *Codex Miskatonicus* with its remarkable textual variants which church authorities had judged best concealed from the ecclesiastical public. I then hastened to extract the volumes I would require for what promised to be a wearying and disturbing afternoon of research.

I thought it most advisable to begin with those works present in the Billington study, many of them medieval magic books of dubious reputation. From the colonial American section I drew forth two volumes. The first was old Abijah Hoadley's *Of Evill Sorceries done in New-England of Daemons in no Human Shape*. Famous in its day, this huge tome, printed in eye-torturing minuscule, rivalled the contemporary *Magnalia Christi Americana* of Cotton Mather as a compendium of superstitious lore. Even less creditable was a smaller polemical tract entitled *Thaumaturgical Prodigies in the New-English Canaan* by a Baptist parson here in Arkham, a Reverend Ward Phillips. Hitherto I, like many moderns, had been in the habit of derisively dismissing the beliefs and fears of these colonial clerics as the product of an unhealthy mix of puritanical repression and the harsh siege of Novanglian winter elements. I now had the uneasy feeling that I would soon be in a better position to appreciate the warnings of the old Calvinist savants.

Gradually a strange pattern of peculiar hints began to emerge from my studies. It became clear that Richard and Alijah Billington had conjured some entity known in the dialect of the Wampanaug Indians as Ossadogowah, or the Son of Sadoquae. The grisly deaths of the enemies of both men had been interpreted by them as the vengeance wrought by this demon once unleashed. It occurred to me as possible that the deaths might have been effected by more earthly means, yet attributed to the legendary Son of Sadoquae for the value this would have in preying upon the superstitious fears of the populace. Perhaps both Billingtons judged this the best method of intimidation in order to protect their privacy. If there had been more to it than this, however, I was in for a major realignment of my views of what the universe could accommodate. Yet, is not openness to such possibilities the most basic precondition for the advancement of learning? Besides, I felt my own safety might now depend upon taking a broader view of these matters.

The resemblance of the name "Ossadogowah" in the pages of *Evill Sorceries* and that of "Tsathoggua" in one of Bates' excerpts from the volume he called *Al Azif, ye Booke of ye Arab,* and which I suspected might be the same as the infamous *Necronomicon,* a volume I had never been particularly inclined to examine, opened up a new line of my investigation that took me ultimately to Philippus Faber's edition of the *Liber Ivonis,* a confusing collection of legends and myths purporting to stem from a vanished civilization within the Arctic Circle, perhaps that hinted of in the ancient Greek legends of Hyperborea. As the hours passed, I came to find much cognate material in the pages of the *Pnakotic Manuscripts,* which to consult was no easy task: Each crumbling parchment page had long ago been preserved between large glass plates to stave off further deterioration. I thought it best to consult the originals since the Miskatonic's Hoag Library has them, rather than the conjecturally restored print versions.

I concluded, long after all the patrons and most of the staff had retired for the night, that the "Sadoquae" of Hoadley's *Evill Sorceries* could be none other than the Hyperborean deity Tsathoggua whose myths loomed large in the *Liber Ivonis.* This Tsathoggua, the legends said, had come down from the stars in earth's primordial past. He had taken up residence in a subterranean realm called N'kai, and been worshipped in the polar regions under the form of a repellent totem combining the features both of a bat and of a toad. Whether extraterrestrial or not, this Tsathoggua cult must have been of foreign origin, since neither frogs nor bats are known that far north. Perhaps it belonged to the myth-patterns of Asia, where both species are common in folklore and religious symbolism. The identity of "Tsathoggua" and "Sadoquae" seemed beyond dispute, especially in view of the latter's toad-like appearance according to Indian descriptions recorded by Hoadley.

These conjectures coincided with others yielded by my reading, namely that in Hoadley's time, some two centuries ago, there was current among the Wampanaug savages the belief that their tribal origins lay far to the north, that they had in fact descended, with some strange admixture only hinted at in his text, from the extinct tribe of "Lamah", which I took to be the exceedingly ancient kingdom of Lomar chronicled in the *Pnakotic Manuscripts,* perhaps identical with Hyperborea. I recalled that old Mrs. Bishop, interviewed with meagre results by both Dewart and Bates, was of half-caste blood, her ancestry containing at least a measure of the Wampanaug. And hadn't Bates quoted her as telling his cousin that this tribe were "more than Indians?" Perhaps the centuried tribal legends survived in her memory. At length I coaxed from this assortment of equivocal texts the disturbing suggestion that the Wampanaugs had not been entirely *human,* that the notorious powers of their medicine men, the famous Misquamacus being the chief recent example, were a result of the fertilization of their line by some ancient blasphemous intercourse with the batrachian-bat entity Tsathoggua; that "Ossadagowah", precisely in his aspect as Tsathoggua's *son,* was the tribe's secret totem, the symbolism of which now took on a whole new meaning.

Oddly enough, the more bizarre and outlandish the results of my research became, the greater grew the disquieting sense of conviction that more than obscure ancient mythology was involved here. Was the Billington madness beginning to affect me, too? At any rate, I could now sympathize with poor Dewart's enthrallment with these matters. And lacking the scholarly resources of Miskatonic's Abner Hoag Library, the fascination of both Dewart and Bates with the mystery must have grown all the greater with their frustration at not being able to delve more deeply into it. The Tsathoggua lore might have made poor Bates' alarm even more acute had he discerned the symbolic significance of the toad-like creatures he thought he had seen through the Rose Window of the study.

Recognizing this for one of those nights I must pass in my office upstairs, I retired there, my overfilled brain still roiling with recondite information and disturbing implications. Bates' reports of old Mrs. Bishop, seemingly confined to her rocker, whispering in darkness, kept returning to haunt me, as if there were some facet of this great enigma that she only seemed to conceal, but actually revealed if only one possessed the key to decipher her cryptic cacklings. Neither Dewart nor Bates had possessed it, yet the interviews Bates had recorded might still yield some clue. I must reread them on the morrow and, if necessary, make the trip to Dunwich to interview her myself.

I lay awake on my cot for an hour or two as the campus clock tower marked them off. My eyes sought the view of the starry heavens through the skylight. I saw the familiar constellations as never before. For the first time in my life, they seemed to me almost to take on the malignant aspect of a threatening void of blackness from which untold horrors might one day descend, or have already descended, to plague mankind. I fancied I heard, at the edge of consciousness, the exaggerated croakings of some batrachian chorus from Euripides. Then I slept.

I rose early, breakfasted at the faculty club, and, after a telephone call to Bates which went unanswered, headed for my apartment. I had awakened with the conviction that I must in fact visit Dunwich to call upon Mrs. Bishop. I spent the morning rereading the transcript of her words, feeling that some clue lay in Bates' description of her, something that should somehow be obvious, yet which would so baffle reason that the mind suppressed the recognition of it. This reading and pondering were done in my apartment, for while my library office might have been a more appropriate or more convenient setting, I had to abandon it temporarily to make way for the University carpenters together with a local Arkham glazier; I had arranged at very short notice some alteration work which suggested itself to me after the last evening's scrutiny of my study skylight. I had business to settle elsewhere on campus, though, and after rereading the manuscript, I paid several calls, arranging with my secretary to cancel appointments, rechecking a few items in the Rare Book collection, and stopping for a visit with the curator of the University's Bowen Collection of antiquities. For so strange a trip as my drive to Dunwich promised to be, one must needs make some rather unusual preparations.

At several points during my busy day I paused to try and contact Stephen Bates, but could never seem to get an answer. I verified his number and tried again, but to no avail. I felt a sense of foreboding at this failure to reach him, yet I reasoned that he was likely out seeking fresh air and convivial company. Then I realized any call of mine would only remind him of his unpleasant visit to the Billington estate, so I resolved not to try him again until I should make some real progress toward a solution.

My age is not so advanced as to prohibit a day full of activities—indeed I am perhaps unusually hale for my years—but it is quite sufficient to make me long for rest at the close of such a day. Back in my quiet Arkham apartment, I had not the slightest difficulty surrendering to Morpheus. The croaking of marsh frogs, only to be expected this time of year, together with the gentle call of the whippoorwills in the nearby hills, only served to lull me all the more peacefully to sleep. Yet I confess to a night of uncharacteristic dreams, undoubtedly the psychic echo of my *outré* reading over the previous days. In one dream I seemed to be ever in shadow, and no matter how or where I ran, I could do naught to escape its confines. Above me sounded the muffled beating of mighty wings, while I seemed to sense rather than hear the upheaval of huge footsteps below the very ground on which I stood. Most vivid and most disturbing of all, however, was the far-off plaintive wailing of a familiar voice. All the stranger was the fact that I seemed to hear the voice in periods of wakefulness between the other nightmares, yet I later concluded I had not wakened at all, but still dreamt, as one often does after dreaming that one is dreaming! The identity of the owner of that voice eluded me until daybreak, finally disclosing itself just as I shook off slumber. And then just as quickly it abandoned me.

Despite my troubled sleep, I felt fit for the long drive into the lonely Dunwich country. Given the usual spring thaws and April rains, the roads of rural Massachusetts can be treacherous, but those leading beyond Dean's Corners to the Dunwich countryside proved to be doubly difficult because of their poor state of repair. Driving was made yet more mentally exhausting by reason of poor visibility. The Dunwich area is peculiarly hilly, the rounded domes of the hills rising abruptly almost from the very edges of the roads. One rounds every bend with a prayer that one may not collide with a less vigilant motorist. At length I attained Dunwich, a more slovenly hamlet than even my own research into Commonwealth history had led me to anticipate. Stopping for directions at a tenuous collection of weathered boards dignifying itself with the name OSBORN'S GENERAL STORE, I ascertained from the muddled-looking shopkeeper the detailed route to Mrs. Bishop's house. Though the inbred region abounded in Bishops, my informant had heard the recent gossip concerning the much-visited Huldah Bishop, as I now discovered she was called, so he knew readily whom I sought. As I climbed back into my waiting Essex, I noted mentally the same abnormality described by Stephen Bates: The shopkeeper had the same goggle-eyes and strangely flaring ears, doubtless the ravages of inbreeding. As I passed through the squalid streets of the town center, I noted with a subtle shock that virtually every individual I saw, whether elderly lounger or cavorting ragamuffin, possessed the same peculiarity, what I began to think of, uncharitably, as the "Dunwich look."

I found Huldah Bishop's house, or to be plain about it, her shack, with little trouble. There as Bates had described it was the post with BISHOP traced on it so crudely that it seemed the painter had copied letters of which he had no familiar command, as if I should try to copy an inscription in Mandarin Chinese. My creaking footsteps on the precarious porch boards announced my presence, calling forth a wary voice from within. "What business have ye, stranger?" The voice sounded oddly flat, or hollow, in tone.

"Huldah Bishop?" I inquired politely, but with a tone of official directness, eliciting no answer this time. I thought it best to continue. "I am Dr. Armitage Harper of the Miskatonic University in Arkham. I am an historian of rural Massachusetts, and my colleague Mr. Stephen Bates, with whom you recently spoke, has told me what a treasure house of local tradition you are. I wonder if you might be kind enough to humor still another old scholar in search of curiosities."

A few moments' silence ensued in which I felt she might be consulting someone with her in the unlit interior. Finally she croaked, "Come on in. Never thought yew college fellers 'ud keer much whut an old Dunnich hag'd haf' t' say." This she found amusing and burst into the phlegmy chuckle Bates had described as an almost batlike chittering. Not so much the sound she made as the aptness of Bates' description of it made me shudder involuntarily as I stepped into the darkened, shaded room and pulled up a chair opposite hers.

I had expected, from the accounts of the two earlier visits, that the room would be swathed in shadows, but I had supposed that window shades would be drawn against the unwanted daylight. Now I was startled to see from the telltale pattern of what little light managed to gain entrance that all the windows of the house had been *boarded up.* In the all-encompassing gloom I could hear but the sounds of the rocking chair and occasional feline purring. Soon my old eyes adjusted somewhat to the darkness, and I could make out the stooped silhouette of the old lady hunched over in her chair. Only the dim reflection of vagrant light revealed her hair to have a silver sheen. Of her face I could see nothing, of her form scarcely more.

"Mrs. Bishop, I hope you will bear with a few questions that may seem childish to one of your obvious knowledge in … ancient matters. Over the past few days I have been reading in some old colonial records as well as various books of magic and legend we keep at the Library. They treat of certain questions that Mr. Bates said you know much about. The name 'Ossadogowah,' for example …."

"Tsathoggua," she croaked, anticipating my question with a star-tling prescience. "Same as Tsathoggua whereof Eibon telleth. My people, the Narragansetts, an' before them the Wampanaugs, did traffick with Tsathoggua and his son of old. Misquamacus knew him, talked ter him face t' face as a man talketh with his friend."

"Clearly, Mrs. Bishop, I am asking the right person! Now am I correct in thinking the tribes you mention believed themselves some-how to be descendants of this toad deity?"

"'Believed'? Why stranger, they knowed it right enough! 'Cause it weren't no 'myth' as yew city folk 'ud like folks t' think."

Instantly I understood her implication, or thought I did.

"Do you mean the famous story of the Goodwife Doten and the ... creature she bore?"

"Yer beginnin' tew ketch on, mister. That wuz one setch, back in '87, but not near an' abaout the only setch. They bin *mixin'* with folk hereabaout s' long as Master sought to come back."

I knew "Master" was the legendary Richard Billington, whom, to judge from the conversations with Bates and Dewart, Mrs. Bishop believed to be periodically reincarnated. I had expected "Master" would come into the discussion sooner rather than later.

"Mrs. Bishop, why is it you refer to Richard Billington, or his wandering spirit, as 'Master?' It was my understanding that you owe him no fealty, that you are a Christian believer."

"That I am, that I am, but so wuz that nosy Ward Phillips, and the good Lord didn't pertekt him none when he got to stickin' his nose where't didn't belong. And the fact is, he is due to be called Master who kin order the Sons of Tsathoggua."

At first the plural gave me pause, until I recalled that in the earlier interviews she had spoken of "Them Things", and that Bates himself had seen at least two of the bat-winged toadlike horrors in his Rose Window hallucination—if that is truly what it was.

"And those are the things that Alijah let in, and that you fear Ambrose Dewart will let in?"

"*Did* let in, mister, *did* let in. I know it, 'cause they're at it agin, a-swoopin' an' a-rippin'. They took yer friend Bates. I heered him only last night, though he wasn't a-speakin' any words you'd recognize."

I must have been visibly shaken. For it came upon me in a flood of realization whose voice it had been that I heard in what I had imagined were my dreams the night before! In my repeated failure to contact Bates, I suppose I had feared something like this, as had Bates himself before he left me. But still, as far as I knew, no corpse had been discovered, and I could yet hold out the hope that the old woman, too, had been dreaming, and that our dreams had simply chanced to coincide. This rationalization sounded hollow even as I sought to use it to dampen down the rising sense of panic I was beginning to feel. Yet I must proceed as calmly as possible. If things were taking as sinister a direction as the old hag's words implied, it was now more important than ever that I learn all I could, for my own protection, Ambrose Dewart notwithstanding.

"I hope you are wrong about Bates, Mrs. Bishop. He was a good man, is a good man, who sought only to help his cousin." Her chittering cackle mocked my naivete.

"D'yer think Master keers abaout thet? All he keers abaout is his plans, plans delayed so long now, and he ain't abaout ter let meddlin' fools git in his way. He let my grandsire Jonathan Bishop lie in his own bed onct he laid it, an' Bates was no different."

"Let me ask about your grandfather, Mrs. Bishop," I interjected, seeking to turn the flow of conversation into what I hoped might be a less alarming channel. "What precisely was he up to? Was he using the Old Ones to enrich himself?"

Again the cackling: "No man uses Them Ones, though some thinks they do. Setch finds they themselves been used. But Jonathan wuz a faithful servant by his lights. He finally got in too deep, an' got careless, but his task was to aid in the *mixin'*."

"Mixing? Of what?"

She shifted in her rocker. For the first time I noticed that she seemed to hold in her lap a half-spread Oriental fan, though she made no motion to stir the air in the clammy closeness of the dark room. "Th' Old Ones can't come back unless they have their children hidin' behind human faces to make ready Their return. Old Jonathan sought to prepare the way. He used the rites to cause the Things to breed in the unseen spheres. He got whut girls from Dunnich an' Duxbury as he kud to help. He called up gold now 'n agin, but just setch as he needed t' make the girls an' their fathers willin'. Them that helped special 'ud git special rewards when things changed an' the Sons of Sadogowah ruled, as wuz their right."

I thought of the mad staring visages of the poor Dunwich yokels and began to wonder if inbreeding were after all the cause of their deformities. *Their semblance no man can know, save seldom in the features of those They have begotten on mankind, which are awful to behold.* Sons of Tsathoggua ....

"Did you ever see any of these activities? Are you sure ...?"

"No, I didn't, I didn't at thet!" Inexplicable tittering, knowing laughter punctuated her words. "But my old mother did! She saw it up close!" My scalp began to prickle, my heartbeat to speed up. "D'yew have a match on yew, Mister Harper? Good, well, go ahead, strike it."

Huldah Bishop held no half-spread fan. The radiance of the match revealed her hand lying across her lap, a hand with inordinately long, pencil-thin fingers, each pair webbed from the tip with a satiny black membrane! I dropped the match; I had seen enough.

I rose to leave, and as I did so, I heard the door behind me creak open all the way. Even so, little daylight entered the room as the doorway seemed packed with bodies. In the twilight I could see the broad faces, the wide gash-mouths, the unblinking eyes, the flaring ears, some, I would swear, pointed at the ends. The whole population of Dunwich must have been gathered there. One or two fists holding aloft menacing rakes or chair legs seemed to bear the tell-tale finger webbing.

I faced the shadowed, grunting mob. Their relative silence implied they awaited further words from the crone who sat behind me. They were not long in coming.

"Master came, an' it wuz right. But then the Bates feller came a-pryin', an' he got his due. Yew got no business here neither, and we ain't lettin' yew take word of us 'n our affairs back aout o' the Dunnich hills." The crowd began to poise themselves, in their palsied way, like hunting dogs barely restrained by the leash. I fought down blind panic, and reached deliberately into my coat pocket. I cleared my fear-constricted throat and spoke hoarsely.

"But I have the Sign," I said, and held aloft the grey-green stone I had contrived to borrow from the Bowen collection. I struck another match and held it beside the star-shaped object so they could better make out the crude tracing of a lozenge shape with a pillar of fire within it. "The Sign of protection. You have to let me pass."

Next I would have tried the elaborate finger sign also mentioned in the old repositories of forbidden lore. I had been reasonably sure one or the other had to be the Elder Sign before which the Old Ones' servants had to yield. Luckily my first guess was correct. Every head bowed in apparent reverence, every eye lowered to the floor. The now quiescent mob parted at my approach, bodies elbowing and stumbling over one another in haste to clear my path, to be out of the wake of the Sign as it passed. Behind me I heard only the renewed sound of rocker treads wearing on the floorboards.

Heaven be thanked none of the dull-witted Dunwichers had thought to disable my motor car, which would have been easily enough accomplished. As I retraced my route through the filth-strewn village streets, I noticed how several houses had windows boarded shut, and I shivered with the thought of what might be hidden away within them. I raced back to Dean's Corners, and finally into familiar ivy-covered Arkham at immoderate speed. No mud-choked, hill-locked roads could retard my pace this time! I drove directly onto the Miskatonic campus, then to the Library and hastened up the staircase to my office. Setting down my valise and tossing my hat and coat onto the sofa, I lifted my eyes to the skylight. It now bore a rudimentary Elder Sign device executed in bars of stained glass soldered onto the original work. (I had told the workmen that the curious design represented a Masonic emblem.) Aesthetically questionable, perhaps, but I felt the addition might prove wise. In view of my late experience in Dunwich, I now felt I had been especially prudent. Whatever had claimed Stephen Bates (I no longer doubted the truth of Huldah Bishop's words) would very shortly be coming for me. Repeating to myself the Arab's phrase "powerless to touch ye Elder Sign and fearful of its great power" as another man might silently chant the Twenty-Third Psalm, I readied myself to retire for the night. I placed the cot directly beneath the skylight and stretched my spare, tired form out upon it.

I think that I slept that night, but at some point I dreamt that I roused at the sound of beating wings above me. Reluctantly I opened my eyes and saw through the skylight two hovering cloudy forms, recalling those Stephen Bates had described. They were vaguely toad-like in outline, but winged, and with a roiling mass of feelers where one might expect a face. The great behemoths were partly translucent, and through their shifting bulks I could catch glimpses of an altogether unfamiliar night sky sprinkled with unknown stellar configurations and nebulae. And suddenly all was as it should be: The monstrous forms had vanished and familiar Orion with his brother constellations smiled down like old friends. Remarkably enough, it was not the insane extravagance of what I had seen but rather my calmness in beholding it that gave me to think I must have been dreaming at the time.

I rose with the sun, feeling much refreshed. Where I suppose I should have been daunted by my visions in the night, instead I actually felt oddly braced and confident. The dream had served to confirm the wild truth to which my delvings, with those of poor Bates, had led me. Having at least the sure sense that I was not simply boxing at shadows, I rose in full force to meet the challenge. First I made notes of my abruptly concluded interview with Huldah Bishop, setting down all as accurately as I could. Why bother with such trifles in such a situation? I realized all too well that Bates' fate might yet overtake me, and I felt I owed it to any future investigator who might take up the trail to provide for him what clues I could toward the resolution of the mystery of Ambrose Dewart.

Now I glanced back over Bates' manuscripts, in search of any possible defensive tactics which might suggest themselves. True, I had for the moment managed to gain sanctuary from the Outside entities who sought my doom, but I could scarcely spend the rest of my days under the skylight, clutching the stone relic. I felt I had some genuine chance at saving myself simply because it had been done before. As Mrs. Bishop told Bates, "Only Alijah outsmarted Master." How had he done it? Alijah Billington's accumulated occult knowledge was past recovery, I knew, but surely the key must lie in the instructions bequeathed to his heirs never to disturb the tower, the stream surrounding it, or the chorus of frogs and whippoorwills that guarded it.

Bates had recorded that Dewart once speculated about exterminating the frogs, but that was moot; their only function was to mark the coming of the Things from Outside, and it was clearly too late for that to matter much. The tower capstone, engraved as my skylight now was, had made the Things' entry impossible—until Dewart, under Master's influence, had disastrously removed it. The last thing to do now was to replace the stone, even if it were possible, since its presence might for all I knew prevent exit as well as entry! No, the more I read, the more I became convinced that the dried-up river surrounding the islet of the round tower was the key. According to the relevant passage in Hoadley's *Evill Sorceries,* the medicine man Misquamacus had managed to imprison Ossadogowah, presumably in the tower. But in what did this imprisonment consist? Had the Indian been responsible for the capstone? That seemed far more likely to be the work of the owner of the property, Alijah Billington. What Misquamacus must have done was to confine the demon to the islet by somehow enchanting the flowing water which encircled it. This I felt certain was the case because of a detail recorded by Stephen Bates, who was sufficiently observant to notice it, but not quite perceptive enough to grasp its significance: In an unguarded moment, his cousin, possessed of the Richard Billington persona, let slip that this minor tributary of the Miskatonic had been called "the Misquamacus", though no modern map retained the name. Local legend must have provided the name in memory of the Wampanaug sorcerer whose incantation accounted for its being important enough to *have* a name. To call it the Misquamacus was as good as to remind oneself that only its circumfluence of the island separated the local populace from their supernatural nemesis. Of course, some years before Dewart's ill-advised arrival on the property the stream had dried up. But in its absence, the graven capstone prevented the return of Those from Outside.

A few calls to the state geological survey division revealed that the stream was believed simply to have altered its course due to soil erosion some miles upstream, and that these days only unusually heavy spring rains ever caused the streambed to flow at all down in the vicinity of Billington's Wood, though few surveyors had ever ventured into that region to be sure. By late afternoon I had come to think I might have the answer: If the Misquamacus could somehow be restored to its old course, its waters might once again perform their old protective service.

During all these deliberations, I could not keep my eyes from wandering again and again up to the skylight with its new heraldry. I really did not expect any overt move on the part of Billington (as I had now begun to think of him who bore the face and form of Ambrose Dewart), at least not through the more spectacular means open to him, while daylight left his actions open to public witness. But might he not, now that I considered the matter, attempt something through more mundane means? There was no doubting, since my visit with Mrs. Bishop, that I must have become at least as unwelcome an object of his attention as the ill-fated Stephen Bates had been. Knowing that my actions must seem increasingly eccentric, I telephoned the campus security office and requested that a patrol of guard dogs be dispatched to the University Library. This request they seemed to regard as most unseemly and were willing to put the dogs in place only after we had closed our doors for the evening.

But I had not finished placing my credibility at risk. Now I asked the campus operator to put me through to the Dean, an old schoolmate of mine. I sought his permission to approach the office of the Governor of the Commonwealth on behalf of a group of the history and geology faculty with the unusual request that men be detailed with picks, shovels, and earth-moving equipment to redirect the flow of a certain tributary of the Miskatonic. Actually such a case was not at all difficult to make, since credible appeal could be made to the benefits accruing to local farmers as well as to the preservation of certain historic topography soon to be threatened irreparably with erosion if the course of the stream remained unaltered. It was less easy to account for the rapidity with which I felt the work ought to be done, but the job was not really complicated and would require few men. In the end, I suspect it was the school loyalty of the Governor, a Miskatonic alumnus

himself, that made him accede to the Dean's wishes. In turn it must
have been personal loyalty to me, his senile-seeming friend, that led
the Dean to grant my peculiar request. In the end, the authorities sent
a chain gang from the county prison farm to do the work under the
direction of one of our senior geology students.

The reason for the urgency of the work, which I could not confide
to my colleagues, was not simply my concern for my own safety. Rather
it was the dreadful sense of certainty I had come to feel from further
researches in the old books Bates had seen in the Billington study. I
was now convinced that Billington and his Indian assistant meant to
open the dimensional gates to the influx of those beings called by the
ancient scribes the Ancient Ones, or Great Old Ones, who individually
bore the names of Tsathoggua, Yogge-Sothothe, Lloigor, and others.
To what realities these strange names might or might not correspond
I did not care to speculate, but the evidence of the recent Billington-
related deaths convinced me that this sorcerous enterprise was
dangerous enough to be stopped, if possible, forthwith. But whence
the urgency? All the ancient books agreed that May Eve, or Roodmas,
was the prime occasion for such blasphemous doings. And Roodmas
was now scarcely a fortnight hence.

I hoped that, essentially, once the work of restoring the Misquamacus to its ancient path was done, nature would take its course.
The work was being done far enough upstream as to escape the notice
of Billington and his confederates until it was too late, or so I hoped.
The same impenetrable blanketing of the ancient woods that hid his
doings from the eyes of outsiders would presumably serve to hide
outside doings from Billington's scrutiny as well. I could only imagine
his surprise when, any day now, the water made its irresistible way
down its old streambed and sealed off the islet, with its tower, from
the surrounding property. If the waters had not lost their ancient
efficacy, I judged that Billington would be cut off from the source
of his power. Then, I hoped, he would be no more difficult to deal
with than any madman who believed himself to be a remote ances-
tor reincarnated.

During the few days in which all I could do was wait and conserve
my energy for whatever contest might come, my sleep was again
troubled by auditions of what I now recognized as the tortured voice
of Stephen Bates. His cries seemed at one moment to emanate from
only inches away, then to be heard with impossible distinctness from
miles and miles above. The voice wept, then laughed, then chanted in

accents scarcely compatible with the human vocal apparatus. *"Iä! Iä! Hastur! Hastur cf'ayak 'vulgtm, gultlagin, vulgtmm!"*

On one such night I was gratefully aroused from my sheet-wringing slumbers by the sudden explosion of canine chaos on the floor below me. The German shepherds, lips retracted in fearsome growls, had cornered a young and ungainly intruder, Lem Whateley, as later interrogation would prove. From his hand dangled a butcher knife. I had a fairly good idea of whom the dull-witted youth had intended for his victim. My eyes strained to capture the details of a second figure who stood just outside the reach of the lamplight filtering in through the stained-glass Library window. I felt sure I could discern the prominent cheekbones and aquiline nose of an Indian, but as soon as the nightwatchman stumbled through the door and turned the lights on, the near-blinding illumination revealed no intruder besides young Whateley, who was soon in custody. Either the old Indian was surprisingly fleet of foot, or I had not shaken off the last vestiges of dream. Or perhaps there were other possibilities that evade rational explanation. At any rate, the wisdom of maintaining a canine patrol at the Library was no more questioned and has continued until the present.

It was April 29, and I knew the denouement of events must come quickly now. The detail of convicts had finished their work on the previous afternoon, and I meant to be present at Billington's Wood, accompanied by a detachment of Arkham and Aylesbury police, to witness whatever would transpire. My nagging sense of reluctance to leave my second-floor sanctuary was dispelled quite dramatically an hour before dawn. Some sixth sense had aroused me from disturbing dreams which, mercifully, I could not remember. As I lifted my age-stiffened frame from off my cot, the silence of the night was banished by the crash of a heavy object hurtling through my skylight! So great was the momentum with which it struck, actually cracking the floor beneath it, that it seemed not to have fallen but to have been *thrown* from above. It took a few moments' examination to be sure, but at length no question remained: The torn and peculiarly *weathered* body of Stephen Bates now lay sprawled at anatomically crazy angles on the floor of my office quarters. I did not even try explaining the situation to the puzzled night watchman, whose duties had in the last week become so much more troublesome. And what, really, did I know? Simply that poor Bates had been Outside.

I spent much of the day in the company of the police captain, apprising him as best I could of what would transpire out at the Billington place around sunset. Of course I had to choose my words carefully, to conceal the real horrors that I myself could only vaguely picture. The police could hardly be expected to send a substantial force of men merely to humor the delusions of a lunatic, even a lunatic on the faculty of Miskatonic University; and a lunatic I must seem should I tell them more than that a potentially dangerous mob of cultists would gather for mischief and moonshine.

About mid-afternoon, several carloads of officers set out from the Arkham police headquarters to rendezvous with a comparable group from Aylesbury. I noted the presence of a small group from the Essex County force as well. We formed an impressive caravan, traveling, of course, without sirens along the rude stretch of road built the previous year at the direction of Ambrose Dewart. Our convoy stopped some hundreds of yards away from the vicinity of the Billington grounds and continued on foot, hoping to maintain secrecy to the last. A collection of junk automobiles confirmed my expectation that a large contingent of Dunwich folk would be present to welcome their Master and Those he served.

The thick foliage of the area provided ample cover for our numbers, and the sounds made by the large number of men were easily drowned out by the startlingly loud chorus of the frogs and whippoorwills, which it seemed Billington had not bothered to eradicate after all. The day had been overcast, ever threatening rain, and now we could hear the rumbling of thunder far off. The incoming thunderclouds made the dusk hour prematurely dark. We filtered slowly through the undergrowth to what we judged a safe distance for concealment.

From our hidden vantage point we could see a gathering of roughly eighty or ninety slovenly-looking Dunwich hill folk, most milling aimlessly, waiting, as we were, for something to happen. A few busied themselves readying large bonfires. The stream was flowing, but it was impossible to tell if it would make any difference, or if any of the gathered congregation thought the fact remarkable. The visitors from Dunwich stood on the near side of the stream, while two distinctive figures stood on the islet before one of the colonnade arches of the cylindrical tower.

For a time nothing happened, save that the bonfires were lit, the cultists unwittingly making our covert observation easier. During this interval, the thunderheads moved closer, finally directly overhead, their cymbal-clashing music growing ever louder, lightning occasionally illuminating the night sky, but as yet without rain. Billington had disappeared within the tower, while the other figure, a stooped man dressed in the distinctive costume of the Narragansett Indians, said something to the crowd gathered opposite him. They in turn began a chant which sounded something like, *"Ngai, n'gha'ghaa, y'hah-Yog Sothoth! Iä! Iä! Nyarlathotep! Ph'nglui mglw'nafh Tsathoggua N'kai wgah'nagl fhtagn!"*

After some minutes of this, during which I observed how the agitation of the hidden police officers gradually heightened, as did the ranting of the cultists, Billington emerged from the tower, swathed in black robes embroidered in gold. Though distance and the unsteady quality of the light made it difficult to be sure, I thought his vestments were decorated with the traditional astrological symbols of the sorcerer. He spoke some words, apparently in archaic English, and I believe I caught the phrase "the million favored ones." He turned to face the tower and began to gesticulate in seemingly random patterns. At this, oddly, my eyes began to ache, and I noticed that when I closed them I saw peculiar after-images as of jetting arcs of flame or lightning erupting from Billington's outstretched hands. But when I opened my eyes again, there was nothing to be seen but the strangely waving hands, the hands it hurt to look upon. Involuntarily I averted my glance. But I listened intently and began to recognize syllables of debased Latin: *"Tibi, Magnum Innominandum, signa stellarum nigrarum et bufaniformis Sadoquae sigillum ...."*

The chanting continued, as did the crash of thunder overhead, until finally it seemed, preposterously, to be *answered* by a great cracking beneath the very earth, almost as if a slumbering giant were rousing. More than a few of the police had drawn their revolvers and made as if to rise and throw off their concealment, but I bade the captain to call for his men to maintain their position a little longer. I knew the most astonishing developments had yet to appear. But we had not long to wait.

At once the chanting and gibbering of the Dunwich folk fell silent, and we, too, involuntarily caught our breaths, as a column of queer greenish-blue light poured up through the tower into the night sky, eerily illuminating the lowering cloud bank that obscured the heavens. How had Billington contrived such a marvelous effect, I wondered dazedly, and what was its purpose? To serve as a beacon for Something whose advent he and his flock awaited?

As we watched, hypnotically transfixed, it seemed that a fragment of the storm cloud dropped lower and detached itself. In the midst of the cloud, vague motion could be seen, as of wildly flailing ropes or tendrils. It came down to meet the crest of the roofless structure and settled about the mouth of the cylinder. The still-flowing light momentarily caused the interior of the pulsating mass to glow hollowly; then the shaft of illumination ceased altogether, and the amorphous mass seemed to be sucked into the tower opening, condensing as it fell.

By the lesser light of the bonfires on the near side of the stream, the form of Ambrose Dewart or Richard Billington could now be seen slowly walking backwards out of one of the tower's arches. Still within the ancient masonry structure was a solid mass of confused outline. It seemed to have huge, folded batrachian hind legs, and to hop obscenely, yet to cover little ground with each movement. After some moments, as Billington and his Indian assistant, both gesturing, took refuge behind two of the encircling menhir stones, the great Thing cleared the tower and waddled into view. It had neither head nor forelimbs that I could see, when I dared look, but only a mass of writhing feelers and sucker-tipped tentacles. It extended great membranous wings that glistened greasily in the firelight.

By now the apish Dunwich throng had thrown themselves prostrate and wallowed in primitive genuflection. Some shouted one thing and some another, none of it intelligible. I glanced to either side of me to see faces frozen in wide-eyed astonishment. The sudden sound of crashing here and there amid the bushes told me that a few of our party of stolid veterans had fainted. I could not blame them, myself saved from the same reaction only by my previous dream-visions of similar entities. No one now made the slightest movement. The night's task had quite suddenly taken on an altogether different coloring.

Now Billington's waving arms seemed to pantomime directions for his hideous visitor to be off and to wing its way skyward again, no doubt for yet another mission of demon-sent vengeance such as had consumed poor Bates. I noted with icy terror that Billington was indicating the very area in which we crouched in apparently futile concealment! He had seen us!

Billington's composure left him abruptly and he began to rave as his entreaties did not meet with the familiar compliance. He turned to the Indian who said nothing but simply pointed to the flowing stream, seeming neither surprised nor eager to venture undoing the enchantment wrought long ago by the ancient wonder-worker Misquamacus. And as Billington turned back to his uncooperative familiar, his Indian companion suddenly plunged into the stream and stumbled across it, making for the side opposite that where the cultists clustered. He disappeared into the black depths of Billington's woods.

Clearly, my guesses had proven out! The flowing stream retained the mystic potency of its namesake: The charmed circle of water imprisoned the Thing from Outside, presumably in the same way old Alijah had done more than a century earlier. Apparently Master's overweening hubris had led him to disregard that fact, though his Indian servant had known, or suspected, better. What might now happen, however, was beyond prediction. But had not the old books indicated that, once summoned, the Son of Sadoquae would not return to its proper realm without the appeasement of sacrifice? And if the Thing could not escape the confines of the islet, must it not seek some sacrifice there, else be confined there as the old wizard Misquamacus had once confined it?

In the twinkling of an eye, the lifted hands of Master Billington ceased from their cabalistic signings as they were each held fast in the coil of a whipping tentacle from the Medusa-like creature before it. Another prehensile limb embraced him stickily, then another, and another, till his form could scarcely be seen.

The effect of this spectacle, so contrary to the fervent expectations of the Dunwich crowd, panicked them as the sudden pounce of a fox will scatter the hens in a barnyard. As the terrified mob took to their heels, some loping with animal speed, others unsteadily shambling back toward their automobiles, the police officers manfully shook off their momentary paralysis and broke from concealment, pursuing the fleeing miscreants, and trying to round them up with a series of warning shots in the air above their heads.

Waiting until the general melee, punctured with wild shouts, meek whimperings, and occasional cries where more than a warning shot had been necessary, passed me by, I headed in the opposite direction, making for the stone-circled islet.

All had changed in an instant. The nightmare creature, which had enveloped Billington in a cocoon of gelatinous tendrils only moments before, was now nowhere to be seen. But prone on the ground between the tower and one of the standing stones was the inert form of Billington. For a moment I expected to find his body a mutilated shambles like that of Stephen Bates, but as he had not been propelled groundward from a precipitous height, I found him intact. The surprise was instead that he yet lived! I stooped and cradled the unconscious form of Billington, or, as I should say, of Ambrose Dewart, for again it was he, as I later determined, freed at last of the malefic influence of Richard Billington's shadow. Old Mrs. Bishop, after all, had said that the entity from Outside consumed not the flesh but the life-energy of its victims, and this time it had feasted upon the essence of Master himself, leaving the physical shell vacant again for its proper occupant, Ambrose Dewart, to inhabit.

I write some weeks later, when things have been more or less resolved. Ambrose Dewart, his memory mercifully wiped clean of most of the strange events that occurred since his arrival at the old Billington estate, is recovering nicely in Arkham's Mercy Hospital. When he has regained his strength, he intends, wisely in my opinion, to abandon our shores to return to his native England. The tower on his property has, with his permission, been dynamited, though he does not know why and seems happy enough to remain in ignorance. The degenerate Dunwich villagers were hastily moved to a government internment camp in the South, where they are to be examined by a team of mystified doctors and ethnologists. There were few complaints from their relatives back in Dunwich, who appear to regard themselves as well rid of their decayed kinfolk. Old Huldah Bishop remains in her chosen seclusion, which her neighbors apparently know better than to disturb. Nothing more has been seen of the elusive old Indian, and I am inclined on that matter to leave well enough alone.

I believe I should wait a while to inform Mr. Dewart of the tragic death of his cousin from, as I shall tell him, a mountaineering accident. And I am not sure I shall ever inform him of another item, namely that the workmen who dynamited the round tower discovered that the structure seemed to be but a minor above-ground extension, a turret really, of a vast subterranean structure, the depth of which no line of theirs could sound.

Dick Lupoff, long a scholar as well as a practitioner of science fiction and fantasy literature, has several Lovecraftian efforts to his credit, including "Discovery of the Ghooric Zone", "Facts in the Case of Elizabeth Akeley", "The Whisperers", "Lights! Camera! Shub-Niggurath!", and the present piece. Lupoff first read "The Dunwich Horror" when he was a whippersnapper of nine years old. It took him fully thirty-three more years to get around to writing his own sequel, "The Devil's Hop Yard." The direct spur was listening to David McCallum's fine spoken word recording of "The Dunwich Horror" from Caedmon Records. The tale first appeared in Roy Torgeson, ed., Chrysalis, volume 2, Zebra Books, 1978. As Donald Burleson and others have observed, the real main characters in Lovecraft's tales are often the locales in which they are set. It is they (or their real-life prototypes) which inspired the sense of strange dread the stories seek to convey, the events and characters serving merely as props. In "The Devil's Hop Yard", the star of the show is the haunted Dunwich region itself, with all of its eerie goings-on. We are just delighted to be there again, like revisiting old haunts filled with nostalgic memories. We almost don't care what Lupoff will cause to transpire, though in fact his fiendish imagination has been at work there as well. Unlike most of the stories in this collection (and in this genre!) there is no interloping scholarly protagonist. We get to see how Dunwich horrors look inside Dunwich.

The Devil's Hop Yard

by Richard A. Lupoff

It was in the autumn of 1928 that those terrible events which came to be known as the Dunwich Horror transpired. The residents of the upper Miskatonic Valley in Massachusetts, at all times a taciturn breed of country folk never known for their hospitality or communicativeness toward outsiders, became thereafter positively hostile to such few travelers as happened to trespass upon their hilly and infertile region.

The people of the Dunwich region in particular, a sparse and inbred race with few intellectual or material attainments to show for their generations of toil, gradually became fewer than ever in number. It was the custom of the region to marry late and to have few children. Those infants delivered by the few physicians and midwives who practiced in the region were often deformed in some subtle and undefinable way; it would be impossible for an observer to place his finger upon the exact nature of the defect, yet it was plain that something was frighteningly wrong with many of the boys and girls born in the Miskatonic Valley.

Yet, as the years turned slowly, the pale, faded folk of Dunwich continued to raise their thin crops, to tend their dull-eyed and stringy cattle, and to wring their hard existence from the poor, farmed-out earth of their farms.

Events of interest were few and petty; the columns of the *Aylesbury Transcript,* the *Arkham Advertiser,* and even the imposing *Boston Globe* were scanned for items of diversion. Dunwich itself supported no regular newspaper, not even the slim weekly sheet that subsists in many such semi-rural communities.

It was therefore a source of much local gossip and a delight to the scandal-mongers when Earl Sawyer abandoned Mamie Bishop, his common-law wife of twenty years' standing, and took up instead with Zenia Whateley. Sawyer was an uncouth dirt farmer of some fifty years of age. His cheeks covered perpetually with a stubble that gave him the appearance of not having shaved for a week, his nose and eyes marked with the red lines of broken minor blood vessels, and his stoop-shouldered, shuffling gait marked him as a typical denizen of Dunwich's hilly environs.

Zenia Whateley was a thin, pallid creature, the daughter of old Zebulon Whateley and a wife so retiring in her lifetime and so thoroughly forgotten since her death that none could recall the details of her countenance or even her given name. The latter had been painted carelessly on the oblong wooden marker that indicated the place of her burial, but the cold rains and watery sunlight of the round of Dunwich's seasons had obliterated even this trace of the dead woman's individuality.

Zenia must have taken after her mother, for her own appearance was unprepossessing, her manner cringing, and her speech so infrequent and so diffident that few could recall ever having heard her voice.

The loafers and gossips at Osborn's General Store in Dunwich were hard put to understand Earl Sawyer's motives in abandoning Mamie Bishop for Zenia Whateley. Not that Mamie was noted for her great beauty or scintillating personality; on the contrary, she was known as a meddler and a snoop, and her sharp tongue had stung many a denizen hoping to see some misdemeanor pass unnoted. Still, Mamie had within her that spark of vitality so seldom found in the folk of the upper Miskatonic, that trait of personality known in the rural argot as gumption, so that it was puzzling to see her perched beside Earl on the front seat of his rattling Model T Ford, her few belongings tied in

slovenly bundles behind her, as Sawyer drove her over the dust-blowing
turnpike to Aylesbury, where she took quarters in the town's sole,
dilapidated rooming house.

The year was 1938 when Earl Sawyer and Mamie Bishop parted
ways. It had been a decade since the death of the poor, malformed giant
Wilbur Whateley and the dissolution—for this word, rather than
death, best characterizes the end of that monster—of his even more
gigantic and even more shockingly made twin brother. But now it was
the end of May, and the spring thaw had come late and grudgingly to
the hard-pressed farmlands of the Miskatonic Valley this year.

When Earl Sawyer returned alone, to Dunwich, he stopped in the
center of the town, such as it was, parking his Model T opposite
Osborn's. He crossed the dirty thoroughfare and climbed onto the
porch of old Zebulon Whateley's house, pounding once upon the gray,
peeling door while the loafers at Osborn's stared and commented
behind his back.

The door opened and Earl Sawyer disappeared inside for a minute.
The loafers puzzled over what business Earl might have with Zebulon
Whateley, and their curiosity was rewarded shortly when Sawyer
reappeared leading Zenia Whateley by one flaccid hand. Zenia wore a
thin cotton dress, and through its threadbare covering it was obvious
even from the distance of Osborn's that she was with child.

Earl Sawyer drove home to his dusty farm, bringing Zenia with him,
and proceeded to install her in place of Mamie Bishop. There was little
noticeable change in the routine at Sawyer's farm with the change in
its female occupant. Each morning Earl and Zenia would rise, Zenia
would prepare and serve a meagre repast for them, and they would
breakfast in grim silence. Earl would thereafter leave the house,
carefully locking the door behind him with Zenia left inside to tend
the chores of housekeeping, and Earl would spend the entire day
working out of doors.

The Sawyer farm contained just enough arable land to support a thin
herd of the poor cattle common to the Miskatonic region. The bleak
hillside known as the Devil's Hop Yard was also located on his
holdings. Here had grown no tree, shrub, or blade of grass for as far
back as the oldest archives of Dunwich recorded, and despite Earl
Sawyer's repeated attempts to raise a crop on its unpleasant slopes, the
Hop Yard resisted and remained barren. Even so there persisted reports
of vague, unpleasant rumblings and cracklings from beneath the Hop
Yard, and occasionally shocking odors were carried from it to adjoining
farms when the wind was right.

On the first Sunday of June, 1938, Earl Sawyer and Zenia Whateley were seen to leave the farmhouse and climb into Sawyer's Model T. They drove together into Dunwich village, and, leaving the Model T in front of old Zebulon Whateley's drab house, walked across the churchyard, pausing to read such grave markers as remained there standing and legible, then entered the Dunwich Congregational Church that had been founded by the Reverend Abijah Hoadley in 1747. The pulpit of the Dunwich Congregational Church had been vacant since the unexplained disappearance of the Reverend Isaiah Ashton in the summer of 1912, but a circuit-riding Congregational minister from the city of Arkham conducted services in Dunwich from time to time.

This was the first occasion of Earl Sawyer's attendance at services within memory, and there was a nodding of heads and a hissing of whispers up and down the pews as Earl and Zenia took a pew to themselves at the rear of the congregation. When the order of service had reached its conclusion they remained behind to speak with the minister. No witness was present, of course, to overhear the conversation that took place, but later the minister volunteered his recollection of Sawyer's request and his own responses.

Sawyer, the minister reported, had asked him to perform a marriage. The couple to be united were himself (Sawyer) and Zenia Whateley. The minister had at first agreed, especially in view of Zenia's obvious condition, and the desirability of providing for a legitimate birth for her expected child. But Sawyer had refused to permit the minister to perform the usual marriage ceremony of the Congregational Church, insisting instead upon a ceremony involving certain foreign terms to be provided from some ancient documents handed down through the family of the bride.

Nor would Sawyer permit the minister to read the original documents, providing in their place crudely rendered transcripts written by a clumsy hand on tattered, filthy scraps of paper. Unfortunately the minister did not have even these scraps. They had been retained by Sawyer, and the minister could recall only vaguely a few words of the strange and almost unpronounceable incantations he had been requested to utter: *N'gai, n'gha'ghaa, bugg-shoggog,* he remembered. And a reference to a lost city, "Between the Yr and the Nhhngr."

The minister had refused to perform the blasphemous ceremony requested by Sawyer, holding that it would be ecclesiastically improper and possibly even heretical of him to do so, but he renewed his offer to perform an orthodox Congregational marriage, and possibly to include certain additional materials provided by the couple *if he were shown a translation also,* so as to convince himself of the propriety of the ceremony.

Earl Sawyer refused vehemently, warning the minister that he stood in far greater peril should he ever learn the meaning of the words than if he remained in ignorance of them. At length Sawyer stalked angrily from the church, pulling the passive Zenia Whateley behind him, and returned with her to his farm.

A few nights later the couple were visited by Zenia's father, old Zebulon Whateley, and also by Squire Sawyer Whateley, of the semi-undecayed Whateleys, a man who held the unusual distinction of claiming cousinship to both Earl Sawyer and Zenia Whateley. At midnight the four figures, Earl, Zenia, old Zebulon, and Squire Whateley, climbed slowly to the top of the Devil's Hop Yard. What acts they performed at the crest of the hill are not known with certainty, but Luther Brown, now a fully grown man and engaged to be married to George Corey's daughter Olivia, stated later that he had been searching for a lost heifer near the boundary between Corey's farm and Sawyer's, and saw the four figures silhouetted against the night constellations as they stood atop the hill.

As Luther Brown watched, all four disrobed; he was fairly certain of the identification of the three men, and completely sure of that of Zenia because of her obvious pregnancy. Completely naked they set fire to an altar of wood apparently set up in advance on the peak of the Hop Yard. What rites they performed before Luther fled in terror and disgust he refused to divulge, but later that night loud cracking sounds were heard coming from the vicinity of the Sawyer farm, and an earthquake was reported to have shaken the entire Miskatonic Valley, registering on the seismographic instruments of Harvard College and causing swells in the harbor at Innsmouth.

The next day Squire Sawyer Whateley registered a wedding on the official rolls of Dunwich village. He claimed to be qualified to perform the civil ceremony by virtue of his standing as Chairman of the local Selective Service Board. This claim must surely be regarded as most dubious, but while the Whateleys were not highly regarded in Dunwich, their critics considered it the better part of valor to hold their criticism to private circumstances, and the marriage of Earl Sawyer and Zenia Whateley was thus officially recognized.

Mamie Bishop, in the meanwhile, had settled into her new home in Aylesbury and began spreading malign reports about her former lover Earl Sawyer and his new wife. Earl, she claimed, had been in league with the Whateleys all along. Her own displacement by Zenia had been only one step in the plot of Earl Sawyer and the Whateley clan to revive the evil activities that had culminated in the events of 1928. Earl and Zenia, with the collaboration of Squire Sawyer Whateley and old Zebulon Whateley, would bring about the ruin of the entire Miskatonic Valley if left to their own devices, and perhaps might bring about a blight that would cover a far greater region.

No one paid any attention to Mamie, however. Even the other Bishops, a clan almost as numerous and widespread as the Whateleys, tended to discount Mamie's warnings as the spiteful outpourings of a woman scorned. In any case, Mamie's dire words were pushed from the public consciousness in the month of August, 1938, when Earl Sawyer rang up Dr. Houghton on the party line telephone and summoned him to the Sawyer farm.

Zenia was in labor, and Earl, in a rare moment of concern, had decided that medical assistance was in order.

Zenia's labor was a long and difficult one. Dr. Houghton later commented that first childbirths tended to be more protracted than later deliveries, but Zenia remained in labor for 72 consecutive hours, and barely survived the delivery of the child. Throughout the period of her labor there were small earth temblors centering on the Devil's Hop Yard, and Zenia, by means of a series of frantic hand motions and incoherent mewling sounds, indicated that she wished the curtains drawn back from her window so that she could see the crown of the hill from her bed.

On the third night of her labor, while Zenia lay panting and spent near to death between futile contractions, a storm rose. Clouds swept up the valley from the Atlantic, great winds roared over the houses and through the trees of Dunwich, bolts of lightning flashed from thunderhead to hilltop.

Dr. Houghton, despairing of saving the life of either Zenia or her unborn child, began preparations for a Caesarian section. With Earl Sawyer hovering in the background, mumbling semi-incoherent incantations of the sort that had caused the Congregational minister to refuse a church wedding to the couple, the doctor set to work.

With sharpened instruments sterilized over the woodstove that served for both cooking and heat for the Sawyer farmhouse, he made the incision in Zenia's abdomen. As he removed the fetus from her womb there was a terrific crash of thunder. A blinding bolt of lightning struck at the peak of the Devil's Hop Yard. From a small grove of twisted and deformed maple trees behind the Sawyer house, a flock of nesting whippoorwills took wing, setting up a cacophony of sound audible over even the loud rushings and pounding of the rainstorm.

All of Dr. Houghton's efforts failed to preserve the poor, limited life of Zenia Whateley Sawyer, but her child survived the ordeal of birth. The next day old Zebulon Whateley and Squire Sawyer Whateley made their way to the Sawyer house and joined Earl Sawyer in his efforts. He descended the wooden steps to the dank cellar of the house and returned carrying a plain wooden coffin that he had surreptitiously built himself some time before. The three of them placed Zenia's shriveled, wasted body in the coffin and Earl nailed the lid in place.

They carried the wooden box to the peak of the Devil's Hop Yard and there, amid fearsome incantations and the making of signs with their hands unlike any seen for a decade in the Miskatonic Valley, they buried Zenia's remains.

Then they returned to the farmhouse where the child lay in a crude wooden cradle. Squire Whateley tended the infant while its father rang up Central on the party line and placed a call to Mamie Bishop at the rooming house in Aylesbury.

After a brief conversation with his former common-law wife, Earl Sawyer nodded to his father-in-law and to the Squire, and left them with the child. He climbed into his Model T and set out along the Aylesbury Pike to fetch Mamie back to Dunwich.

The child of Earl Sawyer and Zenia Whateley Sawyer was a girl. Her father, after consultation with his father-in-law and distant cousin Squire Whateley, named his daughter Hester Sawyer. She was a tiny child at birth, and fear was expressed as to her own survival.

Earl contacted the Congregational minister at Arkham, asking him to baptize the infant according to rites specified by Earl. Once more the dispute as to the use of Earl's strange scriptures—if they could be so defined—erupted, and once more the minister refused to lend his ecclesiastical legitimacy to the ceremony. Instead, Earl, Zebulon, and Sawyer Whateley carried the tiny form, wrapped in swaddling cloths, to the peak of the Devil's Hop Yard, and on the very ground of her mother's still-fresh grave conducted a ceremony of consecration best left undescribed.

They then returned her to the Sawyer house and the care of Mamie Bishop.

There were comments in Dunwich and even in Aylesbury about Mamie's surprising willingness to return to Sawyer's ménage in the role of nursemaid and guardian to the infant Hester, but Mamie merely said she had her reasons and refused to discuss the matter further. Under Mamie's ministrations the infant Hester survived the crises of her first days of life, and developed into a child of surprising strength and precocity.

Even as an infant Hester was a child of unusual beauty and—if such a phrase may be used—premature maturity. Her coloring was fair, almost, but not quite, to the point of albinism. Where Hester's distant relative, the long-disappeared Lavinia Whateley, had had crinkly white hair and reddish-pink eyes, little Hester possessed from the day of her birth a glossy poll of the silvery blonde shade known as platinum. Mamie Bishop tried repeatedly to put up the child's hair in little curls or scallops as she thought appropriate for a little girl, but Hester's hair hung straight and gracefully to her shoulders, refusing to lie in any other fashion.

The child's eyes showed a flecked pattern of palest blue and the faint pink of the true albino, giving the appearance of being a pale lavender in tint except at a very close range, when the alternation of blue and pink became visible. Her skin was the shade of new cream and absolutely flawless.

She took her first steps at the age of five months; by this time she had her full complement of baby teeth as well. By the age of eight months, early in the spring of 1939, she began to speak. There was none of the babyish prattle of a normally developing child. Hester spoke with precision, correctness, and a chilling solemnity from the utterance of her first word.

Earl Sawyer did not keep Mamie Bishop imprisoned in his house as he had the dead Zenia Whateley Sawyer. Indeed, Sawyer made it his business to teach Mamie the operation of his Model T, and he encouraged her—nay, he all but commanded her—to drive it into Dunwich Village, Dean's Corners, or Aylesbury frequently.

On these occasions Mamie was alleged to be shopping for such necessities for herself, Earl, or little Hester as the farm did not provide. On one occasion Earl directed Mamie to drive the Model T all the way to Arkham, and there to spend three days obtaining certain items which he said were needed for Hester's upbringing. Mamie spent two nights at one of the rundown hotels that still persisted in Arkham, shabby ornate reminders of that city's more prosperous days.

Mamie's sharp tongue had its opportunities during these shopping expeditions, and she was heard frequently to utter harsh comments about Earl, Zebulon, and Squire Whateley. She never made direct reference to the dead Zenia, but made cryptic and unsettling remarks about little Hester Sawyer, her charge, whom she referred to most often as "Zenia's white brat."

As has been mentioned, Dunwich village supported no regular newspaper of its own, but the publications of other communities in the Miskatonic Valley gave space to events in this locale. The *Aylesbury Transcript* in particular devoted a column in its weekly pages to news from Dunwich. This news was provided by Joe Osborn, the proprietor of Osborn's General Store, in return for a regular advertisement of his establishment's wares.

A review of the Dunwich column in the *Aylesbury Transcript* for the period between August of 1938 and the end of April 1943 shows a series of reports of rumblings, crackings, and unpleasant odors emanating from the area of Sawyer's farm and particularly from the Devil's Hop Yard. Two features of these reports are worthy of note.

First, the reports of the sounds and odors occur at irregular intervals, but a check of the sales records of the establishments in Dunwich, Aylesbury, Dean's Corners, and Arkham where Mamie Bishop traded will show that the occurrences at the Devil's Hop Yard coincide perfectly with the occasions of Mamie's absence from Sawyer's farm. Second, while the events took place at irregular intervals, ranging from as close together as twice in one week to as far apart as eight months, their severity increased with regularity. The earliest of the series are barely noted in the Dunwich column of the *Transcript*. By the end of 1941, the events receive lead position in Osborn's writings. By the beginning of 1943 they are no longer relegated to the Dunwich column at all, but are treated as regular news, suggesting that they could be detected in Aylesbury itself—a distance of nearly 15 miles from Dunwich!

It was also noted by the loafers at Osborn's store that on those occasions when Mamie Bishop absented herself from the Sawyer farm, Earl's two favorite in-laws and cronies, Zebulon Whateley and Squire Sawyer Whateley, visited him. There were no further reports of odd goings-on at the Sawyer place such as that given by Luther Brown in 1938. Perhaps Luther's unfortunate demise in an accident on George Corey's silo roof, where he was placing new shingles, had no connection with his seeing the rites atop the Devil's Hop Yard, but after Luther's death and with the new series of rumblings and stenches, others began to shun the Sawyer place from 1939 onward.

In September of 1942 a sad incident transpired. Hester Sawyer, then aged four, had been educated up to that time primarily by her father, with the assistance of the two elder Whateleys and of Mamie Bishop.

She had never been away from the Sawyer farm and had never seen another child.

Mamie Bishop's second cousin Elsie, the maiden sister of Silas Bishop (of the undecayed Bishops), caught Mamie's ear on one of Mamie's shopping expeditions away from the Sawyer place. Elsie was the mistress of a nursery school operated under the auspices of the Dunwich Congregational Church, and she somehow convinced Mamie that it was her duty to give little Hester exposure to other children of her own age. Mamie spoke disparagingly of "Zenia's white brat", but following Elsie's insistence Mamie agreed to discuss the matter with Earl Sawyer.

On the first day of the fall term, Mamie drove Earl's Model T into Dunwich village, little Hester perched on the seat beside her. This was the first look that Hester had at Dunwich—and the first that Dunwich had at Hester.

Although Mamie had bundled the child into loose garments that covered her from neck to ankles, it was obvious that something was abnormal about her. Hester was astonishingly small for a child of four. She was hardly taller than a normal infant. It was as if she had remained the same size in the four years since her birth, not increasing an inch in stature.

But that was only half the strangeness of Hester's appearance, for while her size was the same as a new-born infant's, her development was that of a fully mature and breathtakingly beautiful woman! The sun shone brilliantly on the long platinum hair that hung defiantly around the edges of the bonnet Mamie had forced onto Hester's head. Her strange lavender eyes seemed to hold the secrets of an experienced voluptuary. Her face was mature, her lips full and sensual. And when a sudden gust of wind pressed her baggy dress against her torso this showed the configuration of a Grecian eidolon.

The loafers at Osborn's, who had clustered about and craned their necks for a look at the mysterious "white brat", were torn between an impulse to turn away from this unnatural sight and a fascination with the image of what seemed a living mannikin, a woman of voluptuous bodily form and astonishing facial beauty the size of a day-old infant, sitting primly beside Mamie Bishop.

Elsie Bishop welcomed her cousin Mamie and her charge, Hester Sawyer, to the nursery school at the Congregational Church. Elsie chose to make no comment on Hester's unusual appearance, but instead introduced her to the children already present. These included her own nephew Nahum Bishop, Silas's five-year-old son. Nahum was a perfectly normal boy, outgoing and playful, one of the few such to appear in the blighted Miskatonic Valley.

He took one look at Hester Sawyer and fell madly in love with her, with the total, enraptured fascination that only a child can feel when first he discovers the magic of the female sex. He lost all interest in the other children in the school and in their games. He wished only to be with Hester, to gaze at her, to hold her miniature woman's hand in his own pudgy boy's fingers. Any word that Hester spoke was as music to his ears, and any favor she might ask, any task that she might set for him, was his bounden duty and his greatest joy to perform.

In a short while the various children of the nursery school were playing happily, some of them scampering up and down the aisle leading between the two banks of pews in the main body of the church. The two cousins, Mamie and Elsie, retired to the chancel kitchen to prepare a pot of tea for themselves. Although they could not see the school children from this position, they could hear them happily playing in the semi-abandoned church.

Suddenly there was a terrible thump from the roof of the church, then a second similar sound from the burying-ground outside, then a series of panic-stricken and terrified screams from the children. Mamie and Elsie ran from the chancel and found nothing, apparently, amiss in the church itself, but the children were clustered at an open window staring into the churchyard, pointing and exclaiming in distress.

The two women shoved their way through the panic-stricken children until they could see. What they beheld was the body of Elsie's nephew Nahum Bishop, grotesquely broken over an old tombstone upon which it had fallen when it bounced from the roof of the church. There was no question that the child was dead, the sightless eyes apparently gazing upward at the steeple of the church.

Before they could even turn away from the window, the two women were able to hear a light tread, one so light that, except for the total hush that had descended upon the church as the children's screams subsided, it would not have been heard at all, calmly descending the wooden staircase from the steeple. In a moment, Hester Sawyer emerged from the stairwell, her manner one of complete self-possession, the expression on her beautiful little face one of mockery and amusement.

When the state police arrived Hester explained with total self-assurance that she and Nahum had climbed the steeple together, up the narrow wooden staircase that ran from the church's floor to its belfry. Nahum had averred that he would do anything to prove his love for

Hester, and she had asked him to fly from the steeple. In attempting to do so he had fallen to the roof, bounced once, then crashed into the old grave marker in the yard.

The police report listed Nahum's death as accidental, and Hester was returned to the Sawyer farm in charge of Mamie Bishop. Needless to say, the child did not return to the nursery school at the Dunwich Congregational Church; in fact, she was not seen again in Dunwich, or anywhere else away from her father's holdings.

The final chapter in the tragedy of the Devil's Hop Yard, if indeed tragedy is the proper designation for such a drama, was played out in the spring of 1943. As in so many years past, the warmth of the equinox had given but little of itself to the upper Miskatonic Valley; winter instead still clung to the barren peaks and the infertile bottomlands of the region, and the icy dark waters of the Miskatonic River passed only few meadows on their way southeastward to Arkham and Innsmouth and the cold Atlantic beyond.

In Dunwich the bereaved Silas Bishop and his maiden sister Elsie had recovered as best they could from the death of young Nahum. Elsie's work with the nursery school continued and only the boarding-up of the stairwell that led to the steeple and belfry of the Congregational Church testified to the accident of the previous September.

Early on the evening of April 30 the telephone rang in the Bishop house in Dunwich village, and Elsie lifted the receiver to hear a furtive whisper on the line. The voice she barely recognized, so distorted it was with terror, belonged to her second cousin Mamie.

"They've locked me in the house naow," Mamie whispered into the telephone. "Earl always sent me away before, but this time they've locked me in and I'm afeared. Help me, Elsie! I daon't knaow what they're a-fixin' ta do up ta the Hop Yard, but I'm afeared!"

Elsie signaled her brother Silas to listen to the conversation. "Who's locked you in, Mamie?" Elsie asked her cousin.

"Earl and Zeb and Sawyer Whateley done it! They've took Zenia's brat and they've clumb the Hop Yard. I kin see 'em from here! They're all stark naked and they've built 'em a bonfire an' an altar an' they're throwin' powder into the fire and old Zeb he's a-readin' things outen some terrible book that they always keep a-locked up!

"And now I kin see little Hester, the little white brat o' Zenia's, and she's clumb onto the altar and she's sayin' things to Zeb an' Earl an' Squire Whateley an' they've got down on their knees like they's a-worshipin' Hester, an' she's makin' signs with her hands. Oh, Elsie,

I can't describe them signs, they's so awful, they's so awful what she's a-doin', Elsie! Get some help out here, oh please get some help!"

Elsie told Mamie to try and be calm, and not to watch what was happening atop the Devil's Hop Yard. Then she hung up the telephone and turned to her brother Silas. "We'll get the state police from Aylesbury," she said. "They'll stop whatever is happening at Sawyer's. We'd best telephone them now, Silas!"

"D'ye think they'll believe ye, Elsie?"

Elsie shook her head in a negative manner.

"Then we'd best git to Aylesbury ourselves," Silas resumed. "If we go there ourselves they'd more like to believe us than if we jest telephoned."

They hitched up their horse and drove by wagon from Dunwich to Aylesbury. Fortunately the state police officer who had investigated the death of young Nahum Bishop was present, and knowing both Elsie and Silas to be citizens of a responsible nature the officer did not laugh at their report of Mamie's frightened telephone call. The officer started an automobile belonging to the state police, and with the two Bishops as passengers set out back along the Aylesbury Pike to Dunwich and thence to the Sawyer farm beyond the village center.

As the official vehicle neared Sawyer's place, its three occupants were assailed by a most terrible and utterly indescribable stench that turned their stomachs and caused their eyes to run copiously, and that also, inexplicably, filled each of them with a hugely frightening rush of emotions dominated by an amalgam of fear and revulsion. Sounds of thunder filled the air, and the earth trembled repeatedly, threatening to throw the car off the road.

The state police officer swung the automobile from the dirt road fronting the Sawyer farm onto a narrow and rutted track that ran by the decrepit house and led to the foot of the Devil's Hop Yard. The officer pulled the car to a halt and leaped from his seat, charging up the hill with his service revolver drawn, followed by Silas and Elsie Bishop, who made the best speed they could despite their years.

Before them they could see the altar and the four figures that Mamie Bishop had described to her cousin Elsie. The night sky was cloudless and a new moon offered no competition to the million brilliantly twinkling stars. Little Hester Sawyer, her body that of a fully formed woman yet not two feet in height, danced and postured on the wooden altar, the starlight and that of the nearby bonfire dancing lasciviously on her gleaming platinum hair and smooth, cream-colored skin. Her lavender eyes caught the firelight and reflected it like the eyes of a wild beast in the woods at night.

Earl and Zebulon and Sawyer Whateley stood in an equilateral triangle about the altar, and around them there had apparently sprung from the earth itself a perfect circle of slimy, tentacled growths, more animal than vegetable, the only things that had ever been known to grow from the soil of the Devil's Hop Yard. Even as the newcomers watched, too awe-stricken and too revolted to act, the horrid tentacled growths began to lengthen, and to sway in time to the awful chanting of the three naked men and the lascivious posturings of the tiny, four-year-old Hester.

There was the sound of a shrill, reedy piping from somewhere in the air, and strange winds rushed back and forth over the scene.

The voice of Hester Sawyer could be heard chanting, *"Ygnaiih ... hgnaiih ... hflthkh'ngha ... Yog-Sothoth ... Y'bthnk ... h'ehye-n'grkdl'lh!"*

There was a single, blinding bolt of lightning—an astonishing occurrence as the night sky was entirely clear of any clouds—and the form of Hester Sawyer was bathed in a greenish-yellow glow of almost supernatural electrical display, sparks dancing over her perfect skin, and balls of St. Elmo's fire tumbling from her lips and hands and rolling across the altar, tumbling to the ground and bounding down the slopes of the Devil's Hop Yard.

The eyes of the watchers were so dazzled by the display that they were never certain, afterwards, of what they had seen. But it appeared, at least, that the bolt of lightning had not descended from the sky to strike Hester, but had originated from her and struck upward, zigzagging into the wind-swept blackness over Dunwich, reaching upward and upward as if it were eventually going to reach the stars themselves.

Before the bolt of lightning had disappeared from before the dazzled eyes of the watchers, the body of Hester Sawyer seemed to rise along its course, posturing and making those terrible shocking signs even as it rose, growing ever smaller, until it disappeared above the Hop Yard and the lightning bolt winked out, and all sight of Hester Sawyer was lost forever.

With the end of the electrical display the shocked paralysis that had overcome the watchers subsided, and the police officer advanced to stand near the ring of tentacled growths and the three naked men. He ordered them to follow him back to the police vehicle, but instead they launched themselves in snarling, animalistic attacks upon him. The officer stepped back but the three men flew at him growling, clawing, biting at his legs and torso. The police officer's revolver crashed once, again, then a third time, and the three naked men lay thrashing and gesturing on the ground.

They were taken to the general hospital at Arkham, where a medical team headed by Drs. Houghton and Hartwell labored unsuccessfully through the night to save them. By the morning of May 1, all three had expired without uttering a single word.

Meanwhile, back at the Devil's Hop Yard, Silas and Elsie Bishop guided other investigators to the altar that Hester Sawyer had last stood upon. The book that had lain open beside her had been destroyed beyond identification by the lightning bolt of the night of April 30. Agricultural experts summoned from Miskatonic University at Arkham attempted to identify the tentacled growths that had sprung from the ground around the altar. The growths had died within a few hours of their appearance, and only desiccated husks remained. The experts were unable to identify them fully, indicating their complete puzzlement at their apparent resemblance to the tentacles of the giant marine squid of the Pacific Trench near the island of Ponape.

Back at the Sawyer farmhouse, Mamie Bishop was found cowering in a corner, hiding her eyes and refusing to look up or even acknowledge the presence of others when addressed. Her hair had turned completely white, not the platinum white of little Hester Sawyer's hair but the crinkly albino white that had been Lavinia Whateley's so many years before.

Mamie mumbled to herself and shook her head but uttered not a single intelligible word, either then or later, when she too was taken to the general hospital at Arkham. In time she was certified physically sound and transferred to a mental ward where she resides to this day, a harmless, quivering husk, her inward-turned eyes locked forever on whatever shocking sight it was that she beheld that night when she gazed from the window of the Sawyer farmhouse upon the horrid ceremony taking place atop the Devil's Hop Yard.

Ben Indick *is a veteran fantasy fan who bought a copy of Lovecraft's* The Outsider and Others *hot off the press. He carried it with him through the vicissitudes of World War II and even lent it out! For all that, miraculously, it survives today, dust jacket intact. Ben is the unofficial historian of the Esoteric Order of Dagon Amateur Press Association, a group of Lovecraft aficionados who have banded together to share their interest in the Old Gent and his work using one of Lovecraft's own favorite media: amateur journalism. The membership has included most prominent Lovecraft scholars: Don Burleson, Peter Cannon, S. T. Joshi, and Dirk W. Mosig, as well as many fans who went on to become successful fiction authors, like Burleson, Chet Williamson, and David Drake. "The Road to Dunwich" was published in the very first issue of the E.O.D., then reprinted in the small press magazine* Etchings & Odysseys. *Ben set out to write a sequel to one of his favorite Lovecraft tales, while steadfastly refusing to try to pastiche Lovecraft's style. Indick was a close friend of the late Frank Belknap Long, and it is to be hoped that he can someday be persuaded to write a critical treatment of the works of Long. His books include* Ray Bradbury: Dramatist *and* George Alec Effington: From Entropy to Budayeen *(Borgo Press). His essays on* Stephen King *have appeared in* Fear Itself, Kingdom of Fear, *and* Reign of Fear *(Underwood-Miller).*

The Road to Dunwich

by Ben Indick

I have to write this. Not for anyone to see, no. Just for myself, I guess. To get it out of me, and maybe, once in a while, to read again, and remember. I wouldn't even want anyone to see it; some things best shouldn't be seen. Or even talked about. People around here, they wouldn't like it too much, and others would take me for a fool.

Only it wasn't their family, their son, their daughter. That girl was like my own really, even if she was only my son's wife. Before he brought her around, I didn't figure I would even take to her, I'd gotten so used to living alone with my son. I suppose that's why I used to find myself surprised by her. She wasn't like the local girls, with that brightness inside her, always finding something new, and making it interesting. Spirit. Bright.

She was an upstate girl, and even if she was related distantly to the Whateleys, like some folks say, it doesn't matter. They used to live in Dunwich, up the road, and were a peculiar lot. People have pretty much

forgotten them now, and it's just as well. Terrible things are supposed
to have happened to them, so long ago, if one can believe the stories.

"If," I say, and I have to laugh at myself, without a smile. I can believe
it. Still, most folks don't, even those with long memories. My cousin
lived on a farm bypassed by that—whatever it was—*thing* that bowled
over a few places before it disappeared. Some people say they actually
saw it, a great horror, like nothing at all else, but if they did, it was
only through a spyglass. The only ones up close to it, so the story goes,
were some college people, and they never talked much about it
afterward. Well, I can believe anything. I have to. Otherwise, what is
it all for?

I told my son long ago that he would be smart to clear out of here
entirely, find some nice girl somewhere, Iowa, Kansas, say, anywhere
not here, where people don't talk much to each other, and the fields
aren't full of rocks. And the graves of my family. Everybody moves
around so much nowadays anyway, why shouldn't he? It was a waste
of advice, which I knew it would be. For us folks, there just isn't any
other place. Kills us to do our little farming, but it's our land, our hills,
our air. Who would want to leave it? But now my son has, and who
knows where he is?

Go find some girl someplace else, I told him. These girls here, well,
they've been here too long. Maybe eventually he might have listened,
maybe not, but when he met Alice, she was enough for him. She had
come to visit an aunt of hers here; that was Mrs. Whelan, who used to
buy grain from me now and again, and she was a nice enough woman.
She told me the girl had been born here, but the family hadn't wanted
to stay. But maybe these rocks were in her blood, and she was studying
geology, and she came away from school to spend a summer here. They
don't have hills like ours in her part of the state. Enough rock formations
to satisfy any geologist, I suppose. That's when Evan met her.

It surprised me to see how they took to each other, she being such
a lively girl, and he was such a quiet man. Maybe they filled some need
in each other. She had a zest for everything, and he was good at
understanding her, and helping her. Say what you want, I'm proud of
my son. The two of them would take a basket of sandwiches and a
knapsack of tools, and I'd see them ambling up that scraggly road to
the hills past Dunwich, hand in hand. I remember my wife used to
tease me once, why I never took her hand. Well, wasn't Evan took her
hand, I'd say, was Alice took his. Why didn't I take my wife's hand, I
wonder. Never was one for touching. When she took sick and died,
coughing so much, it was too late. Her hand was so warm then ... Alice

and Evan, hand in hand, off hunting rocks. A fool's errand, but there are worse.

After they were married, it didn't change any. They still liked the same things. She came to live with us, and she kept studying the hills. Of course, that's where the trouble started, when she found that unusual stone. An artifact, she said proudly, like a scientist, which she was, I guess, a man-made thing. She put it on the mantel and studied it. Older than Columbus, she said it was, maybe older than the Indians. So who made it, I asked. I didn't know anyone was here before the Indians, but she said it had no relation to Indian art or tribal ritual.

It's broke and buried now, but I can remember that stone. It was very worn, but you could see a design on it, like a sun-shape, with squiggly rays all around it, but they were more like arms or even legs. Truth is I didn't like it, ancient or otherwise. When I looked at it I recalled stories of what had, so they say, happened around here once. She only laughed and asked me whether I was afraid of it.

"You think it's one of those monsters, don't you," was what she said to me, "like once came here to spook everybody?" And she laughed, even making me laugh with her. Then she got serious. "Yes, it probably is one of them, and some artist or priest made it millennia ago, and it represented some terrible unearthly form of power to him."

"And to you?" I asked.

"It's anthropology to me, Dad," she said, "and I think anything people make is interesting." She brushed it carefully and put it back up. "Bet a museum would like it."

She combed the hills for more artifacts, but, aside from a few questionable chunks, didn't come up with anything else. "Maybe when those ancients destroyed the monster, they destroyed all the images too," she'd say with comical seriousness. But I still didn't like the thing; I wished she had sold it to a museum, and I used to tell her. I complained so much, after all, I had a right—it was my house, that finally she put it away and stuck to regular rocks. Good, I thought.

The years passed by, Massachusetts-style. The winters here are so cold that we just accept them and try to forget them. But the spring, and summers, and the fall ... ah, the golden autumn ... we treasure them. Like rich, ripe honey, to savor and sip at. Oh, my lost children, my Susan, whose hand I never took, we'd sip. And sit and watch that old road going past, winding itself into nothing somewhere in the green, gray hills; and that road, itself just like the seasons, sometimes warm, dappled with sunlight, and in worse times cold and strange, with its distant end hidden in shrouds of mist, winding on and on where we couldn't see, and maybe into Hell itself. Evan finally went out on it alone, and where is he now?

I hate the road. I hate its gullies and its pits. I hate it when the sun is bright on it and it pretends to be friendly and inviting. I hate it when it's ugly and leads to Death itself in those rocky hills. Yes, to Hell is where it leads, and where it takes anyone who follows it.

Well. The years passed, and maybe Alice got bored here. She and Evan didn't have any children; they should have, because she wasn't the kind to like staying alone here all the time, but they didn't. She didn't complain, but I guess she ran out of new geology to find, and finally she started driving over to Arkham, to the University. She would bring along her rocks and her drawings, and discuss them with the professors. One day she took along her ancient stone.

"Dad," she said to me, "when they see this, they'll do handsprings. They'll probably name a building after me for such a discovery." She laughed, but when she returned home that night, she looked bothered. Usually she would tell me all about her doings when there was something special, but this time she looked pale and troubled. Evan wasn't the kind to pester his wife, figured anytime she had something on her mind she would tell him in her own good time. Most of us are the same way here. Laconic, you'd call us. But Alice was not just anybody to me, and I asked her. She only shook her head.

"Didn't any of those professors like your monster?" I asked. She only shriveled up a little bit into herself, so I didn't ask any more. I smiled, but she didn't smile back. It was like she didn't see us with her.

After this she went to the University every day. She would take along paper and bring back notes which she would study. And that precious artifact was always with her. She'd ponder over it, and I'd see her making tracings off it, like people do off old tombstones. She would draw these over and over, and even add to the broken endings. It looked like fragments of alphabet-markings around the drawing, and, somehow, what she was adding to them seemed proper.

"Are you learning that chicken-scratch of an alphabet?" I asked. When she looked up at me, I was surprised to see lines around her eyes.

"Yes," she said, so quietly, "there is a language here, and the Library has books which hint at it. This could be a Rosetta Stone of a sort." Then she went back to her tracing and her magnifying glass.

I kept at her. "Alice," I told her, "I think you're in that place too much. Why, I can't even see your eyes for those bags around them. How come you and Evan never go rock-hunting around here any more, and just forget this special study of yours for a while?"

She didn't answer. Truth is, it seemed to me Evan and she didn't talk as much as before, when they did it not with words, which Evan never used too many of anyway, but in all the other ways two young people have. I kept pushing, till finally she just sighed. "Dad ...." And I knew my talk was unwelcome.

So I talked to my son. Evan was my only child. There could have been another, but she didn't live long. She ... well ... Evan was all to me, and we worked the farm together, and knew its problems and its beauty as well. Maybe I took him for granted, and I can see in this useless paper I'm writing I haven't mentioned him much. I don't have to. My son is a fine man, and just what I would want him to be. A father always loves his children, and we were so much alike it was downright easy. Now that he is gone, I have nothing but his picture in my mind, with his quiet face, calm, deliberate, and, because that's how I saw him last, with a darkness across his eyes. The hair falling across his brow, and the eyes withdrawn and no longer the same.

Evan. In those first years I used to bother him why he didn't want to have children; he never had a comment. Later, when I was more insistent, he frowned, and I learned, after he was gone, and I found doctor bills, that they had been seeking medical advice. He never told me though, and so the years seemed barren. Alice only changed the subject when I mentioned it at dinner, and finally I stopped asking. We let things go as they were.

And now she was busy with her hieroglyphics, or whatever they were. When I used that word, she laughed. "The Egyptians were young compared with these." But she was taking to staying overnight in Arkham now, sometimes, busy with her study. When she was home, she would stare up that road into the hills, even wandering up alone now and then. Once Evan offered to go along, but she told him she'd rather be alone. "This time," she apologized, but she still went often-times, to "feel" the place, which is the word she used, to "feel" it. And he didn't offer again.

I must have realized then that whatever warm bond had tied the three of us together up to this time was snapped, and that, in a sad, final way, Alice was lost to us. When a person you love is lost, how can you get her back? You can't demand it, and you can't buy it back, not even with love. My son would stare at her, sometimes coldly, sometimes with quiet longing, but she didn't respond. Maybe a baby might have saved them, at least then.

As it was, Alice kept getting our meals, doing what she had to do about the house, but a housekeeper might have done as much. Her books and paper were more important to her, only it was like an obsession with her. She made a clay model of the stone, but larger, so she could add the letters she had been completing. She didn't show it to us, but she didn't hide it either. That thing which looked like a bloated sun was no sun at all, just a big spherical shape with all manner of legs and arms coming off it, an animal of some sort, but like none I'd ever seen pictured. I remembered those stories told around Dunwich, about monsters, but I never took stock in them. Some horror had existed there, but most likely in the twisted minds of a sick family. Alice's drawing didn't matter to me, but the drift in the family did. I told Evan he should act, say something, maybe take away that stone, or even go away for a time, but he shook his head. He had that kind of love which can't force someone. And yet he did try, only it didn't help.

It was one night, early summer, I think. I was sitting at this table, just like now. I even think I can hear it still, that sudden voice outside, where there was only crickets and birds. I looked out the window and I saw Alice, reading something out loud, in a sing-song way, like a chant. She was standing in the dim twilight, holding her clay model high in front of her, stumbling over strange words she was trying to get out. She would try again and again, and apparently couldn't get the hang of it. She would stop and stare at that thing. I realized Evan was near me, watching her through the screen door, and breathing hard. When she gave up and flopped back on her haunches, he went upstairs. But she tried again the next night, louder, and almost hysterical-sounding. Then Evan came running out, slamming the door. I heard them shouting.

In a way, I was glad. At last he was taking a hand. I looked out at them. He had the stone in his hands, or that clay model, anyway, and he was holding it like he was going to smash it. She began fighting with him for it, actually scratching at him, and screaming all the while, and finally he shoved her back. They glared at each other for a long minute, and she said something I couldn't hear. He looked terrible just then, full of anguish and fear and even hate, but he calmed down, and at last handed the thing to her. She wouldn't move, just stood there, breathless, and at last he put it on the ground. He walked slowly away, his shirt in tatters, and his arms streaked with blood. He came back into the house and walked past me without a word. I watched him go up, and then looked back at Alice. I could see her face, all distraught, staring at her stone, then back at the house. I thought I could see tears on her face. Suddenly she picked up a large rock, and held it high over the stone, but then, with a jerk, she threw it away, and just crumbled down over it. I could hear her sobbing. I still watched. At last she pulled herself up, and brought the stone back into the house. She didn't say anything to me, just put it into the carton she saved for it, and went upstairs.

Here I am, writing all this down, and wondering why I didn't smash it myself. But why? It was only a stone, and it meant so much to her. What right did I have to tell her what I thought best? She could have made another anyway; by now she knew every detail by heart.

After this, Alice would go to Arkham for days at a time. She'd call and just say she couldn't get back yet, and she'd wait a minute, and say goodbye. I tried to get Evan to go up to her once when she called and said she'd be gone a week, because she had to go to the library up at Harvard, as if Miskatonic wasn't big enough! He didn't answer.

I suppose Evan is more Yankee than I am, but then, he had never been a father, to break your heart over a young one's pain. I've been going on here, but I never had too much to say either, out loud. If I had to say it, I'd write it, and later on burn the paper. Maybe I'll burn this too. Or I'll keep it, because I couldn't do it again, and it's my only record of my son who's gone, and my Alice and the two of them, hand in hand. Oh Alice, all that blood! ... But that's later .... That's how it went on for a few months, until one night she called, the last such call, and after midnight, and she was crying and pleading and almost incoherent. She sounded terrified, and I thought she was begging us to help her, but it was hard to make out a word.

Evan was downstairs, on the other line, saying nothing. At last he asked, and you were too cold, Evan!, did she want him to pick her up. She seemed to calm down, and at least we could understand her, but her voice got cold too. No, she said, she'd be home next day. She hung up, but next morning she was home. It was a dark day, raining in gusts. She came in without a word, her notebooks wet like she didn't care about them. She looked at Evan for a minute, and I could see him working to speak, but she sloshed upstairs in her wet things.

At dinner, which I made, she sat without eating, while outside the rain poured down, and flashes of lightning lit up the woods and the road. After a while, very softly, Evan asked her to eat, but she didn't look at him. He got up and went upstairs. Then she got up, very slowly, and, abruptly, without putting on a coat or saying a word, ran out of the house. The door hung open behind her, the rain gusting in, and I ran to the closet and grabbed for her coat and mine. I put mine on and rushed out, calling her name, but I couldn't see anything out there.

There was a crack of lightning and I saw her running, arms out-stretched, face into the rain, chanting again. The thin sound of her voice drifted back through the rain, and I saw her fall over an old stump near the road. I fell myself, and when I got up I could see her in the lightning flash, tearing at her clothes and her hair and twisting herself in agony on the ground, screaming. I heard Evan shout her name and he came running past me, picked her up and carried her back into the house. She wasn't screaming any more. I could see her eyes were closed, but her lips were moving. He put her down on their bed, rain-soaked and all, and stroked her head and held her until she was quiet and sleeping. Later he changed and cleaned her and was at her side all night watching her.

The next two weeks she just lay there, sometimes reviving, but not knowing where she was. Sometimes she would chant that strange language. I've tried to catch it and write it, Lord knows some of those sounds are still in my head, but I can't. All guttural sounds, hard g's, and trilling r's and l's. It sounded like a prayer of some sort in a primitive way. I hated it, like I hate all prayer now. I see I wrote "Lord knows" back there. Maybe if I live long enough I'll forgive God for all he's created, but I don't know.

At last I could see she was recovering, for she recognized me. Her hands fluttered and I tried to take them, but she pulled back and looked at her fingers with fear, even loathing. Evan came in, saw her look of recognition and rushed to her. He took her hands into his and would not free them until at last she relaxed and held him tightly.

She would have no doctor, and since we could see she was recovering nicely, we let her have her way. She took on color, and regained weight. She was soon moving about and smiling, Alice again! I looked at her rounding belly and wondered, and then Evan and I smiled to each other. Best of all, she never seemed to want to look at the stone or her notes, and, of course, we never mentioned that night she ran out into the rain.

This story is almost run. I used to love the spring, the growing things, the new insect life, the birds. Whippoorwills are strong here, always have been. I could hear their twittering all the time. Spring is a beginning to Life, but it was an end here. Sometimes I think Life is a process of losing everything you love, until nothing is left. Alice had been recovering so well that it hurt when she grew quiet again. And it hurt even more when she lugged out that familiar carton and took out that stone. I happened to come into the room, and I recall I saw her looking at it with some kind of fear and even apprehension. She took the stone and went out to Evan in the field.

He smiled to see her, but I could see it become a frown when he saw the stone. I saw her gesticulating to him, pointing to the stone and then to herself. He looked astonished, then angry, and turned away and then back, shaking his head violently. Whatever it was, she kept arguing, pounding the stone with her hand, and he just kept shaking his head. I saw him take a couple of deep breaths and then smile to her as to a child, but she stubbornly pointed to the stone and to herself and finally he flung his hoe down in anger and looked away from her. When she came round him, he waved his head and hands, refusing something.

She came in and sat opposite me, pale and shaking. "Alice," I said, and started to go to her, but she pushed me firmly back.

"Dad, let me talk," she said, and I nodded. She was really so pretty. "You know I love you," she continued, "and you know you love me. What I have to say isn't easy, and it's not so good either. It's my fault. I thought I just wanted to know, to learn some prehistory no one ever knew, but I was wrong." Suddenly she was crying, her words choking out between sobbing that broke me up. "I wasn't learning anything—I was being manipulated! Now I'm pregnant! I know you know it— don't talk, please, you must listen—Evan won't! It's not Evan's, oh God, I wish it was, how we wanted it! But it's not—." Her voice was a whisper. "It's theirs, I know it like I'm sitting here, theirs."

Now she was crying uncontrollably. I took her in my arms and rocked her, and talked to her, of how women get upset at such times, and her having been so sick, and how happy Evan and I were now. But she pulled free, and just went on the same, only worse.

"Dad, you have to believe me." She pointed to her round belly. "This, it isn't human. It's no man's at all …. There are other beings out there, waiting, with terrible power. They used me, used me! I'm afraid of what I'm carrying, and I can't get rid of it." She rose and faced away. "I tried, and I couldn't. And no doctor could either." She faced me again. "They won't let him! But it mustn't live, such a contamination. There's only one way. You must … kill me." And she sat, holding her face in her hands, but not crying any more. She looked up and out the door at Evan, somberly hoeing. Then she went upstairs.

Pregnancy hysteria. I'd heard tell of it. It's living here has done it to her, those old, terrible stories, like Lavinia Whateley, who was, after all, some distant relation to Alice, and who, they said, birthed unbe- lievable things. And poor Alice, hearing all of it, tired and weak, and not being a kid anymore, scared by pregnancy. How could I, an old

man, talk her out of such a fear? Susan had her fears, too, but they were
ordinary. Only time, maybe, could help.

It didn't. The months passed, and she only got worse, always after
us, Evan, me, to kill her. Sometimes she laughed at us. She went to the
closet where Evan kept his rifle, and took it out. She would hold it out
to him or to me, and one night she would cry, and the next she would
laugh. Even if Evan hid the gun, she would find it, and as she got
bigger, she laughed more than she pleaded. Once she even decorated
the gun with ribbons, and knotted them until they hung down like
misshapen arms and legs, and her eyes glittered insanely like they say
Lavinia's did, wandering in her fields. We tried bringing in a doctor,
and once one of those professors from the college, but it was useless.
She'd lock her door and refuse to see them. I was very worried. Her
time was close, and I knew we'd have to protect her somehow, but when
the time came, I wasn't ready.

She came down, one summer day, a bright one, the birds singing
like mad. She had that stone clutched to her breast, and her face was
glowing, and her hair streamed wild. She was singing the chants again,
and she picked up the rifle like a maypole and waddled out with it.
Her face was wet with perspiration, and I started right out after her.
She shouted Evan's name and waved the rifle at him. He got angry, or
maybe scared for her, and ran over and took the gun away. He tried to
take the stone away too, but she ran off with it.

Suddenly she crouched over in pain. "It's time!" she screamed, and
wobbled onto the road. Then she held up that stone and began her
singing again. Her chant got wilder, all those sounds pouring out, and
her body reeling in spasms. She kept repeating a name, and it's still
burned like a cancer in my mind: "Yog-Sothoth! Yog-Sothoth! The
father, he's coming! You wouldn't listen—," and she held up the
stone—"Yog-Sothoth! Take it, it's yours!"

Evan shouted and ran over to her, grabbing for her, but she looked
crazily at him and smashed the stone against his arm. And in that daze
of sun and the deafening sound of the whippoorwills, I heard the gun
go off, and then I couldn't hear anything, except that her singing had
stopped all of a sudden, in a sort of gurgle. She was standing there, her
hands across her belly, and blood was pouring out between her fingers,
on to her arms, her legs.

She crumpled right there. Evan was trying to pick her up, and I ran
over to help, but there was nothing to do. It was like her whole stomach
was torn apart, and I think I must have gone crazy, too, because there
in the blood and torn flesh I thought I could see something there should

never be, something dark and feebly squirming, something, God help me, I thought, like the thing on the stone.

Evan threw his jacket over her, and just knelt there holding her hand. "Oh, Evan," she whispered, "it was the only way ... it had to be .... Oh, Evan ...." After a while, she stopped moving, and her body was still. Evan pulled the jacket over her head, and the sun beat down, and even the birds were quiet.

I can see it like a photograph, Evan, kneeling over her still body, not moving, just kneeling there, in that sun, and not a sound.

We buried her in the field, near my daughter's grave, near my wife's. Evan didn't say a word, but later, as I sat at the table, he put his arms around me. I took his hands and held them until he gently pulled free. Then he picked up his rifle, and walked off down that road. I don't know where he went, and I have heard nothing more from him. He was my only son, and now he's gone.

I've been alone since, just thinking about it all, remembering the blood, and what I thought I saw, and those stories about the Whateleys. Oftentimes, I wish Evan had married a local girl, dull maybe, and she mightn't have been too curious, but she wouldn't have asked for much. Certainly not more than he could have given her. And it would have been enough.

Wilum Hopfrog Pugmire, like Nyarlathotep (of whom he is perhaps an avatar), wears many masks. One of his past identities was as a Mormon missionary in Ireland. This ministry he exited in grand style. Mormon missionaries go house to house, in teams of two, to share the secrets of that long-hidden tome of heresy, The Book of Mormon. As Wilum's partner was explaining how the leprechauns were actually the Lost Tribes of Israel (or something like that), unbeknownst to him, behind him Wilum would flash a set of plastic vampire fangs at their host, who would of course suddenly slam the door! One wonders how long it took Wilum's frustrated partner to catch on!

Already a connoisseur of weird fiction (and of HPL in particular), Wilum eventually made his way to the gay punk scene in Seattle, where he built a local reputation as an author, rock critic, and Boy George look-alike (he looks more like the Boy than George does!). He has edited and published a remarkable zine called Punk Lust for many years now. In the mid-eighties Wilum also edited a Cryptic Publications magazine called Tales of Lovecraftian Horror, which insisted on Lovecraftian ambiance and style but strictly forbade any mention of the Cthulhu Mythos!

His stories have appeared in several anthologies including Cutting Edge and Year's Best Horror. The present tale was one which, read in manuscript, gave me the idea nearly ten years ago to compile the collection you are reading now. Pugmire has written a collection of stories related to "The Tree-House", Tales from Sesqua Valley.

The Tree-House

by W. H. Pugmire and Robert M. Price

John Whateley knelt in the semi-dark attic room that had been his father's study. A thrill of illicit excitement tingled his nerves as he shone his flashlight over the large cardboard box that sat before him. The box contained the journals of his father, Ebenezer Whateley, from the 1920's, the written accounts of a young man's life. His father had planned to destroy them but found it impossible to do so. Although he did not want these records of his life to exist after his death, their destruction seemed almost an invitation to death, as though saying, "I have destroyed the records of my days on earth, now come smother my existence with your unyielding embrace."

Death caught the old man suddenly. He was now nothing but a memory and a putrescent corpse that festered underneath graveyard dirt. John Whateley shivered; the power to his father's house had been turned off, depriving him of warmth or electric light. No matter: What he sought was now before him. He searched through the box and found the journal dated 1928. That year had intrigued John Whateley all his young life. As a child he'd had the odd habit of climbing to the top of Sentinel Hill on certain nights, of sleeping on the great altar stone and dreaming curious dreams. Dreams in which he saw oddly formed shadows. Dreams wherein he heard the muted chants of alien words, words he could not quite remember. And when he was found, and when he spoke of these visions to his kith and kin, he saw faces twisted with horrible expressions; and, always, he heard whispered the date nineteen-twenty-eight.

On the occasions when he tried to learn something of what occurred in Dunwich on that date, he would become exasperated because of his failure. His relatives would pale and order him to be silent. Once he tried to discuss these matters with an ancient crone who belonged to the so-called decayed branch of the Whateleys; but she would merely smile and shake her head. It was from her that he learned of certain books, old books which spoke of fabulous legends. He read her books as best he might, learning bits and pieces of foreign tongues where he could. Once he had taken the trip into Arkham, the university town, and asked to see the most abhorred of the old books. He was allowed, somewhat to his surprise, though a librarian looked on the whole time. As he reverently turned random pages, some of the words seemed familiar, but he was not sure where he had encountered them. And the Latin was to him a blank wall. Soon after, he had journeyed outside the region, to seek the assistance of a Catholic priest to teach him Latin. But John had been naive; barely into the lessons, he had let slip the reason for his interest, and the priest promptly ejected him.

He felt like a man standing in a field in which a treasure had been buried, but possessing no map. He was close to it, very close, but access was barred. So despite his studies, he never learned very much about his ancestral past and the incidents of 1928.

Now he would learn everything.

Old Ebenezer's handwriting was easy to read, and thus he scanned through the journal quickly. Many of the entries for January and February concerned the seaport town of Innsmouth, for which his father had a strong dislike. Mentions were made of the nefarious rumors concerning certain inhabitants of the town, and in February an entry recorded how officials from the federal government made an astounding number of arrests, how whole families were taken away and never heard from again.

The other topic of especial interest was his father's cousin, Wilbur Whateley. It struck John oddly, the way his father wrote of this mysterious cousin. The writing seemed guarded, the words few and carefully chosen, as though to say or hint too much would be a dangerous thing. One entry was of more than usual length:

> I've just learned that Nathan Vreeland had been seeing Wilbur! And again since the disappearance of Lavinia. Damn the fool! I've confronted him about this, and he seemed amazed that people knew of his meetings. He won't tell me much, because—he says—he doesn't know very much. He says that Wilbur sought him out because of Nathan's reputation as a teacher. I guess that Nathan had been reading portions of dangerous books with Wilbur. God, the fool! His mania for occult study blinds him to other things, things that even a dullard like myself can sense. There's nothing I can do; when Nathan speaks of books he has seen in Wilbur's library, especially the English version of the damned N_____, his eyes glow with lust. He won't see reason. He scoffs at the rumors concerning Wilbur and Sentinel Hill.
>
> I'm confused and don't rightly know what to do. People are becoming ugly in regards to Wilbur. I think that more than a few would be glad enough to see him dead. I don't know how much of that I can believe. I've seen, of course, the fires on Sentinel Hill, and I've felt the tremors and heard the rumblings. Nathan won't listen to reason, and we had quite a heated, bitter argument last time I saw him. I feel helpless.

Here it is at last, thought John. Here are names to be researched, and leads to be investigated. Oh, the stirrings of his soul as he read how another Whateley had felt the same attraction to Sentinel Hill. And he knew what the letter N must stand for. As if praying, as perhaps he was, he whispered the name softly: "*Necronomicon.*" The very sound of it had a strange allure. He felt sure that he was on the correct path this time. Somewhere this English version of the book must still exist! With these thoughts whirling in his mind, he read on. The story that unfolded thrilled him with uncanny wonder, almost like what an amnesiac must feel upon the return of lost memory, lost identity.

The enigmatic Vreeland gradually became more than a name. It developed that he had moved to Dunwich years before to keep the hamlet's slovenly one-room school. As the number of students steadily dwindled, Vreeland had begun to supplement his income through private tutoring, willing to travel almost any distance over the rough roads of the region to meet with the woefully backward students. He had been engaged to tutor the much-rumored Wilbur, a strange lad who was at the same time both advanced beyond his years and shockingly ignorant of the most basic knowledge. From various oblique references John began to surmise that Vreeland's calls upon the Whateley household did not decrease even when Wilbur and his grandfather were occupied elsewhere most of the time. Had Vreeland been tutoring the lonely Lavinia, Wilbur's mother? Or had something else been going on between them? But then Lavinia had disappeared one day. Rumor laid this to Wilbur's charge, but John's father had his own suspicions that the older Whateley had discovered Lavinia's true relation with Vreeland and secretly sent her away.

Even this did not put an end to Vreeland's association with the Whateley menfolk, for young Wilbur seemed to have passed some sort of threshold and was ready to expand his home education. Vreeland knew well that most of the youngster's training came from his grandfather's peculiar erudition, but the old man could teach no more than he himself knew. So Vreeland's remedial efforts were again required. Finally Vreeland had himself been initiated into grandfather Whateley's queer curriculum. He had to be at least cursorily acquainted with Wilbur's studies in order to know how to assist him in the basic skills required. This marked the beginning of Vreeland's own obsession with occult lore, into which he began to venture like an explorer in a strange, new country.

When the journal recorded the news of Wilbur Whateley's violent death, John felt a stab of pain inside his soul. He had formed a subconscious link with Wilbur. Damn his father's prudential reticence! How had Wilbur died? And why? Had he at last been arraigned by the authorities for his mother's death?

Suddenly he found, folded between two of the journal's pages, a letter addressed to his father. The flashlight's glow was beginning to dim, and he held the letter near to his eyes, reading it carefully.

Dear Eb,

I know you will not forgive me for the part I played in the horrible events that have taken place. I will not try and excuse my mad behavior. I am ashamed of it, and yet I cannot doubt that in the same circumstances I would do the same again. I will defend nothing and try only to explain certain things.

You told me, during our final, most bitter argument, that when it came to my obsession with arcane books, I lost sight of all else, and this is quite true. I have discovered things, Eb, and this wisdom engenders a thirst for further knowledge. I do more than study these old books. But I do not want to write of this, particularly not now, while the town is in such a state.

If I had realized more clearly who, or rather, who your cousin was, I would never have assisted him, but how was I to have known? Who

in his right mind could have suspected? Despite our conceits, even
you and I still know very little, and the authorities, knowing absolutely nothing of these matters, and eager to keep it that way, are
prone to frown on anyone who is at all interested in Wilbur
Whateley. And I have better reason than most not to want to attract
attention. You spoke of certain visitors from Miskatonic who questioned you concerning certain rare books that belonged to your
cousin. You were under the impression that the books in question
had been misplaced and not yet found. (What I am telling you now
I write hoping that you will destroy this letter after having read it.)
When the shocking news of Wilbur's death came to me by 'phone
from various men I know in Arkham, I acted quickly. There were
three books of vital interest to me sitting on the crude, unvarnished
shelves in the old shed where I met with Wilbur to tutor him in basic reading. Wilbur's grandfather had told me enough that I recognized their unique value, but he had never trusted me to read any of
them for myself. Now I saw my chance.

My desire that those books should not be destroyed or (which is the
same) placed under lock and key at Miskatonic was like some intense fever. And so, in the dead of night, I stole to the farmhouse
and broke into the shed, confiscating the precious tomes. One of
them was Dee's imperfect translation. I acted blindly, with little
sense. You may judge me slightly insane, but who would not have
been after debating arcane blasphemies with Wilbur Whateley?
Over many months of tutoring, absorbed in the work, I had learned
to ignore the stench that oozed from above, the slitherings and fum-
blings and moanings from an unseen room. On that terrible night,
as I invaded the tenantless shed in quest of the books, the sourceless
sounds and the mephitic reek seemed magnified a hundredfold, as if
whatever had kept them in check before had now been taken away
(Second Thessalonians chapter 2, verses 6 through 9). Whatever was
hidden there must have been the thing that soon ravaged the countryside. How little I then understood the magnitude of the risk I
had taken that night! Needless to say, I lingered no longer than absolutely necessary.

Nor will I linger further in this town. I am leaving Dunwich. Some
of your relations may have told you of the Sesqua Valley, out West,
to which they are preparing to journey. I am going with them.
Come with us, Ebenezer. Dunwich is a dead town. Your name marks
you, you must realize that. I need not remind you of what occurred
earlier this year at Innsmouth, of certain families who vanished because their name was Marsh, because of a look with which they had
been tainted. I believe that something of that sort may happen here,
with Whateleys. I have myself had visitors from the government, as
have many others; their furtive questions concerning your family is
what moves me to fear for you and yours. We are young, you and I.

Our lives lie ahead, and they can be good, long lives. Please consider what I have said, and I beg you to destroy this letter immediately.

Ever your faithful friend, Nathan

John Whateley folded the letter thoughtfully. He had indeed found that which he sought. No longer would he suffer familial suspicion or scorn; he would leave Dunwich for the far-off Sesqua Valley. Surely he would find the answers to all his questions with the help of his father's "faithful friend."

II.

Nathan Vreeland frowned at the man who stood before him. He could see in John Whateley's thin nose and dark eyes a semblance of a long-lost friend. But he saw something more in those dark, moody eyes. He saw a longing and a restlessness he had seen too often, years ago, in his mirror. Those eyes gazed at him now, intently, with keen anticipation.

"I was sorry to hear of your father's death, John. He was a good friend in my younger years. We lost contact after I left Dunwich. I confess that I am dismayed to learn that he did not destroy certain letters that I had written; although, from what you say, he may have intended to before his death. He seemed a troubled man after I left."

"Why are you putting me off?" Whateley's irritated voice sounded loud in the small room. "You know from my letter why I am here."

Vreeland's eyes narrowed with annoyance. "I know well enough," he replied in a voice choked with conflicting emotions. He resented the youth's insolence, and yet he felt keenly how much like his own younger self John Whateley was. Vreeland felt almost tangibly the irony that he should wind up playing the role of Ebenezer Whateley, who had once tried futilely to warn Vreeland himself away from the same spiritual dangers. "Your letter quite ... distressed me. You speak of feelings that are familiar to me. *Too* familiar! And yet, in spite of your studies, you seem to have learned precious little. I think your interests are too self-centered to do either of us any good."

"I've been trying to understand these things on my own, in the face of hostility from my family. Things have been kept from me. I feel this hunger inside, and it drives me—"

"That's precisely why they're keeping things from you! The Whateley family has endured one tragedy after another because of that thirst for forbidden secrets. It runs like a congenital disease through the whole family line. Oh, it remains dormant in some—like your father, though I sometimes think he must have been fighting down his own instincts when he opposed my researches so vehemently. But he was right, after all. You are dealing with forces you do not understand. You are being manipulated by things you will never comprehend. Now, in the last years of life, I am only beginning to realize their significance. We fool ourselves into thinking we seek wisdom, when in fact we are puppets in the claws of emotionless creatures who care nothing for us. 1928 was a long time ago, and yet the events haunt me still. And even that wasn't enough to convince me. I've made mistakes since then, terrible mistakes. My greed for knowledge blinds me still. And I am not the only victim. Your visits to Sentinel Hill, that mountain's lure for you—by God, the forces merely sleep, and even in slumber they rule over us, ever-waiting, ever-powerful. We seek their wisdom, but they never satisfy our need. Your own descriptions of the dreams you experienced are so vague—"

"Because I don't remember them clearly. Damn it, that's why I'm here! With your help, with the help of that copy of Dee you stole from my family, I will have the wisdom I crave. You offered your help to a Whateley in the past. Why do you hesitate now?"

"Do you really have to ask? Because of past mistakes! What is it you think happened in 1928? It was bad enough, but nothing compared to what *might* have happened! What in heaven's name are you asking me to do? Go with you to Sentinel Hill and call the frightful Name?" The old man's eyes were wild with unaccustomed emotion. His face was reddening, his breath coming in short gasps. His hands began to shake. He took hold of himself, knowing this was no good for his heart. In a moment he spoke calmly. "Do you really know *anything* of these matters, young man? Or are you merely an impatient child? I think you are like the foolish child who plays with his father's gun, thinking it a shiny toy."

"That's *enough!*" John Whateley yelled, his voice full of wounded anger. "You're just like the others, old fool. You know things I have every right to know! It's my birthright! You stole this knowledge, and now you hold back! You make excuses—"

Vreeland pointed a gnarled finger at his unwelcome visitor. "I take precautions!"

"Then at least tell me where *she* is! If she's still alive, that is. You can't deny me that!"

A new wave of pain crossed the lined face, causing it to assume familiar, if tortured, contours. A tear escaped his eye, but he laughed, too, in a crooked way. "Yes, she lives. But she is quite mad, mad as a hatter. She didn't use to be. People said she was, simply because she knew things the others had only heard about. But now her mind is gone. And ... yes, I believe I'll tell you why. You say the Dee volume ought to be back in the hands of the Whateleys? It *is*, young John, it *is*. I'm only trying to prevent what happened to her happening to you, too!"

John Whateley's colorless eyes widened. "You mean *she* has it? Why the hell didn't you *tell* me?"

"I just *did*, you idiot! *Go* to her if you must! What happens won't be *my* fault! You'll have brought it on your own head. To hell with you!"

Vreeland breathed a sigh of relief, though a shallow one, as his intruder, a living piece of his own past which had come back to haunt him, left in haste, repeating to himself the directions the older man had given him. Vreeland reached for his amber-colored bottle of pills. Life for him had long since become a labor, almost more of an ailment than the heart malady that threatened to put an end to it.

As he sank back helplessly into his threadbare easy chair, he was not aware of the face that watched him from the grimed window, a face which had witnessed the heated exchange, a face set in a grimace of determination and cunning.

III.

It was late afternoon. The sun sat low, filling the valley with softened light. Looking around him, John Whateley admired the dreaming beauty of Sesqua Valley. It seemed an enchanted place. The refreshing wind smelled of forest scents, and the quiet gave him peace of mind, a sensation he hadn't felt in many years. He closed his eyes momentarily and took a deep breath. Looking about him again, he caught sight of a nearby mountain over which a pale mist was forming. The mountain's double peak almost resembled jagged wings folded on the back of a crouching daemon. Its white stone shone in the soft light. John Whateley looked at the mountain for a long while and began to feel a familiar stirring in his soul, the same sort of thing he always experienced when approaching Sentinel Hill in Dunwich. It was almost as if Sentinel Hill had followed him out here to the Pacific coast. That was of course nonsense, John knew, but he could not help feeling as if the mountain were calling to him, flaunting the prospect of supernal wonders to be gained.

Walking casually, he took in the sights of the small town. It was in most ways little different from the many he had seen in his long trip hitchhiking across the country. But one house caught his keen attention. It stood upon a grassy knoll, a huge and ancient mansion such as one

might find in New England. The boarded windows bespoke abandonment, although it had evidently been the home of a wealthy family in
better days. Why had it been allowed to fall into such disrepair? At
one side stood a grove of crooked trees. One of them, he couldn't quite
be sure it was an oak, had been allowed to grow up so close that its
trunk had actually damaged a portion of the antique residence.

He approached the knoll, suddenly realizing he had found his
destination. This must be the house Vreeland had directed him to. Was
it a trick? Obviously no one had lived here in a very long time. But
somehow it felt right nonetheless. The air felt different somehow, like
the rarefied atmosphere atop a tall elevation. Whateley felt a momentary dizziness, and for a second his mind seemed to go blank. It was
quite peculiar. But didn't this, too, remind him of feelings he occasionally experienced when he sat on the great altar stone on Sentinel Hill?
He tried to remember, but his mind seemed disjointed.

As he came nearer the knoll, he saw that a tree-house had been built
on the sturdy branches of the nearest tree. A ladder lay on the grass
next to the tree. On an impulse, John Whateley lifted the ladder and
propped it against the tree trunk's diseased, pebble-textured bark. The
structure looked firm enough. He rapidly ascended the uneven rungs,
then put a cautious foot onto the floor of its one large room. His other
foot found the floor and he stood within.

The place was mostly veiled in shadows, though they seemed darker
than the encroaching dusk should have made them. As his eyes
adjusted he could make out more and more detail. Looking about him,
he smiled at the humble signs of habitation. There was a low table and
a milk crate which served as a chair. In one corner were glass jars filled
with different kinds of powder. From the ceiling, hanging on a length
of strong twine, swung the skeleton of what looked to be a frog, but as he
scrutinized the object he thought the skull was weirdly misshapen.

A battered wooden bookcase was stuffed with disparate volumes.
He thought he recognized a series of dog-eared popular novels, including several of the breezy romances of Robert W. Chambers. Many
others had no titles on their spines, seeming to be privately printed
and crudely bound. But others had titles he recognized in an instant,
though he had never even seen them, much less read them, as they were
written in languages he did not know. These included the Latin *Malleus
Maleficarum* and Remegius' *Daemonolatry*. But many others—the *Mne-
mabic Fragments*, *The Song of Yste*, Yergler's *Chronicle of Nath*, the Marquis
LeMode's *Dark Visions*, the *Black Sutra* of U Pao—all these were
completely new to him. One volume was much larger, and older-look-

ing, than the rest. Its binding had been reinforced with tape many times, and it appeared to lack a back cover. It had been slipped lengthwise on top of a row of other books, being too tall to stand upright alongside them.

He stopped suddenly, his mind whirling: What were these books doing in a tree-house that was apparently the play area of some child? The answer came in the slight, lean form of a boy who had silently climbed the ladder and who now gazed at John Whateley with questioning, yet somehow knowing, eyes.

"Who are you?" the boy asked.

"I'm a stranger," John Whateley replied, then wondered at the oddness of his answer. The boy climbed all the way into the tree-house, and Whateley saw that he was tall as well as lean. The boy was dressed in black, his clothes hanging on him as they would on the thin stick-form of a scarecrow. His shock of wild black hair looked as though it had never once been brushed.

"We don't get many strangers here," said the boy, seeming to phrase his words with hidden intent. "We don't like being *bothered* by outsiders."

John Whateley said nothing, not wanting to betray the defensiveness he felt.

"Looking at the books?"

"Yes. Yes, I was. I must say you've got odd tastes for someone your age."

"I'm …." The boy hesitated, then continued in a strange tone redolent of both offense and amusement. "I'm old enough to study these, and I understand them pretty well, I think. Old Mr. Vreeland has been helping me study them for quite some time."

The mention of Vreeland's name rattled John Whateley. So the traitorous old bastard was still in the business of teaching his secrets, just not to *him*! He must return to Vreeland and confront him. This time he would not be denied. All else momentarily forgotten, he turned to leave.

"Don' t go." The tall, black-clad youth spoke in a quiet voice. John Whateley did not like that voice, or the eyes that stared at him. "Don't go. I'm sorry; I'm not being fair with you. I know why you're here. Maybe I can answer some of your questions. And, yes, you're in the right place." A sly grin played on the boy's lips. Feeling very wary now, still John could not very well turn down a promise of information. Every other channel seemed to have been closed off.

"What's your name?" he asked suspiciously.

"You may possibly know the name: *Whateley*. I'm called Didymus Whateley."

At this news, John began to grow numb. He leaned against the rough wall of the clapboard structure for support. Amid his total disorientation, one seemingly irrelevant observation quietly obtruded. There was something about the shape of the boy's head, he suddenly noticed, the wide forehead and small ears, that puzzled him. He looked at the misshapen skull of the skeletal frog, then again at the mysterious Didymus, and he fancied there was a similarity in form.

"You see, I live here, with ... *her*." With this he pointed further into the shadows of the interior of the surprisingly capacious tree-house. Reluctantly, John turned his eyes in the direction indicated.

There sat, or lay, the shapeless white bulk of her who once fancied herself Queen Mother. No clothes encompassed the obese folds of her translucent flesh. Perhaps she had once worn the tatters of rotten gauze on which she now lay, strewn with her own filth. Every few seconds her corpulent mass quivered in rhythm with some interior tick or cramp. Only wisps of her frazzled hair, almost like old corn silk, remained clinging tenuously to her scabbed and mottled scalp. Yet for the apparent decrepitude, the pink eyes of Lavinia Whateley glowed with a feverish alertness. With these she looked unwaveringly at her newly arrived kinsman. "Ye've come to answer th' Call, hev ye, young Johnny?" The voice seemed to echo strangely, as if coming from a farther distance.

"Why, why ... *yes*, Mother Whateley! I *have*! The old man Vreeland wants to stand in my way, though I guess he knows it's too late now." John's voice, despite his intimidation, grew stronger and clearer as he began to realize that here, for the first time, another had recognized his true destiny, his destined greatness. Then he began to venture much.

"Mother Whateley, everyone else believed you dead. Murdered by Cousin Wilbur. But I knew better. I read Vreeland's letter to my father, and it wasn't hard to read between the lines, to see that you and he— well, that he stood by you when the others thought your usefulness ended. Is he—," pointing now to the young man in black, "is Didymus here your son, I mean, yours and Vreeland's? I suspected something like that must have happened to explain your sudden disappearance, and Vreeland's following you later."

The voice of Didymus broke in. "He is clever, but cleverly wrong." Turning to his cousin John, he went on. "You know much, but as you yourself surmise, there is ever so much more that you do *not* know. That is why you have come seeking the *Necronomicon*. But tell us, what is it you hope to gain by such knowledge?"

"I think you know," John said defiantly. "Or at least Mother Lavinia seems to know. I am the next in line, the rightful heir to succeed Cousin Wilbur in his task!"

Unimpressed, Didymus Whateley taunted him: "See? I told you you are missing crucial knowledge, poor John."

"So *tell* me, damn you! Don't play games with me!"

"All right, but can't you guess? It is *I* to whom that rank, that destiny, belongs. *Mine* is the mantle of Umr-at-Tawil. I am he, the Mahdi of Yog-Sothoth, the Opener of the Gate!"

John suddenly felt childish, silly, as if arguing with a playmate over who would take what role in a school yard pretend-game. He didn't know what to say next. The first thing that came to mind was an unconnected bit of curiosity: "Uh ... why a tree-house? Why hide *here*, of all places? She deserves better than this—"

"The house is built at the exact point of one of the Gates, a small one that occurs just above ground level. Living in the zone is what keeps Mother Lavinia alive, physically I mean. So we had to be up off the ground, you see."

"But," and here John Whateley stepped toward the threshold, looking below, "then why not a simple two-story structure? Why the hell build a defenseless tree-house, for God's sake?"

"*You* called it tree-house, not me, Cousin Johnny. I wouldn't exactly call it a tree-house because it's not exactly a *tree*—"

"I don't care what you call it. It's a far cry from what she deserves, what *you'd* deserve if you were really entitled to be what you claim. Why not build onto the mansion? No use letting it lie empty!"

"Oh, I can assure you it is far from empty. Tell me, wise one, did you know there are goats that bear a thousand young?"

"Look! I've had enough of your riddles! Why are you joking with me? Show the proper respect!"

Didymus only laughed again. And this time, so did the white mass in the shadows. John Whateley was shaken. "But, look! Then what about 'the Call'? Why did you summon me, if not to take what's rightfully mine?" His voice wavered with the futile halfheartedness of one who seeks to argue with bad news.

"Because we knew you'd be trouble. Vreeland knew your father, and he knew what to expect of his son," said Didymus matter-of-factly.

"And," came the queerly resonant whisper, choked off every few syllables by a phlegmy chuckle that erupted into a cough, "*I know* what to expect of *my* son! Y'see, Didymus here is a might older 'n he looks. I guess yew didn't know. Hell, even Papa didn't know. On that night long ago, I birthed a fine set o' *triplets*, an' now Didymus is all I got left. Ain't that so, boy?"

With this revelation, John Whateley, suddenly having crashed down again to mere mortality, began to inch his way toward the door. Meanwhile, the beloved son fell to his knees and went forward into the shadows, arms extended for a loathsome embrace with that which lay festering in a pool of darkness.

But as John gingerly felt for the first plank step in the evening darkness, something found him instead. With breathtaking speed he felt his feet, his legs, then the rest of him tightly wrapped with intertwining tendrils, sucker-tipped, boneless limbs that were not tree limbs as he had first thought. The house perched upon the Atlas-like trunk only shivered slightly, the ground slightly more, as John's collapsing body whipped like a rag doll into the open maw of the gnarled, living trunk of the shoggoth. At least that is what John Whateley thought it was called, though his knowledge of these matters was, after all, a bit sketchy.

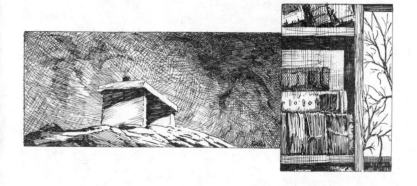

Published in Eldritch Tales as "Windows of the Soul" (not the author's title), C. J. Henderson's "You Can't Take It with You" represented a creative genre hybrid in which the three-lobed burning eye met the hard-boiled private eye. That this surprising combination could work quite well has since been reinforced by the video movie Cast a Deadly Spell, in which a Chandleresque detective named Phil Lovecraft tries to recover a stolen copy of the Necronomicon before a gangster can use it to open the Gates to the Old Ones. Henderson had already made the magic work in this tale of detective versus demon. How can this combination of genres work so well? Maybe because the pessimistic world-weariness of the protagonist-narrator matches so well the cosmic pessimism of Lovecraft's fiction. Both presuppose we are living and acting, perhaps futilely, in an indifferent and inimical universe. Jack Hagee, well known from Henderson's novels and short stories of the character, has a real-life namesake in Henderson's native Carnegie, Pennsylvania.

You Can't Take It with You

by C. J. Henderson

From time to time, I've found myself going back over the past few months, trying to force myself to finally pick and choose, and find at least one story to believe. I've come to realize I'm not going to be able to forget, or even to rationalize, what happened in the Bronx in June, no matter what explanation I choose to accept, or how many bottles I clear away in the morning.

Something killed a woman I cared about. Somehow Lisa was taken and infested and mangled in a way no sane person could ever recount with anything even approaching accuracy. Using words like horrific, or terrifying, or disgusting, to describe the last night I saw her would be as close an analogy as calling Himmler a clever baker.

Of course, maybe it *was* just my imagination. Maybe the strain of what happened to Billy and Francis pushed me over the line and I was only crazy, or maybe the gin had finally done its work and I merely couldn't tell my worlds apart anymore.

Yeah, maybe—but I didn't think so.

It's funny, you'd think that if I can admit Lisa was killed in an inhuman fashion, I could make the jump to who or what it takes to kill in that manner.

I remember the way Billy could never save any money. He'd always spend whatever he had, reminding me, whenever I told him he should save something, that there wasn't any reason to hold onto his cash. He'd always say, "Hey, tomorrow I could get hit by a bus. Listen, if I can have a good time, and make people happy, why should I hang onto every bit that comes my way? After all, you can't take it with you."

God, how I wish everything thought that way.

I remember it all started back in June, back in the hot part of June. I had stayed at my office past my regular hours, waiting for a client who had called earlier. She worked days, and couldn't make it until after 7:00. I'd told her I could cancel my ballet lesson. She hadn't laughed. That worried me. People who need a detective usually at least giggle at bad jokes. It lets you gauge how nervous they are. The more trouble they're in, the more they want to please you, the more they giggle. This girl didn't giggle.

Normally I would have figured that meant someone else was the one in trouble—but something in her voice told me it was the other way around. It didn't matter. I could wait until she came in to tell me what she wanted. It was too hot for second guessing.

She knocked on my door around 8:00, rattling the glass. I told her to come in. Her name was Lisa, Lisa Whateley. She walked through my outer office and sat down in front of my desk, staring at me as if I was what she was scared of. I asked her, "What's the problem?"

She continued to stare at me, her light green eyes growing larger every second. "I need a detective," she said.

"That much is easy," I assured her. "Now comes the tough part. Tell me *why* you need a detective."

"You're Mr. Hagee?"

"Yeah," I growled at her, "Jack Hagee, just like on the door." Heat makes me impatient. "Now, I get the idea something's bothering you. That's okay. That's why we're here. To find out what's bothering you. But if you don't help me, I can't help you. I'm a detective, not a mystic. If you want help, talk; if you want your mind read, go to a swami."

She snapped out of it. Her shoulders squared themselves while her hands rooted through her purse. She said, "I'm sorry; I'm sorry. It's just that I don't know where to begin."

Wondering why everyone seems to learn how to talk to detectives from the movies, I fed her the next line. "Start at the beginning."

She nodded. We must go to the same movies. "I, I think someone is trying to drive me crazy." With a little prodding, I got her to explain. "My family has had trouble with disturbances before. There have been stories, things whispered about us. I moved to New York to get away from them, and it all; for a while, everything seemed better." Her hands finally found what they were looking for. She pulled a photo out of her purse, school graduation size. As she handed it to me, she explained, "I know I'm not making any sense, but this, this might help."

I took the photo, looking it over. It was a picture of Lisa, two, maybe three years old. College. She looked pretty much the same, and yet—something nagged at me. There was something different, something beyond the simple loss of the last baby fat, and a different hair style. True, she looked a lot happier in the photo than she did in my office, but it was something more. I started looking closer.

I turned the small square back and forth, watching the light play on her hair. It didn't help. The layers of chestnut curls looked the same as the shortened, life-size version in front of me. That only left her eyes. The eyes which, if you looked at the photo close enough, you could see were blue. A joyful, summer sky blue. Not at all like the color of the ones she had worn to my office. Those eyes were green, like the color of old money, or the underwebbing of a long dead frog.

I looked into the green eyes, and I knew Lisa was afraid of something she couldn't understand. If I'd had any sense, I'd have been afraid too.

*   *   *

Listening to Lisa's story was like taking a day off to immerse oneself in old pulps. Hitchcock couldn't have orchestrated what was happening to her any better. It had probably started with her family. She had been abused physically as a child. As she had grown older, she'd begun to sense the abuse would become sexual once she was "21 and a woman full", as her father had put it.

She had lied to her parents about her college work schedules, managing to complete the class work load required for graduation in three years instead of four. Waiting out the summer, she passed the months slowly, "lending" those things she wanted to take with her when she left town to a friend. On the first day of the new semester, the friend drove her and her bags to the train station and packed her off to New York.

Things had been all right for her for a few months, but then suddenly a flurry of bad dreams began to plague her. Some were the type that came when she was asleep—others played out before her eyes when she was awake. They were strange, meaningless collages of nightmare, the overpowering images being watery ones—webbed fingers and toes, fins sprouting from human faces, blue eyes hanging in skin-covered bunches like a rubber glove filled with grapes, growing out of the sides of things that belonged on the ocean bottom of some other world.

All in all, Lisa hadn't been getting much sleep.

After the dreams had started their constant roll, however, reality had started lending a hand. Lisa started spotting people, or, as she put it, what she "hoped" were people, watching her. Mostly at home, but also on her way to work, coming out of movies, peeking at her from around corners, out of windows, from wherever an edge or a crack allowed someone to hide and peek and stare.

The thing that kept me listening was the fact I was sure Lisa could tell the difference between those things that were real and those that weren't. Not being an expert, though, I thought maybe her problem could be solved by someone who was. I got my biggest surprise when I asked her if she had considered psychiatric help. She told me she'd already done that, and that her psychiatrist had sent her to me. That one, I told her, needed explaining.

"Actually, I've gone to more than one doctor since I came to the city. At first I was seeing a specialist. She kept telling me that I wasn't crazy, and that all I wanted was attention from someone. Since I wasn't home to get it from my mother, I'd come to her. That was before people had started following me, so I thought, you know, maybe she was right. But later, when things got worse, I—I didn't have the money to go back to her. I had to go to one of the free clinics. That's where I met Dr. Fredriks."

All of a sudden, things got a lot clearer for me. She meant Norman Fredriks, or Billy, as everyone on Eighth Avenue knew him. Billy ran a free mental health clinic in the Village, living off donations and contributions and meals scrounged off an army of friends who didn't want to see him fail. He and I had spent more than a few nights together, pooling our change to try and find a decent meal for both of us in it.

Billy was a good man, I knew he wouldn't have sent Lisa to me without a reason. I asked her if she minded my calling him later. She told me, "The doctor gave me this number. He said if you wanted to call him tonight, not to wait until I was gone."

I took the number. I had a feeling it was wherever his meal ticket was. I was right. A woman who sounded both fairly fat and Italian answered, asking who I was, what I wanted, and if I could hold on. Billy was on the line a few seconds later. "Thought I'd be hearing from you, Jack."

Not wanting his dinner to get cold, I got straight down to the facts. "Is this on the level, Billy?"

"Yeah," he said, "I really think so. I thought so this morning when I told her to call you. I think so even more today."

"Why?"

"Keep a straight face. After the first couple sessions with Lisa, I sent Francis up to her old home town to look things over." Suddenly, Billy got very quiet. "He called me today, Jack. I'm not sure what he's found out; let's just say Massachusetts and the Whateleys have a disturbingly interesting history."

When I asked him to elaborate, he answered, "Not now. Tomorrow. Francis will be back, and we'll be able to go over all the facts together." We said a couple of last pleasantries to each other, and then, just before I could hang up, Billy asked, "Do me a favor, Jack?"

"Like what?"

"Just, well, watch out for Lisa, will you? She seems like a good kid. Maybe we're both getting caught up in something we should know better than to take serious, but, Christ—I, I believe her. I really do."

Looking across my desk at Lisa, sitting there on the other side waiting for me to decide her fate for her, I knew what he meant. I believed her, too. I believed in her dreams, and I believed in her crazy family, and that someone or a bunch of someones were following her and slowly driving her crazy. "Yeah, Billy," I told him. "I'll do my best."

He thanked me, hanging up to go back to his spaghetti. I cradled the phone, looking up at Lisa again. She whispered to me, "Don't turn around, Mr. Hagee. One of those *things* is at your window."

I thought, *Oh goody, just what I wanted to hear.* I love having *things* turn up outside my fourth-story windows that don't have fire escapes. I told her quietly, "When I turn around, you duck behind the desk." She nodded slightly. Bracing myself, I spun around suddenly, catching sight of a blur in the corner of the window. Cursing the shock that held me in my chair for a second, I threw the window the rest of the way open, and risked sticking my head out to scan up and down the building, looking for anything that could explain what we both had seen.

Nothing met my eye—no shadow figures, no human flies or vampires. The only thing outside was hot dark air filled with the scent of garbage. The restaurant on the ground floor had rolled its dumpster out earlier—Tuesday night always meant the trash man—and the summer heat was already helping nature along with its job.

I was sure I had seen a face at the window, but I knew that no matter how someone had reached it, they couldn't have gotten away as fast as they seemed to without leaving a fair sized splatter on the sidewalk.

I was shutting the window to rid us of the invading smells from below when it dawned on me—our pal could have jumped into the dumpster.

Pulling my .38 from its drawer, I grabbed Lisa's hand, dragging her behind me as I headed for the door. "Stick close," I told her. We took the stairs several at a time, hitting the street only a minute after I had shut the window. Leaving her in the doorway where I could watch her, but where she would still be safe, I crossed the sidewalk, approaching the dumpster. I moved forward cautiously, keeping my gun low and hidden, but aimed at its target. Although the sun was still fairly high, it was low enough to allow the buildings around 14th Street to block it. Shadow draped the dumpster, masking it from me, forcing me closer.

For some reason the smell of it was more powerful that night. One can usually avoid the city's odors merely by ignoring them. That night wasn't a usual one. As I closed with the can, the stench of whatever was inside continued to assail me, as if it were a physical force trying to hold me back. If my pal was still inside, he didn't have much of a sense of smell.

Then I saw it, a foot sticking up out of the shadows. Taking a deep breath, I staggered forward through the reeking odor. Thrusting my hand inside at the point where my playmate's chest should have been, I grabbed a handful of jacket and jerked him upward, or at least part of him.

Somehow the force of the jump had split him like a rotting melon— exactly like a rotting melon. As I pulled the jacket upward, his insides oozed out of it, dripping down the front of the can like warm gelatin. I dropped the jacket, backing away from it to where Lisa waited for me. I used the wall to clean my hand, not wanting to befoul my clothes further with whatever it was I had found. Little fish bones scraped away with hair as I rubbed my hand back and forth on the brick. Lisa asked, "What was it? What did you find?"

"We'll talk later," I told her. Taking her arm again, with my clean hand, I pulled her in the direction of the subway. She kept insisting all the way that she wanted to know what was going on. She wasn't the only one.

*   *   *

I took Lisa to my place for the night. I didn't want her going to her home, or to a hotel, or to any place where she would be alone. Not only was I convinced she wasn't going crazy, and that her story was true, I was also sure she didn't know half of what was going on. But then, that was why she'd come to me—to find out.

I showered as soon as we got to my place. Mostly I just lathered and rinsed my arm again and again, brushing free the green and black bits of gelatin which had crusted to it. The running water caused some of it to dissolve; I didn't know how much. I tried not to watch.

After I dried off and redressed, I took the towel and the shirt I'd been wearing and used them to wipe down the tub. Then I threw them down the hall incinerator chute. I wasn't sure why. It just seemed like the best thing to do. Lisa took a shower after I did. With the scene at my office, and the subway ride, and the general mugginess of my un-air conditioned apartment, there was no doubt we both needed one.

After she came out, I told her, "Look, it's almost 10:30; why don't you turn in? I think we should meet with Billy fairly early tomorrow."

"Okay," she told me. "What about you?"

"I'll be fine. I'm used to couches." I am, too. Most nights I never make it home. Between the couch and the hotplate in my office, I sometimes wonder why I bother with an apartment at all. She nodded and went into the bedroom, leaving me to watch the door and the windows, waiting for scratchings and knocks, and all of the other noises one hears when one doesn't want to hear anything.

I sat in my easy chair for a while, watching the windows and the moon outside. It was making a noble try at sending some light down through the smog enshrouding the city. It didn't seem to be making much headway. The way the street lights' illumination reflected from the dirt in the air, it was hard to tell whose light was whose. It didn't matter.

After about an hour, Lisa came out to the front room, complaining she couldn't sleep. I knew the feeling; it was why I hadn't bothered trying in the first place. I had hoped she'd be able to drift off. She couldn't, though. The same restless, despairing whispers that had kept my eyes going from corner to corner had been after her, too. I guess it was worse in the dark. We talked for a while, before she finally ended the charade for us and took my hand and gently led me back to the bedroom, letting me know that she knew what I needed, and that she needed it as much as I did. Human contact can be a despairing thing at times.

We undressed each other and took each other to bed. We held each other for a long time before either of us started moving. It was almost as if we were silently hoping a few minutes of time could blunt the edge of the desperation that had thrown us together in the first place. Fat chance.

Once we started, we were all hands and teeth and movement, rolling each other back and forth with passion but without smiles. We clutched each other desperately, needing the other without really understanding why, wetting each other with summer sweat and tears, refusing to let go.

We made love for a long time, staring at each other, noisily into the night. That way, if there *was* something nearby to hear or to see besides each other, we wouldn't know. Deep down, we both felt something was watching, but we didn't say anything about it. It seemed better that way.

*   *   *

The next day found Lisa and I meeting with Billy and Francis at Billy's clinic. Francis was a perpetual student who eked out a bit of income for himself by doing odd jobs for Billy. His latest assignment had been to go to Lisa's home town and check into her story. It had been his call to Billy the day before that had sent Lisa to me.

Lisa had called her office, reporting in sick. I wasn't sure I wanted her at the meeting, but I was sure I didn't want her out of my sight. Billy straightened out how much he and I and Lisa already knew, and then I told him to give us what he had.

"Here's the scoop," started Francis. "Everyone's heard about Massachusetts. Everyone knows about Salem, and the witches, and all. But, what most people don't seem to know is that Salem isn't the only town in the state with a history. This town, Dunwich, that Lisa's from, and another one close by, Innsmouth, the fairy tales they tell about those places are not to be believed.

"I went to a bigger town which is close by first. Arkham. Now Arkham has a pretty unusual history itself, but I don't want to get too far afield." Francis paused for a moment, his eyes scanning everyone else's. He was taking a mental breath, seeing if he thought he could get his audience to believe something he wasn't sure of himself. Francis wasn't the skittish type, but something about his trip had panicked him and was keeping him that way. He started again with a swallow.

"Strange stuff is supposed to have gone on in both towns back in the '20s. Christ, I know I'm going to sound like the *Enquirer* here, but—well, the stories go that in Dunwich, some kind of invisible monster tore around, wrecking buildings until some doctor found a way to stop it. Innsmouth's claim to fame is a race of fish people ...." Francis read the look on my face. "Yeah, *fish people;* supposedly they're born human and change over the years. Anyway, they, it, *somebody* was practicing some kind of weird rites that stirred up some trouble. The old records say the Navy actually sent a submarine to torpedo a reef off of Innsmouth, and that the F.B.I. destroyed a substantial part of the town's waterfront with dynamite.

"I checked with both the Navy and the F.B.I.; both times I got someone who didn't know anything, but promised to check. I didn't mention monsters or anything. I gave them the old 'article research' bit. Anyway, in both cases, when I got back to my contacts, I got this you're-wrong, we-don't-know-anything, it-never-happened, how-did-you-know, don't-repeat-this, there's-nothing-to-tell bullshit run-around. Now, I'm not saying there really was a monster running around invisibly wrecking houses, or that a bunch of fisherman tried to call the devil down to Massachusetts and got blown apart by the U.S. government, but *something* happened, and no one wants to talk about it."

"What happened to the monster?" I asked. "And to the fish people? Weren't there any bodies?"

"Sure, but they didn't last. When they died, they supposedly just, well, fell apart. Like they were made of jello or something. Nothing left except, like, goo."

No one said anything. Francis flared, "Listen. I'm not making this stuff up. Maybe someone else is, but I'm just ...." I cut him off with the story of the dumpster. Suddenly, nobody had anything to say.

Since I didn't see much purpose in the four of us sitting around looking at each other, I asked, "Okay. Very interesting. But how does this stuff tie in with this case?"

Guiltily not looking at Lisa, he answered, "Well, apparently Ms. Whateley's grandfather on her father's side, Wilbur Whateley, was some kind of key figure. No one liked him much. He made trouble for a lot of people in Dunwich. There was talk of him having kidnaped and killed children who were never found, but nothing was ever proved. But, ah ...." Francis paused again. It was obvious he'd come to the hard part. "Ah, Christ, that doctor, the one who killed the monster, he told people that the monster was Wilbur's half-brother."

The silence came back again, thicker than the summer heat around us. The rest of the story was pulled out in bits. Wilbur's half-brother was never seen again after the monster bubbled down into tapioca. Supposedly, Wilbur himself had died the same way. Lisa quietly admitted that a lot of Whateleys got buried in closed-coffin ceremonies. She added that the ceremonies rarely had anything like a traditional minister or priest in attendance. The quiet deepened. While I tried to straighten out everything in my mind that I'd been told, Francis finished off his report with one final bombshell.

"Jack, I got a lot of this stuff confirmed on the bus on the way back. You see, the bus I was on had some real old types on it, a bunch of them. Well, I thought, might as well ask. I started talking about this stuff as if I took it all for fact, like I was just from the next county.

"Well, they confirmed it, all right. Had a swell time yucking it up over the 'good old days.' Started breaking out the bottles of home brew on the bus; little 'pre-festival celebration', they called it. I went along with it, you know, to keep them talking ...," and then, suddenly, Francis' voice broke, his throat tightening to the point where every other word screeched. "Christ, Jack! They started talking about how we were all going to have a *good time,* a good time this year *for sure!*"

Billy reached out and took Francis' shoulder, trying to calm him. It didn't work. "Jack, they're coming to New York for a mass—they're planning to finish whatever they started in Innsmouth before the government got to them!"

It scared me that I wasn't surprised. Maybe it was the way my pal from the night before had splattered, or the ooze and the smell and the decaying tatters of rot he'd left behind instead of a corpse. Maybe the sweltering heat just made thinking so hard that acceptance was easier. Or maybe it was the look in Lisa's eyes and the green tinge they wore which would have been impossible if Francis was wrong.

Somehow it didn't seem he was. I kept after him, but he didn't have much more. The mass was supposedly set for something called Mid-Summer's Eve—June 23rd in English—two days away.

Unfortunately, even though Francis had found out the when, he hadn't gotten the where. That would take some searching. Reaching for Billy's phone, I called Hubert. Hubert is a leg-man; he deals in facts for the cops, the mob, anyone who needs information. He treads very carefully between his clients, trying not to get anyone *too* angry. Between his looks, his stutter, and the limp he picked up in the war, he isn't left with much to turn over to those he might offend. He picked up after the third ring.

"Hey; w-who I got?"

"It's me, Hu."

"Hey-Hey-Hagee. What's up, D-D-Dick Tracy?"

I gave him a quick run down of the facts he needed, holding back the stuff that sounded like a cheap horror movie storyboard. Getting to the point quickly, I asked him to try and find out where someone might hold an under-the-table midsummer's eve festival of the sort Francis had described. He laughed, "Th-That *all* you want?"

"That should be enough for now."

"Okey-dokey. C-Call you at your place in a few hours. Go have d-d-dinner. B-But don't let your 'meat loaf.'" He laughed again. "Get it?"

"Right, Hu." I hung up in the middle of his second laugh. If I hadn't, the jokes would have continued in the same vein, and I was in no mood then to fend off Hubert's version of "wit." I also knew nothing more was going to be accomplished by the four of us where we were. Francis agreed with me and took off, glad to be out of the office. Billy nodded, saying he would do anything he could to help. He meant it, too.

Lisa and I left together. We had a lot of time to kill while I tried to figure out which answers went to which questions.

*   *   *

The rest of the day and all of the night passed without trouble. Hubert hadn't come up with anything, but promised an answer as soon as he could track down one last lead. I hadn't argued. I hadn't been doing any better. I told him Lisa and I would be at Billy's, for want of a better place to hide. He told me he'd get in touch there as soon as he knew something.

We spent most of the morning thumbing through magazines and moving from one spot to another to try and keep out of Billy's way. Not content to stay outside, the summer heat wrenched its way in past the sputtering air conditioners, loosening ties and top buttons, animating some, leadening others. The patients and the staffers all reacted to the thick layers of toasted air around us, some pacing and prowling the rooms, the rest succumbing to the heat and merely melting into their chairs. The degree intensified throughout the day along with the humidity, turning thought into pain and comfort into a memory filed in the same drawer as gasoline that sold for 30¢ a gallon.

I looked across the room to the chair Lisa had fallen asleep in. Sweat dripped down the wall where her head rested against it. As I stared at her, I wondered what was really going on. The longer it took Hubert to call, the more tales of monsters and fish people and black masses began to seem as silly as they're supposed to. Maybe we *were* all scaring ourselves, I thought. Maybe the Navy had a perfectly good reason for torpedoing civilians while the F.B.I. shot them down in the streets and hustled them off to "detainment" centers. Maybe Lisa was crazy, and Francis took bus rides with nut cases, and people did split apart and dissolve when they fell four stories. Sure, maybe. Maybe the sun was coming up in the west the next morning, too, but I didn't think so.

Hubert's call did not improve my attitude. He had gotten through to his source, but hadn't gotten an answer. He said that would take more time. He calmly laughed about finding me once he knew something, cracking jokes about people making their Easter duty. I hung up, tired of Hubert's jokes, tired of waiting, tired of the heat, and tired of not being able to do anything. Mopping the sweat from my brow, I crossed the room to wake Lisa. Billy was already in attendance, wanting to know what Hubert had told me. I told them both I still didn't know anything, but that I wanted to try and find something out.

"If Francis is right about tomorrow, it isn't hard to figure that we have their guest of honor. Since Lisa's never been given a choice about R.S.V.P.ing, is there anyone who hasn't thought that the opposition might be considering force?" No one answered. "I didn't think so."

"What should we do, Jack?"

"Billy, I want you and Francis to go to my office tonight. Stay there. I'll go to Lisa's and wait for our pals. They haven't been watching so closely since their buddy bought it in the dumpster. If they see the lights on there, they'll probably make their move on me."

"Why take the chance, Jack? Why don't we all just hide?"

She'd asked a good question. It was one I'd asked myself a dozen times. Hoping the answer sounded better out loud, I said, "Who or whatever is behind this, whether they're some sort of agents of Satan, or just a sick bunch of bastards who get off over bloody headlines— whoever they are, they seem determined. Making them miss their date isn't going to put them off. They've got to be stopped. If I can get a hold of them, shake up their party plans, maybe we can put them out of circulation. After all, even if we get them to leave Lisa alone, that doesn't mean they won't decide to elect someone else 'Queen of the May', or that they won't just postpone things until next year, or next week, or to whenever in hell it suits them to postpone things to." I turned slightly, staring directly at Lisa. "You wanted me to find these people and stop them. Is that still what you want?"

She nodded, saying "yes" firmly. Billy interrupted, "What do we do, Jack?"

"You and Francis take Lisa to my office tonight and stay with her. Watch out for her." I flipped him a key; "You know what this opens. Open it when you get to my place, arm yourselves, and stay that way."

"What are you going to do?"

"I'm going to Buddy's Liquors on 18th Street, and then I'm going to Lisa's place to wait for our pals."

*   *   *

Billy called me when he and Francis had Lisa settled in. Opening the back compartment of my bottom desk drawer, they had both taken a weapon and settled themselves in as well. I've kept a number of the unregistered hand guns that have come my way over the years. Such things come in handy sometimes; that night had seemed like a handy one.

I had set myself up at Lisa's about an hour earlier, waiting for something to happen. Pulling a chair around to face the door, I sat in semi-darkness, my own gun and a bottle of Gilbey's within easy reach. Lisa had told me although she had been watched at many different times in many different places, they had always watched her home. I figured if they were going to make a grab for her, they'd have to try her place that night. I'd figured right.

Several hours after Billy's call, the first scratchings came at the door. I watched the entrance, listening to the noise on the other side. It was shallow, a thin slitting sound, as if the door were being skimmed away, layer by layer. I continued to sit silently, watching the doorknob jiggle, listening to the continual, ever-growing scraping as it crawled its way under the door. Sweat rolled down my neck and face; taking a last pull from the Gilbey's, I set the bottle next to my chair and waited.

A few seconds later, the waiting was over. The door swung open, letting gray light filter in from the hallway. The separate sounds I had been hearing pulled together into a voice, the way radio static solidifies into a message when you finally get the station tuned in. It was a dry sound, as if the speaker had gone years without drinking.

This is the time, it told me. *Come to us now.*

I sat. The scraping started again, this time at the windows. As I continued to watch the front door, I could hear the same methodical scratchings peeling away the layers of glass which separated me from the scrapers. I knew they were in the room behind me when the noise suddenly stopped. I stood and turned quickly, just as the first wave swarmed out of the bedroom, knives and bludgeons in hand. Taking a backward step, I raised my .38 and pulled the trigger, firing repeatedly into the horde. Four of them splattered, exploding through the room as if hit by a bazooka. As others poured in the front door, I grabbed one and spun him around, kicking him headlong into the others. As more came up behind me from the bedroom, I punched the first, my fist slamming through its head as its jaw shattered, greening teeth flying in my face.

As blades slashed for me through the darkness, I grabbed hold of one's hair, wrenching him around in front of me. I could feel parts of its flesh giving way as I pulled. Pressing my advantage, I yanked harder, splitting it in two. Ignoring the vulgar reek spilling from the scream-ing, thrashing torso, I grabbed it up in both hands and then used it as a club, smashing my way clear to the bedroom.

Slamming the door behind me, I shoved a chair under the knob and headed for the fire escape. Thuds and scrapings sounded behind me as I clambered out the window and headed for the street. Rusted sections of railing came loose in my hands as I took the narrow metal rungs two, three at a time. I reloaded when I hit the alley, watching for any more of my playmates. Looking up, I saw they had already made it to the fire escape. Some had crawled out the windows, oozing their way down the side of the building toward me. I didn't wait for them to catch up.

Racing around the corner, I ran down one street and then another, twisting and turning, hoping to lose the things following me. Stopping at the first phone booth I spotted, I jammed the door closed behind me, and fished in my pockets for change. As I dropped a dime in the slot, the smell of the fight began to cloud my head. The odors of the rotting flesh and thin, white blood which clung to me curdled upward, gagging me, forcing my hands to shake as I tried to punch out my office number. I leaned backward into the booth's metal corner, watch-ing for my playmates through the glass panels, listening to the unanswering buzz in the receiver.

I hung up after a dozen rings, wondering why no one had an-swered—praying I had only pressed the wrong number. Calming myself, forcing the white fingers of terror to back out of my mind, I reinserted the dime, carefully watching myself press out the same number again. I listened to the buzzes pile up one atop the other, staring around myself in the booth, noting how much it looked like a coffin. Finally I hung up, backing out of the booth. It didn't seem as small from the outside.

I knew something had happened, something more than the three of them stepping out for a pizza. Stepping from the curb, I walked a few feet into the street, hailing at each cab which passed. After a handful of eternal minutes, I finally got a driver not too bored to take a fare to 14th Street. I could hear the sirens as we got closer.

Stopping the cabbie short of my block, I crossed the street, going over to Freddie's. Freddie runs the news stand across from my building. She watches the door, letting me know about anything interesting. I figured she might peg squad cars and ambulances sitting outside as interesting. She had.

She told me, "What goes on in that place of yours, Jack? You better low profile it. They're gonna want answers from you for sure. Musta been some kinda fuckin' war in there. Bodies out the windows, shots, screams, the works." She smiled. "You sure can throw a party."

Freddie always smiles over details. Not much bothered her. Reading too many New York headlines can insulate you from anything. "Lotta gaggin' cops over there. Could smell somethin' over here for'while, but it blew off. Stunk bad in this heat, let me tell you. You don't smell so good yourself." She sniffed at me. "Woouuuch. What the hell *is* that?"

"Sink backed up; I had to wash in the toilet."

"Sure," she laughed, shaking her extra eighty-five pounds, "an' I'm Superman's fuckin' mother." I sat down on a stack of *Daily News*, holding back the anger and tears. Freddie asked, "You need anything, Jack?" Her hand curled around the bottle she was working on that night. I took it, letting two fingers' worth burn the edges off my fears.

I passed the bottle back, saying, "Thanks; how about your phone?"

"Same place as always. Don't be callin' fuckin' France."

I used my dime again. While it rang, I asked Freddie how many bodies they had taken out. She waddled across the street to find out, leaving me to watch the shop, and talk to Hubert. He answered quicker than usual.

"Hey-Hey, w-w-who I got?"

"You find that church yet?"

"Christ, Jack; w-w-what you got yourself m-mixed up in?"

I exploded. "Shut up, Hu. I don't have time for anything but answers. Can you understand that?"

"S-Sure, Jack. Sure. I g-got it." He stammered out the address; his tone let me know he had found out a few things about the parishioners as well as the church.

As I scribbled out the address, I asked him, "What is it, Hu?"

"I, I don't know. Those Massachusetts boys, t-t-there's something wrong with that place. Lots of b-bad history. B-B-Bodies being found—sick stuff ...."

He filled me in on the details he had come across, none of it very pleasant, but I had guessed that much for myself. I told him I had to go as Freddie came back into the stand. Outside of assorted pieces of my splattering pals, they'd only found Billy and Francis. She didn't describe the remains, but the look in her eyes told me all I needed to know.

They'd gotten Lisa. Somehow I knew they would all along.

*   *   *

I pulled up across the street from the address Hubert had given me. Freddie had lent me her car; we both knew mine was most likely staked out by a few of the boys in blue, waiting for me to come to them with an explanation as to what exactly they had found upstairs. That was something I didn't have time for.

I took in the building as I came to it. It had been a decent church at one time, the way Coney Island had once been a nice place. Now it was a shuddering hulk of splintered, forgotten wood, a slanted pile of sticks which no one had bothered to knock over. Probably because no one wanted to get close enough to do it.

It was strange to see a mostly wooden structure in New York. Even in the Bronx, everything is made of stone and metal. Somehow, the First Congregational Church of the Elder Saints had managed to hold off the ravages of progress. The twin apartment buildings it was wedged between were not in as great a state of disrepair as the church, giving the appearance that the decay was spreading from the church itself. Appearances aren't always deceiving.

Figuring subtlety didn't impress the boys from Innsmouth much, I simply went up to the front doors and walked in. That they weren't locked didn't surprise me, just as the inner decor didn't. It was calm inside, calm the way a beach is in winter, the way graveyards are all year long.

Most of the main room was in shadow, the only lighting coming from lanterns and lamps. They burned thickly, giving off a filmy, yellow vapor which smelled like old wet sand. I walked down the main aisle past the rows of seats, no two of them alike. The church was filled with seats—wooden ones, steel ones, leather ones. I walked past recliners, park benches, wheel barrows, patio furniture, kitchen chairs, hassocks, three-legged stools, anything which could support a body.

I listened to the sound my shoes made as I walked, each step either cracking the mucus-like crust which washed over most of the floor, or sloshing where it hadn't yet hardened. I kept my eyes forward, staring at the altar, avoiding eye contact with the things perched off in the dusty fun-house gloom which surrounded me.

Finally, when I was halfway to the front of the church, one of the "altar boys" happened to notice me. It tapped the "priest" on the shoulder. The cowled figure turned around, making the knots in my stomach tighten to the point where the pain made my eyes close. It was Lisa.

We thought you might be here.

Her mouth opened and closed, but her voice didn't come out. The figure moved with a gait barely human, let alone Lisa's. The only part of the thing before me which was still the woman I knew were the large, frightened green eyes, pleading for help. The fear screaming out of them crawled down my throat and touched my bones, chasing away the summer heat with the kind of chill that burns unwrapped meat in a freezer. I'd been trapped in a freezer once before; I found myself wishing I had died in it.

You can stop fighting us now. All is right.

"What's all right? Nothing's all right!"

You have discovered so much, but you know so little. We ruled the world once. My Brothers, My Sisters, My Self. All of the worlds you know of, all the stars you have ever seen—they were Our domain.

Others came, though. Chaotic Ones. Pain givers. Demanding, stirring ones. Young. They took Our ways of order and broke them the way any child will smash a barrier it does not understand. We were slow; We had no understanding of chaos. We were sealed away before We could prevent them from stealing you from Us. Now—it is Our night. We shall return, and you will be safe.

I stumbled away from Lisa's form, inching down the aisle. The voice continued, *Tonight, I shall be born again. I grow here. I shall birth Myself. Soon, We shall all return and dispel the pain givers. Those Ones shall be locked away. You will all be safe again.*

Lisa's hands spread apart, welcoming me forward, allowing the cloak to fall back. Her body seemed twisted now, like a lamp shade someone had kicked too many times. I watched as her skin shuddered, heaving up and down as something dark moved beneath it. My thoughts ranged back to when I had last seen her, and then, amid the memories of our night at my place, my mind flashed further back to my standing in the shower, washing away the slime of the thing I'd found in the dumpster, just before we'd gone to bed together. Somehow the images imposed themselves on each other as the thing before me continued to smile peacefully.

Of course, it said. *Are We not always born of desire?*

I knew what had happened. Lisa was gone; only the shape traveling within her remained. I looked up at the face that once was Lisa's, and said goodbye. As it continued to smile, I smiled too, and then pulled my .38 free, leveling it and firing point blank until I'd emptied it, watching the body jerk backward with each shot.

The parishioners came at me then, squalling in a tongue painful to hear. Using my revolver as a club, I swung at everything that moved, turning their numbers against them, trying to reach the front door. As the howling continued, I threw myself bodily into the thinnest line of their ranks, breaking through into a side corner of the church. As the congregation sloshed forward toward me, I grabbed down one of the lanterns, and smashed it in front of them. The oil within cracked out, igniting the still damp portions of the oily slime on the floor.

As those flaming ran through those who weren't, I took the moment to run from post to post, upsetting all the lamps I could. Before any of them could stop me, I had surrounded us with sheets of flame, the blaze licking up all of the pillars and walls, eating away at the dried wood with a frenzy as unnatural as the calm it disturbed. Running toward the closest wall, I threw myself forward then, through both the flames and the stained glass window beyond. I fell burning into the alley below, sliding downward through the decades of slime which had built up between the church and the next apartment building. Thrashing about in the darkness, I desperately beat out the flames clinging to me, stumbling from the alley, trying not to hear the screams rolling out of the inferno behind me.

Finally, dragging myself across the street, I leaned against Freddie's car, pulling off my smoldering jacket, letting it drop in the gutter. Not many people gathered for the blaze. Most everyone in the Bronx is used to fires, and to minding their own business. Those who had gathered backed off quickly when the doors to the church began to open.

Wrapped in flames, Lisa's body shuffled toward me, leaving a thinning trail of sizzling blood behind it. I watched it as it moved, not knowing what else to do. I had no energy to run with, and no place to run to. I could feel my .38 still in my hand, but didn't bother to reload it. I didn't see where six more bullets would do any good.

The thing stopped several feet from me, staring down as I continued to cling to the car, unable to move. The voice came again. *No order. No order now. Chaos swallows us again. We go—We go. Our mercy on you—you who worship falsely—you have forgotten Us, tool of Chaos; you realize not your actions.*

The eyes of the thing looked inward, and then, raising its flaming arms upward, it looked at me again, saying, *This one, at least, We will save.*

And suddenly, Lisa was back from wherever she had been shoved when the thing had taken her over. I grabbed up my jacket, trying to beat out the flames, but finally stopped. There wasn't any point. Lisa's body was hers again, but her mind, her spirit, her soul—whatever word you want to use for whatever it is that makes us people— was gone; the burning form in my arms was no more human than a gutted porpoise.

Even though I finished the job and put out the flames, she still screamed, the same gurgling howl the things trapped in the church continued to screech. Fumbling through my jacket pockets, I found one last half-moon clip. Emptying the shells into my revolver, I searched Lisa's burnt, hanging face for any sign that could stay my hand. The opaqued green of her remaining eye told me no more than her foaming, blood-flecked lips.

Cursing every god I'd ever heard of, I stuck my gun to her temple and pulled the trigger. The screaming stopped everywhere except in my head.

*   *   *

Somehow I made it back to Freddie's, delivering her car in better shape than I delivered myself. I drank a lot that night. I drank a lot the next night, too. I gave the police my story—letting them know that I didn't know anything, bawling them out for not keeping people and their property safe and unharmed. They weren't really out to blame the mess in my office on me, mainly because they didn't have much of an idea what the mess in my office even was. Truth to tell, neither did I.

I've rolled a lot of ideas around, but none of the answers I come up with make any sense, which is hardly surprising, considering the questions don't make any sense either.

I've found drinking too much to be a wonderful way to sleep without dreaming. Of course, I might be able someday to sleep without dreams without having to drink myself into a stupor, but so far I haven't had the nerve to find out.

I'm not sure I ever will.

S*uppose that not just the legacy of Wilbur Whateley continued, as in the previous
stories, like the widening wake of a boat, but that Wilbur himself came back.
Suppose fate granted him another chance. And suppose further that he reappeared not
in the Lovecraftian world of the 1920's and 1930's, but in a time closer to our own.
What would he make of the world and its changes? A minor point: The updated
Arkham depicted here has evolved in the pages of various Mythos stories from Lovecraft's
day to the present. See if you can place the details with the appropriate writers. One
aspect of the Wilbur Whateley character pointed out by Peter Cannon and others, but
often forgotten anyway, is his function in many ways as a Lovecraftian autobiographi-
cal analogue. Wilbur's being raised by a grandfather instead of a father, his home
education from his grandfather's library, his insane mother, his stigma of ugliness (in
Lovecraft's case untrue, but a self-image imposed on him by his mother), and his sense
of being an outsider all echo Lovecraft himself. Many similar features can be seen in
the figures of Charles Dexter Ward, Jervas Dudley (cf. Machen's Jervase Cradock, a
Wilbur analogue) in "The Tomb", Edward Derby in "The Thing on the Doorstep",
Randolph Carter in "The Silver Key", and Ward Phillips in "Through the Gates of
the Silver Key." They are all in some measure Lovecraft, and thus they are all in some
manner each other.*

This story first appeared in Revelations From Yuggoth #1, November 1987.

Wilbur Whateley Waiting

by Robert M. Price

"Bugg-shuggog ...."

Wilbur Whateley's prayer had been heard. His last incantation
had worked.

He had not chanted to free the unseen Thing from its confinement.
He did not need to; time itself would effect that. As That in the
farmhouse hungered and hungered in the absence of its brother, its
keeper, it would instinctively burst forth, splintering the century-old
hulk of the Whateley farmhouse, like a giant sea turtle for some reason
sloughing off its shell, and go forth to raven and to feed.

What its eventual fate might be, Wilbur Whateley had had no time
to contemplate. It was his own immediate fate that concerned him. He
troubled simply to get the alien syllables right, to sound them at the
right pitch, a pitch which not even he could rightly hear, having too
much of the human in him.

But it had worked. The greedy whippoorwills had abruptly ceased their gloating to flee in chaotic terror. His life rapidly ebbing on one plane, he succeeded in causing it to flow on, or onto, another. As his vast, mutilated bulk began to dematerialize, it would probably seem to leave but a viscous residue on the floor of the Miskatonic University Library, and soon that, too, would be gone. It would have gone to another dimension, that in which the blind and tenebrous Old Ones waited, that into which Wilbur Whateley, a servant of Their servants, had lately sought to recall the earth itself. Ironically, now he himself was going there alone. And like the Old Ones, he must now wait, mayhap for strange aeons, until a Call should come. But in this decadent age, there might be none who knew how to issue it.

* * * * *

Time passed, generations of it, but not where Wilbur Whateley waited, dreaming, sending dreams. Receptive minds on the mortal plane were few, befogged as most were with what is called sanity. Here or there his transdimensional suggestions connected, registered. But none had the knowledge to do what was needful. Some of these became murderers or maniacs, translating Wilbur Whateley's impulses into action as best they could, but in doing so they only dissipated the energy, and it did him no good. More time passed. Wilbur Whateley waited, and dreamed.

* * * * *

In Chorazin, New York, the crazy old man sweated and would have sworn, except that he knew too well not to add any stray syllables to the energy field he had created, which now charged the air in the dusty library in which he worked. He sweated from the effort, an elaborate ceremony now repeated for the twenty-first time, and to no apparent avail. It probably would make no difference if he swore, or, for that matter, if he sang the national anthem, since only his now-threadbare faith told him there was a psychic energy field present at all. Maybe he had made some simple error in his preparations. Or maybe his family had been correct and he was simply out of his mind. Well, nothing to do for it but to redraw the pentacle again, perhaps a different color this time. If this didn't work, he didn't quite know what he was going to do with That in the basement. He was trying to summon someone who would, who must, know what to do.

*   *   *   *   *

On the forty-third try, days later and still no sleep, it did work. First the shimmering white jelly in the middle of the chalk star. Then the stench and the interstellar cold, the sound as of a mighty rushing wind, though the air was still and dead. Then the jelly puffed and bulked. And color and shape entered it.

The librarian's description proved largely accurate. There were the tentacles streaming from the waist, above saurian legs, making the Thing look like a priapan hydra. There was the fur, dense and black and shaggy like a grizzly bear; there was the face which seemed almost accidentally human in aspect. It was all there.

The heap hesitated, as if struggling to return to sync with the rhythm of terrestrial time, and then the breathing began. Strange vein and artery nets began to quiver, and the beaded, reptilian skin began to change colors with the pulses of ichor through the body. And out of the body. The old man had to move quickly to stanch the open wounds of the giant he had called out of the sky. The job seemed simple enough, as the tissue damage appeared trivial. Why such injuries should prove dangerous to such a titan was a mystery solvable only if one knew more about the workings of the fabulous alien physiology than the old man knew. But he did think he knew what to do with the wounds, if the old books were to be trusted. And the very presence of the creature indicated they were indeed to be trusted.

*   *   *   *   *

Wilbur Whateley began to stir. He had come back to the mortal plane from a state of consciousness so indescribably different from our own that to return from it was analogous to waking from sleep. There was simply too much of the human in him for him to retain his ability to conceptualize the Outer sphere once he had returned to the earth.

There seemed to be one of the little humans kneeling before him for some reason, hands clasped in supplication. Shaking with reverence or fear, or more likely both, the old man spoke. "I bid you welcome, O Word of the Aeon, O Great Beast! Shall I ... go on? I am your servant Ezekiel Prinn, and I have brought you back to finish the work you began. It is my work as well, and the work of my family, of Abigail Prinn, and of Ludvig Prinn before her. Being human they all failed, and I have not even the knowledge they had—only these few books, I fear."

Fearing he had said too much, Ezekiel Prinn finished his welcoming speech with a wave of the hand indicating his small collection of mouldering manuscripts and crudely-bound volumes. Through all this, the giant listened, if he listened, in silence. At length the goatish visage rose and the strange eyes met his.

"Yew dun well. Wut books?"

Prinn moved quickly aside, apologetically offering: "They weren't mine; I found them here, and there weren't many still readable." Wilbur Whateley slowly fingered the books and picked one up. The back cover fell away, sprinkling dust. Nervously Prinn continued.

"I only chanced to discover my heritage. Family tried for generations to cover it up. But I guess it was in the blood, and I got curious. I found out who I was, what my task was."

"Where is this?"

"We are in the old Van der Heyl mansion in upstate New York. I read a diary published by the Society for Psychical Research. I don't know if you know what that is .... Anyway, it told of a man who came here and contacted the Outside. The diary said there were books, and I knew I'd need them. But all that were left was what you ... what my Lord sees. Not much. And I have these ...."

"My letters." Puzzlement registered in the strange eyes as he took up one of the yellowed sheets. Here was one addressed to Wilbur Whateley's grandfather, the old wizard.

"Frater Magnum Innominandum, do what thou will shall be the whole of the law ...." It proceeded to describe the very act of planetary sex magic which, with Lavinia Whateley's cooperation, had brought Wilbur into the world the first time, many years ago. It closed as strangely as it had opened: "Love is the law, love under will. Your brother in Almonsin-Metraton, Frater Perdurabo."

Ezekiel Prinn waited, hoping the titan was not annoyed.

"From the wreck of your house. I visited there, too. Not much was left. Destroyed by the Thing." The nature of the unseen Thing Prinn could only guess, though he had surmised its purpose. Both tacitly assumed its destruction. Had it remained in the world, nothing else would have. The humans must somehow have defeated it.

"The meddlers from the University searched your house and they got most everything."

"The Book, too?" Wilbur Whateley mused. He had not been able to steal the Book from the humans, but they had stolen his copy. "Need it. Need more than that."

Ezekiel Prinn wore the look of a well prepared pupil. "I have traveled widely, my Lord. I do have that Other of which you speak. You see, there was Another."

Surprise, definitely surprise, on the semi-human features.

"If you will follow me ...." Prinn led his giant guest through cobweb-shrouded rooms, brushing aside hanging batwings of wallpaper, kicking aside unidentifiable debris, to the basement steps. The cellar was vast and dank and seemed to absorb the glow of the electric torch the old man held.

"I found it in a museum, of all places, in London some years ago. All thought it to be merely an odd bit of surrealist sculpture, but I knew it had been alive and would return to life with the proper Words."

The light now illumined, albeit dimly, a huge and strangely shaped sight. On a throne of stalagmites rested (its anatomy would not allow one to say it *sat*) a globular body supported by six folded crab-like legs. The sphere was covered with puckered cilia and was surmounted by an elephantine snout and a collection of asymmetrical eyes. Something about it reminded Prinn of Wilbur Whateley, though there was really no specific point of resemblance.

"It is Rhan-Tegoth, or so the sign said. Through it the Old Ones can return."

Wilbur Whateley nodded. Perhaps, presumably, he was satisfied. "The Words. Yew know them?"

"My Lord, I do not. They are in the Book, and I do not have the Book."

"Harvard? Miskatonic?"

"I have tried both, and others besides. They all ... ah ... learned their lesson. They have the Book but deny it exists. A legend, they say, or a fiction. But lately I have heard something that gives me cause to hope. South of here there is a place, as yet unmolested by the authorities, that is said to have the Book ...."

"I will go. Clothes."

Ezekiel Prinn hastened to comply. He had intended to undertake the mission himself, but he was not about to argue. Evidently his Master felt the need to finish the task he had begun. This time he meant to return with the *Necronomicon*.

*   *   *   *   *

Hunched over in his seat because of the (to him) low ceiling, Wilbur Whateley found himself taken aback at the view from the train car. On the horizon lay fabled Kadath, or so it seemed. How could the tiny humans have reared the Cyclopean pylons he saw looming up before him? For all his knowledge of lost and elder universes, the human part of him was an isolated country bumpkin who had never glimpsed the like of New York City. It fascinated even him.

The train pulled in and passengers began to disembark, scurrying off in a thousand directions through the huge cavern of the station. Wilbur Whateley consulted his elaborately written directions, comparing them with large posted maps, the intricate and indecipherable colored lines of which reminded him of the cipher-scripts of far-distant worlds. Yet like most who consulted these charts, he could not afford to linger staring at them long enough to decipher whatever cryptic message might lie concealed there.

As he proceeded up the stairs, stepping over an unconscious human heap, he began to study the fleshy tide flowing around him. Most seemed to hover somewhere between soundness and decadence, but there was a diversity of faces and voices here that he had never encountered in rural New England. Like Darwin amazed at the variety of Galapagos finches, Wilbur Whateley was surprised that human beings could take such a multifarious range of hues and forms.

Some of the languages he heard sounded like they were not intended for human vocal apparatus. The loitering knots of youths, the outlandishly garbed eccentrics with their face paint and chopped, tufted hair, the carriers of noise boxes, those selling flowers or distributing leaflets: the rat-faced mongrel hordes repelled him, infesting like vermin the planet that rightly belonged to Those whom Wilbur Whateley served. If he had his way, They soon would have it back, and the metropolis surrounding him would be no more than a corpse city. Yet amid this flood of loathsome humanity Wilbur Whateley was grateful for one thing: no one took the slightest notice of his goat-faced, seven-foot frame, swathed in tent-like garments. Where there is no normalcy, there is no abnormalcy either. For the first time in his earthly life, he need not hide.

He wandered the city streets for hours, wondering that if all went well, all this should be swept away to prepare for Those he served. At length he found his way to the district to which old Ezekiel had tried his best to direct him. The area seemed almost choked with bookshops large and small, these in turn choked with patrons. This surprised Wilbur Whateley, as reading had been an art lost or unknown in the rural backwater of Dunwich. He and his grandsire had been objects of suspicion as much because they owned and read books as because of their occult experiments.

The establishment he sought turned out to be one of the smallest and most squalid, tucked away mid-block on a side street.

A human skeleton hung in the window along with some cheap plaster statuary of gargoyles and phallic witch-gods. On the door a hand-stenciled sign profanely warned away the merely curious and unsympathetic, and a larger sign hanging in the window gave the name of the shop as "The Magickal Childe", which might after all have aptly described Wilbur himself.

He stooped and entered. He would have difficulty threading his way through the two narrow aisles, with his gargantuan bulk. Every inch of available space was stacked with occult paraphernalia, candles, bins of spices and herbs, all labeled according to their supposed curative or aphrodisiac properties. There was a case of jewelry, most crudely forged, all strange in design, some featuring glazed animal eyes as jewels. Wilbur Whateley marveled that such a place as this could flourish openly. Had it somehow escaped the notice of the authorities even in so close and crowded a city? Or had times changed so much in the nearly sixty years of his absence from this earth?

It seemed they had, for as he scanned the shelves, bypassing innumerable cheaply printed pamphlets on astrology and sexuality and whatnot, his strange eyes rested on the impossible.

Several copies of the Book itself!

And for sale in the open like any book might be! Instead of relief or joy, his reaction was one of profound disturbance. Yes, he now could procure the precious volume with no trouble—but so could any fool or dabbler! With the book of Alhazred in so many hands, how did the world still stand? Why did not the Old Ones rule already?

His puzzlement had only begun. Next he noticed that two very different editions were for sale. One featured the title *The* Necronomicon, *the Book of Dead Names* and purported to be a translation of the Dee text, or rather of a coded cipher-fragment of it. The other was larger and bore the one word *Necronomicon* in crude silver lettering embossed on black false leather. (Had he been familiar with such things, he might have thought to compare its binding to that of a high school annual.) This version was longer but not nearly the size of the ponderous thousand-page tome he had consulted sixty years before. It was the rendering of an ecclesiastic of occult leanings, one Simon.

Absorbed in mingled hope and unease, Wilbur Whateley extracted a roll of crumpled bills from his pocket and dropped several on the counter, scarcely hearing the polite chatter of the shopkeeper: "Oh, the *Necronomicon*—that's one of our most popular items. You know, we have classes on it every Sunday night after the Gnostic mass." He left, carrying both books under his arm.

After walking a few blocks under the increasingly clouded sky, he decided to stop in a place called Union Square Park. It was lined with benches, many of which were occupied by oblivious drug addicts and alcoholics. He chose a vacant bench under a lamp post and opened both volumes before him.

In vain he sought to collate the two disparate texts. After an hour or two of laborious plodding through leaden prose he concluded that the books had nothing in common except their title. At first he theorized that since manifestly neither book represented the complete text, he might have two independent fragments. His own copy, long since claimed by the authorities, had been the Dee translation but it was incomplete. Since this new Dee fragment seemed unfamiliar to him, he felt with a momentary thrill that he might have stumbled upon just the passage he had sorely needed. Yet the brief invocation of Yog-Sothoth turned out to be so much nonsense. One was to summon Yog-Sothoth merely to gain worldly wealth.

At this point a suspicion was born in his mind that matured upon closer examination of the other book which seemed to have been mistitled purely and simply. This was not the *Al Azif* of Abdul Alhazred but rather a collection of old Sumerian liturgical chants. Wilbur Whateley concluded he was the victim of a strange joke. He left the useless books on the bench and went in search of a telephone.

He could not squeeze himself into the tiny booths but soon found a telephone attached to a free-standing post. He dug out the paper containing the number of the telephone Ezekiel Prinn had lately had installed in the ancient Van der Heyl mansion. He was relieved to see that the instrument had push-buttons as he would have had trouble fitting his huge fingers into the tiny holes in a dial. Still he had trouble not pushing three buttons at once.

Prinn did not answer, not on the fiftieth ring. This boded complications, trouble. Wilbur Whateley would try to reach him again, but now he wanted to be away and pursuing his changed plans, the plans of which he had meant to inform the old man.

Luckily he had not purchased a round-trip ticket, since he had decided not to return to his point of departure. Instead he would ride the train to the Upper Miskatonic Valley. His next stop was Arkham, Massachusetts.

* * * * *

He was able to ride directly from New York to Boston, but there he had to wait for the ever-delayed Boston-Arkham Local. North Station was tiny by comparison to Grand Central. People rushed through it just as fast, though fewer of them, impatient to be somewhere else. All, like ants in an anthill, were frantically busy at tasks to which Wilbur Whateley hoped soon to put an end, though his increasing sense of foreboding made him doubt his ultimate success. Suppose he could not manage to wipe this world clean: Could he stand to live in it as it was?

Finally the train pulled in and he was underway again. The trip was not overly long, though much time was wasted simply because the route did not cut across country even where this was possible, following instead the crazy, winding path of the Miskatonic River itself. This must be because the track had been laid to connect the various small towns dotting the banks of the river, built there when immediate access to water was necessary for trade.

The train began to slow as it entered the ancient, picturesque town. Wilbur Whateley could make out street names. There were Derby, Hyde, and West Streets, and finally the B & M Station at the corner of High Lane and Garrison Street. He got off the train car and walked across the old brick platform, quaint but in need of repair (like most of the town), to the nearby telephone. He tried to call Ezekiel Prinn. Again there was no answer, and Wilbur now knew something had to be amiss.

Returning the receiver to its cradle, he turned and scanned his immediate surroundings. He had not seen this place for nearly sixty years. He had not felt the passage of time, occulted as he was in another reality; his memories were as if he had visited only weeks ago, but sixty years had wrought many changes. Some of these buildings had been decaying even then. Sometime since they had been refinished in the Victorian Gothic style, something that looked strange even to Wilbur Whateley. He decided to take a circuitous route to see more of the campus, for it was of course Miskatonic University he had come to visit.

He turned right from the station and strode down High Lane, turned left onto West Street and crossed the bridge over the River, passing an island famous for its ancient menhir which had fabulous and dubious associations. Wilbur knew the truth behind these legends. How much, in fact, he could tell the professors in Miskatonic's Anthropology Department, were he so inclined.

He then crossed River Street with its ancient row of warehouses, many of them apparently still in use, though a sign indicated one had been made over into an artist's colony. He proceeded down West past Main to the next corner, where he turned left onto Church Street. This had once been Arkham's main business district, but most shopping had shifted a block northward to Main Street or to the large shopping centers outside the town on the highways. The University faced Church Street on one side and had some years previously bought up the other side as well. Over the protests of many in the community, the mostly bankrupt and abandoned shops had been razed and replaced with new houses, built in the old style (which somewhat mollified the irate antiquarians) for the use of the fraternities. As Wilbur walked down Fraternity Row, he noted a few of the signs posted in front of the gambrel-roofed houses. There were Lam Kha Alif, Kaf Dhai Waw, and others. He did not know what fraternities were, his own education having been restricted to the home.

He turned right onto Garrison Street. The first building he came to was the University Spa on his left, but his attention was immediately attracted by the massive new Administration building across the street. But his business was not here. Down the block was the Library, familiar to him, all too familiar, from previous visits. Here, logically, should be the goal of his quest. Yet it occurred to him at once that the Book might no longer be housed here. Certainly, from what old Prinn had told him, it would no longer be available for casual perusal.

He decided to take the direct approach and walked up the great stone steps into the building. He paused at the circulation desk and waited. A figure of his proportions and demeanor is difficult not to notice, and within moments a prim and intimidated librarian was asking if she might help him.

"I hope yew kin, Miz. I need to see a book I hear tell yew got, call't th' *Necronomicon.*"

"That book doesn't exist, sir. It's just fiction, you know. You know, you're about the tenth person who's come in asking about this book since I've worked here. All I can say is, whoever writes those stories must make it pretty convincing, but it's only just fiction. Why, we've actually had practical jokers come in here and stick phony cards for that title in the card catalogue ...."

Wilbur could tell she believed this. Of course, as a subordinate she would. No one would have told her the truth.

"But I have to do some research on't. Cud'n't yew tell me who *cud* tell me su'thin' more?"

"Well, maybe one of the Literature Department people, or you might try the Foundation. Yes, they might know something. You can find them out the door, to the right, down to the corner, then turn left. You can hardly miss it, it's right past the Pickman Nuclear Lab."

It did prove easy to find. A plaque in the lobby indicated that the new and sparkling building housed a Foundation named for a retired University folklorist, now dead, yet the work of the Foundation was described in vague terms suggesting experimental work in parapsychology. Wilbur surmised that this obscurity was intentional—that it denoted that during the years of his absence the humans had learned quite a bit about Those he served and did not want the public to know too much that might be disturbing.

There seemed to be no one in evidence, so he decided to explore as far as he could before he might be detected. Presumably as a part of the University, the place was open to the public. Voices down the hall indicated that classes were held in the building. He paused outside a door to listen.

"My young friends, these stones, originally the product of an ancient science predating even the Druids, are our greatest technological achievement. We can now reproduce them in our kilns, and like their prototypes, they act simultaneously as a kind of detector device as well as a safety shield. If one of the CCD or their minions were within miles of us, whether in a lateral radius or below, we would both know it and be protected by a shield of psychic force keeping the enemy at a healthy distance ...."

Wilbur could make nothing of this, but as he mused on it, he felt a hand at his elbow.

"Sir, I'm afraid you're in a restricted area. This whole building is restricted, I'm afraid. You'll have to leave." This man was armed, a helmeted security guard. Others now appeared from further down the hall. He apologized and left peaceably.

This had to be the place. If the Book were anywhere on campus it must be here. But instead of filling him with hope, this certainty turned his foreboding into resignation. What could he do now? He did not know where in this vast complex the Book might be secreted. Perhaps they had even destroyed it, as the authorities had done in ages past. And if he had nearly met his doom at the jaws of snarling

Dobermans once, what could he do against armed guards? The Book was now beyond his grasp.

* * * * *

In Union Square Park a furtive figure in a ratty, urine-smelling overcoat stooped over in mild curiosity to examine a book, two books it turned out, illumined by the lamp light. The one on top looked like a high school yearbook, and that's what he thought it was at first, even though he had never been to high school. He flipped it open and saw lists of strange-looking sentences. He studied it for a few moments and began to piece together what, more or less, it was supposed to be. An impulse seized him, and playfully he took up the book; he looked around, and his gaze fastened on a drunk sleeping on a bench a couple of yards away. He began to repeat some of the sentences aloud while pointing to the drunk. He felt silly, but it was kind of fun.

Suddenly his eyes closed against a terrific flash that singed his face. Shading his eyes with one hand and holding the now-closed book in the other, he saw (and heard) that the bum had burst into flame. Not even screaming, the derelict lay there roasting on the bench, the alcohol he had absorbed making his funeral pyre burn brighter.

* * * * *

Before he left Arkham, Wilbur Whateley tried to telephone Ezekiel Prinn one more time. There was still no answer. The reason for this was simple: Prinn lay, drained of blood, in the cobwebs of the Van der Heyl mansion and, naturally, could not hear anything. A day before, eager to further the plan, he had sought to vivify the Thing called Rhan-Tegoth. It turned out that the manuscripts available to him did indeed contain the Words he needed, though at first he had misconstrued the reference. The sorcerer's apprentice had promptly become the Thing's first meal after its waking. Prinn suddenly discovered the purpose of the long proboscis and the thousands of sucker-tipped cilia coating the Thing. He had misconstrued these, too. It was something of this kind that Wilbur Whateley imagined must have occurred. But he never returned to Chorazin, New York. Rhan-Tegoth waited on its stalagmite throne for a priest to bring it new sacrifices, but none did.

* * * * *

There was no bus to Dunwich, not even any signs directing Wilbur Whateley to his destination as he set out on foot down the Aylesbury Pike. All he knew to do now was to head for his only earthly home, or what might be left of it. He reached Dean's Corners late in the afternoon as the sun was beginning to set. He reached the fork where the route to Dunwich branched off. Though all signs had been taken down since 1928, the path was clearly designated by its state of neglect and decrepitude. The moon rose as he trudged on, and by its gleam he saw the familiar stone walls so close against the roadside that they made the road seem almost like an interior hall in some great castle. There was no shoulder of the road to walk on here, but Wilbur feared no automobile suddenly overtaking him. The road had not been used for decades. Frequently individual blocks or whole sections of masonry had fallen out of the bordering walls into the road. It had never been cleared, nor had the walls been repaired. Thick patches of grass and even an occasional small tree grew in the road. Most houses in sight were total ruins, their gray boards falling to dust, a few broken planks still held together only by intertwining vines.

The peculiarly domed hills with their crowning circles of monoliths, now mostly fallen, seemed alive with memories from Wilbur's childhood. He reached the covered bridge and found to his dismay that the bottom had fallen out of it. In the ravine below he thought he could see the rusty remnants of an old automobile. There was nothing to be done about it but to climb down the side and swim the river. He could do that.

Dripping wet, Wilbur Whateley arrived in the town of Dunwich some hours later, near dawn. Despite being cold and wet he felt no discomfort. With his inhuman senses, he could not feel discomfort, at least not from such a source. The crossroads was falling into ruins like the rest of the village, but the people of Dunwich had never had what one might call civic pride, and it was difficult to discern whether anyone still lived here. At this hour no one would have been out and about anyway.

He continued through the town, only a few minutes' walk. The main street dead-ended abruptly at an open field. The end of the road was marked by the fungus-covered, splintering stump of the centuried oak from which the corpse of Wilbur's great-grandfather Oliver Whateley had once dangled, lynched by the villagers forgotten scores of years ago. Wilbur passed by, not sparing it a glance, as if not welcoming this silent reminder of another Whateley failure. He was headed further into the countryside, to the old Whateley farm. He did not expect to find much left standing on the property.

The first rays of dawn revealed the ancient granite hillside against which the farmhouse had once stood. Of this all that remained was some fallen bricks from the chimney. The great wooden structure that had housed the unseen creature had vanished utterly, the shattered boards and beams having long since rotted completely away.

He was pleased to see that the various outbuildings still stood in some fair state of repair. These had been his final quarters once he had devoted the whole of the farmhouse to his unhuman charge. The shabby sheds had been roughly maintained for a few years by some of the poorer Whateleys who had claimed Wilbur's property after his apparent death. Their legal claim having failed, they moved in as squatters, living undetected for years while the inheritance was being slowly settled. Though they were finally driven out, no one ever moved in to replace them. Thus the emptiness, and the desolation, of the place on Wilbur's arrival.

He would stay here and decide what to do next, if anything.

*   *   *   *   *

Weeks passed as Wilbur Whateley waited and considered. All his grandfather's books were gone, appropriated no doubt by the University or the Foundation, the humans at any rate. He had accepted defeat; without the requisite formulae he, even he, was quite powerless. He felt doubly the outsider: If his alien appearance were not enough to isolate him from the ordinary run of mankind, his very reason for being set him utterly at odds with his surroundings. Not even the product of this planet's evolution, he had been bred in the outer spheres for no other purpose than to open the floodgates of the world to the tide of its destruction. If these gates were forever closed, he was trapped inside.

He spent much of his time these days atop Sentinel Hill, sitting on the forlorn heap of stones that had once formed the forbidden altar and menhir, looking out on the rounded hills, steep valleys, and thick foliage now reclaiming more and more of the depopulated region. His strange mind was filled with unearthly memories and dreams. For the first time in his unnatural life he knew melancholy.

One afternoon, Wilbur Whateley risked hiking back to the town of Dunwich. He found that some hardy rustics did after all remain in the village. From then on, he took to entering Dunwich from time to time, visiting Osborn's General Store for what few physical needs he had.

Even in Dunwich no one showed him the slightest suspicion. Most of them had been born since the Dunwich Horror of 1928, and none, it seemed, had even heard of it. None, that is, except old Luther Brown, who had been a youngster at the time. And he never mentioned it, probably having learned his lesson from years of facing the skeptical mockery of the younger Dunwich villagers. Luther himself was no longer certain the whole business had not been a childhood nightmare.

As time passed, Wilbur became less of a recluse and would make the trip down to the village more often than he actually needed to. In fact it was not much longer before he became one of the regular loungers at Osborn's store. Even his great size and odd proportions excited no fearful comments: After so many years of absolute isolation from the outside world, the people of Dunwich had become so freak-ishly inbred and mentally degenerate that some saw nothing physically out of the ordinary about Wilbur in comparison with their own relatives, while others simply could not recognize the unearthly when they saw it.

$$* \quad * \quad * \quad * \quad *$$

Years passed, and still Wilbur Whateley waited, he knew not for what. But he began to fill his time with walks through large tracts of countryside. On these occasions he was more and more lost in memories of his youth, those days when his purpose, his messianic mission, had absorbed every thought and effort. He wondered and wondered again how things might have been different, what he might have done instead of what he did do. If only there were some way for him to have a second chance, he would not fail.

One fading afternoon as the setting sun cast a peculiar golden light on the landscape before him, reminding him of that bright dimension into which he had once hoped to recall a transfigured earth, Wilbur found himself even farther than usual from Dunwich and home. As he returned from reverie, he noticed that he was scaling a hill thickly mantled with elms, a hill overlooking a fallen cottage below. Through the trees he came upon a collection of megaliths, encrusted with lichen and draped with moss, somehow reminiscent of the hilltop stone circles he had so often visited in his childhood. But whereas the Dunwich stones had been artificially changed, these seemed natural, as if the former were the imitation of these latter, as if these stones somehow embodied certain cryptical secrets inherent in the universe, jealously guarded from humanity, yet left enciphered here to taunt the mortal seeker. Wilbur paused to study them, and on a level of consciousness deeper or higher or other than the human part of him, he seemed to understand something of their message.

He set off again, crossing a dried-up stream bed, all the while in the tightening grip of a sense of mysterious expectancy, at last coming upon the mouth of a large cave. Entering, he ran his huge hands along the rough walls to guide him while his eyes took longer than ours would take to adjust to the gloom. The ceiling of the cave was sloping rapidly downward, and even stooping lower and lower he could not avoid frequently bumping his slope-browed head.

At last he was crawling as the cave shrank to a mere shaft's height and width. Despite his giant size he could navigate the small tunnel without much difficulty because of the remarkable elasticity afforded by his alien, almost boneless anatomy. He pressed on, oozed further, because some secret instinct told him something awaited him in a place beyond the darkness and slime and crayfish.

He had not long to wait before the narrow fissure began to grow again, and soon he was standing free in an imposingly large vaulted chamber. Here and there appeared possible signs of workmanship, though if this place had ever known the workman's chisel, centuries or millennia of dripping nitre and water erosion had returned the cavern to its primordial state. Yet as Wilbur Whateley scanned the rock face, looking for something, he knew not what, he imagined he caught sight of a faint glimmer, reflecting dim radiance from some unknown source, perhaps from the luminescent fungi that thinly coated patches of the walls.

Stepping closer, his splashing pad-like feet disturbing the peaceful pool-world of the translucent eyeless fish, Wilbur saw a metal ring protruding from the black and porous wall. Upon examining it more closely, he could see it to be the circular handle of a huge key. Its tarnished surface was minutely carved with cryptic symbols, many of them familiar to him through his childhood studies. Suddenly a whole hitherto obscure chapter of the Book made new sense to him.

Unhesitatingly he reached out his hand and grasped the key with two huge fingers (all that would fit through the handle). Despite the dank cold of the dreadful place, the key seemed to glow with an inner warmth, and even to vibrate slightly. He did not try to turn it, nor did any unseen crack widen into a hidden door.

* * * * *

It was Halloween, and soon the fires would be lit. This night was a happy and exciting one for all children, but for none more than Wilbur Whateley, who unlike most youths knew why he was born and what great thing he would achieve when he grew up. With the boy's uncanny gift of presentiment, his proud mother and grandfather were sure nothing would ever stand in the way of his destined accomplishments. But for now, there was the celebration to get ready. The boy and his mother were both aware of the night air's chill, but soon the raging fires would warm them. Below, a spark, perhaps of lamplight, hinted that down the hill someone might have seen them.

ABOUT ROBERT M. PRICE

ROBERT M. PRICE has edited *Crypt of Cthulhu* for fourteen years. His essays on Lovecraft have appeared in *Lovecraft Studies*, *The Lovecrafter*, *Cerebretron*, *Dagon*, *Etude Lovecraftienne*, *Mater Tenebrarum*, and in *An Epicure in the Terrible* and *Twentieth Century Literary Criticism*. His horror fiction has appeared in *Nyctalops*, *Eldritch Tales*, *Etchings & Odysseys*, *Grue*, *Footsteps*, *Deathrealm*, *Weirdbook*, *Fantasy Book*, *Vollmond*, and elsewhere. He has edited *Tales of the Lovecraft Mythos* for Fedogan & Bremer, as well as *The Horror of It All* and *Black Forbidden Things* for Starmont House. His books include *H. P. Lovecraft and the Cthulhu Mythos* (Borgo Press) and *Lin Carter: A Look behind His Imaginary Worlds* (Starmont). By day he is a theologian, New Testament scholar, editor of *The Journal of Higher Criticism*, and pastor of the Holy Grail Ecumenical Church.

THE SHUB-NIGGURATH CYCLE

Among the most familiar names in the Lovecraftian litany, Shub-Niggurath, the Black Goat of the Wood, the Goat with a Thousand Young, is never met personally in Lovecraft's stories, but is often referred to in rituals and spells. This deity mutated and was adapted as Lovecraft crafted and revised tales spawned by other authors. Here for the first time is a comprehensive collection of all the relevant tales concerning Shub-Niggurath.

$5\frac{1}{2}$" x $8\frac{1}{2}$", 256 pages, $9.95. ISBN 0-56882-017-8; available from bookstores and game stores or by mail from Chaosium, Inc., 950-A 56th Street, Oakland, CA 94608-3129.

THE HASTUR CYCLE

The stories in this book evoke a tracery of evil rarely rivaled in horror writing. They represent the whole evolving trajectory of such notions as Hastur, the King in Yellow, Carcosa, the Yellow Sign, Yuggoth, and the Lake of Hali. Writers from Ambrose Bierce to Ramsey Campbell and Karl Edward Wagner have explored and embellished these concepts and thereby created an evocative tapestry of hypnotic dread and horror. Here for the first time is a comprehensive collection of the thirteen relevant tales; several are rare and (almost) impossible to find. Selected and introduced by Robert M. Price.

$5\frac{1}{2}$" x $8\frac{1}{2}$", 320 pages, $9.95. ISBN 0-56882-009-7; available from bookstores and game stores or by mail from Chaosium, Inc., 950-A 56th Street, Oakland, CA 94608-3129.

MYSTERIES OF THE WORM

New Second Edition, Revised and Expanded. At the end of H. P. Lovecraft's life, the young Robert Bloch was an enthusiastic member of Lovecraft's literary circle. This is a new edition of the long out-of-print volume that collected most of Bloch's early work concerning the Cthulhu Mythos. The new edition includes three additional tales from the period—"The Brood of Bubastis", "The Sorcerer's Jewel", and "The Creeper in the Crypt", previously available only in scarce fanzines and anthologies. Bloch also has slightly revised the texts of three other stories. Seventeen tales, introduction by Robert M. Price, the original afterword by Bloch, and a supplementary essay by Lin Carter.

$5\frac{1}{2}$" x $8\frac{1}{2}$", 272 pages, $9.95. ISBN 0-56882-012-7; available from bookstores and game stores or by mail from Chaosium, Inc., 950-A 56th Street, Oakland, CA 94608-3129.

CTHULHU'S HEIRS

Tales of the Mythos for the New Millennium. Nineteen new stories of the Cthulhu Mythos, never before printed. These range from an ironic tale of a cultist's conversion, to a first-person narration of possession by the thing from beyond itself, to what amounts to a retelling of the Lovecraft classic "The Dunwich Horror" from the inside out. These stories are by turn deft, horrifying, and hilarious, and give new life to the notion of the Mythos. Also, two rare stories are reprinted, one the definitive version of Ramsey Campbell's "The Franklyn Paragraphs." Selected and with an introduction by Thomas A. Stratman.

$5\frac{1}{2}$" x $8\frac{1}{2}$", 288 pages, $9.95. ISBN 0-56882-013-5; available from bookstores and game stores or by mail from Chaosium, Inc., 950-A 56th Street, Oakland, CA 94608-3129.

THE AZATHOTH CYCLE

At the heart of the universe the mad god Azathoth pulses like a cancer. As with the physical universe it created, no purely reasoned argument, no subtle scientific proof, no brilliant artistry, no human love affects the unyielding will of Azathoth. As an entity it is of transcendent power and unthinking immortal sway. It can be avoided sometimes but never challenged. Here are fourteen tales concerning Azathoth by authors as diverse as Ramsey Campbell, Lin Carter, John Glasby, and Thomas Ligotti. The macabre poet Edward Pickmen Derby contributes his immortal "Azathoth", the title piece of his single printed volume. Introduction, exegesical essay, and notes by Robert M. Price.

$5\frac{1}{2}$" x $8\frac{1}{2}$", 256 pages, $10.95. ISBN 0-56882-040-2; available from bookstores and game stores or by mail from Chaosium, Inc., 950-A 56th Street, Oakland, CA 94608-3129.

THE BOOK OF IOD

Henry Kuttner (1914-1958) was a friend of young Robert Bloch and a promising writer in his own right. He also became one of the Lovecraft Circle, submitting plot ideas and draft manuscripts to Lovecraft. He had an important impact on the development of the Cthulhu Mythos, especially with his contribution of a mystical tome, the Book of Iod. This collection of stories comprises all of Kuttner's Mythos tales (including one co-written with Bloch) and a story by Lin Carter about the infamous Book of Iod. Introduction and commentary by Robert M. Price.

5½" x 8½", 224 pages, $10.95. ISBN 0-56882-045-3; available from bookstores and game stores or by mail from Chaosium, Inc., 950-A 56th Street, Oakland, CA 94608-3129.

MADE IN GOATSWOOD

Ramsey Campbell is acknowledged by many to be the greatest living writer of the horror tale in the English language. This book contains eighteen all-new stories, all set in the ancient and fearful portion of England's Severn Valley which Campbell evoked in narratives such as "The Moon Lens." Included is a new story by Campbell himself, his first Severn Valley tale in decades. This volume was published in conjunction with a trip by Ramsey Campbell to the United States.

5 3/8" x 8 3/8", 288 pages, $10.95. ISBN 0-56882-046-1; available from bookstores and game stores or by mail from Chaosium, Inc., 950-A 56th Street, Oakland, CA 94608-3129.